PRAISE

"Wonderful."
—*The Sun*

"Milly Johnson works her magic yet again with this unabashedly heartwarming yet nuanced and relatable tale of resilience against the odds, the power of the imagination and second chances."
—*The Lady*

"Everyone loves a journey and Polly Potter goes on just that in this warm hug of a book... There is much happiness to be found in Milly Johnson's latest bighearted and humorous second-chance novel."
—*Woman's Weekly*

"Warm-hearted and charming—I sank into it like a cozy hug."
—Charlotte Stein, author of *When Grumpy Met Sunshine*

"Witty, wise and wonderful, *The Accidental Rewrite* is a celebration of women, their fragility, feistiness and friendship."
—Jane Costello, *Sunday Times* bestselling author of *It's Getting Hot in Here*

"Gloriously funny, witty, wise and wonderful, this book is a total joy!"
—Alexandra Potter, bestselling author of *Confessions of a Forty-Something F*** Up*

"A delicious warm hug of a book."
—Jill Mansell, *Sunday Times* bestselling author of *Maybe This Time*

"Guaranteed to put a spring in your step—I loved it."
—Jo Thomas, bestselling author of *Escape to the French Farmhouse*

"Gorgeous, heartwarming and moving, [The Accidental Rewrite] is so original and brilliantly written in the typically funny and clever Johnson style."
—Lucy Vine, bestselling author of Hot Mess

"An escapist, uplifting read full of heart."
—Libby Page, Sunday Times bestselling author of The Vintage Shop of Second Chances

"Funny and brilliant and gorgeously warm. Milly Johnson always, always delivers."
—Paige Toon, author of What If I Never Get Over You

"Takes you on a classic transformative journey in the most wonderful and original way. What a joy!"
—Julietta Henderson, author of How to Get a Life

The Accidental Rewrite

The

Accidental Rewrite

A NOVEL

Milly Johnson

The Accidental Rewrite

Copyright © 2025 by Millytheink Limited

All rights reserved. No portion of this book may be reproduced, stored in a retrieval system, or transmitted in any form or by any means—electronic, mechanical, photocopy, recording, scanning, or other—except for brief quotations in critical reviews or articles, without the prior written permission of the publisher.

Published by Harper Muse, an imprint of HarperCollins Focus LLC, 501 Nelson Place, Nashville, TN 37214, USA.

This book is a work of fiction. The characters, incidents, and dialogue are drawn from the author's imagination and are not to be construed as real. Any resemblance to actual events or persons, living or dead, is entirely coincidental.

Any internet addresses (websites, blogs, etc.) in this book are offered as a resource. They are not intended in any way to be or imply an endorsement by HarperCollins Focus LLC, nor does HarperCollins Focus LLC vouch for the content of these sites for the life of this book.

ISBN 978-1-4003-4936-4 (epub)

ISBN 978-1-4003-4935-7 (TP)

ISBN 978-1-4003-4937-1 (downloadable audio)

Without limiting the exclusive rights of any author, contributor, or the publisher of this publication, any unauthorized use of this publication to train generative artificial intelligence (AI) technologies is expressly prohibited. HarperCollins also exercise their rights under Article 4(3) of the Digital Single Market Directive 2019/790 and expressly reserve this publication from the text and data mining exception.

HarperCollins Publishers, Macken House, 39/40 Mayor Street Upper, Dublin 1, D01 C9W8, Ireland (https://www.harpercollins.com)

Originally published as *The Happiest Ever After* in the United Kingdom in 2024 by Simon & Schuster UK.

First US edition

Library of Congress Cataloging-in-Publication Data

CIP data is available upon request.

Art Direction: Halie Cotton
Cover Design: Micah Kandros Design
Interior Design: Chloe Foster

Printed in the United States of America

25 26 27 28 29 LBC 5 4 3 2 1

Dedicated to all those authors who write romantic fiction and those readers who love it and keep us in the job. Be as proud to read us as we are to write for you. A story that floods your heart with joy and an ending that leaves you with hope and smiles does not make it inferior to books in other genres. We do not write lesser books.

#RespectRomFic

Part One

First they ignore you, then they laugh at you, then they fight you, then you win.

—Mahatma Gandhi

The *Daily Trumpet* would like to point out an error in last Thursday's article which should have featured "Karen's Catering" and not "Karen's Carpenters" as stated. Also, Karen has wished us to point out that she won the Leeds Mayoral dessert of the year award for her Eton Mess, not her Elon Musk.

From the Ground Up
A NOVEL

Polly Potter

Characters
  Sabrina Anderson
  Jasper Camward (husband of eight years)
  Linnet (daughter)
  Rina Anderson (mother)
  Ed Anderson (father)
  Dick Germany (boss)
  Note: Sabrina loves black cherries, espresso coffee, cats, cleaning, and red lipstick.

Synopsis
Sabrina Anderson (35) is a successful strategy and operations consultant who has been sidelined in her job at Flying Falcons for far too long by male bosses who take all the credit for her accomplishments—but no more! A total change is needed in all aspects of her life, starting with ending her desperately unhappy marriage and leaving womanizer Jasper for good. But that won't be easy as Jasper can be volatile and she must plan, act quickly, and take only the barest essentials

with her. She has even told her daughter Linnet, currently touring Australia in the footsteps of her recently deceased Aussie grandparents, not to be in contact with her until given the all-clear to do so, because no one knows how far Jasper will go when pushed. Sabrina must get out and flee to pastures new and then begin again in a place where no one knows her, in the old stone cottage she has booked to rent. Will she find her due happiness here? Will she be able to start from scratch and build a career—and herself—from the ground up?

Chapter 1

Seven days to the renewal of the vows ceremony

Being trapped on the big roller coaster at Blackpool, swimming in shark-infested waters while bleeding from a severe paper cut, being sexually compromised by Jeremy Watson at work—these were just a few more favorable alternatives of Polly's to spending time in a wedding dress shop with her partner's sister Camay, a woman who made Hyacinth Bucket look understated. Not for her own wedding—that would never be on the cards, at least not now—but Camay's, or more precisely the renewal of the vows first taken with her husband Ward thirty years ago. Polly hadn't been on the family scene then, but she'd seen the photos of Camay in a blinding white crinoline, looking as if she had just walked off the set of *Gone with the Wind*. Seven bridesmaids in shell-pink satin, a reception at Higher Hoppleton Hall with the Lord Lieutenant as one of the invited guests, more flowers than Kew Gardens. The perfect day, impossible to better; yet for some reason Camay had decided, on a whim, she wanted to do it all again, though on a smaller scale. This time just the one bridesmaid, and that honor to be bestowed upon her dear brother's partner.

Camay, who knew as much about fashion as Polly knew about molecular cell biology, had insisted her bridesmaid should be dressed in beige. Not just any beige, but *designer* beige, and had chosen a frock by a "name" familiar to anyone who sat in the hairdresser's and read glossy mags: Galina de Jong, the queen of the bridal kaftan. If the frock wasn't bad enough, Camay had also chosen for her a feathery fascinator in the style of a swan which had been swimming in murky waters and appeared to be attacking her head rather than sitting on it. This shade of beige made magnolia riveting, and when Polly held out her arms, she looked not unlike a blanched flying squirrel. Camay, peering over Polly's shoulder, was sighing at the reflection in the full-length mirror and seeming to see something Polly wished she could perceive. But then, Camay, as she had come to learn over the years, had always been blinded by a fancy brand name that she could bandy about at every available opportunity: her Louis Vuitton handbag, her Gucci scarf, her Christian Louboutin shoes, not forgetting her fancy BMW.

Camay's wedding gown was a closely guarded secret. All Polly knew about it was that it was plum. Designer plum, of course, and Ward's favorite color, apparently. They'd be like plums and cream together, Camay chortled. Except this wasn't cream; it was the worst kind of beige and it did pale-skinned Polly no favors at all. It was just as well all eyes would be on the bride.

The sales assistant was wearing a name badge that said "Paris" on it. Such a lovely name. Names were so important, thought Polly, who hated hers with a passion. A child had to carry it all their life, and names had powers, both beneficial and detrimental. Paris looked as if she had grown into hers, become pretty and elegant in a way that she might not have if she'd had a name like Polly. Paris was one of those names you couldn't make fun of, unlike Polly and all those putting-kettles-on witticisms.

"I wish I'd chosen one like this for myself instead of something so fitted," said Camay, dropping a different sort of sigh now, a regretful one. "One potato too many and I'm liable to pop a button. This shape is perfect for someone carrying a few extra pounds. Covers a multitude of sins."

Polly tried not to let her indignation show. Okay, she was a couple of stone heavier than her skinny teenage self had been, but she was hardly Mr. Bump. In fact, she had an enviable tiny waist thanks to some lucky family genes, probably on her unknown father's side because her mother had been built like Camay, short and solid with no discernible ins and outs.

"Okay, we're done. Take it off," Camay ordered, giving Polly a little push at her shoulder just in case she'd forgotten where to find the changing cubicle she'd so recently vacated.

Polly couldn't strip it off fast enough. Thank goodness it would all be over soon and she'd never see the photos. Anyone else would have said, "I'm not doing this. Save your money and my pride." But she wasn't anyone else; she was Polly Potter, with a default setting of putting others before herself. She wouldn't ruin Camay's big day. But then, after it was over, it was time to kick against type and put herself first for a change.

Camay's husband Ward was waiting outside for them in his BMW. Camay rarely used the word *car*; she might have done so had she driven an Average Joe vehicle, but she and Ward owned his and hers of the more prestigious models in the BMW range and felt duty bound to insert the brand into conversation at every available opportunity: *I'll pick you up in the BMW. The BMW is having a service. We've just had the BMW valeted. We're thinking about changing the BMW for another BMW.* Camay Barrett-Hunt especially lived to brag. And the sentiment "I have this and you don't and you never will" underpinned every boast that came out of her mouth. Polly sat in the back with the boxes containing her dress, the fascinator, and shoes. The shoes were actually nice, not that she'd ever wear them again after the wedding. Bunion-makers. Her mum lived in high heels. After she'd died, Polly found over a hundred pairs in her cupboard, no heel less than two inches, most not even worn. Her feet were in a terrible state, but still she had crammed all the bulges and bumps into her fancy shoes.

When they got to Polly's house, Camay and Ward came in with her because Camay said they hadn't seen Christopher for simply ages. Then again, Polly lived with him and she didn't see him that much either. She'd converted one of the spare rooms upstairs into a den where she could sit and read and do a jigsaw puzzle in peace because he claimed full TV rights in the lounge. They'd become Mr. Downstairs and Mrs. Upstairs, and it wasn't right. It was one of many things that weren't right, that shouldn't have been allowed to develop, but they had and she was way past the point of hoping for change.

This time Polly didn't blush seeing Camay's eyes rove around the house: the hall carpet with the large worn patch in it, the spaces on the kitchen walls where tiles had dropped off, the missing slat in the venetian blinds, the wonky cupboard doors that didn't sit flush. Polly had given up on telling Chris that she'd had enough of the way the house was and was going to get a painter/tiler/floorer to change it only to get the response that she wasn't because it was his house and he wasn't wasting money on having other people do things he could do himself—except he never did because he was always too busy. Annoyingly, though, if his daughter Shauna ever rang up with a DIY "emergency," he was round there with his toolbox like Usain frigging Bolt. It was a relief not to care anymore.

"Tea? Coffee?" Polly offered.

"Do you have Earl Grey?" asked Camay.

"Nope, just good old Yorkshire tea," replied Polly.

"I'll have coffee," said Ward.

"Me too, then. If instant, I'll take a heaped teaspoon. I like it strong." Then Camay added with a titter, "Like my men."

It was a joke of course. Even Enid Blyton with her vivid imagination wouldn't have applied the adjective *strong* to Ward Hunt. At home he might best be described as a "blundering oaf" who kowtowed to his wife's every demand. At work, in his prestigious banking job, he more than made up for his domestic subjugation by being a misogynistic, condescending bully, if the grapevine was any reliable source of information. Polly knew his type only too well. She was surrounded by them every single day.

The door from the lounge swung open. "Did I hear the kettle being mentioned?" Polly's partner Chris made his presence known. He bent down and gave his older sister a kiss on the cheek. He was wearing his lucky Manchester University shirt. He was always in costume for a match, even if he was sitting in the lounge watching it on the TV.

"What's the score so far?" asked Ward.

"Just finished." Chris grinned. "Three-nil to us." He sat down at the kitchen table with the others. "Coffee for me, Pol."

Please, added Polly to herself. However well you knew someone, they were still worthy of manners. Jeremy at work never said thank you for anything either. Maybe it was a male middle-age thing and had an explanatory Greek term like *manmnesia*. But Chris would have said those two words to a customer, and Jeremy definitely would have said them to Charles the company owner, so it was a deliberate omission not to say them to her. Polly got another mug out of the cupboard and spooned some coffee into it.

"Not long to go now, sis. You must be getting excited," said Chris.

"Yes, yes, I am rather," came the reply.

Polly put a plate of biscuits down on the table and Ward's hand shot out to pick up two at once. Polly often wondered whether, if someone were to cut through Ward Hunt, they'd find *Greed* written through the middle of him like a stick of Blackpool rock. In the time she'd known him, he had grown a little more bloated every year on executive lunches and fine dining until he was this walking barrel of a man, but the greed extended far beyond his gastronomic excesses. He had the perfect partner in Camay, a pair of coveters who had to have the biggest and best and most of everything. They likened themselves to the "Joneses," who set the standard lesser mortals could only aspire to keep up with.

"Are you looking forward to your big day, Ward?" asked Polly, distributing coffees.

"I suppose so," he replied.

"Of course he is," said Camay. "How could he not be, marrying me all over again? And then having a wonderful feast at Maltstone Old Hall." She gave him a poke and his default grumble-face broke into a smile of delight.

"What menu have you chosen for the reception?" asked Polly, leaning against the sink because there wasn't a spare chair for her. The fourth one had broken months ago. She and Chris were supposed to be going to choose a new dining set, but like everything else he'd promised, it hadn't happened.

"Italian bruschetta for starter, fillet of lamb served pink, something with goat's cheese for the vegetarians, I forget what"—Camay flapped her hand in such a way that showed her disdain for anyone awkward enough not to eat meat—"chocolate fudge cake or crème brûlée for dessert." She pronounced the "crème" as if she were clearing a pint of phlegm from the back of her throat.

"Did you really need three courses?" asked Chris, who was the total opposite to his sister in his spending habits. His tone was as tight as if he were footing the bill himself.

"Five. There's cheese and coffee as well," said Camay. "One must do these things right, Christopher. If you're going to have just a select few present, they should have a select menu to match."

"I love lamb," said Ward, spitting out biscuit crumbs as he talked. He ate very noisily always, his jaw clicking.

"Oh God, look at you," said Camay, taking a handkerchief out of her bag, spitting on it, and then reaching over to dab at a blob of chocolate on his shirt.

He tapped her hand away and said, "Leave it for the housekeeper."

"You have a housekeeper now?" asked Chris, eyebrows raised.

"Well, we had to get one. I simply haven't got the time to maintain a five-bedroom house with three reception rooms myself. She's live-out, of course, but she's very good." Camay's eyes dragged from one side of the kitchen to the other. "She'd clean this place up so much you wouldn't recognize it."

Polly felt a growl in the back of her throat. The house was spotless, even though Chris was untidy and could make it look like a trash heap five minutes after she'd cleaned it. He left all that domestic stuff to Polly because it wasn't fair he did housework as well as all the hours he did in his garage, he'd say. In a police lineup, he couldn't have picked out an iron in the middle of a row of mops.

Polly remembered what this house was like when she moved in. There was more fur on the skirting boards than there was on next door's five Persian cats. Once again the idea of a tiny flat or house with just her own mess to contend with made something warm swell up inside her. Maybe she'd find the sort of little cottage that featured in her novel-in-progress, with its old stone walls and doorway framed with sweet-scented flowers. She'd be happy there, she knew she would. She couldn't wait. She couldn't wait for this wedding to be over; she couldn't wait to be alone.

"She's made our porcelain sparkle. Our bidets look like brand-new again," went on Camay, lifting the mug to her mouth with her little finger stuck out like a countess. As always when she was in Camay's company, Polly reaped some killer lines that were the equivalent of gold dust for her creative writing assignments. Polly wondered if that was what professional novelists did: harvest conversations. She'd never be a Catherine Cookson—she didn't want to be—but she did enjoy being imaginative and it was marvelously cathartic to put the world to rights on paper. Her hobby had been a lifesaver this past year. She felt as if she were a god in her own world, a parallel universe where karma was her chief of staff, where people got full credit for what they did and all the notable knob-heads got their comeuppances.

"Waste of money, weddings, if you ask me," said Ward, jaw clicking as he crunched. "All that moolah spent on other people."

"Shut up, Ward," said Camay. "Don't pretend you aren't looking forward to it." There was a threat in her tone. Polly knew he wouldn't dare look anything less than euphoric on the day, whatever he felt.

"I like your mug," Camay commented then, smiling at her brother as he glugged his coffee. "'World's Best Dad.' Shauna or William?"

"Birthday present from Shauna," said Chris. His daughter liked all that sort of tat. There was a "World's Greatest Daddy" trophy on a shelf in the lounge and a "My Wonderful Dad" tea towel in the drawer. There were no matching "World's Best Stepmum" pieces for Polly; Shauna never even sent a card. Chris's son Will, however, unlike his sister, never missed. He'd been thirteen when Polly came into their lives, and that first Christmas he'd bought her a brooch. Chris had made a joke about it, calling it an old-lady present in front of his son, and so Polly had said, to undo the damage, that she loved a brooch but no one ever bought them for her. It became a thing; Will had bought her a brooch every birthday and every Christmas since, and she kept them in a treasure box. And sometimes, when the occasion demanded, she took them out and wore them. It said something that all the brooches were now in her handbag, ready for her to take with her on Sunday.

"How is Shauna?" asked Ward.

"Very well," replied Chris. "She loves her new job."

Of course she did—she worked in the social security office, deciding who received benefits and who didn't. Polly could imagine her in a Colosseum-shaped office, turning her thumb up and down like a female Caligula.

"What about William?" asked Camay.

"He's all right. He's doing some admin or something," said Chris. He'd never shown the same interest in his son as he had his daughter, which was a crying shame because Will was a much nicer person and the only one of them Polly would miss when she left.

"It will be good to see them at the wedding," said Camay. Then she clicked her attention away from him and onto Polly. "Before I forget, the hair and makeup woman will be here at nine on Saturday."

Polly raised her eyebrows in surprise. "A hair and makeup woman? For me?"

"Yes, of course for you," chuckled Camay as if Polly were daft. "I've briefed her on what to do with you. So wash your hair, leave it damp, she'll do the rest. The car will be picking you up at eleven thirty-five. Chris will be staying with us the night before. He and Ward are going to have a few drinkies to celebrate. A mini stag do."

It was the first Polly had heard of it.

"Right then, we're all sorted." Camay stood. "Ward, are you ready?" Ward whipped the last biscuit from the plate as he got up. Polly and Chris saw them out. On the drive, Camay gave her brother an affectionate hug and planted a real kiss on his cheek, then turned to Polly for her usual double air kiss near her ears. Ward didn't do kisses; Polly was grateful for that. It would have been like being slobbered over by a walrus.

Back inside, Chris went to the cupboard to get a Jaffa Cake, only to discover that there were none left.

"Did you have to put them all out, Pol? You know what bloody Jabba's like." Chris's pet name for his brother-in-law was Jabba the Hunt. "Bugger. And no chocolate crumbles either."

"I didn't think he'd clear them all single-handedly," replied Polly.

"Greedy twat," said Chris, having to make do with a digestive. "I hate these." He was grimacing as he crunched. He looked like a recalcitrant toddler. "Next time, don't give Jabba my Jaffa Cakes," he added, reaching for another of the biscuits he hated.

The next time Jabba and his missus come round to the house, I won't be the one making the coffee and putting out any biscuits, Polly thought.

Chris huffed a bit more and chuntered under his breath and then said, "I should have told you about me staying at Camay's on Friday night. I forgot."

Polly carried on wiping down the table with a cloth.

"It's fine," she said. It couldn't have been more perfect in fact. A whole clear evening to pack and take her time about it. For a full month now, she'd been getting rid of what she no longer wanted in her cupboards and the loft, and organizing what she would take with her so she could just sweep it all up and throw it quickly into suitcases. She was banking on Chris being out for the count on Saturday night, and that's when she was going to do the bulk of her packing, quietly, when he was asleep. This arrangement would make everything so much easier. She knew that when she told him she was leaving, he wouldn't be assisting her out with her things and waving her off with a cheery "bye-bye," because he didn't take rejection very lightly. He'd still been dragging a massive bag of luggage around with him when they met—and he'd been divorced for five years by then. Although Charlene Barrett had given him chlamydia, contracted from her sister's husband whom she'd subsequently married. Polly wouldn't be leaving him for anyone else. She didn't want to cause him pain; she just wanted to go and be out of pain herself.

Polly felt Chris's eyes on her, and when she lifted her head, it was to find him staring at her.

"You okay?" she asked.

"Yeah, I'm okay," he replied, then turned and went into the lounge to watch some more sport.

The *Daily Trumpet* would like to apologize to Sue Dyer of Sue's Hair and Beauty for the advertisement that appeared in Sunday's "Treat Yourself" supplement. We inadvertently printed "book early to avoid appointments" when it should of read "book early to ensure disappointments."

Chapter 2

Five days to the renewal of the vows ceremony

"Polly, put the kettle on," said Jeremy, popping his head out of his office door. He grinned as if this was the first time he'd ever said it and not the millionth. He truly was a man of astounding wit. Or at least something rhyming with it.

Sheridan, the office administrator and fourteen years Polly's junior, made a move to get out of her seat.

"I'll do it," Sheridan said, uttering "wanker" under her breath, as if it was the first time she'd ever said it and not the millionth.

"No, you won't," said Polly. "You shouldn't even be working, never mind running around making coffees."

"You do it and I'll never speak to you again," said Sheridan, using her scary do-not-mess-with-me voice. "I need to rub my bum and I can do that in the privacy of the kitchen. Kill two birds with one stone. Bloody sciatica."

She levered her heavily pregnant body from her chair and waddled off in the direction of the small kitchen. Polly would miss working with this young breath of fresh air when she went on maternity leave, and she'd been selfishly glad that Sheridan had decided to work as near to her due date as possible so she could have maximum time with her new baby. Sheridan's maternity cover had already been decided upon. His name was Brock Harrison and he was the business owner's nephew. Polly had already met him and he was exactly the entitled spoiled brat she'd expected him to be. She could forecast what was to come. Like Jeremy, he'd start off as her junior, he'd learn just a little before he began to act like her senior, and long before he was ready, that was exactly what he would be because the male hierarchy would move to promote him above her—and in no time at all, he'd be popping his head out of his office and also asking Polly to put the kettle on.

Sheridan was just emerging from the kitchen with the coffee when the owner of the company, Charles Butler, breezed into the department, speedwalking across the executive red carpet toward Jeremy's office. If Sheridan hadn't made an emergency step backward, both of them would have been splattered in milk froth.

Sheridan followed Charles into Jeremy's inner sanctum. Polly knew she would take as long as possible to deliver the drink and plate of biscuits so she could mop up any gossip and bring it back to her seat. Sure enough, she was wearing a knowing grin on her face when she returned and couldn't wait to lean over the partition that separated their workspaces to share what she'd just overheard.

"You should see the backslapping going on in there, and the handshaking," Sheridan said. "It's all to do with Nutbush's profits. Apparently they are through the roof." Her brow creased then. "I wonder if they'll call you in, Pol, and start thumping you on the back as well, seeing as that was all down to you."

"Let me see," said Polly, tapping her lip with her finger. "I think I have more chance of Leonardo DiCaprio abseiling down the side of the building in the next five minutes, climbing in through the window, and handing me a box of rose and violet creams."

"What are they?" asked Sheridan. "Chocolates? They sound vile." She wrinkled up her nose at the thought of a flower and chocolate combo.

"Don't knock 'em till you've tried them. My uncle used to buy them for my auntie, and whenever I went to visit I could choose one from the box." She smiled at the thought. She always smiled at thoughts of her uncle Ed and auntie Rina. She didn't have a lot of happy memories of her childhood, but the ones featuring them shone bright. A year of warmth and fun and love. Then they were gone and there were no more violet or rose creams or games of Snakes and Ladders or trips out to fairs and the seaside and museums or overflowing buckets of popcorn at the cinema.

"You do know why your star hasn't reached its full ascendancy here, of course," said Sheridan.

Polly did, but she humored her young friend. "Go on, enlighten me."

"You're lacking a dick. Two actually. One in your pants and another growing out of your head."

Polly gave a small laugh, even though it was no laughing matter, because here they were again, same scenario, different company. A business in trouble seeking their help, Polly presenting her best ideas to the panel on how to turn them around. Polly's ideas getting nicked and repackaged, others taking the credit for the success. Polly forgotten.

"Next time you get a company to rescue, feed the buggers a load of duff info and watch them crash and burn, and then stand back and let Germany take the credit for that," said Sheridan, using one of her many nicknames for Jeremy. She rocked on her seat to get comfortable. "I know, I know, before you start on me. You aren't like that."

Polly wasn't. Many of the businesses that came to them at Northern Eagles were desperate enough to invest in their expertise. Old family firms that had no idea how to adjust to suit present markets, or fledgling businesses that had plowed everything they had into their dreams and badly needed guidance. People's livelihoods were at stake, their health as well as their money. She'd felt pride when it was her ideas that had been adopted and made the difference; she still did, but ever since the new regime began just over two years ago, not once had she been given true recognition for what she'd achieved, even though the honors had been handed out too readily to those who had done so little to earn them. She hadn't a clue what she was going to do about it going forward, but she was going to do something. On Sunday a new phase of her life would begin, and she hoped that her newfound freedom would give her the confidence to make changes for herself at work as well as at home. And she'd have a woman called Sabrina to thank for it: a character she had invented in her writing class. Sabrina was everything Polly aspired to be, a new creature springing up from the ashes of her old self, like a brilliant phoenix, no longer happy with her lot and ready to alter things. It was beyond bonkers that Polly found herself stirred by a person who didn't exist that she'd conjured up from her own head and yet who was showing her the way forward. Fictional Sabrina was leaving her cheating shit of a husband Jasper because it was the right thing to do to save herself, and Real Polly was primed to follow in her footsteps.

"Oh you little sod, behave," said Sheridan to her stomach. "I'm as tight as a drum. Braxton-Hicks contractions. To be fair, they don't hurt; it's just your body tuning up for delivery."

Polly knew what they were. "Can I feel?" she asked.

"'Course," said Sheridan.

Polly walked round to Sheridan's side. She placed her hand on her bump, felt the shifting underneath her palm. She closed her eyes and remembered how it was to have a small life growing inside so close to her heart.

"This time next month you'll be holding him," said Polly, removing her hand long before she wanted to.

"And then my stomach will be the equivalent of a deflated balloon." Sheridan sighed. "Just as well, I'm going to fill it up with another one as soon as I can."

She had it all planned out. She'd come back to work for a bit and then get pregnant again and leave permanently to be a hands-on mum. Her husband Dmitri was ten years older and a scientist earning a packet, not that Sheridan ever showed off about their financial status. The only things she liked to show off about were her latest bargain finds from discount shops. She and Polly had a thing that they could only buy each other birthday and Christmas presents from the pound shop.

"So what did you do at the weekend?" asked Sheridan, throwing over a packet of chewy toffees. Polly took one and threw it back. They called this "confectionery tennis." They did a lot of daft things to offset the frustrations of working in this patriarchal black hole.

"Final check on my bridesmaid dress."

"Oh yes, the *dress*," said Sheridan, giving the word a weight all of its own as she held up two fingers arranged as a crucifix. "And does it still fit?"

"That's the problem. It would fit me and half the guests. Look, I took a photo of the whole ensemble for you in the changing room." Polly fished her phone out of her bag, found the picture, and then handed it over the partition.

"Fuck me, it's worse than I imagined," said Sheridan when she realized her eyes weren't deceiving her. "To be fair, it would probably look okay on Harry Styles."

"Everything looks okay on Harry Styles," returned Polly.

"And what for the love of God is that on your head? It looks like a mucky swan."

"It's a fascinator."

"Why does your sister-in-law hate you so much?"

Polly laughed at that. Camay didn't hate her, even though she would very shortly. Camay viewed her as a mere extension of her beloved brother and as such had never bothered to grow fond of her as a separate entity. Polly had always wanted to embrace Chris's family as her own, but his daughter was devious and his sister an inveterate showoff whom it was hard to warm to. Polly was under no illusions: Camay hadn't insisted she be the bridesmaid because they were close—Camay had all her ladies' group cronies for friendship. There had to be another reason, though Polly couldn't for the life of her work out what it was.

"In Camay's eyes, if a price tag is hefty and the designer is well-known, a garment cannot possibly be awful. It's out of the question."

"You have far too nice a figure for that . . . sack, Polly. I mean, why hasn't she chosen something for you that goes in at the middle and shows off that lovely small waist you have?" Sheridan crossed her arms as if she meant business. "I reckon she's jealous."

"I don't think so." Polly refuted that. She wasn't the sort that Camay would envy. She might be if she owned a wardrobe full of Victoria Beckham outfits. Or was tall and willowy like a catwalk model so that everything she wore looked fabulous on her. As it was, Polly was neither tall nor short, neither fat nor thin, with mid-brown, mid-length, poker-straight hair. Once upon a time, though, her tawny eyes shone and she had a smile that could light up a whole city, someone kind had said. The only beauty contest she'd ever have a chance of winning now would be Miss Average Great Britain.

"It's just one day, half a day really, I suppose. I can cope with wearing it for that long," said Polly. "Then I'll gladly take it off and"—*walk away from them all*—"put it in a charity bag."

She had so wanted to share what she'd been planning with someone, and if Sheridan hadn't been pregnant, that's who she would have confided in, but she couldn't offload all that onto her, especially now when the bun in her oven was almost fully baked. She had to be strong for herself, something she should have been long before this.

"Are they having a honeymoon?"

"Apparently so, but she says it's top secret. It'll be somewhere exotic no doubt."

"Benidorm?"

"Ha. I'd put my life savings on it not being."

"I love Benidorm," said Sheridan. "I've had a lot of fun there, both with pals and Dmitri."

"Me too." Polly remembered getting off the plane at Alicante and feeling the blast of hot air almost knock her backward. She'd gone with mates whom she wasn't in touch with anymore. Her first ever trip abroad. It was sensory overload. They'd come home with all the souvenir tat, the Spanish dancer doll, the castanets, the fan, the big furry donkey. And thanks to a young, handsome Spanish waiter and a split condom, Polly brought home an extra souvenir she didn't know about until two months later.

"So who had the affair then, him or her?" asked Sheridan.

Polly stared at her incredulously. "What do you mean?"

"Well, isn't it a thing, that people who have almost buggered up their marriage decide to wipe the slate clean and start again with the vows they've just smashed into smithereens?"

Neither Camay nor Ward was the affair type. He wheezed getting out of a chair; humping some young thing would definitely be beyond his capabilities. Plus, Camay wouldn't allow it. And she would never risk being parted from his pension prospects for an extramarital fling of her own. Unless it was with Richard Branson.

"Maybe, but not in their case," replied Polly. "They're solid as a pair of rocks."

"Seems like a right old waste of money to me then," said Sheridan.

"They have it to burn," said Polly. Camay's plum satin wedding gown and Polly's shapeless beige bridesmaid bag, the cars, the champagne, the hair and makeup woman and pink lamb main course wouldn't even make a dent in their savings.

"I'd love to be super rich, wouldn't you, Pol?" Sheridan sighed wistfully.

Polly nodded. "Of course," she said, knowing that she was going to be *super poor* for the foreseeable future, at least moneywise. Her wealth would be in the form of freedom, and she planned on spending it liberally.

Just after lunch Jeremy bobbed his head out of his office, not to ask for a drink for once, but for Polly to pop in. She followed him and he closed the door behind them and asked her to sit. He plonked himself in his leather swivelly executive chair behind his desk and smiled.

"I wanted to fill you in about Nutbush," he said with a smile so greasy it was a wonder it didn't slide off his lips. She noticed how deliberately he spoke, as if choosing every word with care.

"Okay," replied Polly, not giving away that she'd heard the good news already.

"You'll be delighted to hear that they are on the steepest of upward trajectories."

"That's wonderful," replied Polly. "I knew they would be."

"Suffice to say that they are extremely glad they reached out to us at Northern Eagles."

"Great stuff," said Polly, nodding.

"I'm aware this was initially your client," Jeremy went on. "And you did an admirable job of pointing their ship in the right direction."

It was a slight understatement. Nutbush was a sports company on the brink of receivership. They had a lot of competition in the market, both bargain stores and high-end, and they didn't offer enough to divert custom from either. Polly had gone out to visit them and found their shops a mess. But not beyond hope, *never* beyond; her old boss Alan had trained her to see that there was always that, if they were prepared to listen to expert advice. There was nothing that couldn't be spun around; it was just finding the right combination for the safe holding the treasure, as Alan used to say. And when she did find it, the Nutbush file was whipped from her with the alacrity of a champion greyhound on amphetamines.

"I wanted to formally acknowledge your input," Jeremy went on, pressing his hands together and doing that thank-you gesture that gave her the ick. "I know it was hard at first to get them to accept the changes we suggested, so well done on that."

We. Polly laughed inwardly.

"But I must give you credit where it is due, Polly—you were able to get through to them that ours was the path they should follow. Pretty basic stuff of course, but nonetheless . . . good show."

It wasn't basic stuff at all. It was a massive gamble. Every other business was closing stores and upping their online trading, and that was what Jeremy and his team had expected her to suggest. But Polly's instinct was to do exactly the opposite and expand their high street presence in areas where they were strong, in towns being regenerated where planners wanted to lure people away from their computers to shop in person. She had the vision of making Nutbush a seductive space to wander around. She wanted to make it cool to shop there and deliver an impact that couldn't be felt online. She spent a lot of hours visiting their stores to absorb what the problem with them was, who shopped there now, who might shop there in the future. The fixes she suggested raised eyebrows, but they worked. Retro music pumping through the speakers, less stock on the floor so it looked cleaner with more space, lowered ceilings, warmer lighting instead of the harsh bright white, even a change of coat hangers. Then she discovered there was a premiership footballer by the name of Cedric Nutbush. She wormed her way around his PR. Did he want to help out an ailing sports firm, set up by a young man who'd had a promising football career until a car crash shattered his leg? An inspiration to young kids that there wasn't just one road to success? Could they use his image (for the price of a hefty donation to his underprivileged kids' charity) and the slogan 'Nutbush. No Limits'? Cedric Nutbush went for it and the whole combo worked like magic.

And Polly wasn't even invited to the reopening of their flagship store in Manchester, although Jeremy and his merry band of male managers were. The photo of them, Cedric, and the Nutbush founder ended up in all the national papers. That weekend she took the train to Manchester Piccadilly, walked around the shop, felt the vibe, saw the length of the queue at the till, and felt a massive sense of pride, albeit tainted with some rightful anger and frustration. Her old boss Alan Eagleton would have put her on a pedestal for what she'd done for them, not shoved her in a cupboard out of sight.

"The company owes you," said Jeremy, jabbing his long, thin finger at her. Everything about Jeremy was long and thin: his nose, his chin, his legs, his fingers. He'd have long slim feet with elongated toes as well, she just knew, though her imagination forbade her from going any further than that. "I've had a word with HR and we are upping your salary by a thousand pounds. So what do you think about that?" He beamed. Jeremy beaming was not a good look because his mouth turned into a deranged V shape.

What do I think about that? Polly mused. She could imagine Alan sitting at the desk Jeremy now occupied, raising his shaggy eyebrows and urging her to tell him to stick that grand up his arse, one fiver at a time.

"Good, good." Jeremy didn't wait for her answer but picked up a file from his desk and handed it to her. "Knew you'd be thrilled. Now, if you could take a look at this. You won't have heard of them and that's the point. They have a big budget to spend on improvements. If anyone can make them into the next Warburtons, you can." He stood, signifying their meeting was at an end. He was still smiling, in the way the pope would smile having granted a poor person a blessing.

"What's up, Pol?" said Sheridan when Polly returned and threw herself down on her seat. "Your cheeks are very red."

"I'm cross, that's what I am," said Polly. "Cross enough to storm out of this damned building and never come back."

Jeremy's V-shaped lips were branded on her brain. V for the victory he'd claimed for doing nothing other than regurgitate her ideas, her suggestions, and then he'd had the nerve to fling her a bit of icing from his celebratory cake.

"I've just typed up a letter from Germy for HR. Is it—"

Polly held up her hand to stop Sheridan from saying any more. Her heart was racing, her head full of words unsaid. She'd taken two years' worth of crap from him now, and it was enough. She really did need to be *more Sabrina*. She couldn't wait for her effect to kick in.

During her lunch hour, Polly took the folder Jeremy had given her into the canteen and sat in the corner with it. Confusingly it had "Auntie Marian's Bread" on the front, but inside was a brief pertaining to a very different company—a burgeoning Italian restaurant chain called Ciaoissimo. She unwrapped her sandwich and chewed half-heartedly on it. The catering in this place used to be top-notch, but company cuts had led to detrimental changes. Alan Eagleton was always of the belief that an army marches on its stomach and quality scran was an essential. But then, there was a chasm between the sort of man Alan was and the sort Jeremy was that made the Grand Canyon look like a crack in a pavement.

With an absence of anything else to occupy her, she started to read about Ciaoissimo: *Authentically Italian* it cried, even though it was about as authentically Italian as Bjork.

No wonder they'd asked for help. High staff turnover, low morale, lack of vision, crazy menu, and their mission statement seemed to be "Get the money off the customers, feed them crap, and chuck them out." Negligible number of repeat customers—*no shit, Sherlock*. They were a mess. She opened up an envelope in the back marked *Strictly Confidential* and didn't like what she found there. She hoped this one landed on someone else's pile; otherwise she might actually be tempted to cock it up.

*　*　*

She took the folder back to Jeremy after lunch.

"Ah, straight on it, Polly Kettle; that's what I like to see," he said.

"Well, I would have been had the outside matched the inside," she replied, bristling at the stupid name Jeremy insisted on calling her. She bet he didn't call Jack Jones, the head of Finance, "Jack Spratty," or Marjorie Wright, the head of HR, "See Saw Marjorie Daw." Mind you, with good reason, because Marjorie would have had his balls off. She was fierce but fair: Fools were not to be suffered. Polly had always really liked her no-nonsense approach, and there was too much nonsense in Northern Eagles now. Marjorie was part of the old guard, most of whom had been dispensed with when the company was sold and the new guard came in. Two of her particular favorites had been driven out: Phil Bowery, one of Alan's brightest protégés, and Dave Deacon, a young graduate with a real nose for business. They went to the wall because Charles Butler wanted his own people in, even if they were inferior. Marjorie escaped the firing squad probably because she was female and less of a threat, but she was drafted over from the directorate to Human Resources out of the way.

Polly answered Jeremy's confused, inquiring expression. "The outside says Auntie Marian's Bread; inside there's a business profile of an Italian restaurant chain called Ciaoissimo, not a mention of a teacake to be found," she explained.

"Ah. Not sure how that happened. Just forget about this one; it needs expert handling." Jeremy opened up the big drawer in his desk and dropped the folder in there quickly. "I'll have the proper file brought over to you."

Interesting, thought Polly on the way out, wondering why Ciaoissimo should be classified. Anyway, let one of Jeremy's "experts" deal with it. No doubt he'd run into difficulty and need her input, so it would end up with her eventually anyway. That's what usually happened.

DREAM TRIP FOR GRANNY

The family of May Readman surprised her with a party in her local pub, The Lobster Pot in Whitby, on her ninetieth birthday and a ticket for a fully-paid-for trip to Dignitas. Son Philip said, "We can't wait for Mum to go there; we've been wanting to send her there for ages. Everyone was more than happy to chip in and we'll be delighted to wave her off."

Chapter 3

Polly hated lying. Lies hurt people, lies made holes in trust that could never quite be sealed up again; this she knew only too well. But she allowed herself to lie once a week, and though it was quite an innocent lie, she still felt a bit bad about it. Every Monday she left work early and drove straight to the church hall in Millspring, a village near her home in Penistone, for a creative writing class, and she hadn't missed a single one since she joined.

She had pretended she had to work late on Mondays for over ten months now, not that it inconvenienced Chris, because he was never in before her on that night anyway. He kept open longer hours on Mondays and Tuesdays for emergency jobs and those willing to stump up extra to queue-jump. Those two days were proper money-spinners for him.

Chris had his own body shop garage. He was good at what he did and in much demand, and his charges reflected that because people paid him a small fortune to suck out the dents and touch up the imperfections in their prestige cars. That's where he'd met *her*: Mrs. Jones, the "seven-year itch," he called it, as if it was somehow out of his control, possibly even medical.

On the first day of April (*ha!*) last year, Polly found out about the affair and she'd left him, moved into the first Airbnb she could find that was available. And in the four weeks when they were apart, she started writing down her feelings and found it helped. Sometimes she wrote prose, sometimes her words bent to poetry; both formats took her out of the zone. She hadn't written creatively since she'd been at school and had no idea why she turned to a pen instead of a bottle of wine, but she rediscovered the pleasure of spilling her innermost thoughts out onto paper. Poetry helped put her emotions into a manageable framework; story writing allowed her to climb into the skin of characters, walk in their footsteps, and find some sadly lacking control. Being in charge of a fictitious world helped her deal with a real world in which she had been flattened. Then she joined the Millspring Quillers, which had turned out to be her salvation. Sometimes they wrote haiku or limericks for light relief. One week they'd had an assignment to make a shopping list sexy; they'd even done a letter to an imaginary lover, an exercise in subverting any intrinsic decent values they might have to release a deceptive, self-serving side of themselves, which was pretty ironic given how she'd come to be part of the group. Now they were working through the planning of a novel—the characters, the setting, the dialogue, the plot, the story arc—as an exercise.

She didn't tell Chris about her classes because once, not long after they'd gotten back together, she'd walked in on him and his daughter Shauna reading her "Ode to Old Tom" in her notepad and laughing uncontrollably. Admittedly Simon Armitage wouldn't have felt threatened, but it was a highly personal piece about a cat she'd once been fond of, and she'd poured her heart into it. Their scorn burned her, humiliated her, and when Shauna had gone home, Polly had taken him to task about it. But Chris was politician-skilled at spinning things on their heads, and managed to make her into the bad guy because she couldn't take a joke. So she went underground after that, hiding her creative work out of sight. And she was glad that she'd heeded her intuition not to tell him about the classes, because he'd have put her off or scoffed for he never could see how people got so much enjoyment out of the written word.

Polly found the book project really exciting. In her story she had even reimagined some of her life to bring her comfort. Her uncle Ed and auntie Rina featured as Sabrina's parents, and though gone now, they had enjoyed a long, happy life. Her daughter Linnet was working her way around Australia, having safe and exciting adventures, doing all the things Polly would have wished for her. Polly liked to imagine that as a young adult she was pretty and petite with sun-kissed skin, dark hair, and a voice like a song. Even Tom the cat from next door was in it, and the house Sabrina was escaping to was the cottage her uncle and auntie had rented in real life until they could find one they liked as much to buy. It was bittersweet to write about her lost loved ones, but she found more solace than pain in the exercises.

In her story Sabrina had been pushed too far at work and pushed too far in her marriage. Sabrina was based on herself, but she was much more confident and kickass. Jasper had his womanizing roots in Chris, but he was far nastier, more volatile and toxic. Sabrina was excited about the prospect of being single again. So was Polly, but Sabrina didn't wake up sometimes in a cold sweat worrying about the logistics of breaking free. But both writer and character were united in the knowledge that cutting loose was their only option.

Polly hadn't a clue how Chris was going to take it when she said that she was leaving him, because she knew he thought that everything in the garden was lovely, and it probably was from his side of things. He was looking at flower-filled borders and a verdant green lawn, and all she could see was a barren wasteland; all the seeds and bulbs she'd planted hoping they would grow lay rotten under the surface of the soil.

In hindsight the damage had been done long before his affair, but the affair shone the harsh light on the truth of her relationship, and she saw it now fully exposed. That it was the worst kind of loneliness, to feel alone when you were with someone, and how tiny scraps of shrapnel could do as much harm as big thunderous bullets, even though you barely felt them at the time. Little things that on their own didn't amount to much, but once lumped together made a huge ugly insurmountable mound: never saying thank you to her, taking her for granted, not allowing her to get someone in to put new tiles up or a new carpet down, rolling his eyes at her with exasperation if she told him to shove his dirty clothes in the wash basket instead of dropping them at the side of it, leaving his work bag in a place where she'd always have to shift it. His lack of consideration, his obliviousness to her needs had chipped away at her love but also her self-esteem. She'd been so battered and bewildered, so reduced after the affair with Mrs. Jones, that she didn't know if she'd taken him back more to salve her ego or because she really loved him, though it felt like the latter then. She'd wanted to believe his promises that he'd do what it took to get them back on track. In the first few weeks he tried. He'd even rustled up a couple of meals—pasta in jarred sauce—and had letterbox flowers sent to the house for her that came with free chocolates. She really felt as if a new dawn had come, but in truth it was just a false spring, like the ones in January when the ground warms up and the snowdrops pop out, only for a winter frost to descend and kill them. It all started to slip back to how it was before when she was the only one making the effort in the relationship. And like a worm, in a part of her brain that she couldn't reach to excise it, sat the affair, always there, always hurting.

She told herself that if she still felt the same by the first of May, a year to the day since she moved back in, if his vow to make it all right hadn't come to fruition, then she'd ring the final bell, stupidly hoping that in the meantime, Chris would realize what was slipping away from him. He'd refused to talk things through, he wouldn't listen or change, so she'd kept her promise to herself and set her plan in motion. Then Camay had thrown a spanner in the works with this impulsively arranged wedding. Polly put everything on hold, but it was a mere delay, not a cancellation. She had to leave. She felt herself becoming more and more transparent with every passing day, and if she didn't leave soon, there would be nothing left of her to go.

She had no doubt she would have to absorb the blame for the end of their relationship. Chris would mop up all available sympathy and portray himself as a saint worthy of his own stained glass church window. People who knew him would be flabbergasted that she could leave such a hardworking, good-looking, well-minted family man as Chris Barrett. Was she bonkers? Chris was popular, well-liked, but he saved his best for others, not her.

No doubt Camay would have a lot to say about it and Ward would nod along in consensus. Chris's daughter Shauna would be the most vocal. She'd never liked her stepmother, despite every effort Polly had made to build a relationship with her. Will was a different kettle of fish, a kid with a lovely aura, and Polly liked being around him. She'd helped him with his A-levels when he was struggling and he'd sent her a beautiful thank-you notelet when he passed them all with flying colors. She'd kept it; it was now with the brooches in her handbag.

He and his father didn't have a lot of middle ground, and Chris had been a fool not to try to make some, she'd told him, though he hadn't listened to that either.

In her class that evening, Polly worked on the scene of the big marital split, when Sabrina tells Jasper it's all over. When he'd reneged on his promise not to stick his fingers in his ears and sing loud "la-las" whenever she wanted to talk emotions; when he continued to say that it was unreasonable for him to turn down work so they could go out for a meal or take a holiday; when sex was no longer a giving, sharing thing, but a taking, a mere scratching when an itch presented itself to him. Sabrina had given Jasper a full year to reform, and if anything, he'd gotten worse.

It was all so much easier when you could control the whole thing in your head, like both sides of a chess game. Not so much when playing with only the black pieces and trying to second-guess if the white pieces would erupt, implode, cry, or physically throw her out of the door when her queen checkmated his king.

Chapter 4

On her way home from class, Polly called in at the mini supermarket up the road and bought some chicken Kievs for tea. She sprinkled some frozen mini roast potatoes on a baking tray and stuck everything in the oven along with a carton of cauliflower cheese. Then she poured herself a large glass of chenin blanc from the fridge and sighed as it hit the back of her throat with an icy punch.

When she heard Chris's van draw up, she felt her jaw tighten with tension. Since deciding to leave, she'd felt deceitful pretending everything was running along as always when she knew what was coming. He hadn't noticed anything amiss, hadn't picked up on her awkwardness, hadn't felt the air thickening around them when they were together; sometimes she'd felt it cloying in the back of her throat enough to choke her. She wanted him to suspect something, because at least it would mean he was taking some notice of her, but there was fat chance of that. It wouldn't have changed anything, though, not now. They were too far past their finish line.

"Hi," she called and pushed out a civil smile of greeting when he walked in.

"Smells good," he said. "I'll be down in five for it."

He dropped his bag where he stood. She'd lost count of the times they'd had the subsequent exchange, and they were about to have it again.

"Please don't leave it there, Chris. I'm sick of having to move it."

He rolled his eyes—how she hated when he did this. "Why? Is it in the way of anything?"

Was he blind? "I can't get to the bin, I can't get to the door."

"Do you want to get to the door?"

"It's not the point." He dumped, she shifted, that was the point, and it had been one of the many little things that had helped to wreck their relationship.

He gave it a petulant kick to the left—that was all it took for it no longer to be an obstacle—while chuntering under his breath about not needing this when he'd just come in from work, plus the word *nag* was thrown in for good measure. He then went upstairs to change and Polly checked on how things were in the oven.

He came downstairs shortly afterward in tracksuit bottoms and an old sweatshirt. He smiled at her and she registered the rare phenomenon and silently gulped. He smiled at customers about to part with their cash, he smiled at his daughter, but in all honesty, she couldn't remember the last time she got his full beam trained exclusively on her.

"Want your wine topped up?" he asked, opening the fridge for an energy drink.

"Er, please." He almost never asked her.

She served up and he tucked into his dinner as if he hadn't eaten for a week and made small noises of approval as he was chewing.

"I haven't stopped for as much as a cuppa all day. This is lovely. Tastes like restaurant food," he said.

It didn't. It tasted like what it was, easy and convenient. She used to love cooking for him. She used to put a flower in a vase on the table and try to make their evening meals feel intimate and caring for him after a full day's work, but he'd just bolt down the food and then get up, shove his plate in the washing-up bowl, and go and watch the telly, leaving her to finish her meal alone. She hadn't ever wanted to stop making the effort, but eventually she had. She'd made hardly any meals from scratch over the past few months; fresh had been replaced by frozen and dried, more things were delivered to the table from the microwave, and she didn't want to think how many unappreciated man-hours she'd clocked up in the kitchen over the past eight years.

"Really nice," he went on. "Delicious."

More compliments. Something prickled on her scalp. Looking back, she remembered him being especially buoyant at the time of his fling. Bouncy as a dog with two dicks, not a hint of conflict or guilt. She watched him secretly as he ate with gusto, and she wondered how she would feel if he announced he was having another affair. She wished he would. It would make things so easy because she could say, "Well, off you go and fill your boots." A mutual split would be an ideal scenario.

He wouldn't be single for long, she knew. She'd seen how women flirted with him at the garage, because he looked good in petrol-blue overalls with his perfect stubble, and he had the gift of gab when he didn't have to back it up with any substance. He was handsomer in his mid-forties than he had been in his mid-thirties, and he'd been quite the looker then. He'd always looked after himself, had nice white teeth, and though his sandy-brown hair was thinning and graying a bit at the sides, he wore it short in a cut that suited him. He kept himself trim and toned with weights in their garage and he never had a problem spending money on clothes for himself, even if he had a problem spending it on other things. He always smelled of either his garage or a pricey cologne, both easy on the olfactory nerves of people he encountered. She'd liked that he took pride in his appearance and had enjoyed being on his arm whenever they went anywhere, knowing that other females were admiring him but she was the one he went home to. Until she wasn't.

That night in bed, Chris kissed her. Not a perfunctory peck but a longer kiss that grew in intensity, and she could tell where it was heading. She stopped him before it went to "access all areas" and said not tonight because she was whacked. *Not tonight. Not again.* She didn't even want to sleep beside him anymore—it felt wrong to—but keeping things on an even keel until after Camay's wedding had been her master plan, for right or wrong. It did help that the bed was so wide; it didn't even feel as if they were sleeping together. Chris was snoring softly within five minutes, while Polly lay there imagining herself in a cozy single bed with a springy mattress, not a hard orthopedic one for the back, as had been Chris's choice. Everything was always Chris's way or the highway, and for her that highway was now approaching fast.

The *Daily Trumpet* would like to apologize to Mr. Martyn Eagles of Eagles Carpets, Doncaster, for inadvertently printing that he had "a vast selection of drugs in his 70 percent off May Day sale while stocks last—9am–5pm." This should have read "a vast selection of rugs." We also have to apologize to South Yorkshire police for their having to turn out in force to dispel the crowds that had been queueing since the previous evening.

Chapter 5

Four days to the renewal of the vows ceremony

"Do you think you'll ever get married?" asked Sheridan the next day at work. Then it was as if someone had taken out a foundation stone from a whole tower block, causing it to collapse. Poor Sheridan couldn't have known that Polly would fold quite so dramatically at such a gentle probe. Polly couldn't have known it either: She wasn't aware of how much stress she was operating under. Her head told her she was coping just fine; her body obviously knew otherwise. Her eyes started squirting out tears to the extent that she couldn't wipe them fast enough with her fingers. Sheridan hurriedly took out a pack of tissues from her bag and threw it over the divide.

"Bloody hell, Pol, what did I say?"

Polly looked around her, hoping no one had noticed. It was bad enough breaking down in front of Sheridan, but if any of Jeremy's team were around, they'd attribute any such show of emotion to "women's hormones," "time of the month," or "early menopause," and females in this place had enough of a rubbish deal without handing the males ammunition with which to load their guns.

"Is it that pathetic pay raise? Has it been on your mind?" whispered Sheridan, hoping to jolly her.

It wasn't, but it had its part to play. Another straw on the camel's back, and quite a few of them were bearing down on her at the moment.

"Right, go to the loo, get yourself together, and I'll meet you in the canteen in five minutes," commanded Sheridan. For a woman so young, she was a bossy beggar at times. She waddled out toward the lift, and Polly headed for the ladies' room and did a repair job on her makeup. Nothing could be done about her eyes, which were already puffed up after not much sleep. She'd lain in bed for ages wide awake, putting herself in Chris's head, him imagining everything was fine and dandy and not having a clue that the woman he'd just tried to be intimate with would be leaving him at the weekend. She felt cunning and guilty, and that wasn't a combination that guaranteed a good sleep.

She walked into the canteen and saw Sheridan in the far corner waving. She'd already gotten the drinks and two enormous pieces of tiffin.

"So, spill," ordered Sheridan. She'd never seen Polly cry before and she suspected it must be a big deal if she'd broken down at work.

"Sorry about that, upstairs," Polly began. "I don't know what came over me. I'm okay. Really."

"You're so obviously not; you look like crap. Have you slept? Your eyes were all swollen up when you walked in, not that I would have said anything, although I just have," said Sheridan, who wasn't one for mincing her words. And that was what Polly really liked about her. She was an open book; there was no pretense, no pretensions, nothing hiding in her to leap out and bite you.

Polly really didn't want this, though. Sheridan was about to drop a baby and was full of joy and sunshine and hope and happiness; she shouldn't burden her with her problems. "If," Sheridan then said, through a large mouthful of tiffin, "you are going to give me some bullshit that nothing is up because I'm pregnant and you think I shouldn't be worrying, don't waste your energy. You are not going to bring on my early labor by unpacking what's going on in your head. In fact, if anything, I hope you do, so you've nothing to lose. Trust me, I'm a great listener. I'm also very nosy. So what was it in the words 'Do you think you'll ever get married?' that caused that reaction? Hasn't he asked you—Chris? Is it a sore point?"

When they'd gotten back together, Polly remembered Chris saying in bed once that when things had settled, maybe they should talk about "the next step." She'd become a little giddy about it at the time, when she was all mixed up and vulnerable, presuming he meant marriage, but looking back now, it might have meant joint custody of a pressure washer. He'd never mentioned it since, and she'd never brought it up because if he did propose, it had to come entirely from him to be viable.

"No, he hasn't asked me, but it's not that." Polly swallowed a mouthful of nervous saliva.

"What the hell is it then, Pol?"

Just say it, said a voice in Polly's head. It felt too big to keep in, too weighty and uncomfortable, and she needed to tell someone.

"I'm leaving him."

She had never spoken those words aloud to anyone, and they seemed especially harsh, hanging in the air like a trio of discordant bells. They sounded brutal, heartless, an assault on the eardrums.

"Fuck," said Sheridan, eyes widening. "I thought you were going to say your sister-in-law's wedding had made you feel a bit *why not us?* I wasn't expecting that. Why didn't you tell me before?" Sheridan held up her hand and then answered her own question in a very miffed tone. "You didn't want to offload onto the pregnant woman. I thought we were friends, Polly Potter."

"We are," said Polly. "That's why I didn't want to offload onto the pregnant woman."

"Drink your drink," said Sheridan after tutting at her. "I got you a hot chocolate. I thought it was more comforting than an Americano. You looked as if you needed some TLC." The words nearly set Polly off crying again because it was these little considerations that made the world go round. She'd had so few of them from Chris, whom she wanted them from most of all, that they felt massive, stretched all out of proportion when she received them elsewhere. She'd really miss Sheridan when she left. They'd stay in touch, but it wouldn't be the same as seeing her every day and hearing her irreverent wit and playing their daft office games that made her laugh. She'd been a constant source of joy in her life since she took the office seat next to her two years ago, after Alan had died and the company was going through all the changes and Polly had felt sad and unsettled and in need of a friend. "Can I ask why?" Sheridan shifted to a more comfortable position on the hard plastic chair. "I mean, I've never met your other half, but I kind of got the impression you were okay."

Where to start? With "Me and Mrs. Jones," she supposed. "Chris had an affair last year."

"What?"

Something else Sheridan hadn't been expecting.

"Is that when you lost all that weight and told me you'd been to Slimming World? Polly, you bloody liar."

It was then. And she hadn't said anything to Sheridan at the time because her mum hadn't been well. But even so, Polly had never really been that open a person. She'd had a lot to deal with in her life, things she found too embarrassing and raw to share, so she'd just got on with dealing with it herself.

"Did you know her?" asked Sheridan.

"All I knew about her was that she was called Mrs. Jones. Or maybe she wasn't, but that's the name he'd stored her number under on his phone."

"How did you find out, Pol?"

"We were in his van. It was April Fool's Day of all dates. He'd just filled up with petrol and was paying. A text message from Mrs. Jones popped up on the dashboard display; his phone Bluetooth was still connected, you see. The only Mrs. Jones I knew lived next door to Chris's mum and she kept an eye on her for him so I was worried something must be wrong. I didn't think; I just pressed the 'read out' button."

Sheridan couldn't have been more engrossed if she'd tried.

"This robotic voice read out the message. 'Thank you for yesterday. I haven't come so hard in ages. When are we doing it again? When can you sneak away?'" Word for word, she'd never forgotten it.

"Fucking hell," said Sheridan, more breath than voice. "What did you do?"

"He got back in and I told him what Mrs. Jones had said and he went ape, saying I shouldn't be reading his texts, how dare I? I just got out and walked off."

"Did he go after you?"

"No, he drove off the other way. I spent the night in a hotel. Then I went to the house when I knew he'd be at work, packed some things, and moved into an Airbnb. It wasn't ideal living out of a suitcase. I ignored his calls for a while; then, after a month, I stupidly weakened and answered. We agreed to give things another go, but he said that if we had any chance of repairing we should look forward, not back. What's done is done, no point in raking it all up, blah blah. He refused to tell me anything about her, other than it was finished."

"I bet he did, the bellend," said Sheridan, her mouth contracted into a grim line. "I'd have ripped his bollocks off with my bare hands."

The Billy Paul song "Me and Mrs. Jones" had kept cropping up everywhere in the weeks that followed. It had haunted her. Piped through speakers in the supermarket, playing on the radio in her car, even in a hotel toilet once during a work conference. Especially that line about having a thing going on.

"The Airbnb was awful, I was mashed, and I just wanted to go home. You don't have to tell me I gave in too quickly and let him dictate the terms."

Always his terms.

She'd read countless books about how to heal a broken heart, and they hadn't worked. His affair had altered him irrevocably in her eyes and she'd tried her best to love the changed man she saw him as now, just like the books advised. They said you could build a new stage in a relationship even if you couldn't forgive. And maybe, if he'd put the effort into sewing up the holes that her trust in him had escaped through, they might have had a chance. But he hadn't even bothered threading the needle to try.

Sheridan reached over and put her hand on top of Polly's. "Oh Pol. I wish I'd known all this. Maybe I could have helped you, even if I was just a sounding board for you. But why now, Pol? If he had the affair last year?"

"It sounds dumb, I know, but I told myself that I'd give it a full twelve months from when I moved back in with him on May Day for us to . . . recalibrate; heal, if you like. Some people's relationships reset for the better after something like this"—so said another of those stupid books—"and I hoped that might happen to us; I hoped we could make it right. The idea of splitting up and starting again back then was too big for my head; I was crushed and it was so much easier to stay and hope than leave for good. For a while I really thought we'd recover, but then he just stopped putting the effort in, all the things he'd promised didn't happen, and I realized that after nearly a year of trying, I couldn't forgive and I'd never forget."

"So why the heck did you say yes to being a flaming bridesmaid? You could have been out of it all by now."

"You have to have met Camay to understand," said Polly, though she knew it was a weak answer. "She sort of cornered me in a roomful of family after announcing this mad, impulsive wedding idea"—*"And of course Polly will be the bridesmaid, won't you, Polly?"*—"and I couldn't think of a viable reason why not at the time, other than I was hoping to have left her brother by then. I rang later to suggest maybe she should ask Chris's daughter instead, but she was insistent I was the best person for the job and she would not take no for an answer." Polly rubbed her forehead and groaned, realizing how pathetic she sounded even though Sheridan couldn't begin to imagine how forceful Camay could be when she wanted her own way on things. "I thought about just leaving Chris when I said I would and not even thinking about the wedding, but then the house I'd had lined up fell through at the last minute and Camay seemed so excited about everything and it was all moving so fast and becoming so complicated that in the end I thought, what difference is another couple of weeks going to make? Let her have her day without me spoiling the run-up to it, even if she does scribble out my face on all the photos afterward."

"I'd be scribbling out your dress before your face," said Sheridan. Then softly she asked, "What promises did Chris make to you, Pol?"

"Nothing big," said Polly. "Just that he'd take time off from work so we could go off for a mini break, or the cinema, a meal, even though he thinks eating out is a waste of cash."

"But you like going out for meals," said Sheridan, with emphasis.

Polly swallowed because she knew that what she was about to say would hurt herself.

"When I went back to him, I found a restaurant receipt in the pocket of his suit. He'd taken someone out for fillet steaks, an expensive bottle of wine, porn star martinis, and truffles with their coffees."

"Ouch," said Sheridan with a grimace. "I'm figuring he wasn't such an insensitive twat when you first started going out with him."

"Charm personified. I'd just lost my mum and it had raked up a lot of feelings, so I suppose I was vulnerable. He was ten years older than me and he said all the right things, like 'You need someone to look after you.'"

"Are you sure you didn't mishear and what he actually said was, 'I need someone to look after me'?"

Polly chuckled. "Maybe I did."

"Did he seduce you with fillet steaks and porn star martinis?" asked Sheridan.

"Not even in our early days. I think he bought me a rump once, in a Wetherspoons."

Sheridan's turn to feel teary. "Oh Pol."

"I don't know when we became the couple we are now. I don't know how it happened."

"What about friends, Polly? You never talk about any. Is there no bestie you can call on for some support?"

Polly shook her head slowly. Her once close friends had moved away, had families, found new close friends.

Sheridan took a deep breath that lifted up her shoulders before she exhaled, letting them drop.

"So, what's the plan?"

"I'm going to move into a hotel just outside Wakefield for a week or so. It'll be handy for here until I can find a place to rent."

"If you need any help shifting anything, Dmitri's dad has a van," Sheridan offered.

Polly smiled at her. "Thank you, that's very kind of you." In an ideal world, Chris would play fair and they'd part as friends. He'd store the things she couldn't get in her car until she could move them out, but she was ready to cut and run with only the cases she could get in her car. A punctured ego had the same power as a broken heart to make someone volatile, and she was pretty sure, if anything, he'd be suffering from the former more.

Polly glanced at her watch. "We'd better get back upstairs," she said. "I'm sorry I laid all that on you, Sheridan. It's not fair and—"

"Shut up," said Sheridan. "I wish I could do more to help you. You sound as if you need a good mate."

"Oh, I'll be fine," said Polly, smiling a smile that sat precariously on her lips. A smile she didn't feel. A smile that lied she was all right, when really she was anything but.

An unfortunate error appeared in the Diet and Health supplement of the *Daily Trumpet* on 29 March in which we reported that Mrs. Janet Wilkins had lost four stone by farting for two full days during the week for a whole year. We did of course mean fasting.

Chapter 6

Polly had just gotten back from lunch and was taking off her jacket when one of the young maintenance men came out of Jeremy's office carrying the portrait of Alan Eagleton, founder of Northern Eagles, which had hung on the wall in there for over a quarter of a century. Polly felt a rush of anger sweep through her entire body.

"Excuse me," she called to him. "What are you doing with that?"

"Taking it to storage," he answered.

Polly's hand unconsciously sought out her necklace, specifically the ring that was threaded onto it. She never took it off. It had been her aunt's wedding ring and she'd rescued it from her mother's drawer, where it sat in a bag awaiting a trip to the pawnbrokers. It was the only physical thing she had of hers and as such was beyond precious. Her fingers automatically reached for it in times of stress, when she needed some strength. Her talisman.

Polly was fuming. She tried to channel her focus into Auntie Marian's Bread, but she couldn't. She threw herself out of her chair and headed for Jeremy's office. She knocked but opened the door before he had time to say "Enter," to find him adjusting a new photograph portrait on the wall in the place where Alan's had been. It was of himself in a pinstripe suit, standing with his arm resting on a mantelpiece.

"Like it?" he asked, with the tone of someone who liked it very much. "I look very pensive, don't I? Thought it was about time we said goodbye to old, dead Alan. We don't need him anymore, or his name. Behold a new era, Polly. We are shortly to be rebranded as Business Strength. New logo, out with the eagle and in with the bull."

You're telling me, thought Polly. She didn't offer her opinion on the picture. Jeremy's pointy face looked extra elongated, as if it had been squashed between two lift doors, and the photographer hadn't been tempted to flesh out his mean line of mouth. Polly thought his expression made him look constipated rather than pensive.

"Any initial thoughts about Auntie Marian's Bread?" asked Jeremy, standing back to check for tilt.

"What?" snapped Polly.

"Auntie Marian's Bread? The would-be new Warburtons?" said Jeremy, slowly and patronizingly, as if she were a doddery old aunt with hearing problems.

"Not yet," she said.

"What did you want then?"

She didn't say that she'd flown in here to scream at him, *Put Alan's portrait back on the wall where it belongs, you knob*. The moment had passed and it wouldn't have done any good anyway. Alan's era was long gone and his portrait remaining on the wall wouldn't make any difference.

"I can't actually remember."

Jeremy smirked. "I think you'd better go and get yourself some of that oil of evening primrose, or whatever it is you women take. Anyway, as you're here, any chance of Polly putting the kettle on for me?"

Polly had worked at Northern Eagles for sixteen years now. She'd been a temp drafted in when the head honcho's PA retired and he'd frightened off all other potential replacements. Alan Eagleton had a fearsome reputation, but as Polly was to discover, it was only fools he didn't tolerate. He was a big man in both stature and reputation. He had built the company from the ground up and made a major success story of it because what Alan Eagleton didn't know about how companies worked—and failed—wasn't worth talking about. He was the best at what he did, he knew he was, and he employed people who were passionate, hardworking, and hungry, and he rewarded them for their service and loyalty. Had he lived longer, he would have realized that bringing Jeremy Watson into his crew was a rare mistake.

Everyone expected Alan to eat the nineteen-year-old Polly for breakfast, but he was nothing if not fair, and she gave him no reason to bark at her. She was smart and savvy, picked up his ways and accommodated them. They quickly developed a rapport, and even though she was only supposed to be there until they found a more experienced permanent PA, every interviewee fell short of his expectations. Then one Friday, just before she was due to call it a day, he pulled her into the office and asked her to sit down.

"Polly. Do you think I'm easy to work for? No bullshit now, because I can smell it a mile off."

"I think you have exacting but attainable standards," she answered him honestly, "and you get annoyed when others fall short. You don't get mad for the sake of it."

"I don't get mad with you, do I?" he asked her. "Because you do what I ask and you do it well."

"Thank you." She gave a smile, just a little one because she wasn't sure where this was heading.

"So I'm not faffing about any longer interviewing people, will you be my new PA on a permanent basis?"

He made it sound like a proposal.

"You'll be getting paid more than you get as a temp, plus you'll have all the company benefits, pension, holiday, life insurance, sick pay, et cetera, though I'd appreciate it if you stayed well. I don't like paying people for sitting at home watching telly."

Polly opened her mouth but no sound came out. She'd hoped he'd take her on but never presumed he would.

"Well?" Alan prompted her.

She found her voice quickly then, knowing patience wasn't his strong point.

"I'd be delighted," she said.

"Good. I'll have HR do all the forms and so on, but as from Monday you'll be on the payroll. Now bugger off and have a nice weekend."

And she did bugger off and had a more than nice weekend. And the following Monday started off a wonderful phase in her life, because being Alan's PA became so much more than a job for her. He treated her more like a young trainee, destined to follow in his footsteps. He talked to her about his customers and the problems they were having or what they needed from him, and when she sat in on his meetings, taking notes, she absorbed a lot of information at the same time. Alan nurtured her interest, and one day after she'd been there a couple of years, she walked in to find a brand-new desk had been put in place of her old one—one of the posh mahogany ones all the execs had. "I'm making you my assistant," he said. "More pay, two more days holiday, but you'll be ready for them because I'll work you, lass." And he did, and she loved every minute of her increased responsibilities. They were golden days and she missed them terribly.

Polly took Jeremy a coffee, then exited his office, dropped into her chair, and made a huff noise that cleared all the air out of her lungs.

"You look royally pissed off," said Sheridan.

"I am very pissed off," came her reply.

"Anything to do with that portrait?"

"Everything to do with that portrait." Polly could feel the increased pace of her heart underneath her rib cage. "Storage." She humphed. Alan's daughter was offered the portrait when he died, and she didn't want it, so it stayed on the wall. Alan once told her that they had a fractious relationship. She was stony-faced at his funeral, sitting with his equally stony-faced ex-wife, an older and younger version of each other. Polly had cried buckets. She knew that parent-child relationships could be complicated, blood ties no guarantee of affection, because she hadn't gotten on too well with her own mother. She'd been manipulative and self-centered, but Polly couldn't believe that Alan would be anything other than easy for a daughter to love.

Alan only spoke about his family once to her. It was Christmas and they'd been working late and had stopped for a break: tea and canteen sandwiches in his office. She couldn't remember how they'd gotten onto the subject, but he'd told her that he'd divorced his wife years before, though if he'd known he'd have lost his daughter too, he'd have put up with the loveless state of his marriage. He always hoped the poison she dripped in their daughter's ear would eventually be neutralized by her own judgment as she grew up, but it never was, and that haunted him. She didn't want to know him, though she was quite happy to be acquainted with his fortune: the pony, the private school, the new car when she passed her driving test, the house he bought for her twenty-first birthday.

"I always liked that picture," said Sheridan. "He looked a nice man. Was he?"

"He was great, unless you were an idiot," replied Polly with a fond smile. "He was a brilliant man. Beyond kind."

He gave her as much time off as she needed when her mum played up. For as long as she could remember, she'd been forced into acting as her own parent's parent. No wonder she went off the rails at sixteen and ended up pregnant on that holiday in Benidorm. Maybe it was an unconscious cry to call her mother to arms, but if it was, it didn't work. Her mother wasn't any support to her through any of it. Even when she finally let go of her tiny stillborn daughter and handed her to a waiting nurse, all she could remember was her mother sitting there dry-eyed and saying, "Well, it's for the best."

Then she got the job here and working became her salvation; it gave her the energy to deal with her many responsibilities at home. And Alan Eagleton's presence was like a lit, scented candle in a life that was darker than it was light.

"He was lovely. So well respected," Polly went on. "Everything a man should be."

"You sound like you're talking about your dad. Or a lover," said Sheridan, tossing a Ferrero Rocher over the desk division.

Polly never knew her dad. Her mother only knew him for ten minutes. But no, she didn't think of Alan as a father figure, despite the vacancy. Nor did she think of him as a lover, but she thought she did love him, even though she wasn't sure what sort of a love it was. She couldn't ever see herself in bed with him, but she could visualize them going out for dinner, her arm linking his, talking into the wee small hours, locking the door against the weather and enjoying each other's company in front of a roaring fire and a good TV drama. It was a love that defied a pigeonhole slot, and when he died, it had felt as if she'd lost one of the closest people in her life. She still missed him. It didn't hurt any less, just less often.

"What happened to him?" asked Sheridan.

"He had a heart attack at home. His cleaner found him. He died alone and he shouldn't have. He was too loved, too gregarious for that. He was barely buried when his daughter sold the firm to Charles Butler, and the rest is history. Very few of Alan's people stayed. And Charles, for some reason, really took to Jeremy."

"How can anyone take to Jeremy?" Sheridan stuck out her tongue. That made Polly laugh a little.

"Jeremy's very good at smarm and Charles likes to be flattered, plus he wanted some continuity in the company, someone who knew Alan's ways."

"Like you, you mean."

"Yes, but I'm a woman. So it was Jeremy he elevated to be his MD, leaving him in charge so he could play golf and just poke his head in every so often to see how things were running. They made me apply for my own job, well, at least a role that was . . . much reduced, as was the pay."

Sheridan's mouth opened so wide, she almost lost the piece of tiffin that was sitting in it.

"Jesus Christ, Pol, why did you stay on in this snake pit?"

"Because no other firm would take me seriously without any qualifications, Sheridan. They're all looking for business graduates these days and I haven't even got an A-level. At least here I still had a chance of putting into practice everything I'd learned. Charles Butler was quite aware of the successes I'd had and he thought I was best employed serving Jeremy. I did hope in time they'd come to see what Alan had seen in me and promote me back to where I was."

"But, Pol, they do see that already, but they're not going to give you the top job when they can keep you where you are and just nick all your best ideas. Don't you think you've wasted enough time waiting for things to change that aren't going to?"

That was her life right there in a nutshell: waiting, hoping, nothing.

Polly nodded. Seeing them take out Alan's portrait today hurt her more than she could say. She felt all mixed up inside, angry and sad, as if she were pacing around inside herself not knowing what to do with all the dark energy it generated.

"It's really upset you, that, hasn't it?" Sheridan gave her a small smile of sympathy.

"Yes," Polly answered. It meant the end of something, and there were too many endings occupying her brain at the moment.

Last week the *Daily Trumpet* mistakenly printed that husband-and-wife champion singing duo Vicky and Rob Drew won the South Yorkshire Celebrity Soundalike Trophy for their faultless impersonation of David Icke and Tina Turner. This was not the case. Vicky and Bob won for their impersonations of Sonny and Chair. We apologize unreservedly and are delighted that Mr. and Mrs. Drewp have accepted lunch for two at the Fish Fillies restaurant in Deepcar as due recompense.

Chapter 7

Three days to the renewal of the vows ceremony

The next day Polly didn't get into work until eleven as she had a filling replaced at the dentist. As usual, for anyone who arrived after eight in the morning, there were no spaces available in the works car park, so she had to drive to the large overspill and circle around until she found one, which did nothing for her already elevated stress levels.

"How did it go?" asked Sheridan.

"Ath well ath to be ethpecthed, then it took me ageth to find thomewhere to park," Polly muttered, unlooping her bag from her shoulder. She was numb up to her temple and her tongue was flopping like a dead fish in her mouth. She wished she could lay her hands on something to numb the rest of her for the next few days, until she was sitting in a hotel room unpacking a suitcase.

Sheridan grinned. "I'm figuring you can't have a coffee for a bit."

"Nope," said Polly, giving her a lopsided smile. "I withhh." She did a double take of Sheridan's face. She was pale and her eyes were puffy.

"Don't say it," said Sheridan, because that look hadn't gotten past her. "I've had a very bad night's sleep. I was in bed for nine, but this one would not let me rest." She patted her stomach, which seemed more rotund than it had even yesterday. "I've had enough now, Pol. I just want him out."

She took a bottle of Gaviscon from her filing drawer, screwed off the top, and swigged it. Polly remembered doing the same, totally ignoring the dosage instructions.

"And just to ruin your day even more," said Sheridan, leaning over the partition between them, "you're going to be doing a test. Everyone was delighted—*not*—to find an email this morning telling us we had that to look forward to."

"What?"

"You heard. Remember when Germany went on that psychology day course a couple of months ago and we wondered what it was all about?" Sheridan leaned closer over the partition. "Well . . . it seems he's used his newfound expertise to devise a test for the whole company. And everyone has to do it. Without exception. If you get a wiggle on, you'll catch the eleven o'clock session. They're on the hour. I heard him talking to Marjorie Wright about it earlier. She went flying into his office wanting to know why she knew eff all about it, and he told her that it was nothing too intrusive, just a social experiment to discover personality traits, strengths, weaknesses, and crap like that. He said it would be very useful to know what kind of people work in the ranks and where they need support. Marjorie said that he should have done it in conjunction with HR, if at all. He reminded her that he was the MD and she told him that she didn't give a shit and he was taking liberties. It was comedy gold, Pol; you'd have loved it. She didn't half slam the door on the way out." Sheridan chuckled. "B5, take a pen. No phones allowed."

"Okay then. I'll thee you in an hour," said Polly, picking up a pen from the pot on her table.

"Thee ya," Sheridan batted back.

* * *

Outside room B5 a queue of people were waiting. Polly saw Marjorie just coming away from the coffee machine and gave her a wave.

Marjorie smiled and walked over. She had a real presence, Polly had always thought. She was never seen without a slick of bright red lipstick that Polly wished she'd be brave enough to wear. Marjorie always looked powerful and feminine, assured and glamorous. She wouldn't have looked out of place on the panel of *Dragon's Den*.

"Haven't seen you for a bit," Marjorie said warmly. "How are you doing, Polly?"

"Okay." Polly nodded and pointed to her mouth. "Juth come from the dentitht."

"Ah, so this is merely continuing the joy," she said, the corner of her lip kinking slightly. "Nothing to do with us. This is all Jeremy." She gave his name a sour weight.

People started to move forward.

"Anyway, nice to see you," said Marjorie. "We should have a coffee sometime soon." She sounded as if she meant it and hadn't just issued an empty invitation.

"I'd like that," Polly said with a smile, and Marjorie peeled away and back to her office.

Inside B5, Polly sat down at one of the long tables. Someone's phone made a noise and the adjudicator of the day—Ruth from Finance—had a mini conniption.

"Phones are not allowed. Turn them off and put them out of sight," she said as if she were talking to a bunch of kids about to do a GCSE exam. "Everyone got a pen?"

"I haven't," said the unmistakable voice of Len Champion, head of maintenance, from the back corner.

"You were told to bring one," said Ruth, stomping over with a cheap pen from a box on the front desk, supplied for all the Lens who really didn't want to be here, hoping that the lack of a writing utensil would be their get-out-of-jail-free card. Ruth then distributed stapled sheets of paper, and at exactly five past she said, "You have forty-five minutes to complete the test. A failure to take this seriously will result in a formal warning. Now begin."

Polly wasn't sure if it was legal to threaten someone with a formal warning if they didn't complete a test, but it wasn't for her to argue. She turned over and skim-read what she'd be answering.

Section 1. True or false:
I sleep well whatever is troubling me.
I have lots of friends.
I believe in the universal power of God.
People look up to me.

She could either answer these honestly or put down the answers they wanted to hear. She chose the former, played the game, and wondered how many others would do the same.

* * *

Sheridan was tucking into an egg sandwich when Polly got back to the office. The smell filled the air around her and Polly joke-wafted it away. She couldn't get enough of eggs when she was pregnant. Egg sandwiches with the thinnest white bread she could lay her hands on. She wouldn't eat them soft-boiled and risk causing harm to her unborn child, though. Even at sixteen she'd been conscious of all that health stuff.

"Where's Jeremy?" asked Polly, her speech back to normal now.

"Posh lunch out, which is why I'm eating this here and not in the canteen." Sheridan chewed, swallowed, and continued. "He's with my replacement, that cock Brock Harrison. Good luck working with him. He walked in, addressed my stomach, and said, 'Now then, what have you been up to?'"

Polly's eyebrows lifted in horror. "Did he really? And did you reply?"

Sheridan gave her head a lofty shake. "I decided not to lower myself to his level in case the rapid descent caused a nosebleed."

"Good girl," said Polly. There was a pit of dread in her stomach at the thought of Brock Harrison joining the department, and she knew it was imminent.

"I hope they both choke on their pheasant. Have you noticed how much lighter the office floor feels when Jeremy isn't in, Pol? I feel as if we could all float like astronauts in space."

Everyone noticed it. The air was warmer by degrees too. "I wish you were pregnant as well and we were both leaving at the same time and could meet up for coffees and playdates." Sheridan gave her best beaming smile. "You've still got oodles of time left. So hurry up and find someone nice who'll get you up the duff." *And love you like you should be loved*, she didn't add aloud but wished silently.

"You have such a way with words," Polly replied with a chuckle, though she didn't want to think about having a child because it hurt. When she and Chris first got together, they'd talked about having a baby in time. He'd seemed all for it, for a short while at least. Then he kept putting it off, and then he totally backtracked, said he was happy with what he had and was too old to go through all that "nappy-changing shit" again, though she doubted he'd ever changed one in his life. But being around a pregnant Sheridan had made Polly remember too much: that glorious anticipation, the wonder that a fully grown baby was moving around inside her whom she couldn't wait to meet.

She remembered going for her scan and seeing her cute profile, the little curve of spine. She was perfect when she was born, beautiful, with tiny feet and fingernails, unruly tufts of dark hair. And a little rosebud mouth that would never root for her mother's milk. She remembered all the things she'd bought for her daughter that someone from a charity came and collected from the house in one sad consignment: soft white clothes and teddy bears, blankets, a cot. Her arms had felt very empty for a long time. They still did.

In Monday's *Daily Trumpet* we reported that the family of May Readman had bought her a ticket to go to Dignitas for her nineteeth birthday. This should have read that they bought her a ticket to Disneyland. We are delighted to report that Mrs. Deadman has accepted the gift of a Superlight Flight suitcase as compensation for any distress caused.

Chapter 8

Two days to the renewal of the vows ceremony

"Everyone's talking about that wank personality test," said Sheridan late the next morning as she dumped a cappuccino in front of Polly. "I was listening to Len Champion in the atrium and he reckons they're going to use the results to fire people. He was on about ringing up the union."

"Len Champion would ring up the union if they ran out of cheese sandwiches in the canteen," said Polly. She pressed at her temple because she'd had a headache since she woke up and hoped a second dose of ibuprofen would quickly kick in and shift it.

"Where's Germy today?"

"Day off," replied Polly. A grin bled across her lips and infected Sheridan.

"I frigging love it when he's off. What are you reading?"

"The Auntie Marian's Bread company profile." Polly sighed unconsciously. She couldn't drum up any enthusiasm for it. "It doesn't sound like a very nice place to work."

"I thought as much when I was typing up Jeremy's notes," said Sheridan.

"Hmm," replied Polly with a nod. Some firms were easier to help than others. Some cut unnecessary corners and wouldn't listen to advice they'd paid for, which made her job so much harder. It was usually these sorts of companies that treated their staff like rubbish. Auntie Marian's Bread wouldn't be her favorite challenge; she could tell that already because the owner, Arthur Peach, wanted big changes but at the same time would be resistant to them. Some firms just gave off a rotten vibe, like this one and the Italian restaurant chain she'd read about by mistake.

"I have heartburn like you couldn't believe today, but I don't care," confessed Sheridan over the desk divide. "I was craving spicy food last night and I was craving spicy sex. I was unfillable, Pol. I hope that doesn't go away when I give birth. I'm sure we must have dented the baby's skull."

Polly threw her head back and laughed aloud, then realized she couldn't remember the last time she'd laughed like that. It was almost certainly at work with Sheridan and not at home.

"I'm surprised I can walk."

"Sheridan, please. Too much detail."

"I'm suffering for my excesses, though." Sheridan bent forward with a long *oooh* and rubbed her stomach.

"You all right?" Polly asked her.

Sheridan half chuckled, half winced. "Braxton-Hicks again. I've been having them for a full hour off and on," she said, on a deep breath. "They're really starting to throb a bit."

"Sheridan, love, I hate to tell you this, but Braxton-Hicks aren't painful."

Sheridan's face segued into an expression of horror then. "Oh God, I think I've wet myself." She stood up and there was a stain the size of the Isle of Wight on her trousers, still spreading.

"Sit back down and ring Dmitri," said Polly, putting on her best calm voice. "I'll ring an ambulance. I think you're in labor, love."

Polly got her phone out of her bag and Sheridan got hers and they both made their calls.

"Dmitri's going to meet me at the hospital. He's only five minutes away," said Sheridan. Then she started loading her bag with things from her desk drawers, including her giant bar of fruit and nut chocolate, her notepad, and her foldaway emergency poncho and matching umbrella.

"Leave all that," said Polly.

"Pol, I'm taking my things with me. You and I both know that if I come back after my maternity leave, I'm not going to be sitting at this desk. They'll transfer me somewhere else and Brock the cock is not having my best pens and chocolate." She carried on shoving her possessions into her bag until she was done. "Now if you wouldn't mind, help me get downstairs to reception, will you? Oh my God, I'm wet through."

Holding on to Polly's arm, Sheridan set off for the lift at a comfortable speed.

"I can feel everyone gawping at me," she said, chuckling. "The poor incontinent lady."

"I think they can work out what's happening," replied Polly. "Anyway, never mind about anyone else; you just concentrate on yourself."

"Good luck, Sheridan," someone shouted, followed by someone else and more of the same.

"Thank you, thank you, everyone."

They made their way to reception and sat in one of the quiet corners on the faux-leather seats. Sheridan geared up for another contraction and Polly rubbed her back, hoping it helped. She'd been left to it in the hospital. There had been no one with her, at least in the early stages of labor when she was merely given a dose of paracetamol and a woman's magazine to take her mind off things.

"Brutal," said Sheridan, coming through it. "How bad will I feel if I get to hospital and it's just bad wind after that vindaloo?"

"I've never heard of wind so bad that it breaks your waters," said Polly, pushing Sheridan's long dark curls back over her shoulders.

"Don't, I'll fart," Sheridan said, trying not to laugh.

They sat quietly, waiting for the ambulance or another contraction, whichever came first.

"Oh Polly, I will miss you. We've had a giggle, haven't we, over these past couple of years?"

Polly put her arm around Sheridan and pulled her in close. "Yes, love, we have. And we will again."

"Come and see us at home. I want to know all the goss about Germy and Cock."

"Of course I will," said Polly. She felt stupidly tearful. She remembered her own contractions starting, the strange combo of fear and exhilaration that her baby was on its way. She hadn't had it confirmed, but she knew it was a girl. She'd been in agony, but she didn't care. It meant her baby was healthy and as eager to see her mother as the mother was to see her child.

"Christ, Pol, this hurts. This baby is splitting me in half."

"He wants to meet you," said Pol, squeezing her friend. "You'll soon be holding your baby in your arms and it will be the best moment of your life." She paused then and listened hard. "I think I hear a mee-maw."

Sure enough, there was the faintest two-tone siren in the distance growing ever louder, and then they saw the welcome sight of the big yellow vehicle through the glass front doors. The two paramedics on board were quick to take over.

They loaded Sheridan into a wheelchair and started to wheel her away, but she made them stop so she could hold out her arms to Polly.

"Promise we'll keep in touch, Pol," she said, hugging her tightly. "I need to know how the wedding goes and where you'll be living and if Brock the cock comes into the department and sits on the wet chair."

Polly laughed and embraced her, savoring the warm feel of her. "I will," she said. "Good luck, darling."

Polly stayed there until the ambulance drove off. She didn't know she was crying until she felt the teardrops tickle her cheeks. What a beautiful start of things this was for the Savalas family. She sent up a silent prayer that everything would be all right, that mother and baby would be safe. Everything else would take care of itself if that happened.

* * *

Polly snuck off early that afternoon. And when she was at home, she did a little more secret packing. It made her feel proactive, as if this was really going to happen at last. It would be all change in Sheridan's life, and from Sunday onward, it would be all change in hers too.

Polly woke up the next morning to an email that baby Alexander Michalis Savalas, seven pounds fourteen ounces, had arrived. Mum and baby doing very well.

Chapter 9

The day before the renewal of the vows ceremony

Sheridan's wet chair had thoroughly dried overnight, because when Polly walked into the department, who should be sitting swiveling on it as if it were playground apparatus but Brock Harrison, clicking a pen.

"Seems I'm starting earlier than expected," he said, giving her his best corporate smile. "I hear she's had the sprog."

"Sheridan has had her baby, yes," said Polly, already feeling the hairs on the back of her neck bristling, and he'd only been in situ three seconds. She put her bag down, took off her jacket, and switched on her PC.

"Just before you start, any chance of a coffee?" asked Brock. Polly took a breath and prepared to nip this right in the bud.

"Yes, the kitchen is over—"

Then Jeremy came round the corner.

"Make that two, will you, Polly? Then just bob in for a moment, will you?" Seething, Polly put the kettle on, brought out the two cups. Brock was talking on the phone; otherwise she would have told him that in future he'd be making them because he was the assistant, not her. She was going to be *more Sabrina* at work as well as out of it, and that would start here today.

She took Jeremy's coffee into his office.

"Any ideas about Auntie Marian's Bread yet?"

"Yes, I've had some ideas," Polly said. "I seem to be having trouble getting hold of the owner, Mr. Peach, though. He hasn't returned any of my calls."

"So what are we suggesting to him?" Jeremy templed his long fingers and looked as if he was about to launch into prayer.

"Change the packaging—it's terrible."

"I know, we've just sent him a reworked suggestion. Timon's been hard at that." He smiled smugly.

Timon Cavendish, one of Jeremy's managers. The one who falsely claimed credit for her "Nutbush. No Limits" slogan. If good ideas were dynamite, he wouldn't have enough to stir his nasal hairs.

"I mean change that reworked one. You can't possibly use it."

"Why? Not trying to throw a spanner in Timon's works, are you, Polly?" said Jeremy, looking at her with the amused suspicion of one who thought she had the temerity and shallowness to be jealous.

"Not at all, but it's way too similar to Warburtons, the exact color palette in fact. They'll sue."

"It's an homage," he threw back, rhyming the word with *fromage*.

"It's a rip-off, Jeremy. And it smacks of following, not leading."

Jeremy, however, was not about to let Polly win the argument. "The lettering isn't the same, is it? It's much bolder than theirs. The eye is drawn to that before anything else."

"Yes, I know. He's changed all the capital letters to lowercase."

"Inspired. No one else is using lowercase."

"And coupled with the font he's used, that giant *A* in *Auntie* now looks like a *C*." She tried not to gloat too much. Jeremy pulled his keyboard over and started tapping while looking at his computer screen. When his face registered horror, Polly knew he'd seen it. And once seen, it couldn't be unseen.

"Not a prob," he remarked, though the muscle twitching in his jaw said different.

"They're trying to compete with the quality market and they aren't quality," she went on.

"Well, that's what they want to be. That's what we're going to make happen."

"Won't happen. He went full pelt without market testing his new products and there are better for the same price. He's got too many variations; he needs to streamline, not add to his range. And no, Timon's dictate that I be sure to endorse his 'The Biggest in Bread' as a slogan is not going to happen for reasons that are more than obvious. Anyway, as you asked for, those are my initial thoughts. Arthur Peach won't like them, but he will have to adopt them if he wants to compete with the quality big boys, or he can revert to being cheap and high volume and not spend his money with us, which would be my recommendation because he can't have both worlds, and I suspect he'll want the one that brings him the most revenue. I don't mind telling him."

"Not sure about that," said Jeremy, as expected, because saying, "Keep your cash, we can't help you," wasn't an option Charles Butler would approve of. "And while we are on the subject, talking of Arthur Peach . . . he's not what I'd call a modern man." He pulled a cringey face.

"Meaning?"

"Well, he's already made overtures that . . . he'd prefer dealing with . . . someone . . . male."

Polly's disbelief manifested in a series of rapid blinks. "In this day and age?"

"Sadly, yes. So I'm going to ask you to involve Brock from the off on this one, okay?" Jeremy tilted his head like a confused Alsatian. "He could do a lot of the talking, man to man." Brock was on the first rung. He should be sitting in meetings, taking notes, observing, learning, not "involved" when he didn't know the first thing about putting a failing business back on its feet. She had absolutely no intention of being shoved to one side just because she was female and Arthur Peach preferred talking to a bloke, especially not by a novice too young to grow anything but bum fluff on his chin. She felt her cheeks register an angry heat because Jeremy wasn't asking, he was telling. If she said no, Jeremy would override her. Wasn't happening and she needed to say so. Sabrina definitely would have.

She began. "I really don't think—"

He cut her off. "And then I need to discuss something with you that is a little more sensitive," he continued.

He reached into his drawer and pulled out a stapled group of papers. "The test you did on Wednesday." He flipped through it, refamiliarizing himself with the results, and then flashed an awkward smile before speaking again.

"I'm very concerned about what was . . . uncovered." He slid it across the desk toward her. "This is your signature on the back, isn't it?"

"Yes, it is," said Polly, confused.

"The thing is . . ." said Jeremy, licking his nonexistent lips, "the results of this test are quite . . . quite worrying, I have to say."

"What do you mean?"

"There's no other way of putting this, Polly. I'm afraid you have a personality disorder." Jeremy raised his eyebrows, newly overplucked, and kept them high as he waited for that information to sink in.

Polly hadn't a clue what to say to that. She could feel various responsive expressions tweak at her facial muscles, pulling first this way, then that. What won through was a laugh, a hoot.

"I am serious," said Jeremy, wearing his best serious face. The one he used when he said things like, "*I think we need to hand over Nutbush to Timon. He'll look after the client from here on.*"

Now Polly was serious. "Jeremy, what are you talking about?"

"I've checked the results. They clearly show that, well, basically . . . basically, you show signs of being mentally unbalanced with possible psychopathic traits. And I will have to record this in your HR file. I thought you should hear it from me in person." He turned over his hands, looking from the elbows down like Christ at the Last Supper, and above them like a sneery, pompous twat.

There followed long seconds of silence, then a voice in Polly's head said, *Girl, how much more of this are you going to take?* It was actually a line she'd written for Sabrina in her novel, delivered to her boss, Dick Germany, in a worm-turning moment. The worlds of fiction and fact suddenly blended into one as Polly felt a spiral of fire rising inside her, just as she'd imagined rose inside Sabrina when she was writing the scene.

"So let me get this right, Jeremy. You've been on some sort of amateur day course and decided to subject everyone in the company to a cobbled-together personality test where the results are recorded in indelible ink on our records. And can I ask for what purpose?"

Jeremy's jaw tightened, not expecting to be questioned by the meek and mild Polly, and also not liking that *amateur* word.

"It's an established test," he answered. "I have just added my own guided variations."

"Am I the only psychopath in the company?" Polly asked.

"Actually, no. There are a few with—"

Polly cut him off. "Oh, you don't say. There are a few of us. A group. Maybe a *murder* of psychopaths, because I'm not sure what our collective noun would be. A *derangement*? An *instability*? An *anger*, perchance?"

Anger would fit. She felt very angry, but also his twitching face was amusing her in a situation where she shouldn't be amused. Maybe she was deranged. Who wouldn't be, putting up with this sort of crap day in, day out?

"Your results were by far the most positive. Off the scale," said Jeremy.

"Really?" She leaned forward and noticed Jeremy jerk back.

"Alas, yes."

"You really are a tosser, aren't you, Jeremy?"

Jeremy's mouth dropped into a long O. And so did Polly's. She couldn't believe she'd said that. It was all very well unleashing her inner Sabrina, but Sabrina could afford to walk out of her job and Polly couldn't. She needed it more than ever. She should pull that back, apologize, offer to make some tea and roll out the best biscuits, say absolutely yes to working with Brock on Auntie Marian's Bread, but something inside her was popping like corn kernels and she couldn't keep it in.

"You have systematically sidelined and undermined me since your backside hit that chair, haven't you, Jeremy? You have promoted people above me, you have sent me out to muster up refreshments like a skivvy, but when you want to turn around a business, you'll harvest every idea I have and pass it off as your own, won't you, you inadequate little shit?" Even her inner Sabrina was now standing back in wonder.

"Whaa—" Jeremy spluttered, but Polly wasn't going to give him the opportunity to speak yet.

"Let's take Nutbush as one of many examples. Remember, the shop you were going to shift entirely online. The shop now quadrupling its profits because I told you to do the exact opposite. The project you and your so-called managers took the credit for when not one of you could come up with a single idea that would stop them from going under."

"Nutb—"

Nope, she still wouldn't give him room to talk.

"And now you're revving up to do it all again with him out there, the nephew of the man whose colon you inhabit. You're going to train him up to tell me to stick a kettle on every time he feels like washing down his custard creams and prod him to plunder every idea I have to turn Auntie Marian's Bread around and repackage it as his own. I can't believe I've let you get away with this for so long. You'd have sunk and drowned if it wasn't for me. Nutbush, Fish Fillies, the Gin Lot, Planet, Knock Doors all down to *me*, need I go on?"

Give it to him, Pol. It was a voice that knew she'd been pushed too much, too far, someone who could see what she'd been through in her life, the past heartache, the wrongs she'd endured, and ahead of her only the uncertain path she had been forced to take. And now this insult to add to all the injury: that she was not only being labeled a certified psychopath but one who had to let the office junior handle her account because he was male and not female.

"Well," Jeremy said, when he took advantage of the tiny gap she'd finally left him while she took a breath. "Well, well."

"Then you have the cheek to tell me I'm a *psychopath*," Polly went on. "The fact that you are still sitting there in a chair with a head on your shoulders, Jeremy, should quite clearly prove to you that I'm not. As for putting that on my record, I don't think so."

Jeremy's eyeballs were now in danger of pinging out of his skull and rolling across the desk.

Polly grabbed the papers from his hand.

"That is what I think about your test, Jeremy," she said. There was no point in restraining herself now. She was done here; there was no coming back from this, so she might as well let rip—literally. She tore at the test savagely, letting all the pieces tumble to the floor like giant confetti even though she quickly realized she was playing into his hands. He'd tell everyone she registered as a psychopath on his test and then protested about the results by going psycho in his office, and so he had to get rid of her. How they'd all laugh.

"You aren't fit to sit in Alan's chair," she spat at him as she made to go. But he fired a bullet into her back.

"Oh yes, we all knew what you felt about Alan. It was common knowledge what was going on between you."

Polly stalled, turned around, slowly, beyond angered by that. Alan's name had no place in Jeremy's mouth and she would not let him get away with besmirching him.

"Alan Eagleton was a gentleman and a genius and he'd forgotten more about this business than you'll ever learn."

"I think you'd better go home, Polly, and come back when your PMS or hormonal imbalance or whatever female problem you're going through has subsided. You can come in on Monday with an apology and a fresh outlook. Your job is to train Brock to be your superior. If you can't accept that, then maybe you should resign. My coffee's too cool to drink now." Jeremy flicked his hand toward the full cup. The words "make me another" were unspoken, but she could hear them nonetheless.

"Let me get rid of this for you," she said with her sweetest smile. She picked up the cup and flung the contents in his face.

Polly strolled out into the main office where Brock was still swiveling on the chair and reading the file on Auntie Marian's Bread.

"That was loud," he said. "The whole department heard you."

"Shame the whole building didn't," said Polly. She picked up her bag, slung the strap over her shoulder, and grabbed her jacket from the back of her seat.

"I'm going. Good luck. Not that you'll need it with your connections."

Brock looked rightly puzzled. "What do you mean, you're going?"

"I mean I'm going," Polly said again. "Leaving. For good." She couldn't put it any plainer, but Brock's expression said he still didn't get it. He was a two-watt bulb sitting in a hundred-fifty-watt box. He'd be a disaster let loose on the Auntie Marian's Bread account. He had about as much chance of turning Arthur Peach into the new Jonathan Warburton as he would of turning Jeremy into the new Kate Bush. She knew instinctively how it would all play out. Arthur would shout down every suggestion Northern Eagles made, thinking he knew better. So they'd kowtow to his demands, tailor something to what he wanted rather than what he needed, and it wouldn't work. Then he'd badmouth them for taking his money and changing nothing. Let them get on with it. Good riddance to the lot of them.

* * *

Once Polly had walked out into the fresh Leeds air and the adrenaline had drained out of her system, she realized the enormity of where her rare outburst had led her. At a time when she'd need every penny she could lay her hands on, she'd just thrown in the type of job she'd probably never get again.

Still, said her brain, trying to be helpful by scraping the barrel for positives, it meant she could live wherever she wanted now rather than be restricted by a daily commute to Leeds. Maybe that was what she needed: a total change, not a partial. Maybe she needed to build herself from the ground up. Just like Sabrina in her book.

Chapter 10

Polly couldn't have driven in the jittery-nerve state she was in, so she headed into the city center to one of the coffee shops down a narrow alley that she sometimes popped into, knowing it was the type of basic establishment that no one from Northern Eagles would frequent. It had seen no need to change its 1960s décor since it opened, and maybe it had a point as it was never empty. There was a glass cloche on the counter with the same type of buttercream sponge that had always lived there and a portrait of Tina by J. H. Lynch on the wall, not quite hung straight; she couldn't remember it ever not being at an angle. She came here on her very first lunch break when she joined the firm because she was too shy to go to the canteen. And here she was on her last day: If that wasn't serendipitous, what was?

She ordered a pot of tea and sat in the corner. There was no point in asking herself, *What the hell have you done?* because she knew what she'd done, and the real wonder of it all was that she'd taken so long to do it. When had she turned into this human archery target, happy to let people fire their arrows into her? She'd been a feisty little thing at school, never letting anyone find the truth of a loveless, crappy home life behind her convincing facade. She'd had to handle the loss of her aunt and uncle and the new life she'd been promised, because she had no other choice but to get on with things and then tend to a mother who became more difficult with every passing day. She couldn't have done all that if she'd been weak. But losing her baby had wounded her deeply, maybe more than she'd realized. It took working for Alan to start the slow reconstitution, but she had been changed irreversibly by those nine months of expectant joy and what came after, had become much more vulnerable. She needed someone to be the shell to her fragile oyster, and she hadn't found them.

* * *

She called in at a newsagent's on the way home and picked up a copy of the *Daily Trumpet*. On Fridays they had a jobs section. Best read with caution, considering the number of things they got wrong. The errors didn't detract from its success story, though. Once its distribution was to South Yorkshire only, but now it served the whole of the county. At the present rate, it would be sold in all four corners of the globe by 2056.

Polly sat at the kitchen table and opened the newspaper at the jobs spread. Now freed up from having to live within a commute of Leeds, it made more sense to find a job first and then move to there. It was a plan, and proaction was always healthier for the soul than reaction, she'd come to find. But her heart sank at the offerings. The jobs listed were either on the level of company directors, top management, requiring a list of qualifications as long as Richard Osman's leg, or part-time positions in shops, zero-hour contracts, barmads (she presumed barmaids). There was a vacancy for a "Girl/Boy Friday" at Teddy's, an Italian restaurant in Shoresend. She found herself smiling at it because she knew that little town. It wasn't far from Whitby and that was the only time in her childhood that she'd ever been to the seaside. And she'd been there because her uncle Ed—her mother's half brother—had taken her.

He'd been brought up in Australia but decided to come back to the UK and make a life here. He'd arrived with his Australian wife Rina, the loveliest, kindest person on the planet, and had been shocked to find the chaos in which his sister was living. Until Uncle Ed came on the scene, young Polly Potter hadn't seen anything amiss in being left at home with a comic, a bar of chocolate, and a can full of sugary pop while Sheila Potter teetered off to bingo in her pin heels. In fact, Polly always enjoyed it. She would let in the neighbor's ginger cat, Tom (who'd been named with the same lack of thought they gave to his care), whose old bones were desperate for some comfort rather than the hard, cold windowsill he was usually to be found on, and she'd feed him crumbs of cheese while he snuggled up to her on their battered sofa. Her mother wouldn't let her have any pets. But then, she couldn't look after her own child adequately, never mind an extra animal mouth.

She felt her heart fill up with honeyed warmth whenever Uncle Ed and Auntie Rina called over. Uncle Ed was big and square like a wardrobe—*strapping*, her mum called him—and in contrast Auntie Rina was petite with shiny golden hair and big, beautiful, leaf-green eyes, small-boned and doll-fragile. And they never arrived empty-handed; there was always a book or a bag of sweets or a toy for her. One day they brought a jigsaw puzzle for her and started off her love of them. She found that putting the pieces together, concentrating on building a picture, gave her head somewhere tranquil to go, and she'd carried that pleasure through to adulthood.

One day, after talking about the beach near where they had lived in Australia, Uncle Ed realized that his niece had never seen the sea in person. He arranged for them to go out as a family to the coast the very next day. But Sheila Potter couldn't be roused that morning, however much Polly tried. But when Uncle Ed rolled up, he said to his sobbing niece that he'd had a word with the sea and it was expecting them so they had to go. They left her mother nursing her hangover, and the three of them drove to a place called Shoresend. He and Rina stuffed the day with everything a child's outing to the seaside should have. They bought her a bucket and spade and they made sandcastles and paddled and they helped her collect handfuls of shells to take home, and Uncle Ed had swung her around over his head while she pretended to be a seagull. They had flaky fish and chips soaked in vinegar sitting on the prom, followed by the tallest Mr. Whippy ice cream in the world, covered with strawberry sauce. It was a wonder she wasn't sick, whirling around on the big teacups in the funfair afterward, but she wasn't; she had never felt so well, ever.

The sea air and jollity eventually wore her out and she slept all the way home, cuddled up to the enormous plush cat that Uncle Ed had won for her by throwing darts at a board. He must have carried her in and put her to bed because that's where she was when she woke up hearing Uncle Ed and her mother exchanging heated words.

"I want to adopt her," he was saying. "You aren't fit to have a lovely child like that. I'll take her before social services does."

"Take her then," came her mother's slurred voice by way of response. And the young Polly drifted back to sleep and thought it was just part of a perfect dream.

Not long after, Uncle Ed and Auntie Rina told her they were going to move back to Australia because Auntie Rina couldn't settle here. Would she like to go and live with them there?

It hadn't been a dream. Polly's heart swelled with so much joy she thought it would burst. The wheels were put in motion: Polly Potter was going to become Polly Anderson. But before any of that could happen, her wonderful uncle Ed was driven off the road by a vehicle that was never traced, and just like that, he and lovely Auntie Rina were gone, leaving her only a legacy of lovely memories crowned by that day at the seaside.

A couple of weeks in Shoresend might be just what the doctor ordered, she thought: a place full of happy times and positivity for her, plus a snap of sea air. Yes, she'd head there on Sunday instead of Wakefield. There were loads of hotels and guesthouses in the area; she'd find one when she got there, let fate have a hand in things and see if it did any better than her best-made plans.

On Saturday 6 May, the *Daily Trumpet*'s lead headline read that Skipton couple Myfanwy and Des Gooding were retiring after thirty-three years of dedicated pick-pocketing throughout the whole of North Yorkshire. We did of course mean "litter-picking." This unfortunately had an embarrassing impact on the words that followed: "Both Les and Myfanny said there was more of a skill to doing it than most people realized and they've even held lessons in the village hall." They have, of course, only held a course on picking up litter and not on thieving from people. The *Daily Trumpet* has made a substandard donation to the local community fund in Mr. and Mrs. Gooding's names.

Chapter 11

Chris came back early from work and dropped his bag down by the door as usual, and Polly held herself back from saying anything. It was a symbol that nothing had changed and never would. And when he asked her if she'd had a "Good day?" she replied that it had been fine. There was no point in telling him that she was now unemployed because she'd flung a cup of coffee in her boss's face, and risk Chris lifting a line from the Jeremy Twatson book of sayings by asking her if she had PMS.

"Weather forecast is good for tomorrow," Chris said, kicking off his work boots. She wouldn't be picking them up and putting them neatly with the other shoes again, and that thought came with a joyous spark of relief.

"Sunshine until about two," he went on.

"Great." Though it wouldn't matter, she thought. The beige sack couldn't look good in snow, rain, or a blistering heatwave.

"Cuppa?" Chris said, not waiting for her answer but getting two mugs out. Polly couldn't remember the last time he'd put on the kettle.

She looked at his back as he stood waiting for it to boil and she was hit by a wave of sadness from left field. She hoped he wouldn't be hurt. She hoped he'd miss her enough to realize his mistakes and not carry them forward to a new relationship. His ego would be bruised and he'd have to learn how to operate a duster, but he'd live.

"You don't take sugar, do you?" he asked. After eight years he still wasn't sure. That dried up any internal tears of sympathy for him fast. It was pathetic, their whole relationship had been pathetic, a disaster, and if she hadn't put so much effort into trying to keep it from sinking, it would have drowned and died years before it had.

Her tea was watery with way too much milk in it when he brought it over to the table.

"Should be a good day, I'm looking forward to it," said Chris. He blew out his cheeks. "Thirty years—can you imagine being with someone for all that time?"

"It would be lovely to be with someone for all that time and still want to marry them all over again," Polly replied.

"Some people just rub along in their own way, don't they?"

"Yes," she answered, wondering if he meant Camay and Ward, or did he think that's what they were doing, *rubbing along*, living their separate lives under one roof and it was an adequate arrangement?

"Camay said your dress is nice," Chris went on.

Polly didn't say that it would be an ideal dress to wear if she tumbled out of a plane because she'd be assured of a safe landing.

"So what are your plans for tonight then?" she asked him after a pretend sip of tea. It was awful, like milky witch pee.

"Couple of drinks with Jabba and a takeaway probably." His shoulders rippled with a shiver. "It's cold in here." He got up to switch on the central heating and give the rooms a blast of warmth. He must have been frozen solid to do such a thing. He almost never had it on unless there were icicles hanging from the picture rails.

"We could do with a holiday, don't you think? Somewhere hot like Greece or Italy."

Polly swallowed. What had brought this on? Could some psychic part of him sense what was about to happen and had slammed into reverse thrust?

"Remember that lovely Greek island we went to once, where the cats were all over the place and you were buying tins of tuna for them?" He laughed and Polly recalled that he didn't laugh at the time. He said she was barking. He'd moaned all the way through those ten days that it was too hot, too expensive, too full of schoolkids in the hotel pool, too many fish in the sea, too many towels reserving sunbeds, too many olives in his salad, too many Greeks.

"Yes," she said, pushing out a polite smile.

"Anyway, I suppose I'd better get my stuff together," said Chris, exiting his rose-colored memories with a loaded sigh, and she wondered what it was loaded with.

Half an hour later he came down the stairs hefting a holdall with his suit carrier over his arm.

"Ward's on his way to pick me up, so I'll see you tomorrow then," he said, smiling at her, and she remembered when that smile used to turn on a light inside her. "Break a leg."

"Break a leg?" she questioned.

"Or whatever it is you're supposed to say to bridesmaids," he replied awkwardly.

She was sure it wasn't that. "Hope you have a good time tonight."

"Cheers."

A car pipped outside. He stepped toward her and kissed her cheek and she smelled his aftershave, but it no longer did to her what it used to, like his smile.

She followed the sound of the BMW driving off, and when it dissolved to nothing she let go of the breath she didn't realize she'd been hanging on to. It was all so close now, that "I've got something I need to tell you" moment, and even the thought of it tasted bitter in her mouth. A feeling of dread overcame her. It was so much easier to comply with the devil you knew than to stand up to him: The nearer it came, the scarier it felt. She went to the fridge and poured herself a very large glass of chenin blanc. She wasn't one to turn to alcohol hoping it would smooth out her life, because it hadn't done her mother much good, but at that moment, she wished it would have a go for her. She just needed to get on with things and not think too hard.

She had some money in her savings account that would help greatly, but it wasn't a fortune. It should have been. When her mother died and Polly was going through her paperwork, she'd found that her uncle had left her a substantial sum, which her mother had "managed" since Polly had been a minor. Polly never saw a penny of it; all she had to show for her relationship with Ed and Rina was the wedding ring threaded onto her necklace, and her sweet memories of them. She gulped down half the wine and headed upstairs to pack. She put as many suitcases and bags in her trunk as it would take. The rest were stored neatly in her upstairs sitting room because it wasn't very wise to leave a car on the street with boxes and bags in full view. Everything of true importance was in her biggest handbag: money, phone, bank cards, passport, driving license, documents, her few bits of jewelry. In the event of a dire emergency, if she had this bag with her, she could cut and go without anything else and survive.

When bedtime came, the only thing hanging in her wardrobe was the beige bridesmaid's dress. She put her head on her pillow, closed her eyes, and tried to power down by visualizing her near future. In forty-eight hours, her head would be on a pillow in a little guesthouse by the sea. There would be a lot to sort for the longer term, of course: a new job, a new house, wherever they might be. But for the next couple of weeks at least, she had sea air and the song of seagulls to look forward to.

The *Daily Trumpet* would like to apologize to Mr. Norman Dean Barker for an article which appeared in the Yorkshire Strongman contest article last weekend. Alas, under the picture of the winner was the name Norma Jean Baker not Norman Jean Barker. We apologize to Norma and are happy to report that he has accepted lunch for two at Miller & Arthur steakhouse in Sheffield as due recompense.

Chapter 12

The big day

Polly woke up at six o'clock, and she was glad to be out of her dream. In it she'd been running through air as thick as syrup, taking giant strides but getting nowhere, while behind her a scarecrow lolloped at breakneck speed, dressed in rags and dropping hay in his wake. She'd always had a thing about scarecrows as some people had about clowns. She'd never liked them; even the thought of their grotesque straw-stuffed bodies crawling with insects made her shudder. She always imagined that when she passed one, it would twist its head and stare at her. She couldn't even watch the affable Worzel Gummidge without feeling anxious.

One day she and her mother had taken a bus into the countryside to the spot where Uncle Ed's car had been forced off the road and into a tree, and there in the field at the side was a scarecrow. She could see it now with its hessian flat face and floppy hat, arms resting on a T-frame, tatty legs. Its head was at an angle as if perusing them. Its features were drawn on in thick marker pen, a crooked sly smile and stubby black crosses for eyes, and Polly wondered what was stored in that straw brain. It looked too knowing to be a mere "thing." She'd told Chris about her aversion to them, and though he said he hadn't mentioned it to anyone, Shauna turned up one Sunday with a decoration for their garden that she'd bought at a garage sale—a three-foot-tall jangly scarecrow. She was sure it was no coincidence. Two weeks later, she'd found out Chris had been cheating on her.

Just a dream, Polly told herself. But she couldn't chase away the thought that scarecrows were synonymous with ill portents. She hated them, even the most benign-looking ones with their dopey, friendly expressions.

She had a shower and washed her hair, packing up her toiletries into a bag and taking it out to the car. Then she had a very strong coffee and waited for the makeup woman. Ridiculous expense, but that was Camay all over, never happier than when she was spending money.

The makeup woman, Iz, arrived at nine on the dot. She had a teak fake tan, licorice-black eyebrows, eyelashes she could have tripped over, and only her bottom lip seemed capable of movement. Whatever Iz's middle name might have been, it definitely wasn't "subtle."

Iz dried Polly's hair and put it in rollers and then got cracking on her face: She had a heavy hand where makeup was concerned and totally ignored the rule of not drawing attention to both eyes and lips. There was too much black around Polly's eyes and her lipstick was dark ruby.

"Wish I had natural lips like yours," said Iz with a sigh. Polly's mother had bequeathed her the full-lip gene. She'd had a mouth like a young Debbie Harry.

Polly put her dress on then.

"Oh, that's beautiful," said Iz, sounding utterly convincing.

Polly thought she was either daft, blind, or had been poisoned by Botox.

Iz then took out Polly's rollers and did a lot of painful tugging and backcombing, piling her hair high on her head in a sort of bride-of-Frankenstein tower. Then on went the dead swan fascinator, secured by lots of glittery grips.

The bouquet arrived as Iz was packing up. A large teardrop of purply-red roses, presumably to accessorize with the bride's dress.

Polly put it on the dining table; it would be big enough to hide her handbag behind, which was one good thing. The other was that it would also hide a big portion of her frock as well. Camay really was going to town on expense. After Iz left, there were twenty minutes until the car arrived. Polly checked herself out in the foxed full-length mirror hanging on the wall by the front door, and despite everything, she laughed. How absurd it all was. This ghastly dress, the feathery disaster on her head, the spiders' legs eyelashes. The end to a perfect week of waters breaking, coffee sploshing, Auntie Marian's Bread, Alan's portrait, Brock the cock, all of it in one huge dungball on her head.

Tomorrow couldn't come fast enough. It really couldn't.

* * *

Five minutes later than expected, there was a cheery car pip from outside, and Polly looked out of the window to see a limo with beige ribbons tied on the front. She slipped on her too-tall shoes, swept up her handbag and flowers, and locked up the house. The elderly chauffeur had gotten out of the car to open the back door for her. She wondered if he'd retired from whatever job he had, got bored doing nothing, and found this job to supplement his pension. She liked to guess at people's life stories, as if the curious, writer part of her brain was always on the lookout for ideas.

He smiled at her and said, "Morning, ma'am, Stanley here at your service. You look beautiful." There wasn't a hint of sarcasm in his voice. God bless the old-gent types.

"Nice day for it," he said through the glass partition when he started up the engine. "Rain later, though, so I hope you get your photos done in time."

Polly thought then that she'd never see those photos, thank goodness. She wondered if Camay really would scribble her head out with a biro.

At the traffic lights, they pulled level with an old Volkswagen Beetle festooned in pink ribbons. There was a young bride sitting in the back with a man, her father presumably. She waved madly through the window and mouthed *Good luck* at Polly and stuck her thumbs up. *She thinks I'm a fellow bride*, thought Polly, who mouthed the same sentiment back. She looked happy, excited, as if she couldn't wait to get to the church.

Eventually the limo pulled up in front of the town hall and Stanley once again got out to open the door for her.

"Hope it goes well. I'll see you in a bit. I'll be waiting around the corner." And he pointed to where that was.

"Thank you." Polly adjusted her dress and walked up the steps. A wedding had just finished and the bridal party was posing outside the doors. A young couple with beaming smiles in gothic attire. The bride was in a red lace dress, black veil, and was heavily pregnant, and both she and her new groom were resting their hands on top of her bump as if they wanted their little one to be a central part of their celebration. *I never want to get married unless I'm wearing a smile like that*, thought Polly to herself as she entered the town hall. Camay was waiting for her in the foyer. She had on a long satin plum dress with a bolero, a matching pillbox hat with a veil over her eyes, and she was carrying a posy of purply roses, much smaller than Polly's bouquet. She looked surprisingly understated to be the bride. Polly had expected nothing less than a six-foot train and a crown. Possibly even a scepter. The florist had gotten the two mixed up, it was obvious.

"Slightly late but that's all right. Everyone's in there," Camay said, looking at her Rolex. "Are you ready?" Her shoulders shimmied with excitement.

"Yes, I'm ready," replied Polly. "But I think I have your flowers."

"No, I can't carry those; they'd get in the way," said Camay, grabbing her arm and pulling her. "Come on, the room's just down here."

"Camay," said Polly, stopping dead at the door, because she felt the need to say this, for afterward. "I hope you have a lovely day. I really do. I genuinely wish that for you, so I want you to remember—"

"What are you talking about?" said Camay, too giddy for anything verging on the intense and serious. She opened the huge wooden door. "Get a move on, in you go."

"Shouldn't I follow you?"

"No, you're leading the way," said Camay, giving Polly a none-too-gentle push on her back.

The opening salvo of "Here Comes the Bride" started up from a string quartet in the left corner of the room. Very Camay. Michael Ball would probably start piping up at any moment. Polly walked down the center of the two rows of chairs, Camay behind her. Heads swiveled toward her, lots of heads, lots of eyes.

Surely I should be behind the bride.

She saw Shauna give her the slow once-over as she held up her phone to snap photos or film the event. She recognized some of the lads who worked in Chris's garage and thought, *What are they doing here for Camay's wedding?*

Something wasn't right. The key pieces were in the wrong place. Ward was sitting on a chair to her left; Chris was standing up at the front and looking smart in a black three-piece suit, plum-colored rose in his lapel, his son standing next to him. And then with sudden and terrible clarity, the answer dawned on her, and with it, why she was in the off-white frock carrying the bigger bouquet.

THE GASS FAMILY

The *Daily Trumpet* would like to apologize to Mr. and Mrs. Gass for the misprint which appeared in the Birthday column last Friday in which their son Ethan was inadvertently called Methane. We hope the large sack of toys delivered to five-year-old Ethanol will soothe any hurt feelings.

Chapter 13

Polly drew level with Chris and her feet halted. She was never meant to drift off to the side and let Camay have center stage, because that place was hers today and always had been from the start, and that's why Camay had shackled her to this date. From the corner of her eye, she saw Camay take her seat next to Ward, then heard the creak of many chairs as everyone else sat too. The registrar in front of her was blasting out a wide and welcoming smile, ready to unite two happy souls in holy matrimony, and someone somewhere tipped a cold bucket of water over Polly's head—at least that's what it felt like. She stood there dumbstruck, frozen, icy fingers of dread squeezing her temples like a vise. She had too many thoughts for her brain; they were zapping wildly around the inner wall of her skull as if riding bikes on a wall of death. She could hear her heartbeat pounding in her ears, feel the prickle of pins and needles in the extremities of her limbs as her blood deserted them and rushed to her middle on an emergency defense mission. The wonder of it all was that she was still upright.

Chris was grinning and, as handsome a man as he was, for the tiniest of split seconds, his face looked like the scarecrow's in the field at the side of the crash site with its inane, disingenuous smile.

"Surprise," he said and she heard it in slow motion like a vinyl record played at the wrong speed. Someone behind her tittered and repeated the word.

It wasn't a surprise. A surprise was something that made you shriek in delight. This was a shock, one which pinned her to the spot, as stunned as a baby deer in the headlights of an oncoming juggernaut, who knew that if it didn't move soon, it was going to end up as a venison pancake.

"Dearly beloved," began the registrar. She sounded as if her voice was coming from underwater. The room seemed to shift as if it was getting ready to spin. Polly inhaled a deep breath to stop herself from passing out as she listened to her words. Words she'd heard so many times over the years at other people's weddings, on TV dramas, but never applied to herself. "Christopher, do you take this woman to be your lawfully wedded wife? To live together always?"

Chris was holding her hand. It felt as if he was imprisoning it.

"I do."

A stray clap.

"Polly, do you take this man to be your lawfully wedded husband?" She could feel every eye in the room on her, but it felt like every eye in the world, burning her with their intensity. She heard a rustle, Camay's dress probably, but it sounded like straw scratching against itself, full of field bugs. The registrar continued speaking, her words blurring into each other, though some stood out from the rest: *faithful*, *worse*, *death*.

The registrar was waiting for her answer. Chris was waiting for her answer. Everyone was.

She had to say "I do" for now and sort out this mess afterward. The fallout would be astronomical if she said anything else. But her bags were packed, her new life was waiting for her. She couldn't say it and she couldn't not say it.

"Polly." Chris prompted her by squeezing her fingers. Her mouth opened but nothing came out.

She felt sick. Saying yes would be so much easier. *Tread the easy path.*

She hadn't seen this coming.

Polly, don't say it. Another voice in her head, stronger. Sabrina's voice.

The registrar tried again. "Polly, do you?"

"No."

It was odd because she felt the word leave her mouth, but it seemed to come from someone else and the effect it had was far greater than the sum of its two letters. The room was sucked into a vacuum. There was no sound at all for what must have been moments but felt like minutes.

Ward's boom of a whisper. "Did she say no?"

The registrar was looking at her, waiting for clarification. "I'm sorry, I can't," said Polly.

She tugged her hand away from Chris's, turned, and walked at speed between the seats to the door. She must have dropped the bouquet because she wasn't holding it by the time she got there, only her loaded handbag which she was gripping for dear life. She launched herself from the room, needing outside air and needing it fast, and there was no chance of that with those heels on. She kicked them off, pulled up her frock, and charged forward, ignoring the people who turned to stare, ignoring everything but the large front doors at the end of the corridor.

She blasted through them, out into the midday brightness, her legs propelled by desperate energy. She headed down the stairs like Cinderella trying to beat the clock and to where Stanley said he would be waiting. She could see him standing talking to a taxi driver, taking in the sunshine. He noticed her and waved, his smile closing by degrees as she approached him like Zola Budd with her shorts on fire.

She clambered into the back of the limo and Stanley followed her lead and got into the front with similar urgency.

"You all right, love?" he said.

"Please, just drive," she said. "Take me to where you picked me up from." Stanley twisted the key in the ignition and set off. Through the window, Polly could see Chris at the top of the town hall steps looking around for her. There was a flash of plum behind him. She ducked down.

"Not to Maltstone Old Hall then?" said Stanley.

Oh God, the pink lamb reception at Maltstone Old Hall she'd thought was for Camay and Ward. All that waste. Chris would go bananas. Then she herded her thoughts together; she had bigger fish to fry than bemoaning a load of bruschettas and cake going in the bin.

Polly felt her eyes begin to leak. She wasn't crying, just leaking, as if she had so much pressure inside her that her eyes had decided to take on the job of being the safety valve.

"There's some tissues in the door recess," said the chauffeur, glancing at her through the rearview mirror. "Would it help if you told me what happened?"

Polly found the tissues and blew her nose, which had also decided to be a safety valve.

"I turned up thinking I was the bridesmaid and I wasn't; I was the bride," she said, her throat clogged with mucus.

"Really? Oh bloody hell," Stanley said. "That's . . . that's quite the surprise. You didn't have a clue?"

"Not one." Hercule Poirot's job was safe.

"And . . . I'm gathering you . . . didn't . . . erm . . ."

"I'm all packed up to leave him tomorrow," Polly replied, wondering why she was telling a complete stranger all this. Her mouth, it seemed, was also acting as a safety valve.

Stanley was quiet for a short spell, then he said, "It's a funny sort of thing to spring on someone." He gave a pained laugh. "I mean, I would have thought that a bride would want to plan her own day. And you'd have to be pretty positive that your partner would be up for it before you went to all that trouble."

Precisely. What the hell had possessed Chris to think this was a good idea?

* * *

On the town hall steps, Ward had just asked his wife this same question, after she'd spoken to the photographer who'd been waiting in position to capture the newly wed Mr. and Mrs. Barrett and crew with his fancy camera.

"I did express my doubts at the time when you suggested it to him," he said. He sighed, thinking about that pink lamb which had been his contribution and how now he wouldn't get to have any of it.

"Did you now?" said Camay, arms akimbo, determined not to be blamed for this fiasco. "You must have whispered it then, because I never heard you."

"You did put the idea in his head," said Ward. "You said it would make things right after what happened last year."

"I didn't force him, Ward. I merely mentioned it in passing."

"Plus there's the matter of the forged signature on the marriage notice application form. Highly illegal. A prosecutable offense. As I pointed out—"

"Oh do shut up, will you, Mr. Ruddy Unimpeachable."

Chris appeared at their side, red-faced from running around the building and also from a mix of emotions that ranged from confusion to fury.

"Looks like she's hopped in the limo. This is a frigging disaster."

"Maybe we should just go to the reception place and eat. She'll probably turn up there," tried Ward.

"Jesus wept, all that expense," said Chris, thinking about the meal now, as if his brain didn't have enough to chew on.

"You gave me carte blanche to arrange it for you. You said you wouldn't know where to start," Camay fired back.

"I said make it nice, *but* don't spend too much," Chris said. "I used the word *modest*, as I remember."

"I *didn't* spend too much. I was modest." Camay's tone was an affronted one. "At my wedding, the starters alone were twenty pounds each and that was in the nineties. Your whole menu only cost eighty-three per head."

Chris's eyebrows nearly zoomed into orbit. "How much?"

"That's positively bargain-basement price by today's standards."

"Fiddles and frigging cheeseboards are not modest, Camay," Chris cried.

"Goodness, that's an awful lot of money to waste. Plus the flowers and that awful dress," said Shauna, putting her arm around her father. She never had been one to miss fueling a fire.

"I beg your pardon, young lady," snapped Camay, "that dress was a Galina de Jong. You don't even get an underskirt by her for less than two thousand pounds."

"I hope you're joking," said Chris, before covering his face with his hands. "God almighty, I have never been so humiliated in my life."

"In front of so many people too. It'll probably end up in the paper..."

"Okay, that's enough, Shauna," said Will. He was thinking of Polly and the look on her face when she flew back down the aisle. He'd never thought this was the best idea. They all knew his dad had had a fling and he also knew that his dad wasn't very good at owning blame. He wondered how much work he'd put into actually mending his relationship or if he'd just thrown some paint at the fence, hoping it would disguise the damage. And Will was also cursing himself because the last time he'd seen Polly, he'd almost given her the heads-up on the quiet until, at the last minute, he'd thought better of it, but he really wished he had now.

"She'll have gone home and be waiting there," said Chris. "I know her inside out."

"We'll drive you," said Camay. "In the BMW. Come on, Ward, bring the car round. Chop chop."

Chop chop.

Ward sighed, thinking of that lamb. Shauna was thinking of how much her outfit had cost that now wouldn't be in any photos; Chris was thinking of what people would be saying behind his back and how bankrupt he'd be when Camay handed over all the bills; and Camay was thinking that Polly was a stupid, ungrateful bitch and how dare she do this to her brother after all the trouble she'd gone to organizing this for them? Only Will was thinking what state Polly must be in.

* * *

"Why were you leaving him?" asked Stanley, pulling up at the traffic lights. "You don't have to tell me, but you can if it helps to talk."

Polly blew her nose again. Thoughts were crowding behind a door in her head like zombies, and once that door caved in, she dreaded to think what would happen.

"I don't love him anymore," she said. "He had an affair."

"I see," said Stanley, nodding, then he let out a small, dry laugh. "Blimey, if this was an apology, I think he'd have been better off just saying sorry."

Is that what it was? thought Polly. Was this all instead of not saying the word? Was he throwing a ring at her because it was easier than making the effort to actually love her? It wasn't outside the realm of possibility, it really wasn't.

Polly groaned and rubbed her forehead as if it could soothe the swirl of thoughts beneath it.

Her phone rang in her bag and she took it out.

CAMAY: WHAT HAVE YOU DONE YOU STUPID SELFISH WOMAN!!!
CHRIS: WHERE THE FUCK ARE YOU? HEADING HOME. MEET ME THERE.

She had to get away—now. Away from the shouty capital-letter messages and the anger. Chris wouldn't go back there alone. Camay would insist on being with him and Shauna wouldn't miss the chance to stick the boot in. She couldn't talk to him now. It would have to be later when the heat had cooled.

Stanley pulled up outside the house.

"Will you be all right? Do you want me to wait around?" he asked her.

"I'll be fine," she said. "Thank you. I will, really."

The Barrett family could rock up at any minute; she couldn't risk going in and grabbing more of her belongings.

She had enough with her for now in the trunk; she'd get the rest later if Chris wasn't influenced by his daughter and sister to take it to the tip. They were just things, after all; it was more important she preserved herself.

Her fingers were shaking as they reached into her handbag for her keys. Thank goodness she'd followed the curious hunch to bring it. She opened the car door, slid into the driver's seat, switched on the ignition, and pressed the accelerator. The postcode for Shoresend had already been put in the satnav in readiness.

She was off.

In the 14 May "Focus on Slattercove Churches" edition, there was some unfortunate wording in the passage referring to St. Mary's in which we reported that "vicar's wife Denise Holt made her own wine and is drunk at every communion service." This of course should have read "witch is drunk at every communion service." The *Daily Trumpet* has made a sizable donation to the church roof fun of St. Mary's and we apologize reservedly for any distress caused.

Chapter 14

Ward's BMW rolled up outside the house five minutes after Polly's car had left. Chris opened the door, calling ahead, convinced that Polly would be in there.

Camay, Ward, Will, and Shauna followed behind.

"Dad, sit down, you'll give yourself a heart attack," said Shauna. She couldn't wait to give Polly a piece of her mind. She'd never liked her, though she felt secure enough in her father's affections not to feel jealous of her for any rivalry reason. In a row once, Will had said to her that Polly was a much nicer person than she could ever be, and intrinsically Shauna knew that. So it made her feel better to malign Polly at every available opportunity, none more fitting than now.

"Yes, sit down, Christopher," agreed Camay. "I'll put the kettle on."

"I think something stiffer might be in order. For shock," said Ward, spying the malt whisky on the work surface.

Shauna went upstairs, hoping to find Polly in tears perched on the bed, a sitting duck for a gobful of righteous vitriol, but no such luck. She checked the bathroom and the other bedrooms, then called down.

"Dad, you'd better get up here."

Chris headed upstairs to where his daughter was standing outside Polly's room, the one with the table she'd put in there so she could do jigsaws. Camay followed, anxious to see what her niece had discovered.

Chris walked in to see all the boxes and cases piled up there. "Her wardrobes and drawers have been cleared," said Shauna, trying not to let the smile leak too much out of her lips. "I think we know now why she didn't want to marry you, Dad."

Camay's hand flew up to her mouth.

"Oh my God, she was leaving you, Christopher."

Chris didn't say anything for a few moments. His head was like a shaken snow globe. "Now, why do people usually leave their partners?" said Shauna, being deliberately puckish.

She didn't say the words *for someone else*, but Chris heard them all the same.

* * *

Polly pulled up in a quiet country lane and changed into a pair of jeans, a top, and trainers. There was a large bin nearby, for dog poo presumably. She stuffed the dress and the feathery headgear into a carrier bag and left it at the side, hoping someone would be curious enough to check its contents and discover a designer frock that would fetch a pretty penny on eBay. It would be a shame if it didn't happen, but she couldn't have that outfit in the car with her.

She caught sight of her still heavily made-up eyes in the rearview mirror and saw the tiredness in them. There was no shine there at all, just two circles of dull brown. What a bloody mess. Just . . . why? Surely tomorrow wouldn't have come as that much of a shock to Chris when she said they were over?

Maybe it would, though, because he didn't see things from her side, only his own. He didn't know her at all; he hadn't even really tried to get to know her either. A relationship should be about two people creating a life together, not one deciding for them both and expecting the other to be compliant—this wedding epitomized everything. She'd fit in with his plans all along and maybe, in doing so, she'd reaped what she sowed. Maybe in trying to be easy to live with, she'd made a rod for her own back. Then again, maybe if she'd been with someone who was considerate, who saw her as a person and not an extension of himself, he'd have taken the time to find out what her needs were too.

What were they all saying about her at the house? she wondered. How many pieces had she been ripped into? She pulled her thoughts away from second-guessing what was happening behind her back and screwed her concentration to the road.

After two solid hours of driving, she saw the first signs to Slattercove and Shoresend, so her destination was in sight. Then she spotted a brown local sign to "Shore Heights, beauty spot," and she felt a ghost of warm feelings brush past her nerve endings. She'd been there with her aunt and uncle all those years ago. On a whim, she turned a last-second right up the steep hill that rose and bent, eventually plateauing way above sea level. She came to a stop in the place that had been just bumpy grass back then with a wooden fence to stop people from blowing over the edge. That day the sun had made the waves shine as if they were painted with glitter, and the sky was a wash of bright summer blue with the odd white fluff. Now the sea reflected only dark gray clouds bloated with rain. There were no holidaymakers on the beach below, nor up here, for that matter. No one was utilizing the benches fixed to tables for a picnic, and she saw the fence had been replaced with a more secure one made of iron. It was up here that her uncle Ed had picked her up and wheeled her above his head as she pretended to be one of the seagulls circling around them looking for tourist food.

A burger van was parked nearby with "Benny's Burgers" written on the side. She went over to it, hoping to buy a well-needed coffee, but as her run of luck dictated, there was a notice in the window saying "Back in half an hour," and as there was no way of knowing when that half hour started, she thought she might as well hang on for a while.

She sat on one of the benches, lifted her face to the sky, and let the sea breeze investigate her as a curiosity: *Who is this stranger in our midst? Does she look vaguely familiar to you?* She breathed it in and felt it cool in her lungs and salty at the back of her throat and heard the seagulls squawk and caw and wished she could peel the years back and be here again as a child with those two beloved people. As she closed her eyes, she felt the desire to pray, and her lips moved over words she hadn't planned but which came out nonetheless.

"Dear God, help me because I am lost and I don't know where I belong. Just please guide my first foot on a path, that's all; point me in the right direction and I'll figure out the rest. I know you're busy, but if you could just manage that, I'd be really grateful. Thank you. Amen."

She opened up her eyes and saw a man in the distance looking as if he were on course for the van. Mr. Benny's Burgers, she presumed. Great. She'd done the right thing waiting for him.

Chapter 15

Will loved his dad in a way that filial duty dictated, but he didn't *love* him. He wanted to, but Chris hadn't really done that much to earn his love. He didn't really get his son, he didn't know what made him tick, and he thought it was weird that Will wasn't into football, because he couldn't understand that other people might think differently about things. And that was probably why they were in the aftermath of today's debacle, because his dad wouldn't have considered that Polly might not be up for a surprise wedding. His mother was his dad's female equivalent, self before others always, and Shauna was her mini-me. Will was the family anomaly, and he was glad about that. He wouldn't have blamed Polly at all for leaving his dad, if that's what she was planning to do, and the emptied wardrobes and packed-up boxes rather indicated that she was. Yes, they all knew about the affair because he'd introduced the "new woman" to the family the same week Polly had left, and it was obvious they'd been seeing each other for ages. But two weeks later, she dumped him, and then Polly came home. Will remembered seeing Polly not long after and noting how thin she was, how fragile and sad. A year later that sadness was still hanging around her, a gray aura like a November rain cloud.

"I can't believe she could show me up like this," Chris was saying in a voice that wavered between anger and disbelief. "I mean, how could she do this to me?" he protested, throwing his hands up in the air.

Will was at the end of his tether with his father's victimhood.

"How could you do this to her?" he spat out, unable to stop himself.

"What?" said his father, sister, and aunt in unison.

"You surely can't be on her side," Shauna added.

"It was a weird idea," said Will.

"Nonsense. It was beyond romantic," Camay said to that.

"Ha. That dress, though," said Shauna with a delighted shriek of laughter. "I've never seen anything so horrific in my life."

I have. Your face, Will almost threw at his sister, except it would have been puerile.

"Slightly voluminous, I thought," said Ward.

Camay gave her husband a scathing look. "Thank you, Gok Wan."

"You must have had an idea that she wasn't happy," said Will to his father.

"None," said Chris. "We *were* happy."

"Clearly not," said Ward with a huff.

"Did you ever take her out? To restaurants, the cinema, a hotel? Do coupley things?"

"Will," began his father, an impatient edge to his voice, "when you've come in from work at daft o'clock, the last thing you want to do is get togged up and go out again. Polly wasn't bothered about all that stuff. She was a homebird, like me."

"I'm guessing not that much of a homebird if she's just flown the nest," said Ward, on his third malt. Camay would have to drive the BMW back home. A small compensation for missing out on that lamb.

"When was the last time you said 'I love you' to each other?" asked Will. He thought that might be a quick guide to the state of their relationship.

Chris waved that stupid question away too. "I don't know. We didn't go in for sop like that."

"I think getting your ducks in a row first might have been a good idea," said Ward, fingers creeping toward the Chivas Regal again, "before outlaying all that expense."

"I thought they were," said Chris with a groan. "After . . . last year, I said we should think about the next step." He nodded emphatically.

"What does that even mean unless you're Neil Armstrong?" said Will.

"Well, it's obvious, isn't it?" Chris insisted.

"No, I wouldn't have said so," said Ward.

"Oh for God's sake, of course it is. We're okay for money, we've got good pensions, nice cars, this house, secure jobs—there is *only* one next step. And we'd get a tax advantage being married."

"Tax advantage," Will echoed, deadpan.

"Will, you see things differently when you're my age. You look ahead to the future and . . . security and things."

"Worth doing for tax alone," put in Ward, nodding enthusiastically. "But of course if you had married, all preexisting wills would be revoked, you do know that? She'd have got everything if you popped your clogs."

Shauna gasped loudly and Will tried to hide a smirk. She hadn't been aware of that, then.

"Don't panic, love. I was going to suggest doing new wills to her after the wedding. This is my house and it goes to you and Will when I die."

"And they say romance is dead," said Will. He was ready for running off from them all himself. He knew how Polly felt.

"Look, darling, there were only friends and family there today," said Camay, putting her hand comfortingly over her brother's. "They'll have nothing but sympathy for you. You mustn't dwell on the embarrassment and humiliation, because it will fade away very quickly. And if people are going to laugh at you behind your back, let them. That will say more about them than you."

"Thank you," said Chris, wishing she'd shut up trying to make things better, because she really wasn't any good at it.

Camay kept up the smile as she said, "Mind you, I'll still have to give you the bill, Christopher, even though it was all a terrible exercise in waste. I expect the hotel staff had a good feed."

"Couldn't you have just asked her to marry you, Dad?" asked Will.

"She'd clearly have said no, and then you'd have saved yourself all this bother," said Ward.

"Well, that's very helpful, Ward, thank you," said Chris with a sneer. He poured himself a glass of malt before Ward drank it all.

Shauna slunk upstairs. She wondered if there was something in the room with all Polly's stuff in it that might point to what she had been planning. She hoped she'd find something satisfyingly incriminating.

* * *

Orville Bell had the misfortune not only to be named after a giant green duck but to be known by the contraction "'Orrible." He was a low-level scrote and always would be with that moniker. It didn't bother his girlfriend Tina, who thought it was quirky, but it bothered him more with every year that passed. Others in his orbit had equally insalubrious nicknames: Cockeye, Davy Strong Fingers, Shagger Corbett, but at least theirs had an element of masculinity about them, whereas his was just scummy and also cast in cement, so there was nothing he could do about it. He *did* need to do something about the predicament he was presently in, because he owed Billy the Donk a car. He'd been sent out on an easy steal and he'd smoked too much *herb* on the night in question and missed the window of opportunity. And now he was in trouble unless he came up with the goods—and quick. Or stumped up the heavy cash penalty which Billy had leveled at him for cocking up.

He had an uncle in Slattercove who'd given him more pep talks than he'd had hot dinners, and at the end of every one, Orrible had promised to change his ways, and yet he never had. Uncle Benny had a fleet of burger vans that served the area. He didn't have to work himself, yet he still chose to bring a van up here to this remote spot. Orrible had been wondering why that was for ages, so he'd eventually gone on a detective trail. He'd discovered that his uncle always parked up and stuck a notice in the window that he'd be back in half an hour, but he would go missing for much longer. And that was because naughty married Uncle Benny spent all those stretched-out "half an hours" in a nearby cottage in the company of a blowsy widow with bouncy bleached-blonde curls and even bouncier breasts. He'd hung on to that ace card until he needed to play it—and that time was now. Desperate situations called for desperate measures, and a bit of blackmail had to be done.

So Orrible set off to the beauty spot to catch up with his uncle. But what did he find parked up there but a black car, the type that had a very juicy catalytic converter underneath, and a lone woman sitting on a bench—presumably the owner. No one else around. As he walked toward her, he saw her smile at him and he wished she wouldn't because that was going to make things so much harder.

Chapter 16

Will could tell from Shauna's face when she came downstairs that she'd found a knife to stick into Polly.

"I'm sorry to tell you, Dad," she began, in a voice that said she was anything but sorry, "she's a total slag."

All eyes turned to her.

"I found this in her things. Right in the middle of a bunch of other stuff—hidden away," said Shauna, lifting up a single sheet of A4. "Let me read it to you." She cleared her throat and then began, with badly disguised glee.

"My darling, I cannot live a lie any longer. I have to come to you before my soul fades away and I am nothing. I am yours and yours only. You are the breath in my lungs, the blood in my veins. You are essential as air. If I have you, I need nothing else; no one else means anything to me. I—"

Chris leaped up from his chair and snatched the letter from his daughter. It was typed, but in a scrolling, romantic font. There was no address at the top, only a date of three months ago. He read on silently from where Shauna had been forced to break off: "You are my oasis in the desert. Every night away from you is torture. I may sleep in bed with another, but it is you I think of . . ."

There was more, but he'd seen enough, so he skipped to the end. "My raison d'être, my heart, my everything. XXXX"

Camay wrested it from his hand, took her glasses out of her bag, and read it herself.

"Goodness me," she said, her chins wobbling with indignation. "Well, there you have it, Christopher—proof of what she was up to. Now if anyone wants to snigger at you, you can tell them exactly what she was doing behind your back. Who'll be laughing then, eh?"

"Cuckold," put in Ward, for some reason thinking the word would help. It didn't.

Chris's thoughts swirled inside his head as if they were in a spin-dryer on the top setting. The way his sister was grinning would intimate that Polly shagging another man was some sort of good news; his ego was saying it was anything but. He had not seen this coming. Anger was rising up within him like a vortex, cleansing everything in its path but itself.

"And there's me sitting here worrying about her," said Chris, which made Will cast him a look. "Well, that's it. I wouldn't have her back now if she begged."

"And she will, darling," said Camay, putting her pudgy arms around his neck. "She'll come crawling back on her hands and knees and you will tell her to sling her hook. You've had a very, very lucky escape. And so say all of us."

Will picked up the letter and read it himself. Was it a rough draft of a letter sent, or was it sent to her? He hadn't seen that coming either. He might have had sympathy for Polly, but he couldn't condone her having another man. He didn't want to believe she was doing that behind his dad's back; he'd thought she was better than that and stood on a moral higher ground. He felt let down, but try as his brain might, there was no other way of interpreting it, especially given that Polly was packed up ready to go. With all these clues, it was a convenient truth to think that she must have someone else. And for now, that was all the truth they had.

* * *

Polly's alarm bells started to tinkle a little when she realized the man wasn't heading for the van but for her. The closer he got, she could see how scruffy he was, rangy in appearance, his walk strangely lolloping and wearing a sort of floppy hat that made her scalp prickle. She couldn't have reached her car before he did, even though her instincts were screaming at her to try. She opened her bag and foraged around inside it for something she might use as a weapon. There was only the shaft of her car key or a pen. The trouble was, she'd have to be pretty near to him to cause any damage with either.

"Lady, lady," the man was calling.

She saw he had string in place of a belt and she shuddered.

She got up from the bench and backed away.

"What do you want?" she asked. "Don't you come any closer."

He slowed down but didn't stop. He held up his hands, though, and said, "It's all right, I'm not going to hurt you."

He smiled and she wished he hadn't, because it wasn't a pretty sight. "Is that your car?"

"Yes," said Polly, clutching her bag close to her.

"I'm going to need to take it," said Orrible. "I'm really sorry." Remarkably, he looked it too.

Polly's eyebrows rippled in disbelief. "I'm afraid you aren't," she said.

"I need it. Look, you can get your money back on the insurance. Just throw me the keys, please, and this will all be over really quickly."

It had been a big mistake thinking this day couldn't get any worse.

"Oh, and can you chuck me your handbag as well?" asked Orrible, hopeful smile pinned on his face. Billy the Donk would have the car, but he needed something for his trouble. Polly's adrenaline levels were through the roof. Under normal circumstances she would have just let him take the lot, but these exceeded even the farthest ultraviolet spectrum end of normal. The car he could have, because it was just a lump of metal, but her whole world was in her handbag; it was her survival pack. This horrible little man would rip the back side out of her cards before she had a chance to report them, as well as spend the thousand pounds she had in cash in her purse. Her brain was spinning. She looked around in the hope that someone had left a convenient iron bar on the grass. Or a full can of pepper spray.

"Come on now, let's have the bag, lady," said Orrible. Polly was all too aware she was at a cliff edge, and scrawny as this man was, he had more moves than she did because she didn't have any. He could, at a push, force her through the bars of the fence and tip her over the edge. People robbed you for pence these days.

She took the key fob out of her bag. "Look, take my car but I've got all my clothes in the trunk. There's nothing else but clothes, I promise you. Just please, let me have them and drive off."

She threw the fob onto the grass and Orrible moved to retrieve it. This was the easiest job he'd ever had. But she didn't fool him. He smiled again and wagged his finger.

"You'll ring the police as soon as I've gone—I'm not daft. Please give me the bag, lady."

"I swear to you on my life I won't, but I really can't give you my bag. Just take the car and go. Please."

He didn't believe her. And she had something valuable in that bag or she'd have given it up with the ease she'd given up her car. He calculated that all that was separating him from the bounty it held was a minor tussle at most. She was scared stiff; she'd let go as soon as he touched it. He had never mugged anyone before and he really didn't want to start now, but Billy the Donk was one bad MF and . . . needs must. He stepped forward and made a grab for it, but he'd underestimated Polly's desperation. She twisted and elbowed him in the rib. He folded, but it wasn't enough to make him give up. He stretched out his hand again and this time his fingers gained full purchase of it; Polly grabbed it back with a mighty pull. Orrible threw himself forward, and Polly dropped it on the ground in her haste to remove it from his reach. They both made a dive for it, but Orrible tripped over Polly's foot, kicking the bag as he struggled to right himself, and they both watched it skid to the end of the cliff and tumble over the side.

They yelled, "Noooo!" in unison, leaning over the barrier to witness the bag slide down the rocky edge, then come to a sudden stop as it snagged on a sticky-out plant branch that only an osprey could have gotten to.

Angry now, upset and cheated, Orrible grabbed Polly by the shoulders and shook her in frustration.

"You stupid . . . flipping . . . twerp," he yelled, pushing his face into hers. She inhaled his rank breath, saw his blackened teeth, his beady little eyes, his flippy-floppy hat nodding on top of his living, breathing scarecrow head, and panic drenched her like an Arctic wave. She felt her heart race, her lungs empty of air and struggle to pull more in to replace it. Her head felt light through lack of oxygen, it started to spin, her legs crumpled from beneath her. Orrible let go and watched the woman's face bounce into the metal railing before she hit the ground, and he winced for her. She lay there still on the grass and Orrible thought she was playing dead until he tried to lift her up by her arm with a rousing "Lady, lady, lady," before realizing she was totally out cold.

"Shit, shit, shit," he said, looking around for witnesses and then up for a drone. People sometimes used them around here, but the skies were clear of everything but smoke-gray rain clouds preparing to burst.

He rolled her into a rough version of the recovery position because he didn't want to be responsible for her choking to death. Then, noticing she had a nice watch on and three rings on her fingers, he decided to relieve her of them. He couldn't go to hell any more than he already was. It would offset some of the pain of having missed out on the bag.

He legged it to the black car. There were some cases in the trunk, but he didn't have time to look through them now and confirm that they had only clothes in them as she'd said. *Sorry, lady.* He started up the car and rejoined the road, concentrating on nothing but presenting his spoils to Billy the Donk. It was dog eat dog in his world. Even if he was a scruffy mongrel serving the pedigrees.

* * *

The heavens opened five minutes later, and twenty-five minutes after that, a very sex-satisfied Uncle Benny of "Benny's Burgers" walked jauntily back to his van to find a sodden unconscious woman on the grass. She looked as if she'd had a bash to her face. If he'd seen someone attacking her, they'd have been lying at the bottom of the cliff now. He checked for a pulse in her neck and thankfully found a strong one throbbing. Then he took out his phone and called an ambulance.

Part Two

It is never too late to be who you might have been.
—George Eliot

The *Daily Trumpet* would like to apologize to artiste Alison Baker for reporting in last Tuesday's edition that "so many people said that she looked and sounded like Maradona that she made it into a career." Alison wishes us to point out that this should have read that she looked and sounded like Madonna.

Alison has released a cover of Madonna's hit single "Beautiful Strangler" to raise funds for charity, available for download from all major streaming services.

Chapter 17

"I'll have to go," said Diana, putting her cup and saucer down on the coffee table with a sigh of regret. "Doug's not a hundred percent at the moment and I feel I should be with him."

"What's the matter with him?" asked Jackie, snatching another custard cream bun from a plate on the table. Homemade with Bird's custard powder, lethal for the waistline. She'd have to do half an hour on the treadmill when she got home to burn off just one, and she'd had five.

"Irregular stools," said Diana with a wince. "They're of concern. He likes them to be consistent."

"Ikea," said Bev, walking in on the conversation from the loo. "If he wants consistency, there's no place better. We got six for our island and they're solid as a rock. Just how a stool should be."

She didn't understand why her comment was greeted by an uproar of laughter. "What?" she asked, her eyes flitting from one friend to another.

"Not that sort of stool," replied Marielle.

"What other sort of—" The penny dropped then, and Bev chuckled. "Oh, I see. Then Ikea might not be able to help."

Diana thought, *Thank God for these women.* She always felt so much better after meeting up with them, putting their various worlds to rights in their safe space. She looked forward to their "Mad Cows" get-togethers so much. It was Jackie who had conjured up the name. A group of menopausal friends who had gravitated together, like planets.

They'd all said it at some point: *How did I ever cope without us?*

"Look at us sitting around talking about men's stools," said Sylvie. "Was this ever on our list of aspirations as sweet young things?" At sixty-eight she was the oldest in the group, not that anyone from the outside could have guessed that. Her life had been revolutionized by HRT over a decade ago. She'd only been on it a couple of months when she turned her humdrum existence on its head, left her useless lump of a husband, and found a hot lover twelve years her junior. Hormone replacement hadn't just made her life more livable, it'd given her a life, she said. And she was riding it—and him—like a horse in the Grand National.

She took one of the last custard creams and nibbled on it like a duchess might have nibbled on a cucumber sandwich. Jackie took out her phone and snapped a photo of the bun on her plate. "For Instagram," she explained. "I'm going to make your custard creams an internet sensation, Marielle."

"I love to look at food on Insta," replied Bev, who was on yet another diet she wouldn't stick to. She knew she ate too much comfort food.

Diana stood up. "I'd best be going. I want to make us something nice for tea tonight and take his mind off things. Doctor's first thing Monday morning."

"I hope he gets on all right," said Marielle, and the others nodded or made noises intimating the same.

"I'm sure he'll be fine, but best to check these things, eh?" Diana smiled, but she knew her matter-of-factness wasn't fooling anyone. Doug was twenty years her senior, and after a life of perfect health things were starting to go wrong with him. He wasn't a man who made a fuss, and the fact that he was worried enough to tell his wife that he had concerns said a lot.

"Put it in the WhatsApp group chat when you know," said Jackie.

"I'm sure Doug would love that the details of his bowels are in everyone's phones, Jackie."

"'Course he will. He's a bloke—he'll love that women are talking about him."

Bev nabbed the last custard cream and sighed. "I really shouldn't be eating these. I'll end up driving around on one of those mobility scooters because I'm too fat to stand up." It didn't stop her stuffing it down in one, though. Bev always said she wondered why she wasn't featured in *Guinness World Records* as the woman who had gone on the most unsuccessful diets.

Jackie rose from the sofa. "I'd better go as well. I'm on nana duty tonight. Scott and her are off to the theater and then they're staying in the Hilton." She snarled at the mention of the daughter-in-law who wasn't good enough for her son by half, in her opinion.

"What are they going to see?" asked Marielle.

"An opera." Jackie's nose wrinkled up. "She'll only be going because she thinks it makes her cultured. Our Scott's idea of a night out is darts and curry. He'll be asleep as soon as the orchestra starts up."

"Look on the bright side: You'll have Pip all night," Bev said.

Jackie's features melted. "I can't wait. We're having chicken and then we're going to snuggle up on the sofa and watch *Die Hard*."

"Bit young for that, isn't he?" said Sylvie with a laugh.

"Five's thirty-five in dog years," replied Jackie.

"God knows what you'll be like if they ever have a real child as well as a dachshund," Diana said, opening the door. "Right, definitely off now. Bye."

There was a lull after she'd gone; then Marielle said what they were all thinking.

"She's worried sick, isn't she?"

"Doug's immortal—she should stop worrying," said Jackie, looping her bag around her shoulder.

"He's not, though, is he? None of us are, and that's why we should enjoy it while we can."

Chapter 18

The Krayfish fish-and-chips emporium was a small but thriving business in a hamlet just north of Whitby. The mainly older customer base who queued up for the OAP soup, cod or haddock special with tea, bread, butter, and a sherry trifle dessert had no idea they were contributing to the upkeep costs of a "front" for a nest of criminals whose offices were tucked covertly behind the kitchen, hence the tongue-in-cheek name. The leader of this northern division of a much larger organization, Billy the Donk, was rather proud of thinking up that one. The two worlds of the pensioner genteel and the lawless existed side by side in sweet symbiosis and had for a decade and more.

Orville Bell was in the back office as summoned by Billy. Sitting on the bus, he'd imagined Billy clapping him on the shoulder and saying, "Well done, boy, you are officially off the hook." He might have even reached into his desk drawer and taken out two shot glasses and his favorite Irish malt whisky, nudging one toward him, or invited him for a game of pool in the other room with the big telly and the massive sofas. This, however, was quite different from the reality of the side of his head being flattened against Billy's desk while Square, Billy's "muscle," held him in an armlock. Square, aptly, was as wide as he was tall and had the jawline of a shoebox.

"Not exactly a high-performance motor, is it, though, Orrible?" Billy said, after puffing a mouthful of cigar smoke in his face. "I gave you an order of a Range Rover—a Range Rover, mind, just sitting there waiting for you, couldn't have been easier, and you miss the time slot and bring me a piddly little thing pensioners go shopping in—are you having a giraffe?"

"It's got a catalyptic convert—" Orrible squeaked, but Billy cut him off.

"I know it has, and that *catalytic* converter is the reason I'm only going to break one of your arms today," he said with a bone-chilling grin.

Orrible made a noise of pain that ordinarily only bats and dogs could hear.

"Oh, let him go, Square, before he busts my eardrum," said Billy, to Orrible's relief. Square gave his arm a sneaky extra twist before finally relinquishing his hold. Orrible straightened up and rubbed at the sore spot left by the imprint of Square's fingers.

"Was there anything in the trunk, Billy?" asked Orrible, grovelingly. "I never looked. I just brought it straight to you."

"Ah yes, the luggage," said Billy, leaning back in his chair, taking another puff of his fat Cuban cigar. "I have to salute you, Orrible, for *the luggage*."

Orrible didn't see Square grinning behind him.

"I know you didn't look in it, Orrible, because you'd have taken the Krugerrands out, wouldn't you? A very nice little haul."

Damn, thought Orrible. He hadn't seen them when he had a forage.

"And the emeralds," said Square. "Don't forget the emeralds, Billy."

Billy smiled widely, showing off the full piano of his teeth: Simon Cowell white interspersed with Goldie gold.

"And that diamond hiding right at the bottom, the one that makes the Cullinan look like a sequin."

The penny dropped. They were lying. Orrible didn't know if that made him feel better or worse.

Billy leaned forward and his leather jacket creaked menacingly. "Shall I tell you what we found in the cases, Orrible? Knickers, bras, socks, skirts, blouses, a brush, toothpaste, some makeup. This old lady going on holiday, was she?"

"I don't know, Billy, she never said," answered Orrible, before realizing his mistake. He'd told Billy he'd taken the car from a car park and found the keys resting conveniently on the front tire.

"Ah, so now we're getting to the truth." Billy's eyes darkened; it was what he was renowned for, as well as his love for donkeys, hence his nickname. The light drained out of them when he got mad and they transformed into shark's eyes. "Where did you really get the car, Orrible?"

"I found it, Billy." Panic set into his voice as he felt Square's hand grab his barely recovered arm.

"Come on, Worzel, I really don't want to have to hurt you again," said Square, which made Billy chortle. His crew always said that if ever there was such a thing as a walking, living, breathing scarecrow, it was Orville Bell.

"Okay, okay, I'll tell you. I went to see Uncle Benny up at the beauty spot above Slattercove and there was a woman up there on a bench, looking at the view. Sitting duck. I told her to give me her keys and she did." He nodded and let the truth, minus a few choice details, sink in.

"Just like that, Orrible? I'm impressed," Billy said eventually, his eyebrows lifting as far as the Botox would allow, which was farther than usual because he was due for a top-up.

"Well, yeah. She obviously felt *freatened*."

A beat and then Square, Billy, and Big Charlie, who was adding up some receipts at the desk in the corner, burst into laughter at the thought of this lanky streak of piss being able to threaten anyone. Then Billy snapped off the laughter and Orrible shuddered.

"Talk me through the truth, Orrible. And I warn you: Lie, and Charlie will damage your bollocks."

Orrible gulped because Charlie had form for damaging bollocks. It was his signature modus operandi.

"Okay, well . . ." Orrible paused to wipe the sweat fast forming in beads on his forehead and top lip. "So Saturday, I thought I'd go and see my uncle Benny, say hello like. He weren't there but that woman was, just sitting on a bench. There was no one else there. I couldn't have missed that opportunity, could I? She did ask me to leave her the luggage in the trunk, but . . . well, I wasn't going to do that, was I? There might have been valuables in it that I could have given to you."

"There might indeed," said Billy, nodding sagely.

"I asked her for her handbag because I didn't want her ringing the police on her phone. But there was a bit of a . . . sort of a . . . scuffle, and it ended up . . . sort of flying over the cliff edge." Orrible gave a horrible smile, his teeth the stuff of Billy's nightmares, and an eel of revulsion rippled down his back.

"What happened to the lady, Orrible?" asked Billy, his voice low, his eyes still black.

"Well . . . she sort of . . . fell."

"Lot of 'sort ofs' in your recounting," Square said. "Did she fall or didn't she?"

"Well . . . I . . . she sort of fainted. And she banged her face on the iron fence as she went down. Not hard, though, just a bit." Orrible was at pains to point that out, because for all his faults—and there were many of them—Billy did not condone violence toward women. He had three daughters he doted on, a wife he adored, and a mother he idolized.

"Where is this woman now?" asked Billy.

Orrible shivered. The air seemed to have chilled by degrees in seconds. "I dunno, Bill. She just . . . sort of . . . slumped. I left her in the recovery position, though, and I knew my uncle Benny was due back any minute. He'll have sorted her, I know he will."

Billy let all that sink in before he began to speak again. Orrible felt sweat slide between the hairs on his head and slither down his neck.

"I'm not liking what I'm hearing, Orrible. What have I told you about shitting on your own doorstep? Too many people know you in Slattercove, including the police, and you're going to be on their radar when that lady goes to them and tells them some manky little prick in a stupid hat and string round his middle has nicked her car, presuming she hasn't come to permanent harm. If anything about what you did on Saturday leads back to me, you and Charlie will be taking a trip up to the beauty spot for some flying lessons, if you get my drift."

"Yes, sir," said Orrible.

"You'd better find out where this woman is, Orrible. I want eyes on her."

"Yes, Billy. I'll find her."

"Thank you for the *catalyptic* converter. But you still owe me a car. Now piss off," said Billy.

Orrible got out of there as fast as he could. The rings on the woman's fingers had all been just silver, not white gold or platinum, and netted him a mere tenner at the pawnshop. They'd laughed when he'd asked how much for the watch. All that for nothing. He hadn't thought this through at all. Then again, if that woman had gone to the police and given them a description, they'd have been round at his and Tina's house in a flash. So why hadn't they? What if she'd somehow rolled off the cliff? A cold wash of dread claimed his scalp. He took out his phone to ring Uncle Benny for a "Hi, long time no see. Anything interesting been happening?" chat. He figured he'd leave the blackmail for another day.

* * *

Bev left not long after, but Sylvie had no intention of following her for a while. She sat back against the cushions of the sofa and bided her time. Out of all of their houses, she liked Marielle's the best. This big, open-living kitchen with the sea view and the huge squashy sofas. More than just the furniture, though, it was filled with an ambience that was quite simply "Marielle." She'd long thought someone should capture it and make it into reed diffusers. She'd buy the lot and put them in her salon.

"Come on then, what's on your mind?" asked Sylvie when Marielle didn't automatically confess what was on her mind, because something definitely was.

"Oh, it's nothing," said Marielle, waving her concern away. "Want a top-up? Coffee or wine?"

"Do you need to ask?" came the reply. "And don't kid a kidder."

Marielle got out two glasses and filled them with malbec. She took them over to the sofa, set them on the coffee table, and then sat down heavily. The two women had met only ten years ago, when Marielle tried out Sylvie's salon, but they both felt as if they'd known each other for so much longer.

"Is it Cilla? I know she's on your mind," said Sylvie.

Marielle's cousin was often on her mind, even though she didn't deserve to be in Sylvie's opinion. She couldn't do with high-maintenance people who were a drain, and Cilla was the sort of person that the word *diva* was created for.

"No, it's not her," said Marielle. "I didn't want to say and bring the mood down, but it's Teddy and those damned . . . bastards."

Sylvie raised her eyebrows. This was only about the third time she'd ever heard Marielle swear, and never anything more than a mild expletive.

"Of all the places they could pick to put another one of their rubbish restaurants, why a little town like Shoresend? Ha. Authentically Italian, my eye. Why not Leeds or Nottingham—somewhere bigger, not next door to us," Marielle went on.

"Because they are a big, greedy chain and they don't give a toss about the little guys, that's why," said Sylvie. "Anyway, the people who frequent that type of crappy shove-it-in-a-microwave restaurant will not be the sort that want what Teddy can offer: *authentic* authentic Italian."

Sylvie hoped she sounded convincing, because she wasn't sure she was right. Teddy's food was premium and his prices reflected the quality he strove for, but there were plenty of people who'd compromise if there was a much cheaper alternative nearby.

"I hope so, Sylvie."

Marielle hadn't lost her worried look, and Sylvie could see there was more on her mind because she knew her so well. She hadn't emptied her soul by a long chalk.

"Come on then, what else? Because there is something."

"No, that's all," said Marielle.

"Liar."

Marielle let out a long sigh. If she couldn't tell her best friend, who could she tell? But even then she was wary.

"You know I visit the old people up at the hospital? Well, last week they admitted a woman to the ward. She's only mid-thirties I'd say, and she was found unconscious at the beauty spot by the man who has the burger van up there. She hadn't a clue how she got there, poor lamb. She's very confused. She can remember her name and that's about it, but it's not shown up on the database."

"Drugs?"

"Nope, no drugs or alcohol in her system."

"Haven't there been a couple of jumpers up there?" asked Sylvie.

"Years and years ago," replied Marielle. "There's big iron railings up there now because it's like a wind tunnel in bad weather, so God knows why the council installed all those picnic benches alongside all the danger signs. Bonkers."

"Well, that's Slattercove and Shoresend council all over, isn't it?" said Sylvie, who'd had a few run-ins with them over the years with various businesses she'd owned. It was one rule if you were on the council or had friends serving on it and another rule for everyone else, and she fit in the latter category. "Left hand doesn't know what the right hand is doing with that lot, but I could take a guess at what the right hand *is* doing. Bunch of wankers."

"Naughty Sylvie," said Marielle. "Anyway, she'd taken a bump to the face, but the brain scan didn't show any trauma."

"No ID on her at all?"

"Nothing. Just a wedding ring on a necklace around her neck. She had jeans and a top on but loads of makeup and all her hair was pinned up with pretty little pins. She looked like a different person above the neck to below it."

"Where's Miss Marple when you need her?" Sylvie reached over to squeeze her friend's arm. "You worry too much about other people; I can feel it coming off you in waves. You can't save the world, Marielle. Teddy will be on top of the restaurant thing, and as for the lady in the hospital, well, it's sad but I'm sure she'll remember where she comes from. And if she doesn't..." Her voice carried a heavy note of caution in it. "Promise me you won't do anything daft."

The *Daily Trumpet* would like to apologize to Mr. Yannis Drakos for an advert which appeared in last weekend's "Best Places to Eat in West Yorkshire" in which we reported that his Wakefield restaurant Zorba's was renowned for its Greek mess. This should have read "Greek *meze*." Mr. Drakos will give everyone who orders one of their famous messes at Zorba's, and brings this article with them, a five pounds discount to end of June.

Chapter 19

Marielle had a large hold-all with her the next time she went up to the hospital. She smiled as she approached the nurse's station and saw her favorite ward sister, Tessa, on duty. Tessa used to go out with her son Teddy—not for very long, though, which was a shame because Tessa was the sort of woman Teddy should have settled with. Thank goodness the one he was going to marry met someone else and emigrated to the Antipodes, which still wasn't far enough away in Marielle's opinion.

"Hello, Mrs. B," said Tessa, a smile of greeting flashing on her face as she clocked Marielle. "Lovely to see you as always."

"I thought I'd bring a few things for the Lost Lady," said Marielle. The Lost Lady was what one of the auxiliary staff had named the patient in room four, and it had stuck. The Lost Lady said she was called Sabrina Anderson. She didn't know where she lived, though, or how she had ended up unconscious at the Shore Heights beauty spot.

"That's sweet of you," said Tessa. Marielle Bonetti had to be one of the nicest people she knew, and she wished she'd had her as a mother-in-law instead of the old bat she did end up having. When Marielle had retired from nursing, she couldn't keep away and so became one of the "friends of the hospital," visiting patients to keep them company. Too many old people had either no visitors or short visits from relatives who were off as soon as they'd satisfied their duty gland. Marielle chatted to them, helped to feed them sometimes, did puzzles with them, and should have been on prescription. The Lost Lady shouldn't really be in this ward with geriatric patients who had pronounced memory loss, but there were no other beds, and she had to go somewhere for now.

"How is she?" asked Marielle.

"Just the same," said Tessa with a regretful smile.

Tessa was as professional as they came, but she might have just dropped a tad more information to a trusted and respected ex-nurse like Marielle than she would have to any of the other volunteers. Of course, there was always the possibility that Sabrina, if that's what she really was called, was deliberately withholding information, because it wouldn't have been the first time someone had feigned amnesia, usually for nefarious reasons. But they also had to consider she was in danger from something or someone and that was forcing her to keep her details to herself. Often in these cases, a patient "suddenly recalled" things like allergies and a past medical history if it meant that by not remembering them, they might be at some risk, but Tessa did have to admit that Sabrina was either a genuine case of memory loss or a damned fine actress. There seemed to be no medical reason why she couldn't remember, so if she wasn't pretending, the block had to be a psychological one, and that could be very tricky to unlock, especially if serious trauma had caused it.

"Is she still in the same bed?" asked Marielle.

"We've had to move her into bay three as we needed the private room," said Tessa. "Try and work some magic for us, will you?" Marielle walked into the bay of six beds and over to the bottom corner where the Lost Lady was sitting by the window reading a newspaper.

"Hello, Sabrina," she said. "Up for some company?"

Sabrina looked up, recognizing her voice. Her mouth curved into a smile at the sight of the kind woman with the dark auburn hair and the bright blue eyes.

"Hello, Marielle. How lovely to see you again."

Marielle pulled over a chair and put the hold-all on the bed; then she unzipped it and took out what was inside.

"I've brought you a few things," Marielle said. "If they aren't right, I can change them." There were a couple of soft flannelette nightdresses and two packs of pants from Marks and Spencer, a waffle dressing gown, a pair of cozy slipper-moccasins, a loose boho top in pinks and blues, and some gray marl jogging bottoms. There were also a couple of books and a bag of pick 'n' mix. Marielle put them in the storage cupboard by the bed for her.

"Thank you." Sabrina sounded both humbled and crushed, not how Marielle had intended to make her feel.

"They're just bits and they cost hardly anything," Marielle said.

"It's very kind of you."

"What are you reading?"

"A days-old newspaper," Sabrina replied. "The *Daily Trumpet*. My goodness, the spelling mistakes. I don't know how they're in business."

"The *Daily Trumpet* is renowned for its mistakes," said Marielle, picking it up and reading out the headline: "*Sheffield Woman Bitten by Cobbler on Indian Holiday.*"

"Surely they mean *cobra*," said Sabrina.

"You'd hope so," replied Marielle, thinking that if she'd never heard of the newspaper, she couldn't have come from Yorkshire, though her accent suggested she was from somewhere up north.

They were interrupted by the tea lady trundling her trolley through the ward.

"I don't like milk in my drinks," said Sabrina, sipping her coffee. "So I know that about myself."

"Well, it's good you know some things." Marielle chuckled. "More will follow."

"I spoke to a consultant today," said Sabrina. "I think they're satisfied I'm not lying when I say I really can't remember anything of what happened. I wish I could, I really do . . ." Her voice trailed off, and she shook her head as if she was having a small inner battle with herself before she started speaking again, but more quietly this time. "Marielle, I do know more than I'm letting on, though."

"Ah." It wasn't a surprise. "Do you want to tell me?"

Sabrina licked her lips nervously. "Please don't say anything to anyone . . . I know I'm a business analyst," she said with absolute surety. "I know I have a daughter and that she's out in Australia, and that's good because I know she's safe, and I know I ended up here to get away from what was happening in my life and that I'm absolutely sure no one will think to look for me in this place."

Marielle knew that she arrived with a wedding ring on a necklace. She'd taken it off her finger for some reason and put it on a chain. She waited for Sabrina to say more, but all she got was a regretful smile.

"That's it. That's all I have. Other than an overpowering feeling that I don't want to go back to wherever I came from."

Marielle had been expecting more, and she wasn't quite sure if what Sabrina was telling her was true because it did sound a little dramatic, although she seemed convinced of it herself.

"It must be very frightening for you," said Marielle.

That was putting it mildly, thought Sabrina. Why did she remember just these few details about herself, and that she had run from someone and she didn't want him to find her? Somehow she had to make a cake of the rest of her identity using only those random ingredients.

"I asked the doctors what will happen to me, and they said that I might be in hospital for a while. Apparently they'll set up social care and get the safeguarding adults team involved, and that can take ages."

"That sounds about right." Marielle nodded.

"I had indents on my fingers, apparently, where some rings must have been. They think I was mugged."

"It's certainly a possibility if you had no handbag with you. And that's quite a distance up the hill where you were found. No one would walk up there"—*in their right mind*. Marielle cut off her words because they were insensitive under the circumstances.

"The police came to see me, but I wasn't exactly helpful." Sabrina gave a little laugh. "They took notes, but I don't think they really know what to do with me. For now anyway. No one's reported a woman like me missing."

She got the feeling that the cynical policewoman who had interviewed her didn't believe that she didn't know much about herself. She couldn't really blame her. Especially when she said she didn't want to go down the route of getting the press involved to put out an all-points bulletin in the hope that someone would recognize her. She didn't want to be recognized, not until she could uncover more about herself and why she had washed up in a small seaside town on the east coast of Yorkshire.

"I can't stay in hospital for weeks on end—I'll go mad. Especially when there's nothing wrong with me physically." Somewhere she had friends, a bank account, possessions, a job waiting for her. She *needed* to remember why she'd forgotten everything—and why she felt that she had to lay low. The consultant had asked her if she had been under a lot of recent strain, because that might have triggered it. Or maybe even something small sparking off long-term stress—like a match to a load of dried hay, was how he put it. She wished she had a pound for every time she'd said "I don't know" this past week; she'd have enough money to start a new life in San Tropez.

"You're in the best place for now," said Marielle kindly, reading the despair on her face. "You will remember little pieces and they'll come together like a jigsaw puzzle. I promise."

Chapter 20

"Ya what?" said Sylvie, horrified.

"You don't approve of my plan, I take it?" said Marielle.

"If you do that, I'll have you bloody sectioned."

"Do say it as it is, Sylvie. Please don't hold back."

"Marielle, you don't know this woman from Adam. What if the reason she's lost her memory is because she's killed someone and it's all too traumatic to bring back?" Sylvie shook her head. "Marielle Bonetti, do *not* do this."

"She hasn't killed anyone, silly," said Marielle, and though she couldn't be wholly sure of that, the odds were against it. "She's rotting in hospital."

"Good, let her rot," said Sylvie, "and I'm not being callous. I would just rather it was her at a disadvantage than you."

"Well, I'm not listening to you. My mind is made up."

"I'll tell Teddy. You give me no choice."

"Then if that's your answer, I'm going, Sylvie Sampson." And Marielle reached for the jacket she'd taken off not long before.

Never once had Marielle walked out of Sylvie's house on bad terms, and they weren't going to start now. Sylvie stood up to block her way. "I'm sorry. Please don't go."

"I'm sixty-three years old, not some child who doesn't know her own mind, and you're threatening to tell my son on me." Marielle was angrier than Sylvie had ever seen her.

"Look, Marielle—love—I'm only thinking about you." Sylvie swapped the heat in her voice for concern. "Come on, you can't blame me after what happened last time when you let that woman stay in the flat and she ran off with everything that wasn't screwed down."

"I made a mistake then and I admit it, but Sabrina is a very different case. I'll let her stay in the flat for just a little while, I promise. I'll keep the door between us locked. She's not making any headway in a hospital environment, and the sooner she does, the sooner she can go back to her life. They've tried all sorts of things on her this past fortnight. She hasn't even responded to hypnotherapy, so whatever it is, is very deep-seated—"

"Or she's making it up," Sylvie said, unable to stop herself, then, seeing Marielle's expression, apologized quickly. "Okay, I'm sorry. But surely she's better off in hospital?"

"I don't think she is. I think I can help her break down the wall she's built up inside herself," said Marielle.

"And what makes you think you can do that?"

"Because I was a nurse for forty years and I've done it before," Marielle answered. "When I was working in the hospital in Naples, there was a young woman on the psychiatric ward who couldn't remember who she was, very similar circumstances to Sabrina's. She was in there ages and it did her absolutely no good at all. So she discharged herself even though she had nowhere to go, and Sal and I took her in. She lived with us and she'd help out, cleaning, cooking, and just by doing banal things that didn't take up any headspace, her brain must have started turning over in the background, and she began to remember bits and pieces. Like when you can't think of an answer in a crossword and you can't force it out, but it'll come to you if you go for a walk or do some ironing. To cut a long story short, we discovered that she was traumatized after losing her child. She had a family in Turin going mad to find her and we were able to reunite them. So whatever you say, it's happening. I'm going to try to help Sabrina my way."

The doorbell rang; the others were arriving for the Mad Cows get-together.

"Then do me one favor, Marielle. Just run all this past everyone else and see what they say. I promise you, I'll keep my mouth shut. Now you get the glasses and I'll get the door."

Sylvie wasn't even going to bother putting on the kettle. The Mad Cows were going to need something a bit stronger to wash that down with.

Sylvie didn't do baking, she never had, so when it was her turn to host, she bought cake from the posh deli in Slattercove, but it was never as moreish as Jackie's filo tarts, Bev's French fancies, Diana's scones, or Marielle's simple, moist homemade custard creams. But the food always played second fiddle to the camaraderie. They were a vacuum-safe space, nothing was out of bounds to talk about, and no one ever felt judged, and that's why Marielle's cousin Cilla Charlesworth would never be a Mad Cow, even though she'd done her best to elbow her way in.

"I saw Cilla in Waitrose," said Diana, daintily lifting up a forkful of cake to her lips. "She couldn't wait to show me her tan, which was, I have to say, very impressive."

They all knew Cilla from old. Bev had known her since school, Jackie lived a few doors down from her, she frequented Sylvie's beauty salon, although there was always something she found to complain about and press for a discount, and she used to go to the same book club as Diana before Cilla drove out most of the people with her outspoken ways and it closed down.

Marielle had been eleven when her mum's feckless sister died, leaving behind four-year-old Cilla, so her parents had adopted their niece. They'd spoiled her, ruined her, overcompensating for her less-than-ideal start in life, and in the process made their daughter feel second-best. It was, all the Mad Cows agreed, no wonder that Marielle had buggered off to Italy at age seventeen and married the first man to give her some love and attention. Cilla had been a thorn in her cousin's side when they were kids and she still was, even though Marielle was too kind to admit the full extent, even to her besties. She'd recently come back from a cruise in the Bahamas with Hugo, a new man on the scene whom she'd found on the internet, and Marielle didn't trust him as far as she could throw him. Any attempt to warn Cilla to be careful had been rebuffed with an accusation of pique, and so Marielle had decided to back off.

"She said the sun shone every day, Hugo was the perfect gent, and the caviar and champagne flowed," added Diana.

"Wonder who paid for all that then?" asked Jackie, but it was a question they all knew the answer to. Hugo's money was all tied up in long-term investments, Cilla had told Marielle and Marielle had told her friends. He had to give a stupid amount of notice to access his funds, so while they were waiting for clearance, so he didn't lose any interest, Cilla stumped up for everything.

"She's a grown woman. Let her get on with it," said Bev. "Even at school she always knew best."

Marielle blamed her parents for that, giving her a false sense of her own importance. Cilla could do no wrong growing up. The result was that the spoiled, entitled child grew up into a spoiled, entitled woman.

"I don't want to talk about Cilla anymore. How are Doug's bowels?" asked Marielle.

Diana smiled. "He got his results back this morning: no action. And it might help if he stopped eating beetroot and scaring himself stupid."

Bev raised her glass. "A toast to Doug's colon." And everyone else followed suit.

"Any other business?" asked Jackie.

Sylvie, who by now was on her second glass of malbec, reneged on her promise and dropped Marielle right in it.

"Marielle's taking in another woman of no fixed abode," she said, then clamped her hand over her mouth. "Whoops."

There followed a stunned silence.

"You're fecking joking," said Bev, breaking it.

"What's Teddy said?" asked Diana.

"Oh, bugger Teddy," replied Marielle in a hard voice she seldom used. "Why does everyone think I haven't got a brain but my son has?"

"I'm sorry, Marielle," said Sylvie, wishing she'd never opened her mouth. "Just tell them what you told me."

So Marielle told them all the story of the Lost Lady, and they listened without smart comments or interruptions until she'd finished.

"How come she's not forgotten how to eat or walk or sleep?" asked Diana.

"Can you forget how to sleep?" questioned Bev.

"Because it's psychological, not physical," Marielle explained. "There's no brain damage, but something is keeping her from remembering things, probably some trauma. The brain works in odd ways, and hers is obviously trying to protect her from recalling something probably very unpleasant until it thinks she can cope with it, so it's set up its own internal blocking system."

No one said it, but they all thought that Marielle might be as capable of fooling herself with the "Lost Lady" as Cilla was with "Internet Hugo." They also all thought that they'd be watching this Sabrina character like a hawk, and woe betide her if she was as rotten as some of the others Marielle had tried to help.

"How long are you going to look after her for then?"

"What if she never gets her memory back?"

"Will the hospital just let you take her out like that?"

"Surely social services should be looking after her, not you."

"How are you going to explain her to Teddy?"

"How old is she?"

Questions missiled at Marielle, and she had to hold up her hands to stem the flow.

"She's about thirty-five, and no, I don't know what will happen if she doesn't get her memory back. We'll have to cross that bridge if we get to it. Yes, I know I said I wouldn't do this again, but she's different from the others. Yes, I'll make sure I'm on my guard, but I know that I'm doing the right thing—there's not a doubt in my head. Yes, it took a bit of jiggery-pokery to get her out of hospital because they weren't happy about her wanting to discharge herself against all their recommendations and safety orders, but they could hardly stop her if that's what she wanted to do."

"Be careful, darling," said Diana, not wanting to be too judgmental. Her friend had a heart of gold, and none of them wanted to see her good intentions blow back in her face.

"I hope we're going to meet her," said Jackie, by which she meant she insisted they did so they could suss her out.

"Hang on. You used the past tense," said Sylvie. "You said it *took* a bit of jiggery-pokery." She raised her eyebrows in question.

"I did," replied Marielle. "I brought Sabrina home this afternoon. She's making herself comfortable in the flat as I speak."

Chapter 21

Sabrina stood by the large picture window in the small flat adjoining Marielle's house, looking out to the sea in the near distance. There was something about this view that was acting like aloe vera on her soul. It made her think that the sight of the sea was connected with happy thoughts, and that's why she had come to it. She had little to go on other than feelings at this present time. She knew she hadn't just materialized at . . . thirty-five, she was pretty sure she was that age, but she couldn't remember anything of importance before waking up in the hospital, just faint flotsam and jetsam, and then being asked if she wanted chicken supreme or a baked potato for her tea. As one stunted sense makes the others more powerful, her intuitions and sensitivities seemed sharpened by the loss of her memory, and she had little choice but to trust them.

There was an adjoining door to Marielle's house, and her temporary landlord had been really apologetic about keeping it locked, but then she explained why. Sabrina wasn't in the slightest offended and agreed that it was wise for her peace of mind; there was nothing for Marielle to feel guilty about.

Trust should be earned; it was too valuable to be given away flippantly. She felt that too. What a kind woman she was, thought Sabrina. She'd bought her clothes and magazines and helped engineer to get her out of hospital and into this pretty flat, the home environment she was convinced would speed her recovery. It was cozy-tiny with an all-in-one lounge and kitchen, a bathroom with a corner shower, and a bedroom with a single bed that Marielle had dressed for her with some clean, flowery sheets and a cloud-soft duvet.

Marielle had also brought her a box full of food: a large bar of Galaxy chocolate, butter, bread, milk, coffee, cheese, and other staples. She'd left her in Little Moon to familiarize herself with her new surroundings, relax, watch the TV, whatever she wanted to do while she went out to meet with friends. The main house was called Big Moon and Marielle told her she'd named it so because on the first night she spent in here, framed in her sitting room window like the most beautiful picture, there had been a huge, bright supermoon in the sky. She'd never seen a moon so large before or since, and she'd stood staring at it for ages in wonder.

It wasn't even seven o'clock yet, but Sabrina changed into one of the flannelette nighties, waffle robe, and fluffy slippers that Marielle had bought for her. When normal service was resumed, Sabrina would pay her back and more for her generosity, touch wood, because psychological memory loss was an unknown quantity, apparently, and there were no guarantees. Luckily, weighing in at the other end of the scale was Marielle's success story about the young Italian lady. Sabrina had to hope that her brain would eventually let go of its secrets, because if it didn't—what then?

She made herself a drink and switched on the television, flicking through the channels until she came to a film she instantly recognized: *Breakfast at Tiffany's*. She knew she'd seen it at least five times and what the story was and who starred in it. Why was her mind holding some things back and not others? She tried to stop thinking and just let the lovely story wash over her. Then at the end of it, the TV announcer said:

"*Following on with our Audrey Hepburn evening, we have* Sabrina *with William Holden and Humphrey Bogart.*"

She hadn't heard of that film. How strange it was her name. Then what popped into her memory, like a little bubble carrying a treasure, was that she was named after her late mother Rina. She knew she had died only a few years ago, but in her mind's eye she was petite with golden hair, young, not old. That didn't matter though; what did was that something had slipped through the barbed-wire fence in her head and it meant that more was sure to follow. She smiled with relief and caught sight of herself in the mirror hanging on the wall. She felt that the woman staring back at her hadn't smiled for quite some time.

* * *

When Marielle returned, she knocked on the adjoining door, gently in case Sabrina should be asleep. She wasn't, and called "Hello" in response.

"Is it okay to come in?" asked Marielle.

"Of course, it's your house."

When Marielle unlocked the door, it was to find Sabrina smiling in a way she hadn't seen her do before.

"I remembered something," she said. "It isn't much, but I know I was named after my mother Rina."

"That's wonderful," said Marielle.

"I was watching the film *Sabrina* while you were out, with Humphrey Bogart and Audrey Hepburn, and it must have pushed out a memory."

"I know it," said Marielle. "It's a lovely story."

She'd watched a lot of those old black-and-white films when she was younger. Her mum loved them. They'd snuggle up on the sofa together every Sunday afternoon when her dad had gone for a nap after his big roast lunch. Then Cilla had come along and she'd snuggle up with her mum instead, and Marielle had to sit in the armchair because there wasn't room enough for all three of them on the two-seater.

"Come through to the house and have a cup of hot chocolate with me to celebrate," said Marielle. "My son bought me a Velvetiser for my birthday and I'm addicted. I've got white chocolate, Black Forest, or orange."

"They all sound nice," said Sabrina, but she plumped for Black Forest. She was giddy as a kipper about remembering something, and Marielle didn't think for a minute she was putting it on.

"Tell me about yourself," said Sabrina, her hands drawing warmth from the mug as she sat on Marielle's squashy sofa. "Since we met, everything's been about me and all I know about you is that you're some sort of an angel." A sweet-faced angel with kind blue eyes and lovely dark red hair.

That made Marielle chuckle. "I'm no angel, trust me. I'm a very ordinary sixty-three-year-old mum of one. When I was seventeen I went over to Italy as an au pair, not knowing a word of the language, but I picked it up very quickly. I stayed with the family for three years, and then I became a nurse in Naples. And at the hospital there, I fell for one of the maintenance men—Salvatore Bonetti. He was gorgeous—and he knew it. We married and then came my son Teodoro, though everyone has always called him Teddy. We came back to England when he was eighteen as my mother wasn't well, and I found a nursing post in the hospital where you were. Four years later I lost both her and Sal within weeks of each other, and I've been on my own ever since."

"That must have been hard, losing them so close together," said Sabrina.

"Yes, it was," replied Marielle. She'd had to split herself in two, working and nursing them both. Cilla hadn't pulled anything like her fair weight to help, considering all her adoptive mother had done for her. She was a widowed mum herself then with a two-year-old daughter, but she still could have helped more. Marielle had had to rely on Teddy far more than she'd wanted to. He'd been at catering college then, and when he wasn't studying, he was working in restaurants to get experience. He'd been a rock for her then and he still was.

"Happy marriage?"

Marielle puffed out her cheeks. "We stayed together," she said, "but he caused me a lot of pain."

"What sort of pain?" Sabrina lifted her mug up to her lips. It was black, with the word *Teddy's* written on it in a scrolling font over an Italian flag.

"Other women sort of pain," said Marielle. "I can't tell you how many times I took off my wedding ring to fling at him. I stayed with him because I didn't want to break up my family, not until Teddy was grown up anyway. He wasn't the best of husbands to me, but he was a wonderful father to our son. I planned to come back to England alone, but Teddy wanted to come with me, and Sal said he wanted to as well. I don't know what happened, but here he became the husband I'd always wanted him to be and we had four fabulous years. Then he fell ill—nothing serious we thought. But weeks later he was gone and I'm sorry that I didn't have enough of that Salvatore."

Her eyes had gone glassy, Sabrina noticed. "What about your son? Does he live close by?"

"Yes, and he has his own restaurant in town. It's a bit of a family affair. His two young cousins from Naples live over here and are waiters—very good-looking boys, they're having quite the time of it—and my cousin's daughter Flick is our, well . . . everything: receptionist, waitress, sommelier, sometimes sous chef, sometimes washer-upper. They're always so busy, she has to wear a few hats. My son is thirty-eight, she's nineteen, but I have to stop and ask myself sometimes who's the oldest because she doesn't half rule the roost."

Flick was someone Marielle seemed fond of; Sabrina could tell that by her voice.

"And has Teddy given you any grandchildren?" asked Sabrina, because if anyone would make a perfect granny, it would be this woman sitting next to her.

"Oh Sabrina, the one thing I wish I could go back and change is that Teddy grew up seeing a very dysfunctional template of a marriage," replied Marielle with a sad smile of regret. "You try and hide your unhappiness from your children, but they know. I cried too much, we rowed too much, it was probably no wonder that Teddy almost married someone who was giving him the runaround. It was like watching myself and Sal, only with the sexes reversed. I don't mind telling you I couldn't have been more relieved when they broke up, and I'm not sure he's been out with anyone since. He always says he's too busy for a relationship, which is a real shame because you should never be too busy for love. So, one day, I hope..."

"Families are complicated," said Sabrina, though she wasn't sure if she just knew that as a general point or was speaking from experience. "I bet even those picture-perfect ones on Instagram who make their own jam from fruits they've grown in their gardens end up throwing teapots at each other sometimes."

That made Marielle smile. "I threw all sorts of things at Sal. I'm not proud of it."

Sabrina bit her lip in thought, recalling something Marielle had just said which might kill two birds with one stone. "You said that your son's restaurant is always busy. Do you think they'd like another pair of hands to help out? I could do with a bit of pin money to earn my keep and pay you what I owe you."

Marielle shook her head. "You don't owe me anything. It's all freely given."

"I know, but you said the girl you helped in Naples got her memory back by doing some jobs and keeping busy. I'd like to at least try that," said Sabrina.

Marielle thought about that for a minute. There wouldn't be as much to keep Sabrina busy here as there had been for Viola in Naples. She'd thrown herself into helping with young Teddy and Sal's parents, cooking with Sal, cleaning their large house while they were both at work.

"I can ask for you, if that's what you want."

"Yes, I do," said Sabrina. It couldn't do any harm—only good—and she'd feel better repaying her debt, whatever Marielle might say to that.

The *Daily Trumpet* would like to apologize to animal behaviorist student Murphy Benson for inadvertently reporting that his professor at Cambridge was "mightily impressed with his feces, so much so that he insisted it went into the Cambridge University Library as a shining example to others to replicate the standard." This, of course, should have read that he was "mightily impressed with his thesis."

Murphy has kindly agreed to accepting dinner for two at the "Dog and Boner" pub in Knaresborough as fair recompense for any embarrassment caused.

Chapter 22

Teddy Bonetti was in a very bad mood the next morning. Next door there was a lot of activity going on in the empty building that would soon be a rival restaurant. Also he'd had to tell the drivers of a builder's van and a flash Mercedes who had parked up on his private land to shoo. It was clearly marked for patrons of Teddy's and it wasn't the first time this had happened, nor would it be the last. He'd been so distracted that he'd cocked up a batch of ice cream which had ended up more like soup. Felicity Charlesworth, affectionately known as Flick, put up with him grumping about all morning like a grizzly bear with an ingrown toenail, until she reached satiation point.

He was her second cousin, but she'd always thought of him as more of an uncle and that's what she called him.

"Right, that's it, Uncle Teddy. Be quiet or go and have a smoke outside."

"I don't smoke," he said, looking at her as if she were insane.

"Well, start. You might find it helps. I thought most Italians smoked anyway." She didn't stop wiping down the tables as she admonished him; she was quite capable of doing the two jobs simultaneously.

"It's a myth. Like Nero fiddling while Rome burned and bulls hating red. And the earth is flat like a pizza."

Flick tried not to chuckle. Uncle Teddy was at his funniest when he was on one. His accent was a strange hybrid of Yorkshire and Italian, but when he was impassioned, it veered toward the latter, and his hands started flying around as if he was conducting the Philharmonic Orchestra playing "Flight of the Bumblebee."

"Ah look, someone to cheer you up," said Flick, seeing Marielle coming through the door.

"Good morning, love," said Marielle, looking around for Teddy.

"He's in the kitchen, but watch out, Auntie Marielle—he's *irato*."

"I heard that," said Teddy. "You need to go to whisper school."

"I'll get you a coffee," said Flick. She loved Marielle, and though she tried not to admit it to herself, she thought she loved her more than she did her own mother. Her feelings for Cilla were complicated, while her feelings for her aunt were straightforward, because she was a far nicer person. Auntie Marielle lied in the kindest way too, like making it sound as if Flick would be doing her a favor by living in her little holiday flat when she wanted to move out of her mother's house because Hugo had moved in.

"Teddy, come and spare me five minutes, will you," said Marielle, sitting down at a table.

Teddy wandered out of the kitchen, and Marielle thought as he walked toward her, *How did we produce this man between us, Sal and I?* He had Sal's thick, dark hair and her blue eyes and he had the height and build of his maternal grandfather, but he was a much warmer, kinder person. She was so proud of him, and protective. He might have been less than two years away from his fortieth birthday, but he would always be her baby, and she was ready to fight anyone who was threatening to hurt him and destroy what he had taken years to build.

Teddy scraped back the chair opposite and plonked himself on it.

"Okay, what have I done?"

That made her laugh. "I'm not here to tell you off. I'm here to solve one of your problems."

"It's solved. She's going to university in September."

"Oh very funny," said Flick, giving him her best middle finger.

"I know a lady who needs a job and I think she'd be perfect." Marielle let that sink in as she took a sip from her coffee.

"Can she string sentences together?" asked Teddy. "Because I've interviewed God knows how many people so far who can't."

"Yes, she can, quite adequately. She's a business adviser," said Marielle, though she wasn't quite as sure as Sabrina about that, but it did make her sound trustworthy and hardworking.

Teddy tilted his head at his mother.

"A business adviser," he repeated flatly. "What would I want with a business adviser?"

"Well, there's a reason she can't do that job at the moment and would like something lower key."

Teddy sat back and crossed his arms, waiting for the big reveal, because his mother was about to hit him with something he wasn't quite sure he'd like.

"Presently, she's renting out Little Moon from me." Marielle smiled at him.

Teddy's eyes narrowed. "You don't rent that flat out, Mum. You lend it out free to people you don't know, who fleece you and then run off."

"Oh Teddy, shush, it was only one . . . two. Listen to me. This lady has been in hospital." Teddy opened his mouth to close this conversation down, but Marielle wouldn't let him. "She has a few gaps in her memory but not about anything that would affect her doing a job."

"She won't forget to put her clothes on then, and turn up naked?" said Teddy.

"You wish," said Flick.

"She wants a job and you need some help and I can vouch for her. If she can't do the job adequately, then you have my permission to let her go, but I'm asking you to give her a trial run."

"Mamma . . ." Teddy put on his best beseeching expression while rubbing his forehead and muttering a string of Italian expletives.

"Teddy. Hear me out."

Marielle pleaded her case further, reminding him of how she'd helped the woman in Naples. He listened in silence, although throughout, his expression shouted that he was convinced she was setting herself up for another disaster. But she was his mother and he wouldn't just turn her down for the sake of it. There was a caveat, though.

"Okay," he said at the end of her appeal. "I will see her, but if she doesn't fit in, she goes. Everyone has to, even someone who cleans the toilets. Deal?"

"Deal," said Marielle, beaming now that she'd gotten her own way. She polished off her espresso and stood up. "I'll go and fetch her now and introduce you to each other. No time like the present."

She left quickly, before her son changed his mind, which was entirely possible if she gave him too much time to think.

* * *

"Are you sure you feel fit enough to do a job, Sabrina?" asked Marielle, as she watched the woman putting on the trainers she'd been found wearing. Even if the trauma to her head hadn't been physical, her brain was obviously psychologically impacted, and that could cause a lot of fatigue.

"I feel perfectly fine, Marielle. I just don't feel very smart for a job interview." She had a sudden flash of herself in a suit, heels, kickass red lipstick. She had a large mahogany desk at work. Granted, her present getup didn't exactly scream she had executive status and could turn the fortunes of companies around.

They set off out of the house and down the winding streets. "I think this might be a really good idea of yours," said Marielle. "He runs a tight but happy ship and he always feeds his staff well after their shift. He's kind and calm and even-tempered . . . I bet you'll get on like a house on fire."

Outside Teddy's restaurant a well-dressed woman paused, let her dog take a dump on the pavement by the front door, and then moved on, pretending not to notice. But Flick, looking through the window, had.

"Teddy, she's done it again. I'm going to say something."

"I don't believe it," said Teddy, rushing to the window. "I warned her. If she does it again, I will make sure she doesn't do it again. Flick, out of the way, darling. Let me do the talking." He asked his pizza chef, George, to throw him a yellow washing-up glove from the sink, and when he'd caught it, he burst out of the front door.

"Hey, you, lady, I know who you are," Teddy shouted at the woman's back. She ignored him and tried to continue on her way, but her spaniel hindered her by squatting for a wee. "And I told you what would happen if your dog did it again. So I'll give you to the count of three to turn back and pick it up."

The woman didn't acknowledge his count, but tugged impatiently on the dog's lead and they walked on.

Teddy scooped up the poop with his glove and with a pitcher's skill worthy of a place in the World Series hall of fame, he lobbed it through the air in the direction of Councilor Stirling's wife. Even he was surprised by his accuracy, because it hit her squarely on her brunette French plait with a horrifying splat. She touched her hair to see what had been thrown at her and screamed when she found out.

"Maybe now you don't do it again," Teddy called after her, wagging his dirty rubber glove at her.

"You animal, I'll have the police on you. That's assault," shouted Wendy Stirling, half shouting, half retching, shaking her head, shaking her hand.

"And it's a fifty-pound fine for you. Every time your dog drops a poop here now and you don't move it, you'll be wearing it five seconds later and I'll make sure you pay up the money." Teddy gave her his best smirk.

That was the moment when the two women rounded the corner, and that was Sabrina's introduction to Teddy Bonetti.

When Sabrina walked into "calm and even-tempered" Teddy's

restaurant, she picked up on the good vibe, as if years of happy times had pressed themselves into the air and colored it. There was a wonderful aroma of fresh coffee and the tables were all wearing cheery red-and-white coverings. A first-time customer would think they'd made the right choice as soon as they entered; a repeat customer would feel comforted by the familiarity. She felt as if she could be in Italy, rather than on a sunny street in a Yorkshire seaside town.

She sat down at a table and waited, looking around, taking in the place while mother and son were in the kitchen part of the restaurant in heated conversation.

"Teddy, you do know who that was?"

"Yes, Mamma, I know exactly who that was."

"Councilor Stirling is someone you really don't want to upset."

"I don't give a toss about him. What about him upsetting me? I can't tell you how many times his wife has done that outside. She even has an attachment for the poo bags on the lead, but never does she pick up her dog's *cacca*. I'm sure she's trained it to do it there and nowhere else."

He had a strange accent, thought Sabrina as she listened, mainly neutral, then it took a sharp turn into Yorkshire and then veered off at an Italian tangent. Strange but charming.

"Teddy—"

"No, I'm right on this, Mamma. I warned her last time what would happen. And I am a man of my word. That's how you raised me, so it's your fault."

"Don't you dare blame me, Teddy Bonetti, for splattering Mrs. Stirling's hair with her own dog's doings."

There was a beat of silence; then they both dissolved into laughter and neither could get the conversation back onto a serious plane again. Sabrina's attention was snatched away by a coffee cup being placed in front of her by a young woman. She was tall and slim and looked as if she could have been Teddy Bonetti's daughter with her brown-black hair and blue eyes.

"He's gone full-on Tony Soprano today," she said, jabbing at the kitchen with her head. "That's never a good sign."

"Thank you," said Sabrina. The coffee looked thick and strong and delicious.

"I can get you some milk if you like."

"Thanks, but this is perfect."

"Flick," said the girl, holding out her hand and smiling with full lips that must have caused jealousy in other girls who coveted such a natural pout. Sabrina thought she remembered the same happening to herself, but the memory skidded away before she could fully appreciate it.

"Hello, Flick. I'm Sabrina."

"It's Felicity really, but . . ." Flick stuck her tongue out as if that constituted her opinion on her name. Flick suited her; it had attitude.

Teddy and his mother had finished talking and were coming over to the table. He looked like a chef, Sabrina thought. One of those who took his food very seriously. One of those who was on the right side of wild.

He slammed himself down on the seat opposite her while Flick and Marielle peeled off to a far table and left them to it. He held out his hand, and it felt so much bigger than her own when he squeezed it in greeting.

"Hello, Sabrina, my mother tells me you need a job. So have you worked in a restaurant before?"

Teddy tried to see the woman in front of him as a business adviser in a suit and he couldn't. He was expecting her to spin him some bull and he was ready to see through it. It was the morning for *cacca*—dog or otherwise.

"I don't think so," Sabrina answered. "Did your mum tell you that I can't really remember much?"

"She did. You think you can set tables, empty a dishwasher, polish glasses, maybe even cut some vegetables?"

"Yes, I can do all those things."

"Hmm," said Teddy, like Alan Sugar in the boardroom. "You being here for a while would save me from having a regular turnover of useless, unreliable temps. You'd be doing anything that needed to be done, and that includes a lot of cleaning: floors, toilets." He had no intention of glamorizing it. If anything, he was hoping to put her off.

"That's great, thank you. I'd like to pay your mum something back for her kindness to me."

The cynical part of Teddy thought she would say something like that, trying to appear plausible and sincere. He'd be watching her.

"Okay, I'll give you a trial," he said. "No uniform needed, but if you've got something black, that would be ideal. Start tomorrow at nine. I'll need your bank details."

Her expression segued into one of a pained apology and he sighed. This was already too complicated.

"Well, cash it will have to be for now. I won't make you work a week in hand."

"Thank you, that's very good of you."

He stood up, the interview at an end. He turned and walked back to the kitchen, giving his mother a look as he passed her. In return she grinned at him.

On the way home Marielle stopped at the cashpoint and pulled out a hundred pounds, which she handed to Sabrina, who tried to push it back.

"You need to buy yourself some clothes for work," she insisted, stemming the protestations coming her way. "There's a couple of clothes shops in the center and a big Primark. You're bound to get a few black tops and trousers there. Take it."

She watched discomfort cloud Sabrina's expression and thought again how utterly dreadful this must be for her. But why wasn't anyone missing her? She'd googled every day to see if there was anyone trying to trace someone called Sabrina Anderson, but there was nothing.

"Come on, I'll go with you. Let's see what we can find," said Marielle, taking Sabrina's arm and propelling her forward before she started having a bit of a weep herself.

Chapter 23

Sabrina bought two pairs of black jeans and a set of three T-shirts plus some more underwear. There was change, and she offered it to Marielle, who wouldn't take it. "You'll need it for something, I'm sure. Are you hungry? Let's go and have some fish and chips for lunch, shall we, and celebrate your new job?" She pointed across the road. "The Mother of Cod is the best one around."

As they neared the restaurant, the smell of fish and chips hit their nostrils and Sabrina's stomach keened with a hunger she didn't know she had.

Marielle pushed open the door and walked in. The restaurant was full, and the waitress was just about to tell them they'd have to wait for a table when she heard a familiar "Cooee." Sylvie was waving from near the back, sitting with Diana at a table for four.

Poor Sabrina, thought Marielle, knowing she was in for some more grilling. She led her young friend over and sat down with her old friends who were enjoying the last of their lunch.

"How lovely it is to meet you at last, Sabrina," said Sylvie, wearing her fixed smile, the one that spelled danger. Diana's expression was in much the same mold, and her eyes checked out every square centimeter of the younger woman. If she'd had an X-ray machine handy, she would have checked her insides as well.

Sabrina sat down. She didn't blame any of Marielle's friends for giving her the once-over. She had nothing to hide, and she'd do what it took to make them realize she was genuinely grateful. She had no intention of outstaying the welcome extended to her. As soon as she remembered enough information to return to her *context*, she'd leave and work everything out from there. As soon as she knew what was and wasn't safe, because that was the most important thing.

"Sabrina, this is Diana and Sylvie, two of my closest friends."

"We're all Mad Cows," said Sylvie.

"It's the name of our club," Marielle explained. "Diana and I used to work together at the hospital. She was a physiotherapist. Sylvie owns a beauty salon. I started going there because I heard it was very good."

"It still is," said Sylvie. "You should visit. I'll make sure you have a deep tissue massage on the house. Have you ever had one before?"

The interrogation commenceth, thought Marielle. The Gestapo would have nothing on Sylvie when she got started. "Let's order," she said as a timely waitress appeared at their side.

"Just fish and chips for me, please," Sabrina said.

"Twice, then," Marielle told the waitress. "Tea, bread and butter, please. Mixed white and brown."

"Thank you," said Sabrina, then asked where the loo was.

She needed to go even though she knew she'd be picked apart in her absence.

"Different from what I was expecting," said Diana, spearing a chip.

"Seems decent enough, but then, a practiced con artist would," added Sylvie. She anticipated Marielle's disapproval and so quickly added, "Just looking out for you as a true friend. Allow me some cynicism until I've been proved wrong."

"She's going to be working for Teddy for a while," said Marielle.

"Good. He'll suss her out. Or Flick will. She'll not be able to fool them." Diana realized her faux pas immediately. "Not that I think you—"

"Look," said Marielle wearily, because she was getting a bit fed up with all this now, "I've taken a chance on her because I believe her.

I'm pretty sure this woman wants to prove who she is and get back to her life more than anything else, so please stop it, will you?"

Diana dropped her eyes, slightly shamefaced. Marielle had a right to be annoyed when her friends, however well-meaning, were treating her like a simpleton. She could try to make up for it.

"Marielle, are you doing anything on Sunday night?" Diana asked.

"Yes, I'll be in hospital with stab wounds from Sabrina," she replied.

"Okay, I'm super sorry, forgive me. I've got two tickets for the theater in Slattercove. They were given to Doug, who really doesn't want to go. I thought Sylvie might have them, but she's said no as well."

"God forbid," said Sylvie as her shoulders shivered. "They'll go to waste if I don't find a home for them. An acquired taste I grant you, and certainly not my sort of fun evening."

"What is it to see, a brass band?"

"If it had been, Doug would have gone there like a shot. No, it's a psychic. World-renowned, apparently—at least that's what it says on the tickets. Psychic Pat." She fished around in her Mulberry bag and pulled out an envelope. "What do you think? You and your new friend could go. You never know, Psychic Pat might pick her out and tell her something interesting."

"Yes, I'll go to that. Anything's worth a shot," said Marielle and reached over the table for the tickets.

* * *

Sylvie and Diana said their goodbyes and left the two women to their lunch.

"I really don't mind that your friends are curious about me," said Sabrina, pouring the tea. "It's nice they think so much about you and are protective."

"Yes, I get that, but sometimes it goes a bit far," said Marielle. "I'd like to think I was a good judge of character, but I did get taken in by a couple of people I lent the flat to. The last one broke the lock, got into my house, and ransacked the place looking for valuables. She didn't find much because I have a safe, but she did leave a heck of a mess."

"Then you really can't blame them for worrying. It's horrible when your trust is broken."

Trust. Broken.

That feeling again that her own trust in something was broken. It brought with it a pain deep in her chest this time, the echo of a persistent ache. She remembered sitting on the edge of a double bed crying, pressing the ring on the chain around her neck so hard it dug into her hand. Her wedding ring, she presumed. She'd taken it off to signify the end of her marriage maybe. But that didn't tie in with why her fingers reached for it often to bring comfort.

The fish and chips were wonderful, the batter crisp, the fish white and flaky, the bread thin and spread with real butter.

"Teddy doesn't usually throw things at women in the street, least of all a dog's dollops," said Marielle. "I did want to point that out."

"He must have terrific aim, though, to have landed it so perfectly on that woman's hair. What a talent," replied Sabrina. Both women smiled.

"It's all part of a much bigger story," said Marielle. "My son is about to be driven out of business. Next door to him was an empty shop. He and the newsagent on the other side own their properties, but the rest of the row are leased from the council. There was an agreement in place that none of them could trade in direct competition with each other. But the council have reneged on that and are allowing an Italian restaurant to take it over, one from a relatively new chain that seems to have set up in Yorkshire. Not only that, but they're attempting to take our car park away from us for them to use, digging up some nonsense about the legality of the wording on the deeds which might allow them to serve us with a compulsory purchase order. Even if it's rubbish, it will cost us money to fight it and we'll need a specialist solicitor. We can't get any help from our councilor, the one who got all the votes by promising to serve his ward. No surprise really as he happens to be the brother-in-law of the deputy leader of the council, James Stirling, although he seems to be more in charge than the leader from what I've heard. He and the council cabinet are just one big old boys' club, and no one would ever dare vote against him on anything. You met Stirling's wife this morning, along with his defecating spaniel."

"A chain, you say? Which one?"

"Ciaoissimo. Have you heard of them?"

Ciaoissimo. Why did that name ring a bell? Why did it trigger off an image of herself sitting at a table, eating a sandwich, reading about them? And why did the memory come with a sensation that wasn't particularly pleasant?

"Of course, Councilor Stirling will get the police onto Teddy if he hasn't already. I have no idea why he and his cronies are being so bloody hostile. I tell you, if I ever find out they've been given a backhander by Ciaoissimo, I'll go for their jugulars. All we've heard from them by way of an excuse is that they want to encourage healthy competition. It's a travesty. They're making things up as they go along."

"Councilors have to have declared any business interests, surely," said Sabrina. "They can't manipulate and overturn decisions to fill their own pockets."

"It seems they can do what they want if they cover their tracks well enough. There has to be some murky secret, but how can you find out? Stirling could hide behind a spiral staircase, he's that twisted. The dirty tricks campaign against us started with the decision to install Ciaoissimo next door. You should read the vile reviews about us on the internet that have suddenly sprung up. There has to be a connection."

A man's voice in Sabrina's head: *Forget about this one.*

"Are you okay, Sabrina?" asked Marielle. Sabrina looked suddenly far away, tangled up in thoughts. "Sabrina?"

Sabrina snapped back into the here and now. "Yes, I'm fine," she said.

* * *

As they left the Mother of Cod, a police car passed them and Marielle said a very heartfelt "Oh no," because she had an inkling where it was heading.

"Do you mind if I just check . . . ?" she asked Sabrina, quickening her pace.

"Of course." Sabrina fell into step with her.

Sure enough, when they got to Teddy's, the police car was parked outside and Teddy was talking to the two policemen occupants on the pavement away from the sight of his diners. Flick was also out with him, putting in her two penn'orth.

"How long have you known me, Craig? Am I the sort of person to throw turds at women's heads without good reason?"

Marielle recognized Craig immediately. He'd been at catering college with her son before deciding to change tack and join the police. The older policeman was Constable Travis; everyone in the town knew him, respected him, and liked him. He was a solid, fair, seasoned copper whom they sent into schools when they needed someone to make warning speeches and actually be listened to.

"I hear what you're saying, Teddy, I really do." Craig was scratching his head. His hands were clearly tied and he was trying to wriggle out of the binding.

"Dog fouling is against the law and the council give a fifty-quid fixed penalty that does not exclude councilors' wives," said Flick. "This is not the first time she's done it either. In fact, she's making quite a habit of it. It just happened to be the first time we caught her *in flagrante delicto*."

"She said it *was* the first time and she hadn't noticed the dog had done it," said Craig, which caused Flick and Teddy both to burst into laughter.

"She says she always clears up and showed us the poo bag holder attached to her lead as . . . evidence," Travis said in a way that suggested he was skeptical of her account.

"Ah, well, if it's evidence that you want," said Flick, fumbling around on her phone, sweeping the screen with her thumb until she found what she was searching for. She held it up to them. "Here's a film of some CCTV footage."

Teddy flashed her a look of amazement before he viewed the film with the policemen. It was of Wendy Stirling walking slowly past the restaurant, loitering, doubling back, clearly giving her spaniel every opportunity to empty his bowels. It looked crystal clear that she was very aware of what was happening, staring into space just after the dog had crunched itself into position. The footage continued until Mrs. Stirling started threatening and flapping her sullied hand around.

"One hundred and eighty!" said Craig, clearly impressed.

Travis turned to Teddy. "I think that's plainly an offense on the part of Mrs. Stirling. Maybe, Teddy, if you stick to collecting evidence in this way rather than lobbing spaniel shit at women who think they're above the law, it would make the situation so much more clear-cut. Neither of us wants to arrest you. Stirling can cause trouble in an empty house; don't give him bullets for his gun, lad."

"Thank you," said Teddy, appreciating what they were saying to him.

"Where did you get that footage from?" Teddy asked Flick when they'd driven off.

"Simon." Flick thumbed toward the newsagent next door. "When I was picking up some milk, I overheard him saying that he'd had some new state-of-the-art CCTV cameras fitted at the front, so I thought it was worth a shot asking him if he had any footage. Might be an idea if we get some. Anyway, back to work." And she sauntered off back toward the restaurant.

"You need to put that girl's wage up," said Marielle. "Go on, Teddy, you have customers." Teddy gave his mother a kiss on her cheek and then returned to his duties.

"What next?" said Marielle, shaking her head. Because she was sure as eggs were eggs, there would be another offensive to follow.

In Monday's edition of the *Daily Trumpet* we reported the story of postman Barry Ratcliffe who was causing uproar in Hatfield, Doncaster, with his continual wrong deliveries. We stated that Ms. Linz Hennegan, chair of the Hatfield Residents Society, had "chased him down the street on numerous occasions in order to shake her lettuce in his face." This should have read "shake her letters in his face." We apologize to Ms. Hennegan for any embarrassment cause and have made a donation to the Hatefield Residents Society fund in recompense.

Chapter 24

When they got back to the house, Marielle's hand paused when opening the door, and she turned to Sabrina and said, "Do you fancy a little drive? I just thought you might like to see where you were found. Perhaps it might dredge up some memories for you."

"It's worth a go," Sabrina answered her. She got into the passenger seat of Marielle's car and clicked herself into her seat belt.

"You're really seeing the best of my son, aren't you? Throwing dog muck at women and then nearly being arrested," Marielle said to her with an uneasy shot of laughter.

"Bad things happen to nice people," Sabrina said. "I'm not judging."

Five minutes later, the car turned up the hill signposted "beauty spot."

"It's a misnomer in my opinion," said Marielle. "It can get dangerously windy up here, which is why it was madness that the council should make this into a designated picnic spot. They've got far more money than sense. It's always given me the shivers, this place."

They pulled in at the top in the exact spot where Polly Potter had parked her car three weeks ago, and when she saw the nearby burger van, she felt a tremble in her muscle memory. "I came here in a black car," she said, letting the image come to her so she didn't scare it away. She could see herself sitting on one of the benches, waiting, but she didn't know what for. Sabrina and Marielle walked over the bumpy grass toward the railing. There was a sign in the burger van window, "Back in half an hour." She'd been waiting for it to open; that's why she had sat down.

"Benny Prince, who owns the van, was the man who found you," said Marielle.

"I should seek him out and thank him." Sabrina looked around her as if he should magically appear.

"Benny Prince is someone people get out of the way of, not go and find. You wouldn't believe how many of these vans there used to be on this stretch of the coast until Benny moved in, and then, bang, all the competition was gone. That said, he does sell really good burgers and ice creams. It isn't always the way when the big boys move the little boys out and quality becomes a thing of the past." Her countenance grew grim, and Sabrina knew she was thinking about her son.

"I could at least write him a note," said Sabrina. "I don't suppose you have any paper on you, do you?"

Marielle had a pocket pad and a pen in her bag. Sabrina sat at one of the picnic tables and wrote.

Dear Mr. Prince,

My name is Sabrina Anderson and I was told you very kindly rang an ambulance for me after finding me up here three weeks ago. I have no recollection how I came to be here and am just out of hospital, so please forgive this much overdue thank-you. Hopefully my memory will return one day and the mystery will be solved. I did hope to see you in person to deliver my thank-you and I hope that one day I may catch you to be able to do that. But in the meantime—again, thank you for your kindness.

My very best wishes,
Sabrina Anderson x

There was the slightest gap in the van window that she could push the note through, though it took a few attempts; then it sat on his counter where he wouldn't be able to miss it when he got back.

It was kind of Sabrina to do that, thought Marielle, even if Benny Prince was a likely culprit to have taken her missing handbag and rings. Or maybe she was being unfair to him. Life was making her bitter and more cynical. She'd end up giving Cilla a run for her money if she wasn't careful.

A lone seagull wheeled above them, checking them out for snacks and squawking with annoyance when he saw their hands were empty. Sabrina looked up and felt dizzy and lightheaded, as if she were whirling around. The sound of the seagulls was tied up in her head with the smell of doughnuts sugaring the air, fish and chips, sunshine, laughter, a big man and that small woman with gold-blonde hair.

"What is it?" asked Marielle. "You're smiling."

"I think I must have come here with my parents," said Sabrina, feeling it rather than knowing it. She closed her eyes, hoping to find more, and a soft June breeze caressed her face. She could sense her own happiness here, as if she'd left some of it behind years before to reclaim, and she wondered again why here, why this place? Why was it so special to her?

* * *

That evening, Sabrina joined Marielle in Big Moon for a glass of wine, some cheese, and company.

"We have a lovely farm shop nearby," Marielle explained, loading a water biscuit with some buttery, crumbly Wensleydale. "I always spend far too much in it. Teddy buys his cheese there, too, for the restaurant. He won't use any cheap ingredients. He couldn't cut a corner, that boy, if his life depended on it, and I hope it's not the undoing of him."

"It has a very happy air, the restaurant," said Sabrina.

She'd picked up on that as soon as she'd walked through the door. But something in her brain clicked in and began looking at it through an analytical eye and decided, though she could appreciate why it was a popular place, there was definite room for improvement.

"Sal had Teddy working in the kitchen with him before he could talk, and he loved it. Apart from a spell when he wanted to be the goalkeeper for SSC Napoli and a brain surgeon, he never wanted to do anything other than have his own restaurant." Marielle laughed at the memory of young Teddy with his toy doctor's case and his makeshift hospital in his bedroom. "Teddy's was always booked out; people travel for miles to eat there. Probably why those horrible people think there are rich pickings to be had. They make me sick." Marielle drained her glass, and while she was thinking she'd better slow down, she was reaching for a top-up at the same time. She'd had nearly a full glass before she'd asked Sabrina to come through.

"Flick seems to have her head screwed on."

"Doesn't she just," replied Marielle. "We all love Flick. She's wonderful, and so bright. She's had a gap year to earn some money, and in September she'll be off to university doing business studies. We'll miss her, but it's only right and proper that she go."

"You said she was your cousin's daughter?"

"Yes. My cousin Cilla." Marielle took a long drink. The wine and the chat were taking the edge off a not-too-great day. How dare that despicable Stirling woman get the police involved.

"Her mum was my mum's sister. When my auntie died, Cilla would have had to go into care if my parents hadn't taken her in. It would have happened sooner or later because if Janet hadn't died of a drug overdose, she would have ended up in prison." Out of all her friends, only Sylvie knew that detail, and Marielle had no idea why she had just told it to a relative stranger rather than to those who were closest to her. "I was eleven, Cilla was four when she came to live with us. I was so excited about having a little sister in the beginning." She sighed then, in such a way that Sabrina could tell her idealistic expectations hadn't quite turned out the way she thought they would.

"She was like a blonde, blue-eyed Shirley Temple, a china doll; butter wouldn't have melted in her mouth. My parents tried to make up for everything she'd lost, and it felt to me as if their whole world revolved around her."

"That must have been hard on you, being an only child and then suddenly having to share," said Sabrina.

"It was," said Marielle, then she realized she must be coming across as resentful and unkind. "Ignore me, Sabrina." The wine was loosening her tongue in a way she didn't like.

"No, please go on," urged Sabrina, because it sounded like whatever was inside Marielle needed to come out.

"I shouldn't be saying these things," said Marielle, gulping back more wine. "Yes, it hurt. I wasn't supposed to say anything because I was 'the grown-up one who hadn't known anything other than a nice bedroom and lots of toys.'"

"Well, you weren't exactly grown up at eleven," said Sabrina. "I would have thought you needed more love at that time, not less."

"She used to lie. Oh God, did she lie. They'd believe her before me and I'd be the one who got the slap. And I remember one Easter they bought her an egg bigger than mine. Isn't that petty of me to have stored that in my head for fifty years?"

"The fact you have stored it up for fifty years says it was important to you, Marielle. It's the paper cuts that hurt the most."

Marielle hadn't even told Sylvie all this silly stuff that she'd kept hidden because she didn't want to be judged as an awful person. The fact that Sabrina seemed to *get* it made her feel vindicated in a way she didn't think possible, and she was beyond grateful that her deeply buried pain was seen to have some validity.

A tear slid down Marielle's cheek and she dashed it away too late for it not to be seen. There was so much more that could come out: how one year when her school prize-giving had clashed with Cilla's play, her mother had gone to the latter. No one had been there to see her pick up her award for excellence, and though her cup had pride of place in the sitting room, the shine had been taken away.

"Did you keep in touch with your family when you went to live in Italy?" asked Sabrina, ready to cut the questions because she could see Marielle was upset.

"Yes, we kept in touch. And they came over occasionally to visit. They doted on Teddy, of course, and it was lovely to see, but I wanted some of that for myself."

Tears, thick as syrup, were trickling down Marielle's cheeks now, and she couldn't wipe them away fast enough.

They felt hot and sour, as if they'd been inside her too long and fermented.

"When I came back to live here because my mother wasn't well, she told me one day that she was sorry if I'd ever felt pushed out, that she'd done a lot of thinking over the years about why I'd taken off at just seventeen. We're all a lot wiser in hindsight, though, aren't we? I never told her it was because I didn't feel loved. I didn't want to hurt her."

Sabrina could well imagine that. Marielle had kept the weight on her own shoulders rather than offload it. She was one of life's givers, that was clear.

"Cilla had a very short-lived marriage. He took off long before Flick was born, and then he died soon after, before they could even start the divorce, so she copped for the whole of his estate. Then when Flick arrived, Cilla said she couldn't cope alone with her, so rather than palm her off on child-minders, we looked after her a lot of the time."

"Blimey, Marielle, did you ever have any time to yourself?"

Marielle shook her head. "Flick was such an easy baby, no hardship at all. Sal adored her. Sometimes she felt as much my own child as Teddy was, though I was always very careful to make sure he knew he was my number one." Marielle took another drink, then another.

"Sal left me well provided for," she said after a thoughtful pause.

"Our house was way too big for one, so I bought this place and a holiday flat to rent out, even though Flick's staying there at the moment because she didn't want to live with her mother's new boyfriend. Mum left half of everything to me and half to Cilla, no surprise there, but she still wasn't satisfied. She took Mum's engagement and wedding rings, even though she denied it. I *know* she has them. It was pure greed. *I* was her daughter. They were precious."

Sabrina realized she was touching the necklace with the ring on it again, and somehow, at that moment, she knew that it wasn't her own ring but her mother's. And that's why she touched it so much and drew reassurance from it.

Marielle put her head in her hands, ashamed.

"Oh, what must you think of me, Sabrina? That I'm a horrible person, no doubt."

"You couldn't be more mistaken," Sabrina said gently. "And how are you and Cilla now?"

"As good as we'll ever be. She's infuriating, but ironically I can't help worrying about her. And I worry about Flick because Cilla has got all her priorities wrong. She gives these transient flash Harry boyfriends more attention than she does her daughter and it's unfair. This latest . . . thing, she says he's loaded, but I don't buy it; it's straight out of the textbook of gullible women and romance scammers. He says his money is tied up in long-term investments, so she pays for everything. He said his huge pile in the Home Counties is being renovated and he won't take her there until it's all done. He says his car, which just happens to be a vintage Rolls-Royce, is waiting for parts to be shipped from overseas. There's nothing about him on the internet because he's ex-military intelligence and has to fly under the radar. I mean"—Marielle threw her hands up in the air—"who believes all this . . . crap? But people do. We've all seen the TV programs and still they think it's *different in their case*. I'm waiting for him to suddenly announce he's got a serious illness, because that's what they do, isn't it, these . . . vampires. She bought him a car to run around in, but did she give her own daughter so much as a penny toward one when she passed her test? She says Flick has to learn the value of money, which is a joke if ever I heard one, seeing as she barely earned a penny of hers."

"She's not in your Mad Cow group, I'm guessing," said Sabrina.

"No. In our little group we all trust and like each other, and I've said too much. I'm not being kind."

"You're allowed not to be a saint, Marielle. I'm sure there are people in my life I don't like." Sabrina wished she knew who they were and who the people were that she did like. "Besides," she went on, "anyone who walked in here could tell from the ambience that it belongs to someone very lovely."

"It does have a nice feel to it, doesn't it?" Marielle replied, looking around. "I loved it as soon as I walked in. The old man who'd had it before me used the flat as a storage space, but I liked the idea of it being somewhere I could have people stay. I had more than enough money to do it up. And I gave Mum's money to Teddy so that one day he could buy his restaurant, and that's what he did with it." She topped up her glass again, wondering how it had gotten so empty so quick. "And now those Ciaoissimo bastards want to take everything away from him."

Ciaoissimo. Again that feeling that Sabrina knew the name. It was somewhere in her head, like a splinter in her brain.

"I'm sorry," said Marielle. "I've drunk too much and I'm going to make us both a coffee now." After two failed attempts on her part to get up from the sofa, Sabrina got up instead and said she'd make them. By the time the kettle had boiled, though, Marielle's head had dropped forward and she was snoring softly. Her arm was still out to the side, glass in her hand, and Sabrina rescued it just in time from falling to the pale blue carpet.

She cleared the drinks and the plate of nibbles away and closed the curtains. Marielle's house was an upside-down construction, so she had to go downstairs for a quilt and a pillow. There were three bedrooms and a bathroom on the lower floor, the largest of the bedrooms being obviously the one Marielle used. It smelled sweet, like freesias, Sabrina thought. There were photos on the bedside cabinets. In one, a young Marielle with long dark red hair held a smiling toddler, and at her side was a man who had to be Teddy Bonetti's father because the family resemblance was so pronounced: handsome, rugged, dangerously good-looking smile. On the other cabinet was a photo of a heavily pregnant Marielle, Salvatore's arm draped around her shoulder. They were looking at each other and laughing joyously. Sabrina touched her stomach and remembered being pregnant, remembered putting her hands on the swell and feeling her daughter flutter underneath. She'd named her Linnet, after the small, bright bird with a voice like a song, and she was presently living her best life, traveling, just as Sabrina had wanted for her. But she couldn't see her face in her mind's eye, no features discernible, and she asked herself for what reason was her brain also keeping her child from her?

Chapter 25

Sabrina was outside the restaurant at a quarter to nine sharp the next morning. She'd checked in on Marielle before she left. She was still on her sofa and hadn't woken to take the two ibuprofen or the glass of water Sabrina had set out for her. She really was out for the count.

Flick rounded the corner within five minutes, her ponytail swinging as she walked with her long stride.

"Morning," she said and opened up the front door, turning off the alarm and lifting the electric security blinds with practiced hits on switches and buttons.

"First job in the morning is very important," said Flick. "Putting on the coffee machine. I drink gallons of it. You can have a coffee whenever you like, by the way. Come on and I'll show you how it works."

She was just doing that when Teddy walked in, his face bearing a not-too-happy expression.

"*Buon giorno*, Teodoro," said Flick in an affected Italian accent. "Whatsa uppa with you? You have the face of a decomposing crab."

"Tripadvisor, that's *whatsa uppa*. More bad reviews." Teddy ripped the phone out of his pocket, found the page, and read, "'Rude waiting staff, cold inedible food that we had to wait half an hour for.' . . . 'Dirty toilets. Inappropriate sexual comments from waiters toward my wife.' . . . 'Found foreign object in pasta.' . . . A nice mix covering all the ground, don't you think? Oh look . . . 'Cold mozzarella sticks.' We don't even serve mozzarella sticks."

"Blimey, that is bad," said Flick, closing up her happy morning smile.

"Have you answered them?" asked Sabrina.

"Sorry?" said Teddy.

"Have you replied to them? Asked them to contact you to give you more details about when they were here? I'm presuming they're fake reviews, aren't they? If other people see that you've answered them and . . . called them out basically, they're less likely to see them as gospel. And definitely make the comment that you don't serve mozzarella sticks. Also put up an announcement that you're getting fake reviews and are currently liaising with a technical expert to uncover where they're being generated from . . ."

Sabrina's voice tailed off. She wasn't sure if Marielle had told Teddy what she did for a living. If she hadn't, then he was going to think that his new cleaner had a right gob on her.

What he said was, "That's actually a really good idea that I hadn't thought of. I presumed the best plan was to ignore them."

"How do you know all that?" said Flick, well impressed. Sabrina gave a small, almost embarrassed shrug of her shoulders. "I've come across it before."

Flick picked up her coffee. "I'm going to get onto that straightaway," she said.

"Can you tell me where the cleaning stuff is, please?" asked Sabrina. Whatever she was in her other life, this was the only one she was living at the moment, and she guessed she needed to start with scrubbing the toilets.

While Flick was in the office, Sabrina cleaned the loos and put in fresh loo paper from the storage room, filled up the soap containers, and emptied the bins. She was introduced to the sous chef Antonio, who was actually Tony from Whitby, but he wanted to be Italian, so they'd made him an honorary one. She mopped the restaurant floor, polished the cutlery, and set the tables. She did jobs she wasn't asked to but thought they might need doing, like wiping down the laminated specials menus, giving the stainless steel coffee pots a good polish, and watering the plants.

Teddy's cousins—their father Luca was Salvatore's younger brother—Niccolo and Roberto turned up just before twelve and greeted her with big curves of smiles. They were young, good-looking Italians who didn't take life too seriously, and Sabrina liked them on sight. She guessed, despite their flippancy, they were hard workers because she didn't think Teddy would tolerate slackers, family or not.

George arrived then, whose job it was mainly to make pizzas in the wood-fired oven in an adjoining room. "Proof that anyone given the proper training can make good pizzas," Teddy explained to her. "Even an old Greek."

"Less of the old—I'm only sixty-one," George threw back with some choice words of Greek, and Teddy threw a mouthful of Italian back at him, and Sabrina thought that this must be how it always was between them, this cheerful banter disguised as warfare; it smacked of people who were fond of each other.

When the first lunch customers turned up, Sabrina's duties were transferred into the kitchen. Teddy set her on cutting up onions and peppers and mushrooms and grating garlic because he never crushed it, he said, and crossed himself as if it was on some sort of sin scale to do so. While she was chopping, she was observing. She liked the buzz, the theatrics of the waiters conversing with each other in their native tongue, even though Teddy told them at least twice to tweak down the volume. She noticed how many people seemed to be grabbing a quick lunch, no starters, no desserts, and she noticed how many were walking in only to be turned away because no tables were free. And she knew that whatever was blocked in her brain, the corporate analyst part of it was running as well as it ever was.

They had a break at two thirty. Teddy said that she could go or stay until five. She stayed and ate with them all around the big table and absorbed the chat, also answering the odd question, even though they all knew she'd lost her memory and was working here in the hope it would help her get it back; she was glad they knew because she had nothing to hide from these kind people. She turned down a pudding, though Flick didn't: a slice of lemon cheesecake that was the size of a house brick. Then when the others, all except Teddy, went off until the dinner shift, she carried on cleaning.

"You don't have to," he said.

"What else am I going to do?" she replied. Whoever they'd had in cleaning before had done an okay job, but her standards were higher.

She thought he should have dimmable lights for the evening customers—the lights were too harsh at present—and candles with real flames rather than the battery-operated ones. It was all good, but it could be better. There was a much more intimate feel to the evening, and little touches and changes would add to that.

The last diners left at ten, but no one rushed them to finish; no one shut the door as soon as they were out of it and bolted it; there was no air of *We've got your money, now on your way*.

"You look knackered," said Flick to Sabrina.

"I'm fine," she said, but she did feel very weary now. She started to lift up the chairs and put them on the tables, but Teddy told her to stop.

"Do that tomorrow," he said. "We don't open Sundays; we just get ready for Monday. So ten till three, please."

"I'm not in," said Flick, stretching her long arms up and yawning. "Just you and Uncle Teddy. Won't that be nice for you, Sabrina? Right, I'm off to bed. Good night, everyone."

"Okay, I'm coming," said Teddy, darting out of the kitchen to escort her.

"Oh for God's sake, I'm only around the corner."

"I know this, but it's late," he said and followed her out, and Sabrina thought what an enviable relationship they had, so close.

She was just putting her jacket on when he returned. "I'll give you a lift," he said, picking up a pizza box from the counter. "Here's your supper."

"It's fine, I—"

"Don't you dare turn down one of my pizzas," said George, wagging his finger at her.

"Okay, I won't." She smiled in return.

Everyone filed out and said good night, Teddy locked up, and he and Sabrina walked out to his Golf in the restaurant car park.

"I pass by my mother's house, so it would be stupid not to drop you off. And even if I weren't, it would be about a minute out of my way," he said, getting in.

"Well, thank you, it's much appreciated. Do you live nearby?" she asked, clipping in her seat belt.

"A mile away," he said. "I'm renting somewhere at the moment so when I find a house I'm not in a chain. I sold mine recently. No doubt my mother told you that I bought it with someone who dumped me less than a month after we completed."

"No, she didn't actually," said Sabrina.

"Ah, sorry then, I thought she might have because she tells everyone." He laughed. "And also that my ex-fiancée emigrated to Australia, and it still isn't far enough away for my mum."

Australia. Her daughter was there. She had a strong feeling she'd told her she'd be in touch as soon as she was settled and not to worry if she didn't hear from her in the meantime. But that was before all this happened.

"You okay? You look deep in thought," said Teddy.

"I was thinking about my daughter. She's over there now and I don't know what she'll do if she needs me and can't get hold of me."

"Well, I'm sure that would trigger a full-on search for you," he replied. "I know Mum checks the internet every day. Do you know whereabouts in Australia she is?"

Sabrina shook her head.

"Maybe *you* should contact the newspapers—"

She cut him off. "I can't. And I can't tell you why, either, because I don't know." She dropped her head into her hands. All she had to go on were feelings, instincts, intuition, and it wasn't enough. She *had* to remember more.

"It must be awful for you," Teddy said. He thought he believed her story a little more than he did yesterday, though he wouldn't commit wholly yet.

"It is."

He pulled up outside his mum's house.

"Thank you, Teddy," Sabrina said, unclipping her belt and facing him. "I'll see you in the morning."

"'Night," he said. He hadn't meant the word to sound dismissive, but that's how it came out.

She reached for the door handle and then turned back to him.

"I know you're concerned about your mum—she told me what happened when the last person lived in the flat—but you have nothing to worry about from me. I just need to remember a little more and then I'll be gone. Marielle has been beyond kind, and I swear to you that I'll pay her back for everything she's done for me, somehow."

He looked into her eyes. He couldn't tell what color they were in this light, but they were clear and large and lovely, and they really didn't look like the eyes of someone who was out to take advantage of his mother.

"Good night, Sabrina," he said, imbuing his tone with warmth this time. "Enjoy your supper. George makes the best pizzas I've ever tasted."

"Thank you, I will."

He waited until she had opened the door to Little Moon before driving off. He hoped to God his mother was right about her.

Chapter 26

Sabrina slept a deep, dreamless sleep, and it felt much later than half past eight when she awoke. She had just dressed when she heard a knock at the adjoining door. She opened it to find Marielle there with a very apologetic look on her face. "I am so sorry about Friday night," she said. "I can't remember the last time I was drunk, because let's face it, I was . . . absolutely . . . gone." Sylvie would have said *bollocksed*, she thought then. "I woke up with the most awful hangover and I couldn't get rid of it and I had to go to bed early and—" Sabrina interrupted her before she beat herself to a pulp.

"Oh Marielle, please don't worry another moment about it."

"It doesn't take a lot these days to send me cuckoo. I bet I bored you to death, didn't I?" She looked mortally embarrassed.

"No, you didn't," replied Sabrina with emphasis. "You talked, and I think sometimes it's easier to talk to a stranger than a friend."

"Thank you. That's so kind of you to make me feel better," said Marielle, meaning it. "How did you get on at work yesterday?"

"Good—at least I hope I did. It's a great place, really nice atmosphere."

"I think so too."

"Coffee?"

"No, I'll let you get on. I didn't want to interrupt you. I just wanted to say I'm sorry."

"No need." Sabrina smiled.

"Don't forget we have a date for the theater tonight. We'll set off at six thirty."

"I won't forget," said Sabrina. She wasn't sure what to expect, but it couldn't do any harm and may even do some good. She needed to remember, and as hypnotherapy hadn't worked, cleaning loos, cutting up pepperoni, and visiting a psychic all had to be worth a go.

* * *

Sabrina had not long left the house for work when there was a hard knock at Marielle's door, the sort of knock a debt collector with a serious grievance might employ. She looked through the spyhole and saw the sour face of her cousin there. Well, that took longer than she thought it might. Shoresend may have been a town, but it was full of village gossipmongers.

Cilla Charlesworth marched in as if she were carrying a mace and a brass band was following behind.

"Are you stupid, Mari Bonetti?" Cilla was the only one who ever shortened her name and it had always irritated her.

"Pardon?"

"You've done it again, haven't you? You're about to make a proper fool of yourself." Cilla was walking around expending nervous energy while Marielle watched on, waiting for her clockwork to wind down.

"Cilla, what are you talking about?" said Marielle, though she knew; of course she knew.

"Letting some . . . tramp into your house to stay and rob you. Possibly even slit your throat while you're sleeping. What sort of idiot are you?"

Marielle stiffened. She might have been touched if she'd thought this was Cilla concerned for her welfare, but it wasn't; it was about seizing a chance to belittle her, something Cilla had never been able to resist.

"I have a guest staying with me, yes." Marielle forced herself to remain calm.

"Ha. That's what you call her, is it? A *guest*."

"How did you know?"

"Someone saw you buying clothes with a woman in town on Friday. So I rang Felicity to make discreet inquiries and she told me you had *a friend*, as she put it, staying with you and working at the restaurant. It wasn't hard to join up the dots."

"Why is this any of your business, Cilla?"

"Do you have to ask, Mari? I am family and as such I'm more than qualified to be worried. Can't you remember what happened last time when you let someone rob you blind? How you weren't killed in your bed is anyone's guess. Everyone was saying as much."

Well, that little speech played straight into Marielle's hands. "I'm so glad, Cilla, that you brought up how worried we should be about each other as *family*"—she overloaded the word with enough sugar to make her kidneys cry—"because this Hugo of yours is very concerning. You barely know him and there you are splashing out eight grand on a cruise with him."

Cilla's neck shot back in indignation.

"How do you know I spent that on a cruise?"

"Who doesn't know? You've told everyone. Plus a car because his Rolls-Royce is in the garage, and Lord knows what else you've forked out for."

"Not this again," said Cilla. "If you're trying to insinuate he hasn't got a Roller, then you're wrong, because I've seen photos of him in it."

"Oh Cilla," scoffed Marielle, "I bought Teddy a Ferrari experience last Christmas. We've got photos of him in it, but it doesn't mean he owns one."

"I'm not here to talk about Hugo."

"No, but while you are here, we will," Marielle threw back at her because she was cross and she wasn't going to miss this golden opportunity to drum some sense into the woman.

"You do know he went to Eton and he can absolutely prove that, not that he needs to," said Cilla.

"So did Lord Lucan."

"Oh for God's sake."

"Are you so desperate for this man to be genuine that you're swallowing any old tripe that comes out of his mouth?"

"Don't be ridiculous. I love him and he loves me—it's indisputable." Cilla was unexpectedly on the back foot now, and she didn't like it at all.

"Because he's good in bed? Yes, you've told everyone that as well. Haven't you ever seen those programs where gullible women go to foreign climes and are seduced by hot young men? Don't you think they can switch on being sexually attracted to some overripe desperado if they can squeeze the life savings out of her?"

"Overripe?" Cilla took great exception to that.

"Not you, them. They're always lonely, grateful women who think if they cough up it'll somehow make all those 'I love yous' genuine. Love brings gifts, Cilla; gifts don't bring love. That's a basic fact. *Sweetheart scamming*, that's what it's called."

Cilla had seen those programs and she always thought those women—and men sometimes—needed a good shake.

She wasn't anything like them. Hugo didn't want her for a passport, and he wasn't thirty years younger than her either. And he didn't fake anything in bed; he made sure she was very well taken care of. He was a giver, not a taker.

"You're very wrong," Cilla said. She didn't want to listen to any more in case Marielle's venom burned through her skull and put doubts in her head. A relationship was nothing without trust; Hugo had said so many times.

"Cilla, please, do me one favor . . . ," Marielle implored. Even though Cilla drove her barmy, she didn't want her to get hurt and she didn't want Flick to have to pick up the pieces. "Please don't give him any more money. If he is genuine, and I really hope he is, for your sake, then he will not press you for it. Yes, I think he's taking you for a ride, but I would be delighted if you proved me wrong." She let out a long breath by way of a full stop. Looking at Cilla's face, she realized she'd probably been too brutal, more than she ever had before, and it didn't sit well with her that she might have truly upset her cousin. "Come on, sit down for five," she said with a smile. "I'll put the kettle on."

She walked across to it, picked it up from the work surface, and went over to the tap to fill it.

Cilla stood stock-still, heart racing, furious. She hadn't come here to be taken down and then have to sit here and drink tea as if nothing had happened. How dare she? Marielle was the one being duped, not her, and she was trying to spoil things for her because she was jealous.

Except deep down, Cilla knew she wasn't, because Marielle had a much better hand than she had in life, even without a man, and the river of jealousy flowed only one way. Cilla resented the easy, loving relationship Marielle had with her son and how Flick seemed to be more fond of her than she was of her own mother. She resented that Marielle had friends who had never invited her into their inner sanctum. She resented that Marielle was respected and liked in the community for being a good nurse and a kind and generous woman. Cilla had been born with a seed of envy in her soul, and over the years it had flowered into bitterness.

While Marielle was hunting in the cupboard and twittering on about biscuits or something, Cilla noticed the handbag on the floor, between the dresser and the bookshelf, the zipper open. She saw the corner of a purse poking out of the top and she took the chance to shut up her oh-so-self-righteous cousin once and for all. While Marielle was pouring the water into the teapot, she made a quick snatch for it and shoved it in her own bag; then she stepped away from it to create distance. She wasn't anywhere near it when Marielle turned to bring the teapot over to the table.

"I came here because I am genuinely worried about you, whatever you might think," said Cilla now, her voice subdued and a sniff added for effect. "I did not come here for you to turn on me and attack me for my choice of partner. If you think about it, only one of us has a history of making the same mistakes over and over again where personal safety is concerned."

Marielle had to concede she was right. She had never told anyone that when one guest left Little Moon, she'd found a nasty-looking knife under the mattress which wouldn't have been used for taking the peel off apples.

"I'm sorry if I shouted," she said. "Please sit down. Look, I've got the best mugs out." She tried a smile, but it didn't work.

"No, I think we've both said enough, so I'm going," replied Cilla. "But please think on when you're lecturing people about being a good judge of character that you've been lied to and conned more than anyone I know. Don't say I didn't warn you."

And with that she turned to go.

LOCAL MAN ADMITS THROWING STONES AT BIRDS

The *Daily Trumpet* was in court to hear Orville Bell, 83, of no fixed abode, deny that he was throwing stones at birds on Slattercove beach. He said he was in training to enter the Commonwealth Games as a put shotter. In his defense Bell said that he loved birds and always had turkey for Christmas. Bell was bound over for six months.

Chapter 27

"Well, well, well, you're a hard man to find," said Billy the Donk as Orrible's head slammed into his desk with such force that Billy's Lotus Biscoff biscuit jumped off his saucer. Billy slid the *Daily Trumpet* toward him so the eye not currently having a close-up view of the inlaid leather could read the entry in the paper.

"I must say, Orrible, you're looking pretty good for eighty-three. I'd have put you at least ten years younger. Let him go, Square. I want to ask him what face cream he uses."

Square hoisted Orrible to a standing position where he withered, making himself look as small as possible—a primal defensive move—and reverently averted his eyes from gaining contact with Billy's. Instead they roved around his office walls, taking in the photos of his daughters, his mother, and his surgically enhanced wife with her rubber-tire lips, and all the donkeys he sponsored in a sanctuary, and then the huge oil painting of the Kray twins taking up half the wall behind him.

Billy's mother was rumored to have had an affair with Reggie, and Billy himself was the product of their many liaisons. The dates tied up and it was a story Billy chose to believe. Then again, when this information was eventually relayed to him by his mother, she'd been going a bit doolally and also told him she was Catwoman in the original Batman series with Adam West and had invented the Crispy

Pancake. Given his mother could burn water in a kettle, Billy was selective about her culinary claims, but the Kray connection suited him, and enough people believed it, which greatly enhanced his hard-man reputation. Despite moving up to Whitby many years ago, Billy's accent had never lost its East London inflection, and the tenor of his voice was soft, like theirs, but no less menacing for that.

"Now, Orrible, what part of 'keep a low profile' are you not getting, you muppet?"

"I'm sorry, Billy," said Orrible, shrinking even further. "I was only throwing stones. Not at anything, just chucking them. For a laugh. I didn't know that there was birds nesting. Ocelots or sumfink."

Behind him Square snorted and Big Charlie made the comment that David Attenborough better watch it or he'd be out of a job soon.

"Orrible," said Billy with his smile, the one that made Orrible's bowel clench, "do you know what the love of my life is? Apart from my girls? And my donkeys?"

Orrible ruminated, desperate to get the answer right. "Cigars?"

"Nope."

"Fine... Scotch? Oh no, I know... Cognac?"

"Cognac," Big Charlie said with a snort, trying to hold it together.

"I'll give you a clue: Think wings," prompted Billy.

Orrible thought about it for a long moment, then grinned in triumph. "Got it—Paul McCartney?"

"Oh for fu—. Birds, Orrible, *birds*." Billy nodded in the direction of the left wall where there was a massive framed photo of himself with a Steller's sea eagle perched on his arm, gigantic talons gripping his falconer's glove, wings extended, all two and a half meters of them.

"Oh, birds. Wow, he's a biggun, inne?" said Orrible. Luckily he stopped himself saying he bet it would feed a family of six at a Sunday lunch.

"That's Tiny," said Billy.

"He's not, Bill, he's frigging massive."

"That's his name, you moron. Dear God, where were you when

they were giving out brains? Scatterbrook Farm, having tea with Aunt bleedin' Sally? Let's start again. You might learn something even though your gray matter is about as spongelike as a slab of concrete. Tiny there has claws capable of crushing a man's skull like an egg," said Billy.

"Bit like me," said Square with a grin that would have turned milk sour.

"However, unlike you, Square, birds are among God's prettiest creatures. And to think that anyone would throw a stone at one of them breaks my heart. There they are, flying around being beautiful and majestic, minding their own business, and some lowlife with a rock decides they're target practice. Do you know how angry that makes me, Orrible?"

Orrible coughed. "Very, I would imagine. But—"

"Especially when the person chucking rocks is someone I've told to keep a low profile. Because who knows what that person might say to get out of trouble if apprehended by the law? Who knows whose name he might just drop into a policeman's awaiting ear?"

Orrible saw now where this was going. "Billy, I wouldn't—"

Billy cut him off. "I haven't finished speaking, so you stick a peg in your lips, you gimp. Now not only does this idiot get himself arrested and bound over and featured in a county-wide paper in the space of days, but Square here, yesterday, was taking a leisurely stroll along the beach with his lovely Helena, and who should he see in the distance throwing rocks up at the cliff?"

Orrible gave a nervous laugh, jiggling his shoulders up and down in a very unconvincing "no idea" gesture.

"I'd have said hello, but you ran off," said Square. "Don't even try to say it wasn't you, Orrible. I could recognize you if you stood at the Kent end of the Channel Tunnel and I stood in France."

"Now, Orrible, can you give me one good reason why I shouldn't come down on you like a ton of bricks?" asked Billy. "You're a liability. And you know I don't like liabilities. I don't *need* liabilities. Or animal abusers."

"I wasn't chucking stones at birds, honest, Billy." Orrible sniveled. Billy slammed his spade-like hands down on the desk and bellowed, "Then what were you doing, and why are you continuing to do it?"

"I was trying to get a handbag," Orrible cried. He couldn't remember what story he'd told Billy, but it didn't matter anyway; he just needed to get himself out of this present scrape—and only the truth was going to do that. "That woman whose car I nicked at the beauty spot, her handbag fell over the cliff, but it snagged on a sort of tree thing and it's too far down to reach from the top, but I thought if I threw rocks I just might be able to dislodge it." He slumped then, as if telling the whole truth and nothing but the truth had emptied him.

"Right, I see. This is the unconscious woman your uncle Benny helped get to the hospital. The woman his nephew robbed and assaulted. I'm presuming Benny doesn't know this, does he? Not sure he'd be too pleased about that for pretty much the same reasons I'm not."

Orrible grinned. "I meant to tell you, Billy, she hasn't got any memory. She wrote Uncle Benny a note and shoved it through the window of his van. She can't remember anything about how she got there or how she ended up in hospital."

"Well, aren't you a lucky boy then?" said Billy. "But memories are funny things, aren't they? They can be brought back by triggers. What if she looks in the newspaper and sees a photo of a scruffy twat who looks like he just walked out of Ten Acre Field, who's been nabbed for chucking stones at an 'ocelot's nest' and she *rec-og-niz-es* you and it all comes flooding back to her?"

"It was a really old photo, Billy. I had all my teeth then—"

"You won't be able to compete in the Commonwealth Games with broken arms, will you, Orrible? I think your chances of a *put-shotting* gold medal would be slightly scuppered. I could, however, leave your arms alone and let Charlie here loose on you. I do believe they're looking for sopranos in the Shoresend ladies' choir."

A damp patch started to appear on the front of Orrible's trousers and Billy made a face of disgust.

"Jesus, get him out of here before he stains my Wilton. I'm warning you, son, I want you as invisible as Harry Potter with his magic cloak on. Leave that handbag where it is to rot on the cliff, do you hear me?"

"Yes, Billy. I hear you loud and clear."

Outside, Orrible straightened his clothes. Every time he went in there, he thought there was a big chance he wouldn't walk out again, but he always did, and the resulting relief felt like a shot of joy administered directly into a major vein.

He sauntered off in the direction of home and Tina, but that big fat handbag hanging on the cliff would not leave his mind. He'd been obsessing about it since he'd seen it snag on the branch. He fantasized about it in bed at night, opening it, reaching inside and pulling out all the rich pickings: gold, cash, cards, diamond jewelry, the latest iPhone. There was real treasure in it, he knew, and he had to get it before someone else did, no matter what Billy said.

Chapter 28

The woman was a worker if yesterday and today were anything to go by, thought Teddy, and everyone seemed to like her. It was important to him that everyone fit in with each other in his restaurant, even though he knew it wasn't likely she'd be here long. He really couldn't get his head around it all—a so-called expert in business matters with barely any memory of her life before ending up here and being oddly reluctant to find out who she was and at the same time desperate to do so. There was something he wasn't seeing, he was sure of it, but for now he'd take it all at face value and wait for more to show itself.

"Sabrina, take a break," he called, pouring out a coffee from the jug. "You want a piece of cheesecake with this?"

"No, no thanks, I'm okay," she said, standing up from scrubbing the corners of the floor and straightening out her spine.

Teddy brought two cups over to the table, and despite her turning it down, he'd cut two pieces of cheesecake as well. His specialty, black cherry, with a thud of clotted cream on the side.

"Eat it, it's my recipe. Come on, sit. You got the job, you don't have to impress me by flogging yourself to death," he said. There were just the two of them here; he could sound her out under the guise of being benevolent.

"Thank you," Sabrina replied. She sat down at the table and picked up the fork. Black cherries—her favorite flavor. And at that moment it came to her that she also liked espresso coffee and cats and red lipstick. Why had all that just landed as one big lump in her head?

"You can use the computer in my office if you like, to try and find yourself," he said, then realized how stupid that sounded and tutted. "You know what I mean."

She smiled at that. "Thank you. Your mum lent me her iPad and I've been looking," she replied. Nothing had rung a bell, and she couldn't find her daughter on any social media either, which struck her as odd. "If I could just remember the name of the place I worked, that would help. This cheesecake is really good, by the way."

"I know it is," said Teddy. "So you're some sort of business adviser, then?"

"Yes, I help businesses that are failing and I advise new ones that want to start up, but mainly the former."

Teddy noticed her lips, full and dark pink, and thought it must be their natural color.

"Someone must be missing you," he said. "Family, work, friends, partner."

"I'm starting to wonder if I'm an alien and they'll find an abandoned spaceship in a bush somewhere."

He smiled at that, involuntarily. She had a small blob of cheesecake on the edge of her mouth, and the cynic in him wondered if she'd placed it there artfully to tempt him to lean across and wipe it away with his thumb.

"Mum tells me she's taking you to see a psychic tonight." He rolled his eyes. "Do you believe in all that nonsense?"

"It's worth a try."

"Don't expect too much. I think Mum is hoping to hear from Dad. If he comes through, trust me, he'll be singing. Dad thought Pavarotti was an amateur."

"I'll look out for that." She wiped her mouth with a serviette. He noticed how genteel her actions were, the way she ate and picked up her cup.

He took a mouthful of his cheesecake and made a mental note to put a bit more lemon in it next time. He was always refining; there was always room for even a little improvement.

"Okay, so tell me," he said then, preparing to test her, which was a bit bad of him but he couldn't resist, "what would you have me change in my restaurant?"

She knew he was testing her. How could she blame him?

"I'd have to study you in depth."

Of course you would. Nice get-out.

"But from first impressions, yes, I'd suggest some . . . tweaks."

"Really?" He hadn't expected that. "Such as?"

"Well . . . the kitchen is only half open to the public; it's neither one thing nor the other. They can see your torsos but not your heads. Why not open it up more so people can see their food being prepared? It would work well here."

"Go on, what else?"

"I don't want to say in case—"

"I give you full permission."

"Okay, I think your food is wonderful; people obviously love it." A beat. "But your décor doesn't scream at me that you are authentically Italian. Also, an intimate ambience isn't automatically made by putting tables too close together. You need to rearrange the layout. You could add in three tables and still have more free space than you have now and improve the intimate setting. Your light bulbs should be warm white, not bright white, and dimmable. Put real candles on the table. Don't tell your waiters to lower their volume; your customers seem to enjoy their theatrics. I notice table four has a wobbly leg, and that's so off-putting—"

"Whoa, whoa," said Teddy, jumping in to stem her flow.

"You did ask," said Sabrina, loading up her fork with more of her cheesecake.

Teddy looked over at the working area. He'd been thinking himself that they should either block it off completely or open it up for the reason she'd said, that it was neither one thing nor the other, but he couldn't decide which way to go.

They ate in silence for a minute or so, and then Sabrina said, "I really hope I find something out tonight. Maybe a few details will make everything else just fall into place. And trust me, if I were you, I would find it very hard to believe me too."

"I'm sorry," said Teddy. "My mother's heart is too big for her body. She's really helped some people, but not everyone has been so kind to her in return. One time she didn't realize her card had been cloned until the bank contacted her to check if she was in Spain or not. Then she let someone stay just for a night but they took the TV from the flat and ran off with it. After that last time, when her house was trashed, I told her that enough was enough."

"It's not things I'm after, Teddy; it's memories—my own," said Sabrina, hoping she sounded convincing. She did, but still, where his mother was concerned, Teddy wouldn't be letting his guard fully down yet.

* * *

"Do you think I look all right?" asked Sabrina later. She had a pair of black jeans on, her trainers, and a white T-shirt. She'd bought some cheap mascara and lipstick from a bargain store in Shoresend which made the best of her light brown eyes and full lips. She'd left her hair down for once, and it lent a softness to her face that the practical ponytail she wore for work didn't.

"You look more than all right." And she did, thought Marielle. Why wasn't someone doing everything they could to find this woman? "We'll get off in a minute, shall we?" She went over to the drawers in the dresser, opening one after the other.

"Have you lost something?" asked Sabrina.

"It'll turn up," replied Marielle, abandoning the search after noticing the time. She couldn't find her purse. It was always in her handbag. She'd had it with her on Friday to pay for the fish and chips, but when she came home, she remembered distinctly that she'd taken fifteen pounds out of it to pin on the noticeboard in readiness for the window cleaner's due visit. She hadn't been out since, so it must be in the house somewhere.

She'd have a good look round later; she was sure she'd find it, but still, it was odd that it wasn't where it always was.

* * *

Slattercove Theater was a building of faded grandeur and had kept all of its original features, though Sabrina thought that people in the last century must have had smaller bums, because the red velvet seats were snug and legroom between rows was sadly lacking. They had the two end seats in the middle section, six rows from the front, which had a good view of the stage. Psychic Pat was obviously very popular, because when people began to pour in after the three-minute warning had been given in the bar, there weren't many empty seats.

The stage was set with a leather Chesterfield chair, a small wine table at the side with a glass and a jug of water on it, and all along the back, large drop-down posters featuring pictures of a short, round woman in pink with vaguely recognizable celebrities.

The lights dimmed, and a disembodied voice broke over the speakers.

"Ladies and gentlemen, please make sure your mobile phones are switched off and in your bags as Slattercove Theater proudly welcomes the world-renowned, the one and only . . . Psychic Pat."

To tumultuous applause, a short round Weeble of a woman in a glittery pink caftan entered stage right. She was wearing a Madonna mic so she could use both hands for gesticulating. Her nails were long as eagle talons and painted in a shade of fluorescent pink that could be seen from Mars.

Pat used to work on one-to-ones, asking people to hold a crystal ball, press their essence into it so she could pick it up and work with it. She'd always been very good at reading people, telling them generalizations that were open to much interpretation, until she'd had a bang on the head in a freak accident. As if a door to real psychic abilities had been broken down in the process, she found that she really could tune into the spirit world and interact with those who no longer existed on the physical plane. Her readings shifted from the "one size fits all" to the tailored, and her popularity ballooned as a result. She no longer operated from her pink front room but in theaters all around the country where she was, more often than not, totally sold out.

"Welcome, loveys," said Pat in a voice that was pure Vera Duckworth. If she ever made it to a Vegas stage, they'd need a translator on hand. "Now the way I work is quite simple. Spirits are here, and they know you're here because they follow you around, so that's nice, isn't it? And if I come to you, they need to hear your voice so they know you're interacting. No nods, no *mmm*'s, a nice clear voice. That all right, loveys? I said, IS THAT ALL RIGHT, LOVEYS?"

The audience returned a resounding and sibilant YESSS.

"I can only tell you what they tell me, and they sometimes aren't as clear as they could be, so if something doesn't make sense, take it away with you and think about it, all right? They can be a bit cryptic, and your guess is as good as mine why that is." Now Pat went to the far right of the stage.

"You there, in that flowery top. Does the name Steve mean anything to you?"

"He's our window cleaner," came the reply, which caused a titter to ripple across the room.

"It's not him. He's closer to you than that," Pat snapped. She would not have her gift rubbished, though plenty of smart-arses had a go. "He's a man who liked a pie. A pork pie, he's saying. Lots of brown sauce and—"

A gasp. "Oh my God, it's my uncle. But we always called him Uncle Steph, because it was spelled with a *ph* and not a *v*."

"He's been in spirit a long time, hasn't he? He's sending you love and he's saying don't worry about your mum. That's his sister, isn't it. He says he's not coming for her yet." A gasp from flowery top. "Oh, and are you redecorating your front room?"

"Yes." A sniffle now.

"He said don't go for the stripy one, go for the bright colors."

"Oh my God, we couldn't decide."

"Can I leave you with that then, lovey?"

There was a ripple of applause. Pat moved her attention to the back. "Lady there, with the scarf on. Yes, you. Who's connected to class-A drugs? Does that mean anything to you?"

A hearty "Yes."

The woman next to Marielle turned to her and raised her eyebrows.

"Not sure I'd have admitted that," she said.

Pat carried on. "He's in court, isn't he? He'll be okay. His grandad will be right there with him. He's standing here now saying he has to clean up his act. He says he doesn't like the smell in the attic. *'It's my attic'*—ooh, he's cross. All those plants growing."

Marielle's neighbor said, "I hope there's no police in tonight."

"I'll come to as many people as I can," called Pat from the stage. "I obviously can't get around to everyone, but here, in this area, who's Stanley? He's got big glasses on like bottle bottoms, black frame. He's saying, 'Put me a bet on that horse.'"

A woman right at the back on the other side said, "I think that might be me dad."

"Is he in spirit, lovey?"

"Last week."

"You put a bet on a horse for him, didn't you? On the day he died."

A hiccup. "Yes. It came in at ten to one."

"He's sending love. He says you've promised not to put your mum in a home but you might have to, lovey. Don't promise what you can't do. You'll realize now he's gone how much he kept from you about your mum, and he doesn't want you to take on the burden. Think on. She'll be okay. He leaves you with love."

"What I can't understand," said Marielle's neighbor, who had obviously been chewing on it, "is why would a spirit come through and start talking about wallpaper?"

Marielle hunched up her shoulders. "Maybe to prove something personal?" was her only suggestion.

"Somewhere in the middle. You in the brown top. I'm seeing a little boy and a problem with social services."

* * *

After an hour and a half there was a break. Marielle asked Sabrina if she wanted a drink in the bar.

"Only if I can get them then, out of the money left over from buying the clothes," said Sabrina.

They went into the bar and she took a tenner out of her pocket. Marielle wondered if it had come out of her purse and then slapped the thought down.

"So what do you think?" she asked, when they'd found a seat at a table.

"It's fascinating," replied Sabrina.

"Would you like her to come to you?"

"The trouble is, if she does, will I know if she's right? What about you, Marielle?"

Marielle tilted her head from one side to the other. "The answer to that changes every thirty seconds. I'll leave it in the lap of the gods to decide for me."

They went back in after the interval and were ten minutes from the end when Pat walked from one end of the stage to the other and drew a circle in the air which encompassed them.

"Have I got a Polly here?" No response. "A Molly? A Dolly?"

"I'm a Wally," said a man farther back, which caused a wave of laughter. "Short for Walter," he added, realizing that people thought he was making fun.

"No, it's a woman here. Polly or Molly." Pat circled the area again, almost impatiently now because she was adamant she was within it. She turned to the side and appeared to be listening to someone before she spoke again.

"I've got a young lady here, and she's with a man in spirit. Big strapping fella, loud, full of love. He's saying, "I'm sorry, I'm sorry we let you down by leaving you too early." He's trying to show me that he's got her, he wishes you could see that."

To Sabrina's surprise, Marielle pulled in a sharp breath and said aloud, "I think it's me." *Molly, Mari*, she wanted it to fit.

"She's all right, you don't have to worry," Pat said, holding the flat of her hand up to Marielle as if to push away her doubts. "She's happy. And they're watching over you and keeping you safe. Aw, she's beautiful. He's telling me she's so like you."

Tears were rolling down Marielle's cheeks.

"They'll always be with you, lovey." Pat's palm patted the base of her neck as if it was trying to touch something there. "And your mum. Is your mum in spirit, lovey? Well, they're all together and sending love." Pat was still patting. "Is that all right?"

Marielle nodded, unable to speak, and Pat moved on to someone at the back with a visiting spirit called Jeff who worked in a factory in his earthly manifestation and had a penchant for Kit Kats.

Marielle fished in her handbag for a tissue. "I had a miscarriage after Teddy," she explained to Sabrina in a low voice. "They told me it was a blighted ovum, but it was always a baby to me. Sal's got her." She smiled even though her tissue was saturated. *Loud, full of love*, though she wouldn't have described him as strapping, but it had to be him; no one else in the audience had claimed him. And her mother coming through too, trying to make amends. She was beyond comforted by what Pat had told her. She only wished that someone had come through for Sabrina too.

In Saturday's *Daily Trumpet*, when reporting on the bakeoff at the country fair at Ren Dullem, the wording underneath the photo of champion "Janice Micklethwaite and Her Fat Bastards" referred to her prizewinning buns and not her husband and two sons who appeared in the picture with her. We apologize for any distress caused and are happy to report that the Micklethwaites have accepted a weekend at Center Parts by way of compensation.

Chapter 29

Teddy asked Sabrina the next morning if a ghost had appeared to his mother singing "O Sole Mio," and Sabrina had done as Marielle had told her to and denied they'd been the recipient of any of Pat's revelations. Marielle didn't want anyone to pour scorn on what she'd been told, especially her cynical son. She wanted to hold it close to her and savor it.

That night in the restaurant there was a loud man who was impossible to please. The wine was corked, he said. He sent his starter back, then his main, saying that his medium-rare fillet was too rare. He demanded another, cooked from fresh, and he sent that back too. Teddy himself took the third steak out to him. "This is medium rare," he said. "I have cooked enough medium-rare steaks in my time to know what they look like."

The man started eating. All seemed okay. The mains were finished with, desserts were served, and then there was a loud shriek from his table. The man spat into his serviette; his mouth was bleeding and he dabbed at it, wincing.

"Are you trying to kill me, you bloody idiot?" he screamed at Niccolo. "Look." He raised his hand so the whole restaurant could see the piece of broken glass he was holding. "This was in my zabaglione. If anyone else has it, I advise you to stop eating it immediately."

Two customers who were eating theirs froze. Niccolo swept them up and took them out of the way. Flick tried to smooth things over. She had no idea how this could happen, absolutely none. The piece of glass was too large to be missed when anyone was pouring the zabaglione into dishes. She told the noisy man that of course his food was on the house.

"You didn't think I was going to pay for it, did you?" he scoffed, scraping his chair back dramatically from the table. "You'll be hearing from my solicitors." The woman and the other couple he was with stood also, slowly, squeezing all the theater they could out of their leaving while the rest of the restaurant watched. On the way out, he pushed past Flick and knocked her into a table, sending the customers' drinks spilling.

Teddy flew out of the kitchen as if rocket-propelled and caught up with him at the door.

"Hey, you, you don't push my staff."

The man's face registered incredulity on an industrial scale. "You're worrying about that when I could have been seriously injured? Do you realize what would have happened if I'd swallowed that glass?"

People were listening; they couldn't help but overhear because the man had turned his volume button up to max.

"That glass was not in the zabaglione we served you."

The man let rip with a loud, dry laugh. "I beg your pardon? Do you think I brought it in with me?"

Yes, that was exactly what Teddy thought. This smacked of the dirty tricks brigade, but proving it was a different matter.

Teddy sighed resignedly.

"Please leave your name and address."

"I absolutely will not." The aggrieved customer swept out into the street with his party behind him. The diners carried on eating, but the atmosphere had changed. Only a couple lingered after coffee. They closed earlier than they had done in a long time, and when the staff sat around the table afterward eating pizza, they were all touched by the somber cloud of awfulness that had descended on the place.

"I wouldn't be surprised if that were something to do with Ciaoissimo," said Teddy, who wasn't eating anything because his appetite wasn't there. "*Ciaoissimo*—ha! It's not even a real bloody word." He sighed and shook his head. "And now I have to look forward to solicitors."

"I wouldn't bet on him instigating legal action," said Sabrina.

Teddy looked up. "What do you mean?"

"If it is something to do with sabotage, then he won't want to take it further. Did you notice how reticent he was to leave his details? What name did he book under?"

Flick got up to look at the reservations record on the reception podium.

"Jones," she said, finding it. She clicked her fingers, remembering something. "When he rang, he wouldn't leave a number; he said I wouldn't need it. So when I came off the phone, I one-four-seven-one'd and the number had been withheld."

"Interesting," said George.

"But not definitive proof, is it? I'll have to sit back and wait to see if I'm going to be sued," said Teddy, sounding glum.

"He was very loud and damaging," said Sabrina. "I think he was a plant."

It was a hunch but, she felt, an informed one. She remembered standing in front of an audience, giving a talk to a roomful of people about combating deliberate attempts to sabotage businesses, such as contamination of foods, the wrecking of professional reputations by both rival firms and individuals seeking freebies and compensation, the holding of companies for ransom.

In the car on the way home, Teddy was quiet, things obviously turning over in his mind. Sabrina presumed it was to do with the events of the evening. When he parked outside his mother's house, he said, "You don't think I should be worrying about legal action?"

"I really don't," she said.

And it was beyond odd that he believed her.

In last Monday's *Daily Trumpet*, we apologized to Ren Dullem Bake Off Champion Janice Micklethwaite and her family for the misleading wording that appeared underneath their photo. We would like to point out that the winning buns are called Fat Rascals and not Fat Bastards as stated.

Chapter 30

When, after a week, no solicitor's letter arrived and no newspaper reporter turned up on the doorstep to get the inside scoop on glass in their puddings, Teddy finally let himself believe that it wasn't going to happen. But bookings were down, and for the first time they hadn't been full on Friday and Saturday night. Teddy couldn't help feeling the negative impact of bad reviews was starting to kick in—was this the beginning of the end of everything he had worked for? And there had been a few hoax bookings too, one for a party of nine who didn't turn up. If that wasn't bad enough, that Monday morning the street was filled with builders working on the premises next door. They were parked on the double yellow lines outside, although they had council clearance for being there, and dust was blowing everywhere and coating the windows. No one would be sitting at their outside tables and having lunch today.

"I bet Ciaoissimo has got one of those hotshot business firms in to advise how to make them a massive success story," said George when they were all sitting around after their lunch customers had left: a record low of fifteen people. Sabrina really liked George; he was the quietest of the crew but had the driest wit. He became much smilier when Marielle was there, she'd noticed. He was always the one who brought her a coffee, a biscuit sharing the saucer with the cup. He more or less leaped to the machine to be the first to make it for her.

"Maybe you should get someone in as well, then," Sabrina said to Teddy.

"Have you any idea how much they cost?" he threw back.

"Yes, actually, I do."

He smiled and wondered again if she was what she said she was. The disbelieving part of him had reasoned that the few ideas she'd given him so far to improve his business could have been thought up by anyone with a modicum of common sense and a reasonable interest in interior design. But she was certainly right about "glass man" not pressing charges, and he would have, surely, if he had a genuine grievance.

Teddy wanted to believe her because he liked her; she fit into his team well. George had taken to her, and he was the most difficult to please. He'd even entertained her with some of his table magic and practical jokes one night. She'd shrieked with genuine delight when he "spilled" the cup of fake coffee over her after pretending to trip. The coffee was a lump of plastic molded to the cup, which was attached to the saucer by a chain. Teddy took George as a benchmark because he was always the last to melt. Sabrina didn't try to court anyone's approval; that was the interesting thing about her. She just got on with her duties, was last to stop for a break, and was first to start work again. Niccolo and Roberto were two daft pups who liked everyone, but Sabrina was the first one they'd tried to teach Italian to, most of it dodgy. She would think she had just learned how to say, "Where is the beach?" but really she'd be asking, "Where are the hot studs?"

Teddy knew that she knew they were taking the mick, but she played along. Flick adored her, it seemed, and that was unusual for her because she was always more comfortable with male company, apart from his mother. Cilla had done a real number on her daughter, constantly letting her down, putting her fancy men first. Flick was drawn to Sabrina's light, he could tell. And there was light in her and kindness, and he really wanted proof that it wasn't an illusion.

As for himself, his guard was up and then it went down again on a continuous loop. When it was down, though, he felt sorry for her, because she seemed like a nice person, gentle and uncomplicated, and she intrigued him, possibly because almost every other woman he'd been involved with was anything but, and he was expecting to be hit from left field with a nasty surprise.

"Okay then," said Teddy to her, unwrapping a biscuit. "You've been here long enough to study the place, so tell me what else you'd alter apart from the lighting and the table arrangement and knocking down half the kitchen wall so people can see my head."

Sabrina laughed. *She has a laugh like a tinkly bell*, he thought, and deep dimples that appeared when she smiled. And really beautiful eyes, light brown with golden flecks in them. He hadn't ever seen anyone with eyes that color before, and it added to the mystery surrounding her.

"Okay, well . . ." Sabrina tried to make it sound as if she hadn't been chalking up a mental list since she'd started here. "You're always booked up so far in advance that you miss out on customers who might just be here for the day. Why not set aside a couple of tables for walk-ups?"

"Why would I keep tables empty when I could fill them?" Teddy asked her.

"The amount of people who come in and have to be turned away? They won't be empty, trust me."

"I've had plenty of room for walk-ups this week," said Teddy with a grumble.

"Normal service has been interrupted, I know. It'll recover, but you may have to recalibrate."

Teddy tilted his head. "What do you mean?"

"If this other restaurant does open, you'll have to give your customers something they don't."

"Like?"

"Like . . . I've been thinking. Those pizzas that George makes, they're incredible."

"My darling," said George, blowing her a kiss across the table, which made her smile.

"I think people would want to see them being loaded into the pizza oven. Open up your kitchen, as I told you before. Let people watch you chatting and laughing and enjoying creating your dishes—it makes everything taste better."

She was crazy, *pazza*.

"How can it make the food taste better?" asked Teddy.

"Psychological effect. Trust me, it works. Those cupboards in the corner could be shifted next door; they're only housing pots and pans. You'd lose about a foot of worktop, but the payoff would be enormous. Move George's oven into your main kitchen. And also . . ."

Niccolo nudged Roberto and they started chuckling at Teddy's gob-smacked expression as Sabrina reeled off more of what was wrong with his restaurant.

". . . Plus I don't like that blue wall. Blue is a color that doesn't occur naturally in food, and that can put people off. I'd go for a nice earthy tone, personally."

"So you're Laurence Llewelyn-Bowen now?" Teddy was smiling lopsidedly as he said it, though.

"Not quite, but I know what tricks the mind. Weirdly, blue makes customers thirstier, so if this were primarily a bar, I'd tell you to keep it."

Teddy tossed her ideas around in his head like pizza dough; then he drained his cup, stood, and said, "I'll think about it."

* * *

Sabrina didn't go straight home after her shift. She finished at six that night, and it was still light, so she walked down to the beach. It was cool for late June and the sand was deserted, not that it ever got as full in peak season as the livelier seaside destinations such as Whitby or Scarborough or the recently rejuvenated Slattercove. Shoresend had an air of stepping back in time about it, and as such was a magnet for people who liked a more demure sort of holiday. It was a hidden gem, with its caves at one end of the shore and its suntrap beach and rock pools at the other, and Sabrina knew that whatever had made her come here had done her a big favor. She sat on the steps that led down from the promenade to the sand and let the noise of the sea fill her head, swoosh around in it. There was someone farther down with a metal detector, and she wished she could have the brain version of one of those, to find all the missing valuable pieces in there.

Bits were coming back to her, but they were too small, too banal to be worthy of mention, like the outer frame of a jigsaw, pieces of grass and sky, a seagull flying in it, but nothing that would hint at what the full picture might be. Whatever had shut her down would be the key to opening her back up again, she was sure of that. But having to leave this place would be hard. She knew she couldn't stay in Shoresend forever, but she liked the people she'd met here; she liked the simplicity of her present life. She felt privileged that the waiters teased her with their fake Italian and George tested out his magic tricks on her. She enjoyed talking to Flick, and she wondered if she and her own daughter had discussions the way they did—why couldn't she remember if they had? How could she not bring to her mind something that would be so important to her?

As for Teddy Bonetti, she really wanted to help his restaurant because it didn't deserve what it was getting. But more than that, she wanted to help *him*. She liked being near him. She liked being near him a little too much.

Chapter 31

"Do you think I'm bonkers wanting to go to uni?" Flick asked Sabrina as they were having their morning break that Thursday. "Mum thinks I am, and that a degree is going to be no use at all and is just going to saddle me with a lifetime of debt."

"Do you want to go?" Sabrina answered.

"Can't wait," said Flick. "I want to get back to studying."

"Then no, I don't think you're mad. You're bright and keen and you seem pretty sure that's what you want to do."

"Am I that bright, though?" asked Flick, scrunching up her nose. "The suggestions you made to Uncle Teddy about this place, a lot of them seem so obvious and I can't believe any of us missed them. Why didn't I see them?"

"Because I'm seeing it more objectively, maybe? And with years of experience behind me."

"I'd love to be one of those people who goes into somewhere and says, 'You need to do this and this and this,' and turn them around like a superhero just when they're on the brink of bankruptcy. You've really revved me up, Sabrina. I hadn't thought that's what I'd use my degree for, but listening to you, I'm sure that's the direction I'd like to go in. I want that intuition like you have, and I clearly haven't got it."

"Intuition isn't magic; it comes from learned experience, Flick. I couldn't have just walked into a company knowing nothing about how the business ran and started to make suggestions on my first day on the job like some sort of psychic. You have to build up your knowledge and your expertise and learn how to assess what works and what doesn't, and even then it's not quite an exact science. But the more you know, the more informed you are, the more accurate your subconscious calculations will be—in time. Be an expert in your field. The more you know, the more of a toolbox you have at your disposal to utilize."

"You sound like you had good teachers," said Flick.

"I had the best," replied Sabrina. It was out before she'd realized what she'd said. She remembered someone, an older man, a mentor. He entered her brain on a float of warmth. He'd been special to her and he was someone who was gone now, because she felt that she missed him in that way.

Teddy listened to them talking and saw how much his young cousin believed that Sabrina was exactly what she said she was on the tin. He wasn't far behind her. Why was no one on the planet looking for her? She must be a loss to someone: It was puzzling, but more than that, it was sad. Her early jokey theory that she might have fallen from outer space was becoming more of a believable possibility with every day that passed.

Now they were both talking about where the other Ciaoissimo restaurants were situated.

"Whitby. And there's also one in Scarborough," Flick was saying. Her eyes widened with an idea. She whipped her head around to Teddy.

"Why don't you and Sabrina check out one of them as mystery customers so she can go in and make an assessment."

Niccolo whistled and Roberto made a lewd but funny in-and-out gesture with his hips.

"Not on a date, you knobs," said Flick.

"That's not a bad idea at all." Teddy mulled it over. "Sabrina? You up for that?"

"Yes, I'd be happy to," she said. She felt a too-wide smile spread across her lips. A body language expert would have read a lot into that.

"Tomorrow lunch then. George and Antonio can easily cover." He felt a smile spread across his lips and keep spreading and wondered what a body expert would have read into that.

* * *

After work, when Sabrina got home, she could see the light on through the adjoining door between Little Moon and Big Moon and she knocked. She hadn't seen much of Marielle since they'd been to the psychic evening. Marielle had already said she didn't want her to feel she was a pest, invading her privacy all the time, but Sabrina missed her company. It was probably her imagination, but she was sensing something between them was ever so slightly off. She hoped she was wrong; otherwise she'd be giving Psychic Pat a run for her money.

Marielle unlocked the door.

"Hello, love. Nice to see you," she said, although she didn't move aside and invite her in.

"I'm just knocking to say hello," Sabrina replied.

Sabrina could see the flowers she'd bought for Marielle with her wage, sitting in a vase on her dining table. Marielle had refused to take any money from her, even though she had tried to push it at her, so she'd bought her a large colorful bunch of bigheaded blooms and scented freesias instead. "Marielle, I'm going to check out a Ciaoissimo with Teddy tomorrow. I'm getting up early to find something to wear. Are there any charity shops in town?"

"Yes, there are a couple in the square and one or two in the arcade."

"Great stuff," Sabrina said.

"We'll have to have lunch or dinner together again very soon," said Marielle.

"I'd like that. I don't mind doing the cooking. I'm sure I can throw something edible together," replied Sabrina. "Would you like a coffee or a tea?"

Marielle yawned. "Sorry, I'm a bit tired tonight. Another time."

"Okay then, good night," said Sabrina, and smiled, though she thought that yawn had been put on.

Marielle's suggestion they have a meal together was what Sabrina needed to hear to put her mind at rest. She was probably being daft thinking that anything had changed between them. There was no reason why it should have, and Marielle couldn't have been kinder to her. She'd even found that Marielle had left a bag of toiletries on the bed for her. But still the feeling persisted, like the faint buzz of a mosquito she could hear but couldn't see.

* * *

On the other side of the door, Marielle sighed heavily. This was awful. She liked Sabrina so much, she liked her company, and if this purse thing hadn't happened, she doubted she'd have bothered locking the door between them anymore so Sabrina could come and go as she wanted, have a bath whenever she needed instead of having to ask permission.

She didn't want to come right out and accuse her of taking her purse, but she'd looked everywhere for it—everywhere—and it was nowhere to be found. There could be no other explanation, unless she had a poltergeist, than that Sabrina had taken it. Only two people—Sabrina and Cilla—had been in her house that weekend, but Cilla couldn't have done it because she and Marielle were together the whole time they'd been in that room. She wished Sabrina would just admit she'd made a mistake: She wouldn't have made a big thing about it; the woman had been through a lot and maybe she'd done it without thinking. She'd given her ample opportunities to put it back, but it hadn't happened. Sabrina had carried on interacting with her as normal, without a hint of awkwardness, and that's what hurt, because it smacked of practiced wiliness. It was getting in the way and she couldn't bear that it was, but nor could she forget it and allow Sabrina that one, single, isolated blip.

She'd tried to bring it to a head, asked Sabrina if she'd happened to see the purse anywhere when she'd brought the flowers over. She'd said that it was an old thing with just a few pounds in it and a bank card, but Flick had bought it for her years ago, so it had sentimental value. Sabrina had merely offered to help her look for it. Was she a fool, as Cilla had accused her of being? She didn't want her friends and her son to shake their heads at her standing in the "vulnerable, gullible idiot" corner. Not again.

Marielle looked at the flowers on the table. It had been kind of Sabrina to buy them for her with her first wage from Teddy's, but they reminded her of Jody who'd lived there before, who broke into the house only hours after buying her a bunch of tulips. *"Just as a little thank-you for your kindness,"* she'd said, more or less the same words Sabrina had used, as if it were a sign. Marielle loved flowers, but these ones made her sad, however lovely the scent that drifted from them. She lifted them out of the vase and pushed them headfirst into her kitchen bin.

Chapter 32

At nine in the morning, Sabrina was up and dressed and heading for the town center square in search of a charity shop. She found the best one up the arcade—the Maud Haworth Home for Cats shop, a large double-fronted building with rails of clothes in both windows. There she found some very nice Lee jeans still with the tag on, a pair of barely worn navy suede ankle boots in her size, a blue stripy Breton top, and a longline blue linen jacket, all going for a song. It was a bit of a blue overload, but it looked smart as an ensemble and, anyway, she wasn't going on a date, only a recce mission. Marielle's car was gone by the time she got back—she was obviously out somewhere—so Sabrina couldn't ask her if she passed muster when she put on her new clothes. She applied a touch of makeup, some black eyeliner and mascara to open up her light brown eyes and some pink lipstick a smidge darker than her natural color. She left her hair down, then put on her new boots and checked herself out in the mirror.

The woman staring back at her was both familiar and a stranger, and she wished she knew her story.

At twelve exactly Teddy's car pulled up outside. She hurried down the stairs to meet him, and at first he thought it was someone else who skipped out of the flat, not her. She looked young, bright in stripes and blue instead of the customary black, her hair loose, falling past her shoulders in a rich brown sheet.

She opened the Golf's front passenger door.

"Hi," she said, climbing in. "Sorry if I look a bit like a sailor. It was all I could find."

"You look . . ."*Lovely* was the word that came first to mind, but he said "fine" instead. He caught a scent of her as she twisted round to clip in her seat belt: clean, fresh, soap. Nothing like his ex, who used to clog up his lungs with her heavy, cloying sweetshop of a perfume.

"I'm quite excited," said Sabrina as they set off.

"I'm not looking forward to giving them my money," grumbled Teddy.

"Be worth it," she said. "You can claim it back on your taxes as essential research." The journey to Scarborough took just under half an hour. They didn't talk much, but that didn't matter; the silence wasn't at all awkward. Sabrina was content to look out of the window.

They passed a sign for Robin Hood's Bay, and Teddy asked her if she'd ever been.

"No idea," she said with a strained laugh. "It doesn't ring any bells. I think I would know, like I knew that I'd been to Shoresend when I was little. I remember my dad whirling me around his head while I pretended to be a seagull." She laughed and he thought again what a lovely sound it was. Natural and clear.

"Robin Hood's Bay is lovely," said Teddy. "All steep streets." He'd taken his ex-fiancée Matilda there to show it off to her, but she wasn't that impressed. She hadn't seen the winding narrow streets and the tiny cottages, the cliffs, the rock pools, and the rolling sea through the same eyes as he had. Plus she'd stupidly worn high-heeled shoes and had almost broken her neck on the cobbles.

They parked up in a multistory car park and walked down into the busy town center. The air was a cocktail of salty sea, fried doughnuts, hot dog onions, and sugary candy floss. There was an energy to the place, a buzz and vibrancy that she liked, but she much preferred the volume-down, less commercialized Shoresend. They passed a crammed fish-and-chip restaurant with a queue waiting outside, then rounded the corner and carried on up a long road, right out of the main part of town, to where Ciaoissimo was situated. It looked massive from the outside, plenty of room for all the holidaymakers who didn't want to queue anywhere, but when they walked in, they found fewer than half the tables occupied.

"First impressions?" asked Teddy.

"Looks more like a transport café than an Italian restaurant," Sabrina answered. "Cheap tables and chairs and too many of them, no space between; terrible layout, designed to cram in as many diners as possible without giving a toss about their comfort. Every surface is hard: the walls, the furniture, the floor, so any sound is going to amplify, nothing to soften it."

Teddy stopped the "Wow" coming out of his mouth because it would have sounded puerile, but she seemed to know her stuff. The general hubbub was indeed harsh on his eardrums.

They were waiting a considerable time before anyone turned up to attend to them.

"I'd sack Flick if she took this long," Teddy whispered, bending to say it into her ear. There were only two waitresses on the floor zipping around; the place was clearly understaffed.

Eventually they were shown to a table and given oversized laminated menus. When Teddy attempted to open his up, he had to peel one page from the other because it was sticky. He and Sabrina both pulled "yuk" faces.

The choice of dishes was extensive, though. There was everything you could hope for on it. Teddy whistled; Sabrina wasn't as impressed.

"Too many choices," she said immediately. "Too many words, each dish with its description. It's over the top; it's actually off-putting."

"Surely it appeals to a broader base? I always feel we don't have enough on our menu."

"You've got it right, whether you meant to or not. A good standard menu with wide appeal and enough specials for variety. If you put too many dishes on a menu, people start to wonder if they should have picked this or that; it unsettles them. They'd rather have three, four, five dishes they like and have to pick between them, not forty. It will take people an age to decide what they want otherwise."

"Well, that's made me feel better," said Teddy.

"Their spoilage costs must be eye-watering," said Sabrina, shaking her head. "The chefs I bet are tearing their hair out. They can't pour love into every one of these meals."

"Love is poured into every one of mine," said Teddy. "I wouldn't send anything out that I wouldn't eat myself."

"Precisely. And imagine Niccolo and Roberto having to learn about all of them in order to answer any questions."

Teddy cast his eyes over the menu again, calculating how many ingredients there must be. "They couldn't supply all this fresh on order, could they?"

"No, so imagine how much is frozen, tinned, shipped in from outside. They cannot possibly make this the same way you make yours."

Eventually a waitress turned up at their side.

"Sorry," she said, pushing her hair out of her eyes. "We're so busy. Now can I get you some drinks?"

"Excuse me," a woman shouted across from another table. "How much longer is his main going to be? I've nearly finished mine."

The poor waitress didn't know who to sort out first. Teddy made it easy for her and told her they'd wait.

When she darted off to the kitchen, Teddy grinned. "I'm liking this. It's terrible."

"I think I'll have the Bolognese for main," said Sabrina. It was a popular staple and she wanted to know what Ciaoissimo did with it.

"Have whatever you like; you don't have to pay today," said Teddy. "I'll deduct it from your next week's wage."

Her eyes flicked up from the menu, believing him for a second, and he laughed. And she thought what a lovely laugh he had; a *generous boom*, she decided.

"Sorry, I am joking," he said then. She smiled and he thought what a beautiful mouth she had. He wondered what her lips would taste of, and that rogue thought shocked him because he didn't think of her in that way, and he didn't want to start either. He plunged his attention back to the menu and decided on a pizza.

"Have you noticed how many people have a one-course pasta main at lunchtime in your restaurant?" Sabrina asked him.

"There's a big business park five minutes away. A lot come in to grab a quick bite."

"Then you should have a takeaway service, something like 'Fasta Pasta.' Something they can whiz in for, pick up, and go back to the office with. Maybe they'd send a runner to collect a bulk order. Or 'Piece-a-Pizza.' You do takeaway pizzas, I presume?"

"No, we don't," said Teddy.

"You should think about it. You're shut on Sundays, but not everyone wants a roast dinner. You should shut on Mondays instead."

Teddy looked at her across the table in something resembling awe. This woman wasn't a bluffer or a phony; he'd bet his week's takings on it. "You really do know what you're talking about, don't you?"

"Yes, I do," she replied.

* * *

In Diana's beautiful lounge, the Mad Cows were salivating over her clotted cream scones. When it was her turn to host, in came her mother's recipe and out went any diets.

"I can't stand going out for an afternoon tea when they don't give you butter," said Jackie, spreading one of her scone halves with a curl of Lurpak before loading it with jam and clotted cream. She made a noise of delight when she bit into it.

"Ey up, Jackie, you nearly had to unhinge your jaw then to get it into your mouth. You looked like a snake about to devour an antelope." Bev laughed. "Ooh, and talking of snakes, I saw Cilla and Internet Hugo in Wellem on Monday."

"Did you stop and chat?" asked Diana.

"Well, it wasn't exactly a chat. She said, 'Bev, I didn't recognize you. You've put a bit of weight on since the last time I saw you, haven't you, but I have to say it suits you.' I mean, who says that?"

There was a collective gasp and a mass "She didn't!"

"She bloody did. I thought of a million comebacks in the car on the way home, but all I could say at the time was, 'You're looking well, though. That cruise air must have done you good.' I've done nothing but gnaw on it ever since. Like a dog with a bone."

"She's not exactly Twiggy herself," said Jackie. "She's got one of those arses that would wipe out her own footprints in the snow. You should have told her that."

That made them all laugh, except for Marielle, who was in a world of her own today. Jackie gave her a nudge.

"Earth to Marielle. You okay?"

"Sorry," replied Marielle, "I was away with the fairies then." She picked up her scone. This interruption of her relationship with Sabrina was taking her over. She'd have to sort it one way or another.

As if Bev could see into her head, she said then, "How's your lodger? Sylvie said she seemed very nice."

"She is," said Marielle cautiously.

"I must admit I was quite surprised," said Sylvie. "I actually felt quite assured having met her."

"She's working in Teddy's restaurant, isn't she?" said Jackie, loading up the second half of her scone. "How's that going?"

"Good. Teddy says she's a hard worker."

"If I'd had a son, I'd have wanted one just like your Teddy," said Diana, who hadn't been able to conceive and it had caused her a lot of heartache over the years. "I can't understand why he's still single."

"Me neither." Sylvie nodded. "He needs to get a move on and give his *mamma* some grandchildren. I do hope Waltzing Matilda didn't put him off."

"I hope so too, but I try not to quiz him," said Marielle. "If he wanted to tell me about his love life, he would."

"Deep as a flipping well, aren't they, blokes?" said Bev. "You can't tell from their faces what's going on behind them."

Some women were just like that as well, thought Marielle, trying not to let her sadness show.

* * *

The Ciaoissimo starters weren't great. Some of the prawns in Sabrina's cocktail were still frozen, and she'd sent them back and had creamed mushrooms instead, which were okay, though she'd had to wait a couple of minutes for them to cool down because they'd been over-nuked in a microwave. They were molten; she could have cauterized wounds with them. Teddy's bruschetta was beyond bland, more or less tomatoes on toast without any effort to sex it up.

The mains were mediocre too. The crust on his pizza could break teeth and he found the ham slimy. George certainly had nothing to worry about. No one offered Sabrina a hearty grind of black pepper or a snowfall of freshly grated Parmesan for her spag bol. She abandoned it halfway through after finding the second bit of gristle in the meat. Cheap mince, clearly. When she picked up the salt pot, she found it coated in dried sauce.

"I'd love to see their kitchen," said Teddy. "I'm sure it passes muster, but it won't be to the standard of my restaurant. I've always had top hygiene ratings. But I have to say, you've brought an extra shine to everything, Sabrina."

He meant it literally, but it sounded flirty. He needn't have worried because she didn't notice. "There's something really satisfying about scrubbing at things and getting them clean," she replied.

"Maybe you're . . . subconsciously trying to scrub at your life to find out what's hidden?" Teddy suggested.

"Or maybe I just like cleaning, who knows?" She smiled, but she did think that she must have liked it in her other existence too.

Eventually, after a very long wait, the desserts arrived: tiramisu for Sabrina and a cheesecake for Teddy—brought in, he could tell.

"I bet you'll be lost without Flick when she's gone to uni."

"I will. She's very keen to go. I think you've given her ideas. How's your tiramisu?"

"Horrendously sweet. And flavored with a nasty rum essence."

"Can I try?" asked Teddy.

Sabrina pushed the dish over so he could stick his spoon into it.

"Everything tastes cheap, doesn't it?" was his judgment.

"Because it is cheap. They aren't focusing on quality. Cheap and cheerful, except they need to seriously work on the cheerful part. I wonder if they have a mission statement. Do you, Teddy?"

"Yes, to get through every shift without killing someone," he replied, grimacing at the first mouthful of his cheesecake.

"You don't mean that."

"You're right, I don't." Teddy put his spoon down. "I can't eat any more of this *merda*."

"You're very passionate," she said, adding quickly for clarity, "about your food."

"I'm passionate for the things I care about, Sabrina," he said with feeling. "My work, my people."

She had a sudden flash thought of what he might be like in bed and shooed it off before it brought a blush to her cheeks. She imagined he would be a lot more satisfying than her tiramisu. Teddy paid the bill with his card but handed over a generous cash tip and told their waitress that it was just for her. Sabrina liked that he did that.

"Ooh, cheers," said the waitress. "We aren't supposed to keep tips, though. We have to shove them in a jar and they go toward a Christmas night out." She pulled a face. "I'll not even be here then."

"Are you leaving?" asked Sabrina, seeing a good opportunity for some info.

"I've got another job." The waitress looked at her watch and made a quick calculation. "In twenty-nine hours exactly, I'll be walking out of that door and never coming back." Her tone suggested she was really happy about it too.

"You looked rushed," Sabrina said, in her best sympathetic voice.

"No staff. They can't keep them. It's shit here. Shit food, shit hours, shit conditions, shit pay, shit bosses . . ." She gasped then. "Oh God, you aren't mystery diners, are you?"

"No," said Teddy, smiling at her. "Don't worry."

"Shame really. I wouldn't mind being sacked on the spot."

"Good luck," said Teddy. "And do keep the tip for yourself."

"Interesting," said Sabrina as they walked out. "High staff turnover rates are very telling and don't add anything to stability." Then she noticed something she hadn't seen on the way there. Across the road was a vacant building with signage indicating it was a commercial property available to rent. In faded lettering above the door was the name "Luigi's."

A little restaurant bullied out of business by the big boy across the street? It looked very much like that.

The *Daily Trumpet* would like to apologize to Mrs. Brenda Buttershaw for an unfortunate error that appeared in the "Focus on Nurses" on Thursday 15 June in which she was described as a "geriatric nit nurse" and not a "geriatric unit nurse." We apologize for any unintended insult and hope the bouquet from Keighley florist Floral Sex is due compensation.

Chapter 33

When Northern Eagles had been bought out by Charles Butler two years ago, everyone thought that Marjorie Wright was pushed from the directorate over to HR, a lesser position, because she was a woman. In fact, she had chosen to head it up. And she got what she asked for because she knew where many bodies were buried. Also she was having a reckless but very useful affair with Charles Butler at the time. She couldn't save the people who were blown away by the winds of change, but she could at least make sure they got the best of references and overgenerous severance payoffs in her new capacity. She was on a very good number, but she'd had enough. She had a big nest egg stored away, no mortgage, and was just putting together an early retirement package for herself, which Charles would agree to of course.

Working for Alan Eagleton had been a privilege, but the new regime were a bunch of useless wankers headed up by Emperor Wanker himself, Jeremy Watson. It had been his brainchild to rename them "Business Strength" with its new BS logo and the head of a bull. Good grief, had no one realized how that came across?

There was a knock on the door. Oh my God, she was going to enjoy this. She counted five long seconds before saying, "Come in." Psychological tactic to make him think he wasn't more important than the task she was engaged with.

"Ah, Jeremy, do sit down."

Her office was bigger than Jeremy's, which rankled because Charles told her Jeremy had said so. He'd still jump back into her bed if she let him, but she wouldn't. Occasionally she hinted that she might, though. Dear God, she could be a player.

"Something wrong, Marjorie?" Jeremy asked with a twisted smile of puzzlement as he took the chair at the other side of her desk, crossing his long legs and ostentatiously sticking out his shiny shoe. He wasn't happy at being summoned to her office like a naughty child to the headmistress.

"You could say that. I've had a complaint," said Marjorie, trying to pace her glee. "About you."

"Me?" Jeremy's face registered shock.

"Yes, you, Jeremy. In-ap-pro-pri-ate conduct." She gave each syllable a weight of its own.

He waggled his head in bafflement, so she enlightened him. "Where to start? Bullying, belittling, sexual language . . ."

"What?"

"Systemic prejudices can and will be winkled out in Northern Eagles, Jeremy. Sorry, Business Strength now. Big mistake in my opinion, ditching a name that is synonymous with stellar service and replacing it with a very anodyne one." Her tone smacked of a contempt that made him bristle with annoyance.

"Charles likes it very much," said Jeremy, his mouth a tightly gathered moue of indignation.

Charles also put a prick like you in charge of the company, so he's hardly infallible, she thought but kept to herself.

She leaned back and tapped her fingers together. "What happened to Polly Potter, Jeremy?"

He huffed impatiently. "I sent you an email. She had a meltdown last month, threw a cup of coffee over me, and stormed out of the building, never to return."

"And what triggered this supposed meltdown?"

"I think it was Alan's portrait being taken down, if you must know. Got very emotional. Wonder why?" He smirked.

"You accused her of having an affair with him, didn't you?"

"Oh, she's put in a complaint, has she?" He laughed at how ludicrous that was. "And no, I didn't accuse her; she's obviously misinterpreted my words."

"It wasn't Polly who put in the complaint."

"Well, it couldn't have been anyone else seeing, as there was only her and me in the room when I said it." He realized his mistake and went for damage limitation: "That thing she thought she'd heard."

"Maybe you just have one of those voices that carries." Once one disgruntled person in the department had come to see Marjorie, it had set the rest off singing like a choir of canaries.

"Also, Jeremy, maybe something to bear in mind for the future, that people in glass houses really shouldn't throw stones. Or should I say . . . *rocks*."

There was something knowing about the way she said the word that unsettled him. She couldn't have known about his fumbles with the temp Roxanne "Rox" Smith, whose knockers arrived in the office three minutes before the rest of her did, could she? Shame how her contract had ended when she started to get a bit clingy. He could feel his cheeks beginning to heat. This was excruciating. Marjorie fucking Wright was loving every second of this takedown, he could tell.

"Anyway, I can't have been the only one that thought it about her and Alan," Jeremy said. "Why else would he have her by his side all the time?"

"Maybe because she was very good at her job and he recognized that. She's had a lot of success stories attributed to her over the years, but funnily enough hardly anything since you became managing director. Amazing what you unearth, though, when you do some deep digging."

Jeremy uncrossed and recrossed his legs.

"She had a few good ideas that were implemented, but she was hardly the company cornerstone," he snapped.

"Nutbush, Fish Fillies, the Gin Lot. They've got her stamp all over them. There's a detailed paper trail of her research and suggestions—I've read the files. I've seen everything. Let's take 'Nutbush. No Limits,' for instance. Why did Timon Cavendish take the credit for that tagline?"

"Well . . . because . . ."

"Be quiet, Jeremy, it was a rhetorical question. I already know the answer. Because Polly was discriminated against. And why was she discriminated against . . . ? Because she is a *woman*."

"Absolutely not," Jeremy rebutted. "Is that what she's said?"

"No, she hasn't. I haven't spoken to Polly. Yet. But I have spoken to a lot of other people. Little people, you'd probably call them, the ones you breeze past every morning because they're too insignificant to acknowledge, the people far below you who, amazingly, have eyes and ears. And I've also spoken to a few psychopaths," Marjorie then added with her tongue firmly jammed in her cheek. "You have no idea how many of them we employ in this company."

That stupid test. Marjorie hadn't interfered with that because she wanted to see what he'd do with the data collected. She hadn't imagined the mess she'd have to sort out when she was tasked with updating people's records with "proven" psychopathic diagnoses, other personality disorders also available. It wasn't going to happen on her watch. Polly Potter was about as psychopathic as Basil Brush. She'd had to talk Len Champion from maintenance out of forming a picket line.

She hadn't wanted to interrupt Sheridan Savalas's maternity leave, but she'd rung her hoping to fill in some missing gaps in her findings. Sheridan had been only too delighted to share some of Jeremy's overloud and public comments, including how he wished the company wouldn't keep employing temps who were fat and forty, and how she'd overheard him and Timon Cavendish laughing about her "very small tits being a decent size now she was up the duff." And how Jeremy was renowned for talking to women's breasts, how he denigrated Polly Potter, calling her Polly Kettle in front of others to embarrass her, while taking every credit for her triumphs . . . and more, much more, spilling her guts as if she'd been waiting a long time for such an opportunity. And Sheridan had let it drop that in a brainstorming session for Zingo lemonade, in which she was taking notes, Jeremy had suggested the tagline: "As bitter as Marjorie Wright's minge."

Polly had clearly been pushed to her limits. Sheridan said that she couldn't get hold of her; neither could Marjorie, and she just hoped Polly hadn't had a full-on nervous breakdown.

"So here's where we're at, Jeremy," said Marjorie, smiling like a hungry hyena at him. "I'm going to send you on a workplace discrimination and equality course where you will be educated on conduct befitting the mission statement of Northern Eagles, which has been adopted, as you know, by"—she couldn't help but roll her eyes—"BS."

"I'm the bloody managing director," said Jeremy, no longer trying to keep a lid on his chagrin. In fact, he'd ripped off that lid and hurled it across the room like Captain America's shield.

"Precisely. And unless you want to be a managing director without a job, you'll go on the course. Charles insists. Can't really have its MD going against everything the company stands for, can we?" She'd made it very clear to Charles that this needed to happen or they'd have some very unwelcome press, so he had to back her up. She'd had him by the balls for three years, and she wasn't ready to loosen her grip yet.

"Is that all?" asked Jeremy, standing up.

"No, it isn't. You'll personally write a letter to Polly Potter offering to reinstate her with no penalty nor break in her salary if she hasn't already consulted a solicitor to pursue a claim of constructive dismissal."

Jeremy was incandescent. "You're bloody HR, you write it," he said.

Marjorie didn't miss a beat. "Write the letter, Jeremy. It's not a request. Oh, and one more thing: Don't ever malign the character of Alan Eagleton again. He was a professional; he didn't cross boundaries. He was a man of principle and a gentleman and he didn't talk to women's breasts or liken their minges to bitter lemonade. And if he were here now, he would have kicked you out of this building with his own right foot up your arse and I'd have polished the shit off his shoe for him once he'd done it. Do close the door when you leave."

Chapter 34

"You okay, my lovely?" asked Sylvie, giving Marielle an affectionate nudge. "You're quiet." Marielle cursed herself for being so transparent. Every time she'd met with her friends recently, she'd been like a joy killer. But she couldn't tell them what was really troubling her this time because she'd get a proper earful of "I told you so's" and she couldn't bear that. She'd learned the lesson now, and when Sabrina finally left, she would be letting no one stay in Little Moon unless they were people she knew inside out. She gave Sylvie an alternative believable reason why she wasn't the life and soul of them today.

"I had a bit of a . . . *setto* with Cilla last week. The day we went to see Psychic Pat." Everyone seemed to lean forward then, as one, to hear more.

"She stormed round to tell me that I was an idiot and the worst judge of character on the planet, more or less," said Marielle with a tired huff.

"You aren't at all," Bev said to that. "Look at who your best mates are."

"She meant those I've let stay in the flat."

"Well, we can all make mistakes," said Diana kindly.

"I'm still married to mine," said Bev. "I don't know why I've stayed with him. I don't even like him. Do you know, we haven't had it off for seven years."

"I haven't had it off for over seventeen years," said Marielle. "At least Cilla's getting some good sex while she's being duped."

"Oh Marielle, we need to find you someone nice. That's too long to be sat on the shelf gathering dust. You're still a young woman," said Jackie.

"You can have Harry if you like," said Bev, "although don't expect any foreplay. He will give you a run for your money at *Tipping Point*, though."

Everyone laughed at that.

"How was the psychic?" asked Diana.

"Interesting. I think Sal came through for me. She said he was watching over me." Everyone nodded and smiled, but only Bev believed in that sort of thing.

"Well, Sal isn't here anymore and you need a good man's company," said Sylvie. "Maybe he'll send you someone if he's watching over you."

"Isn't there anyone you've got your eye on, darling?" Diana inquired.

"No," said Marielle, though it wasn't strictly true, but she'd keep that to herself too.

* * *

"Are you in a rush to get back?" asked Teddy when they reached the car. He found he didn't want the day to end yet. He'd enjoyed Sabrina's company; it had been a long time since he'd gone out for a meal with a woman who wasn't his mother, and even though this was never meant to be a "date" date, it felt as if it could have been. It was nice to sit across the table from a woman and eat—even substandard Ciaoissimo food—and talk and laugh and feel that she enjoyed his company too. He worked stupidly hard, but when he stopped, like today, he realized that he missed having someone special to care about.

"No, not at all," said Sabrina. She was glad he asked because she hadn't had enough of today yet. She'd liked spending time with him, just the two of them, and when she talked she noticed how intently he listened to her. It felt like a novelty, as if whoever she had left behind hadn't valued her enough.

"It's a lovely day—we could have a stroll on the beach. There's plenty to choose from."

"Sounds great," she said.

"I'll even throw in an ice cream."

"Ooh. Extra great." She grinned with an almost childlike delight that made him grin too, and he felt something inside him, like a frisson of warmth against sensitive nerve endings. It was unexpected but no less pleasant for that.

Teddy set off, heading out of Scarborough on the north road. He knew which beach he'd take her to: Briswith, with all its pretty fishermen's cottages painted in different colors and higgledy-piggledy streets, but without any steep hills, unlike Robin Hood's Bay.

"Loads of mermaid tales—excuse the pun—around here, you know," Teddy enlightened her. "Did you know they sank lots of Spanish ships that sailed here in the Armada?"

"I think I remember doing the Armada at school," said Sabrina, "though I can't recall them ever giving any mermaids credit for the scuppered ships."

"They obviously didn't fit the narrative."

Sabrina took in a sharp breath, and the noise made Teddy's head spin round to her. "You okay?"

"I just . . . just remembered sitting on a sofa with a big ginger cat on my lap." She had no idea why her mind had leaped from Spanish-hating mermaids to that image.

"Maybe you were reading a book about mermaids when he was with you?" suggested Teddy.

"Maybe," she answered, but she didn't think it was that. Maybe it was the same sort of comfort she got from him as she was getting here, in this kind Italian man's company, but she couldn't exactly say that without sounding flirty.

They were shortly in Briswith; Teddy parked up on a street and they got out, walked down a small incline, and they were there on the beach.

"Hang on," said Sabrina, perching on the arm of a bench while she stripped off her boots and socks. "Ah, that's better," she said, putting them in her shoulder bag. "I only bought the boots this morning and I think I might know why someone donated them to a charity shop. They're agony."

So she'd been shopping to dress up for today. Probably blown her wages on clothes. That made Teddy feel a stab of guilt because he was only giving her a minimum wage.

"Don't worry, they were cheap," she said, as if hearing his thoughts. "I got the whole outfit for thirty quid."

She made her ensemble look more expensive than that. She exuded quiet class and Teddy wondered if, in her other life, she was the sort of person who spent all her money on expensive clothes or was happiest in jeans. She looked *really* good in them, he had to say. Anyway, he didn't want her to be out of pocket, so he'd put an extra thirty quid in her next wage packet and lie that it was tip money.

"What's good for the goose," he said and kicked off his trainers and ripped off his socks too. The sand felt good underneath his feet. The beach was on his doorstep and he never went.

They strolled along and he wondered if people they passed thought they were a couple, if they gave off that vibe, or else friends or siblings. He liked her being at his side. He wouldn't have minded if people bracketed them together. He imagined what it would be like if they were. He missed being a "two." He missed sex, missed the intimacy of sharing his bed with a woman. Sharing anything with a woman actually: a meal, talking at breakfast across the kitchen table, watching a box set, the excited packing for a holiday. He missed that giddy expectation of first going out with someone, of wanting to get to know her, of wishing the date would never end and stringing it out for as long as possible.

Sabrina edged toward the sea and squealed as the cold water hit her skin. Teddy thought that it was like being with someone who had never been up close and personal with the sea before and was experiencing it for the first time. He thought it was sweet, especially as she went back for more and squealed again.

"Come on," he said, taking her hand without even thinking about it and pulling her up the beach. "Ice cream time." He held it for not more than ten strides before letting go, hoping he hadn't overstepped a mark, pretending it wasn't a big deal. It wasn't a big deal, so why did he like the feel of her hand inside his so much?

He bought her a cornet with a flake and strawberry sauce; he plumped for chocolate, and they sat on a bench looking out to a sun-sprinkled seascape in a companionable silence while they ate.

"Sabrina," Teddy asked eventually, breaking into her reverie, "do you really think a lunchtime 'Fasta Pasta' initiative might work?"

"I don't see why not," she said. "People eat on the go these days, have lunch at their desks. There's often someone in an office who is sent out to collect breakfast or sandwich orders, so I can easily imagine one of the big firms nearby ordering pasta pots from you and getting a runner to pick them up. And if they're not quite hot enough when they arrive, the container would be easily microwavable, one quick minute blast and Bob's your uncle. You wouldn't need a massive takeaway menu: a few standards, a vegan option, and a changing special. Same with pizza slices. A single giant triangle. I even thought about pizzas in the restaurant shaped like an initial for special occasions."

"Now that idea I like," said Teddy.

"You'd have to use the same amount of dough for an M as an I, of course, to avoid any complaining. Just brainstorming; I expect some of my ideas to fall on stony ground, but not many."

Teddy smiled at her, a lopsided smile that set off a small, warm incendiary bomb inside her that she wasn't expecting. She wasn't being bigheaded, he knew. She was more confident in her work than she was in herself, that was clear.

"You really are an enigma," he said.

"Tell me about it," she replied.

"Okay, playing devil's advocate, what would you do with Ciaoissimo if they ever came to you and told you they wanted to take over the world?"

"I wouldn't work with them," answered Sabrina. "Knowing what I know."

"No, really, humor me."

"Okay," she began slowly. "I'd go back to basics with them. I'd make sure I had a mission statement which was at the heart of my business. What do I want to do? I want to bring Italy to Yorkshire, give my customers an unforgettable dining experience—"

"It certainly does that," said Teddy with a sneer.

"It hasn't got its fundamentals right, but it's forged ahead nevertheless. So there's a Ciaoissimo in Whitby and one in Scarborough, yes?" Sabrina asked him.

"That's right. The one in Shoresend will be the third."

"They're spending their money on all the wrong things. Who owns it?"

"A group, that's as much as I know."

"If they're a limited company, you can access their records."

"I did; none of the names mean anything to me," said Teddy. "What do I do?" he went on. "Sell up and move? I don't want to. Why the dirty tricks? Why do they feel the need to drive me out to set up themselves?"

"Because it's run by people who aren't as business savvy as they think they are and they see you as competition that has to be eliminated when really you could, at a push, coexist because your clientele base, with some crossover, of course, is quite different. I was thinking you could ask your customers when they leave to give you a positive review online and if they do, they can have a free dessert or coffee the next time they come for a meal."

"Is that ethical?" asked Teddy.

"Well, it's a sort of bribery, yes, but you do need more good reviews. It's a negative age and people are more likely to publicly complain than praise. You'd just be asking politely if they'd take the time to do that for you if they've had a nice meal. Most people won't have thought about doing it and they'll make the effort once you tell them it would help your business. You're not exactly forcing anyone, just rewarding some kindness."

"Yes, that's a good idea."

"Ciaoissimo as a company is obviously not community-minded, which will do them harm with locals but not so much with holidaymakers. They seem to be throwing investment at it at the moment, like a hobby . . . a racehorse venture, but if it doesn't start earning its money back soon, either it'll fold or they'll get someone in to turn it around. That's when they might up their game and become your real direct competition."

"And then it's goodbye, Teddy."

"You never say never; there's always hope." Sabrina remembered someone very special telling her so at times when she'd doubted they'd ever be able to rescue a failing business.

They sat on the bench long past the point when they'd eaten the last of their cones, just enjoying the sunshine and people watching. A little girl in a frilly swimming costume and a pink hat was attempting to make a sandcastle but spilled every shovel of sand before it reached her bucket. Sabrina wondered if she'd ever taken Linnet to the beach, and she tried to force her brain to bring just one memory of that forward, but there was nothing. Sometimes walking round and round in her head got tiring. She could have closed her eyes and gone to sleep in the sun and hoped that the seagulls that featured in her memories and her dreams would take pity on her and bring her some clues about her other life on their wings.

She felt at peace here, soaking up the warmth and the seaside sounds and the easy company of this man at her side. She hoped the day would kick against the clock, force its hands to brake so she could rest longer in this lovely solid oasis where everything felt certain and uncomplicated.

But time had rules to abide by, the sun began to drop, and Teddy fetched two coffees from the kiosk where he'd bought the ice creams.

"I think George has a thing for your mum," said Sabrina. "Did you know?"

"Everyone knows but my mother," replied Teddy.

"You should tell her."

"And have George lording it over me as my stepdad?" Teddy gave her a look of horror, but she knew he was only pretending.

"She's been without your dad a lot of years, and she's still a young woman."

Teddy hadn't thought about his mum being lonely. She had her friends and her volunteering up at the hospital, and she was always busy. But then, he was always busy, and that disguised his own loneliness. He felt slightly ashamed that he hadn't thought of that parallel before and recognized the similar void in his mother's life.

"His jokes are great. Kids would love them. You should let him out of the back to do his table magic occasionally. You won't get that at Ciaoissimo."

"He won't have time; he'll be too busy doing takeaway pizzas." Teddy smiled again and realized he'd smiled so much today that his face had begun to ache. Muscles he hadn't overused for a long time.

"George lost his wife when he was just a young man; no children," Teddy told her. "He likes to garden when he's not working. We get all our herbs from him and a lot of vegetables. Mum likes to garden too." Now that he was thinking about it, he realized that Marielle and George had quite a few things in common. They both liked the theater, the cinema, sunny holidays, days away, museums, eating out. He'd always thought it was funny how George behaved around his mum; he hadn't really considered that real, serious feelings might be involved. Maybe he needed to look outside his restaurant occasionally. It was his everything and if he lost it, he'd have nothing.

Sabrina polished off her coffee then put her socks and boots on. They'd end up back in the charity shop, for sure. She was reluctant to stand up in them, expecting the discomfort to kick in straightaway.

"Here, take my arm," Teddy said, crooking it for her. It felt sure and strong under her hand. She was almost glad her boots were uncomfortable enough to force her pace to be slow as they walked back to the car so she could squeeze some extra time with him out of the day.

"Are you okay?" Teddy asked her.

"I'm so sorry about this," she replied.

"I could give you a piggyback."

"I'd break your spine." She chuckled.

He didn't mind that they were taking an age to get to the car. He couldn't recall the last time before today that he hadn't rushed or darted or strode anywhere. It was nice to stroll with someone on his arm, someone at his side.

They drove home the longer, scenic way. Teddy tried to convince himself he'd chosen the route because it would be quieter, but it wasn't that at all. He was a teenage boy again, stringing out an enjoyable time for as long as he could. The day had not turned out as he'd expected it to; it had been much better, and he had learned more about himself than he had a rival restaurant. He felt a downturn in his spirits on seeing the "Welcome to Shoresend" sign.

He braked outside the door to Little Moon.

"Sabrina, thank you for today," he said.

"It's a pleasure." She turned to him, smiling again, and he knew she felt it too, that the air in the car felt suddenly as thick as honey. Something had grown between them today, like a small shoot poking out of its seed but then wondering where to go next. He felt his blood gain pace inside him.

Sabrina's hand crept slowly to the door handle, giving him the opportunity to say more before she got out. Then he opened his mouth and did say more.

"Obviously I'll pay you for today. You were working after all; I do recognize that." If he'd wanted to kill whatever was warming the air between them, he'd just done it. Stone dead.

"Oh, thank you, that's . . . great then." She opened the door. "I'll see you tomorrow. Bye." She hopped out too quickly for him to say that he'd had a really lovely time with her, lean across and kiss her cheek, because he had wanted to do that, to let his lips have contact with her.

She was aware that he was watching her until she was safely inside, and she tried not to walk as if her boots had a vendetta against her feet. She unlocked the door, went quickly in, and heard him drive off, and she was glad that he had.

Oh God, she was lucky she hadn't made a fool of herself, read too much into the ease they'd shared. She'd picked up on something that wasn't there, her intuition evidently not as tuned as it was in a work environment. She thought back, hoping not to find something she'd said that came across as inappropriate. But then again, said a kind voice, he wasn't exactly champing at the bit to get home either. But then *again*, said her own voice, he was a good man and he probably thought that it was due recompense for her business analytical services to take her for an ice cream and a coffee at the seaside. There was nothing more in it than that. What else could there be?

Chapter 35

When Sabrina arrived at work the next morning, Flick was already designing something on a laptop on one of the tables. "I presume this is your idea," she said to Sabrina, beckoning her over. "What do you think?"

> HAVE YOU ENJOYED YOUR MEAL AT TEDDY'S? IF YOU HAVE, TELL THE WORLD (WELL, TRIPADVISOR). EMAIL US A SCREENSHOT AND WE'LL GIVE YOU A FREE DESSERT OR COFFEE WHEN YOU COME BACK (PLEASE MAKE IT SOON X).

"Perfectly pitched, succinct, and witty." Sabrina nodded with approval. Flick beamed. "Niccolo will be really good at getting women to do this. 'Come back soon so I can see your beautiful face again,'" she said, putting on an exaggerated accent.

Teddy appeared briefly in the kitchen doorway, dropped a "*Buon giorno,*" and then disappeared again before Sabrina could return the greeting. It was as if yesterday had never happened. She headed for the toilets to begin her routine.

Well, that wasn't awkward, thought Teddy. Sabrina was back in her customary black cleaning getup, hair in a ponytail, but he'd dreamed last night that she was in nothing but his sheets and he'd woken up half convinced that if he rolled over, that's where he'd find her in reality. He was so out of practice with anything beyond the platonic, it was pathetic. Something had changed between them yesterday, and it unsettled him. Did she sense that he'd been on the brink of leaning over and kissing her cheek as they were about to part, and that's why she'd run off at a rate of knots, which at least had stopped him from making an arse of himself? If he'd done that, and she'd let him, he would have said, "Shall we go out for a drink one night?" because it would have followed as naturally as breathing, but it hadn't happened, and it was probably for the best because this wasn't a normal situation. She was vulnerable, she was lost, confused. Them being anything other than what they were was a complication she obviously didn't want and he really didn't need.

Flick put "Operation Review" into practice that same day, and it could be no coincidence that two fresh five-star reviews had been posted on the internet by the time they'd said goodbye to the last lunch customers.

"George, Sabrina thinks I should let you out of the kitchen to show your magic to customers," said Teddy as they were sitting around eating today's special, *polpette di carne*.

"I will have to speak to my agent," said George.

"Yes, yes, do it, Georgy," said Niccolo. "But wear a mask so you don't frighten the children."

"All Italians want to be Greek," said George and presented his profile to the boys. "See, from the side we are like Elvis. You can't compete with your Roman noses. Roamin' all over your face."

"Oh God, it's kicking off," said Flick, but loving the floor show.

It had been a jolly day so far, which fortified them all for the evening shift. The bookings were few, but the restaurant had filled up from walk-ins. A party of eight had come in for a seventieth birthday. The lady had embraced the fuss and the two dishy waiters serenading her, and the whole of the restaurant had joined in the singing when it came to "Happy Birthday." The atmosphere had been wonderful.

"And I think you could splash out on some merchandise. Some

souvenir mugs: Maybe the wording 'I had my birthday at Teddy's.' Or something like that," said Sabrina, the thought coming to her as she lifted up her coffee cup when they were all unwinding around the table.

"Or what about 'I wanna to go to beddy with Teddy,'" said Niccolo, hamming it up. He and his brother were so playful, thought Sabrina. Their mother must be so proud of them. She would have been had they been her sons.

"Well, I'll just leave it with you," said Sabrina, wondering if she was interfering too much now. The more she suggested, the more she was implying that what he had was lacking.

"There isn't one single thing you have said that I haven't thought would be an improvement," said Teddy. He felt comforted that they appeared to be back to normal, any awkwardness gone. "I am going to open the kitchen up and move the pizza oven so everyone can see more of the handsome chefs."

"And George," said Niccolo.

George gave him yet another mouthful of choice Greek and Sabrina thought again what a fantastic set of people they were, the dynamics between them all perfect. She would miss them when the time came to leave them, and she both hoped that would be soon and also not. She'd not outstay her welcome, but she doubted that anything she had in her other life could be this joyful; otherwise why would she have left it?

"You look tired," said Teddy when he dropped Sabrina off at Little Moon that night. That was putting it mildly; she looked shattered actually. "Take the day off tomorrow; there's hardly anything to do."

She didn't want to take the day off. It was just the two of them who went in on Sundays. She could only presume that he was trying to gently push her away; maybe he suspected she had misread his intentions and wished to put some distance between them. She took the hint.

"Okay," she said. "Thank you."

* * *

"Well, isn't this nice," said Cilla. "Yes, it is."

Flick was at her mother's house for Sunday lunch, some overdue mother-and-daughter time while Hugo was playing golf, said Cilla when she'd rung to invite her. The house used to be Flick's home as well, but she and her mother butted heads too often and Hugo moving in six months ago gave her the cue to move out. She much preferred having her space in the flat, and she would never move back home now. It was better that when she came here, it was just to visit. They were less likely to fall out if they only saw each other in small doses.

Cilla was an excellent cook, and the lunch had as many trimmings as a Christmas dinner. Her mother had gone to an awful lot of effort, and Flick was touched by that. She really wished she and her mum could get on better, but that would never happen while Cilla thought she knew everything and was right about everything and emotionally manipulated people. It was lucky that Flick had a strong will and would not be dissuaded from going to university. She had no idea why her mother didn't want her to go. Sometimes she wondered if her mother was a bit jealous of her. She was an odd woman and her own worst enemy. She didn't have many friends, which said a lot, and the ones she had were nothing like her auntie Marielle's Mad Cow friends, who were brilliant, down-to-earth, and kind. Marielle would never say things to her like, "I think that haircut is a bit short for you, Felicity," even if she thought it. Nor was it "a mum thing," as Cilla excused herself, to think she was still five and didn't have opinions of her own that just might be valid. Cilla rarely gave the respect to others that she automatically expected to receive herself.

"Is that Vivienne Westwood?" asked Cilla now, studying her daughter's top as they were sitting eating.

"Yep," said Flick.

"I thought you were saving up for university, not buying designer clothes."

"I got it from Vinted dirt cheap," said Flick, then, when her mother's face showed puzzlement: "Secondhand shop online."

"Ah, I see. I've made a peach trifle for dessert." Cilla smiled at her. "If you're not dieting."

"Why would I be dieting? My BMI is perfect," returned Flick, bristling. Her mother was a human needle designed to get under skin. As for peaches, she wasn't keen on them, though she'd eat the trifle to be polite. She would never eat peaches as a child because even the thought of their furry surfaces made her skin crawl; she would have thought her own mum might have remembered that.

"How's Hugo?" asked Flick, spearing a roast potato. Dialogue with her mother had always been strained. They never spoke to each other like adults or had proper conversations like she did with Auntie Marielle and, recently, Sabrina at work. She really liked Sabrina and felt inspired by her. She was keener than ever to go to university now and maybe take her career down the same sort of path that Sabrina had. She hoped that they'd stay in touch when Sabrina went back to wherever she'd come from, and while she knew she was being selfish, she wished that wasn't until she herself had left for uni.

"Hugo is wonderful, Felicity. He's very good company. You should come around one night and talk with him, and then I think you'd warm to him. He knows how to address counts and barons and any dignitary you can name."

"I'm sure that comes in handy in Shoresend," said Flick, sounding more sarcastic than she meant to, so she generated a compliment to balance it out. "The beef's lovely. Really tender."

"Thank you. When you get some spare money, which will be a long time off I should imagine, with all the student debt you'll incur, you should think about having a private pension," said Cilla. "The earlier you start, the better, Hugo says. He's very on the ball with financial matters and has investments and stocks and shares spread everywhere. I always wondered if people really had Swiss bank accounts, and now I know they do. Anyway, he told me to pass on his advice about your pension so that you won't be sorry in later life."

"I'll bear it in mind," replied Flick. If Hugo had a Swiss bank account, she was Taylor Swift.

"Have you got an investment account?" asked Cilla after a few forkfuls of buttered cabbage.

"No point in me locking my money away, is there, when I'll need it for university."

Cilla nodded. "Of course, of course," she said. Her speaking voice had become even plummier since she'd been hooked up with Hugo, and it was bad enough before, thanks to all those elocution lessons she'd had as a child.

"Worth mentioning, though, that the longer you do lock your money away for, the higher the interest rate you get. Hugo's money is all in long-term investments because he didn't imagine he'd need to access it sooner. He said he never expected he'd meet someone that he wanted to share his life with. Isn't that sweet?" Cilla tittered. "Now I've put him in a whirl and totally upended his plans. He's had to give a year's notice to get to his own money, can you believe, or he'll be stung with the most ridiculously heavy penalty fees."

Flick could feel the cold wind edge into the room. She didn't comment, leaving the silence clear for her mother to fill it.

"More gravy, dear?"

"Thanks, I'm fine, Mum."

"There's plenty of meat, so do tuck in."

Flick hadn't been invited here because her mother was missing her; there was something else afoot, she could tell. She didn't have long to wait for the big reveal.

"Felicity, darling, the money I deposited in your name for tax purposes, I wonder if you could transfer it back to me."

It was said lightly, as if of no more importance than the surfeit of roast beef available for consumption.

Flick didn't miss a beat. She cut up a slice of meat and put it into her mouth, chewed, swallowed.

"Did you hear me, Felicity?" Cilla's voice, honeyed and sweet.

"I heard. You told me that was your emergency fund," said Flick. "Under no circumstances was it to be accessed unless you were either very ill or a disaster had occurred." She cut more meat, chewed, swallowed.

"Things change, though, don't they? I gave it to you for safekeeping until I needed it, and now I do."

Flick registered the note of steel that had crept into Cilla's voice, but still she answered, "No, Mum."

"What do you mean, *no*? It's my money. Mine."

"Not legally it isn't. It's in my name."

Cilla gave an open-mouthed gasp of astonishment. "You've spent it, haven't you?"

Flick gasped in turn at the accusation. "I haven't touched a single penny of it."

"And that's because you know it's mine." Cilla's volume was rising, the honey replaced by acid.

"Yes, but you told me to keep it safe for a dire emergency."

"It's mine and I want it. Now. You will kindly transfer it to me with immediate effect."

"I kindly won't." Flick put down her fork. The food had stopped tasting good now anyway.

"Felicity Charlesworth, do not cross me."

"Mum, you told me that unless you were—"

"*Give me my money.*" Cilla dropped her cutlery onto the plate with an angry clatter.

"No." Flick more than matched her mother in sound level. "You just want it to give to him, and I'm going to make sure that you have at least something left for when you realize he's bled you dry."

"How dare you?" Cilla's face was screwed up now and very red.

"You'll thank me one day."

"You little shit. You think you can tell me what to do. You think you're in charge here, do you?" Cilla was screaming now.

Flick had never seen her mother this angry before. She looked demonic. "Mum, I think you should calm down."

"Don't you *dare* tell me to calm down. Who's put you up to this? Marielle, I suppose—ha? Yes, I'll bet. I suppose she's been dripping poison into your ear about me, telling you I'm stupid and that I haven't got a brain to think with, the frustrated, shriveled-up cow."

Flick had no idea where all this vitriol was coming from. "Mum, Auntie Marielle hasn't said a—"

"She's *not* your auntie!" shrieked Cilla. "She's a dried-up old bag who has got no right to tell anyone else how to run their life. She's jealous of me; she always has been. It's colored our whole relationship, Miss High and bloody Mighty. How can she of all people have the nerve to dictate to me? If she were such a good judge of character, she wouldn't let people into her home—*her own home*—who rob her blind. And she keeps doing it; she doesn't learn any lessons. What sort of idiot does that make her? They keep taking advantage of her, like that bloody woman there now. Ha!"

"Sabrina, you mean?" said Flick. "She's not like that; she's lovely."

"Lovely, is she?" snarked Cilla. "I bet your *auntie Marielle* didn't tell you that *lovely Sabrina* had the barefaced cheek to steal her purse from under her nose *and* then deny it when it couldn't have been anyone else. No, I bet she didn't, and she's so weak and pathetic that she's *still* letting her stay in the flat because she's beyond dense, because she's frightened what people would say if they knew. And she really thinks she knows better than me?"

The words hung in the air, long tails on them. The hush broken by a single note of disbelief, a small sound from Flick's throat.

"That's not true," she said eventually.

Cilla realized her mistake immediately. What if Marielle hadn't said anything to anyone about the missing purse? Cilla then couldn't have known. But the thought was quickly dismissed, because Marielle didn't keep anything from her friends, especially Sylvie, and she could blame the leak on them. But just in case, she should cover herself.

"You absolutely must not say a word; I was told this in strictest confidence," Cilla said. "You must swear to me you will forget this conversation happened."

Flick had been brought up to know that you didn't break a holy swear. Her mother, in spite of her faults, was God-fearing at heart. Or sort of. She believed that if you went to church for the communions, believed in Christ, prayed before bedtime, and always took swearing on the Bible seriously, you would glide up to heaven one day on a golden escalator.

"Your auntie Marielle would be destroyed if this got out." Cilla threw a little emotional blackmail into the mix for good measure. "I'm sorry if I overreacted. It's only because I'm frustrated by her too-trusting generosity. So mean it when you swear."

"I swear," said Flick, her voice wobbly. Her heart was beating in her chest, a horrible mix of adrenaline and disappointment. She felt rocked, disorientated, as if someone had pulled the whole floor from under her.

"Now let's continue on a new footing without talk of money—yours, mine, or otherwise. I wanted to have a pleasant lunch with my daughter and it's taken a sour turn. I'm sorry that we let other people spoil it. Have some cauliflower cheese; I don't want any wastage."

It would wait, thought Cilla, picking up the dish and handing it to Flick. If her money was safe with her daughter, she'd get it later. For now she had to concentrate on erasing this conversation from history.

The *Daily Trumpet* would like to apologize for a misprint that occurred in last Friday's edition in which we misnamed Flora Exley's floristry business as Floral Sex. We apologize for any intended error to Ms. Sexy and have made a donation to a charity of her choosing.

Chapter 36

Flick wasn't her customary sunny self the next day. She didn't even have her morning break with everyone but took herself off into the office, and then she went home rather than have lunch there. Teddy had asked her what was wrong and she'd said she hadn't slept well, but she was the same on Tuesday and Wednesday too. Sabrina had also asked if she was okay and she'd answered in a very strange, clipped tone that she was perfectly fine, thank you, and just had "things on her mind." She obviously wasn't fine, but Sabrina reckoned if she couldn't offload to her uncle, whom she was close to, she wasn't going to confide in a woman she barely knew, and so she backed off.

Things on her mind was an understatement. Flick had been stewing since that conversation with her mother where she'd revealed that Auntie Marielle's purse had been stolen. By Sabrina. *It couldn't be.* But then again, it might explain why Marielle hadn't been in the restaurant for at least a week, which was unheard of. If people found out that Marielle had been robbed again, they really would have something to say, so it was in her interest to make sure no one knew and had a go at her for being daft enough to let someone she didn't know stay in her house. The pieces fit together too well, but Flick didn't want them to. She had sworn to keep the secret, but it was bursting out of her, too big to keep in because she was really hurt. And when Sabrina asked her if she was all right, she'd wanted to scream at her that she *knew*.

Sabrina looked different now in the light of this information. Flick had always judged her at face value, but it was entirely likely that she was a practiced con artist, working hard to impress them and being nicey-nicey all the time and spouting obvious crap about how to improve things so they'd really believe she was a business expert. Even more than she was angry at Sabrina, Flick was angry at herself for being taken in by someone so flaming easily. And to think she'd actually pushed Sabrina and Uncle Teddy together to go out to a Ciaoissimo, hoping a spark between them might light. She was glad it hadn't now. And maybe the reason Sabrina was here, saying she'd lost her memory, was because she'd run off from cheating someone else and was lying low. That would also fit. Surely if she could remember what job she did, she'd remember where she came from as well. It made Flick's brain ache to try to unravel it all.

She had this information, but she didn't know what to do with it. She couldn't tell Uncle Teddy—he'd go ape at Auntie Marielle—and she didn't want to confront Sabrina because right now she didn't want to talk to her ever again. So it sat inside her and continued to fester until it was black and rotten. Everyone felt the impact of her mood on the atmosphere, and Teddy pulled her into the kitchen after the lunchtime diners had gone because he'd had enough of her face tripping her up. It wasn't like her at all. For one thing, she always told him when she had a gripe; she used him as a sounding board, so the fact she wasn't on this occasion was significant.

"What's the matter with you, Flick?"

"Nothing," she said defiantly, looking so much younger than her nineteen years.

"Look, take the night off. There's obviously something wrong, and if you can't tell me, then why don't you go and see my mum and talk to her?"

There was no way Flick would do that. She wasn't supposed to know what had happened; she'd sworn not to tell anyone, so Auntie Marielle was the last person she could go and see.

"I don't want the night off. I need the money. I'm going to uni soon in case you've forgotten."

"No, I haven't forgotten. I'll pay you anyway. Just go. We can do without you for one night." Flick silently walked away from him, took her sweater off the peg, and slunk out the front door. She really didn't want to be around Sabrina. She'd trusted her. But really, could anyone be that nice without an agenda? She only had to think of her mother, making her a lovely Sunday lunch because she was trying to manipulate her into handing over money.

She left the restaurant feeling as if she was carrying the weight of an unexploded bomb inside her, and she knew that if she went straight home to the flat, she'd fill the air in it with so much toxicity she wouldn't be able to breathe. She would have gone down to the beach to clear her head. She liked to walk on the sand and let the breeze play with her long, dark hair, but the skies were thick gray dumplings and rain was leaking out of them in fat, intermittent drops. She decided to go and buy herself some comfort food and hole herself up with *The Sopranos*, hoping to replace the violence and dysfunction she felt inside with their violence and dysfunction. Plus a Furio Giunta–heavy episode never failed to take her to another place.

The post office had a great food section at the back supplied by the farm shop. She opened its door absently with way too much force and almost knocked the woman behind it off her feet.

"Careful," said the woman crossly, then, when she saw who it was, her tone instantly warmed.

"Flick. What are you doing in such a rush?" Of all people, Sylvie.

Flick opened her mouth to answer but nothing came out. Tears did the talking for her, though, forming, shining, falling.

* * *

Sabrina worked the reception for the first time, and she was as polished as if she'd done it since the place opened. They weren't fully booked that evening, but they had a couple of walk-ups, including a group of six who thought a vacancy would be a hope too far and were delighted that it wasn't. They had every course and seven bottles of wine between them. And they wanted to take two pizzas home. Sabrina poured them all a complimentary Limoncello as she handed out Flick's invitations to leave a positive review. They said they'd definitely be back to claim their free puddings.

Teddy had asked George to hang back for five minutes after the other staff had gone.

"I've got two tickets for Slattercove Theater," he said, taking them out of a drawer and wagging them in the air. "They gave them to me in exchange for putting a poster up in the window to advertise a show: the stage version of *My Big Fat Greek Wedding*."

George chuckled. "Of course I'll go with you. I'm flattered you thought of me."

"That would be my worst nightmare, for many reasons," said Teddy. "But my mother would love it, I'm sure." He shut up then and waited for George to get his meaning.

George looked puzzled. "Go with me, you mean?" he said eventually.

"Be a shame to let the tickets go to waste."

George's hand came out slowly toward them as if he expected Teddy to pull them back at the last second.

"You could make an evening of it," Teddy went on. "Have something nice to eat. She likes Chinese, Thai . . . even Greek."

"Okay," said George slowly, as if he wasn't quite sure if Teddy was joking or not. "If that's all right with you."

"Please don't tell me you've been waiting for permission." Teddy shook his head.

"I would have approached you first, as a matter of respect. And I was judging when would be best to . . . ask." He mused for a moment. "She can only say no, right?"

Teddy realized then that love didn't get any easier or less complicated. It was always a step into fog, and you just hoped that you had solid ground beneath your feet.

* * *

When the table of six had gone and Sabrina had locked the door and closed the window shutters, she turned around to find that Teddy was pouring out two glasses of red wine. Thinking about George and his mum together had pushed him to say something to her that wouldn't sit still inside him anymore. He was glad the last customers had lingered; it gave him the opportunity to send everyone home and have some time alone with her.

He gestured that she take the chair opposite. "You hungry?"

"No, I'm fine," she replied. "But this will go down well." She raised her glass. "*Salute.* I hope that's right, unless Niccolo has been lying again and I've actually just said *knob*."

Teddy chuckled. "No, it's right." He returned the greeting, drank, and then said, "I just wanted to have a word with you. About last week, when we went to Ciaoissimo."

"Oh?" she said, feeling a cocktail of curiosity swirling around in her stomach with the wine.

He jumped in with both feet. "Did I say something to upset you? You seemed to leap out of the car really quickly."

"No, not at all," she said, trying not to look as if she were lying. Then again, he hadn't really. The fault was hers, imagining a spark that wasn't there. Stupid of her.

"I had a great day," he said.

"So did I." Her smile was flickering, unsure.

"I mean I had a great day with you, Sabrina." Did that mean what she thought it meant? She didn't answer straightaway because she didn't want to get it wrong.

Teddy wasn't sure how to interpret her silence. What he did know was that when you started opening up to someone, all your gauges lost their bearings, so a little clarity wouldn't go amiss.

"Sabrina, I am really out of practice, so if I'm overstepping the mark here, I'm so sorry. I don't want to put you in any awkward position, because I know your situation, but I enjoyed your company so much. I can't say more—it wouldn't be fair to you because, well, I don't think I have a right to, you know, say what I feel. This may not be what you want to hear and I don't want to confuse you or get in the way of what's . . . what's waiting for you . . . back home, but . . . I really like being around you because I really like you. I'm not expecting you to say a word back to me and I won't say anything more, and please feel free to totally ignore it, just strike it from the record. But I needed to get it out. Okay . . ."

He let out a long breath at the end of his monologue and wondered if he'd been talking nonsense. Then he noticed her stunned expression, which made him wish he could pull every mangled word back. He took a nervous glug of wine and was a nanosecond away from standing and saying that he'd drive her home and was sorry and they should erase the past few minutes from history, when she spoke.

"I feel the same."

He coughed in his glass and sent wine sploshing all over his face and his chef whites.

"You'll need some Vanish for that," she said, smiling a smile that lit up her lovely brown eyes.

"I don't know what to say now," he said, wiping his face with a serviette.

"Me neither, if that helps."

"Look, I don't think . . . either of us can . . ."

"We can't." She shook her head.

"So . . . let's just park it there and . . ."

". . . forget it for now. But also keep it in mind." *Does that even make sense?* she thought.

"We can just . . . have it . . . with us, inside." *What the bollocks am I saying?*

"I think it's for the best."

"Let's leave it to the gods. The Roman ones, not the Greek ones. They haven't a clue."

She laughed.

He leaned across the table, picked up her hand, and pressed the back of it to his lips. He felt her gasp and joy spread inside him like warm syrup that he'd had that effect on her. That was two things he'd set in motion tonight. One of them a slow but sure burner, the other . . . a mad, reckless leap into the unknown that could end up being the best gamble or the worst mistake of his life.

The *Daily Trumpet* apologizes to Darren Cartwright of Cartwright Decorating Services in Doncaster for an unfortunate error in our local tradesmen's directory. Mr. Cartwright has been an interior decorator for thirty-three years and not an inferior decorator as printed.

Chapter 37

"Well, this is a nice impromptu surprise," said Marielle the next morning in the tea shop. "What's the occasion?"

"Nothing, I just fancied having a breakfast special here, and I thought who better to share it with than my fabulous friend?" said Sylvie.

"But she wasn't available so you asked me." Marielle grinned.

Sylvie grinned back. What a gorgeous, kind woman her old pal was; she deserved much better than she got.

"How's Tim?" Marielle asked, looking at the tea menu. How could she possibly choose between forty variations?

"Rampant as always," said Sylvie.

Marielle hooted. "Are you complaining?"

"I certainly am not," said Sylvie adamantly. "I consider myself very lucky. Not sure what'll happen when I start losing it and dribbling, but I'm enjoying myself for now."

"You shouldn't be wondering about what's to come when you have no need," said Marielle. "I wouldn't have wanted to even consider that Sal would leave me a young widow. You have to believe you'll live forever."

Sylvie smiled sympathetically. She'd never met Salvatore, which was just as well really because she didn't do "lovable cads." A cheat was a cheat in her book, and they weren't to be forgiven. But it wasn't her judgment call. Marielle had been happy with him in those last years, and Salvatore had finally realized what he had in her.

The breakfast special arrived, three tiers of cake plates with warm croissants, *pain au chocolat*, and cinnamon whirls on the bottom, potato rosti cakes with bacon and poached eggs in the middle, and scrambled eggs with avocado and tiny glasses filled with various yogurts and muesli on the top.

"We'll never eat all this," said Marielle.

"Let's give it our best shot," replied Sylvie, cutting into a croissant and smothering it with honey butter. "How are things with you? Any news about the Ciaoissimo bastards?"

"No. Sadly they haven't gone bankrupt and no freak meteorite has landed on their property."

"Nothing more from Cilla?"

"No also to that. I think we're best staying away from each other for the time being."

"How's the lodger? Has she managed to remember anything else?"

"Bits and bobs," replied Marielle, with an unconscious sigh that Sylvie registered. "Not enough to get her back to where she should be."

"I hope she isn't outstaying her welcome. She's been there longer than anyone else has." Sylvie bit down on her croissant with unaccustomed savagery.

"Not at all," replied Marielle. If it hadn't been for that missing purse, she thought she could have quite happily let Sabrina stay in the flat forever. She had been such unassuming, gentle company, at least before it had gone wrong. She had even tried to forget it and move on. There was only thirty pounds in the purse, and when she'd rung the bank to stop her card, they'd told her no one had attempted to use it. She wished now she'd just had a conversation with her face-to-face about it before it had gotten so big in her head. She was too soft; everyone was right about her, that she gave people far too much scope to hurt her.

"You know you can talk to me about anything in confidence if you ever need to," said Sylvie, suddenly serious.

"I know," replied Marielle. "And the same goes for me with you."

"I would always turn to you first," said Sylvie, glancing upward at the clock on the wall. They'd be there now. By the time they finished this breakfast, Marielle's problem, the one she wouldn't share with them because she was likely too embarrassed about it, would be long gone.

* * *

Sabrina felt stupidly cheerful that morning, as if some of yesterday's early sunshine had lodged inside her and was sloshing around, and it was all the fault of Teddy Bonetti. Though he hadn't really done much to cause her to feel as if she had springs in her shoes, other than to say he had enjoyed spending the day with her and he liked her.

He had driven her home last night and she thought he might have kissed her on the cheek as she said good night, but he didn't. But she could see that he wanted to and had held back for the reasons he had mentioned in the restaurant—and that was enough to make her smile all the way up the stairs to the flat like a teenage girl whose heart started thudding every time she caught so much as a glimpse of a certain teenage boy. She smiled all the way through her shower and through the cup of tea she made in an effort to unwind, because the fizz in her veins wouldn't be letting her go to sleep anytime soon.

When she did get to bed, she wondered if the translation of all those stutterings was that he meant she had a place in this life if the other one—the real one—turned out to be somewhere she didn't want to go back to. After all, she'd left it, hadn't she? But had she *left* it? Forever?

She couldn't stay in this limbo for much longer. Whatever was trying to protect her had done its duty; now it had to let her into the truth of who Sabrina Anderson was. Whatever bad stuff was behind the door, her daughter was there too, and if that meant she had to break it down to find her again, then so be it. She was strong enough now, she was sure of it.

The last thing she'd done that night was pray.

"Dear God, I'm ready to know everything now. Please help me." That was all she needed to say to him if he was listening.

* * *

She was just getting her shoes on for work when the flat doorbell rang. She walked down the stairs to answer it. She opened the door just a little to see who it was, but as soon as she had, it was pushed hard from the other side and Diana, whom she'd met in the fish-and-chip restaurant when she and Marielle had had lunch there, barged in, followed by three other women.

"Good morning," said Diana. "Can we have a word? It's about Marielle."

"Of course," said Sabrina, slightly confused because Diana didn't sound half as friendly as she had the last time they'd met. She went back up the stairs into the flat with the women following behind her.

"Lovely in here, isn't it?" said Jackie, looking around.

"Yes, but everyone Marielle lets into it seems to take advantage," said Diana. Sabrina didn't know what to say to that, but the air was full of threat and she hadn't a clue why.

"Now, Marielle won't tell you this herself, so I'm charged with doing it for her," said Diana, hard-smiling. "Kindly pack up your things and leave." She turned to her left. "Jackie." Jackie pulled an envelope out of her pocket and handed it to Sabrina.

"There's two hundred quid in there. The bus stop is on the front just by the deck chair rental; you'll need the number sixty-four. There's a women's refuge in Slattercove. Beach Street, easy enough to remember, but I've written it on the envelope. Ask the bus driver to tell you when to get off."

Sabrina's head began to whirl. "Marielle wants me to leave?"

"Got it in one," said Bev, who wasn't smiling in any shape or form.

So it wasn't her imagination then. Marielle *had* been off with her. Had she outstayed her welcome and she hadn't dared tell her? What else could it be?

"Of course I'll go."

"Aren't you even going to ask why?" asked Diana, taking the fact she hadn't as a sure sign of guilt.

"Does Marielle feel that I've taken advantage of her? I never wanted that to happen." The women looked at each other, exchanging amused glances.

"Just get your stuff," said Diana. "We'll wait."

Sabrina felt as if something had reached inside her and scooped out her center. Her thoughts were tumbling over themselves trying to work out what she'd done to Marielle that was so bad she couldn't say it to her face but had sent a posse of people round to speedily evict her. She walked into the bedroom and picked up the black bag she'd been putting her dirty laundry in and loaded it with her work clothes and her blue ensemble that she'd worn to go on the Ciaoissimo trail with Teddy. It didn't take long to collect all her worldly possessions, and they all fit in that one bag. She exited the room for the last time, leaving the envelope on the bed. She had no idea what this was all about, but she had done nothing to be paid off for.

She walked past the file of women, feeling their eyes boring into her. They followed her down the stairs and out the front door. It was raining heavily, and Sabrina's charity-shop blue jacket wouldn't afford her much protection, but it was hard for any of the women to find sympathy for her. They were all thinking a variation of *As ye sow, so shall ye reap.*

"Bus stop's just down there," said Diana, pointing. "I'll take the key, thank you." Sabrina put it in her awaiting palm, and Diana's fingers snapped shut on it like a Venus flytrap. She started walking, then turned back to find them all waiting to make sure she'd gone. "I really don't know what I've done to upset Marielle, but would you please just tell her that I'm so grateful for what she did for me. I'll pay her back every single penny."

Well, if that isn't an admission, what would be? they all thought collectively.

"On your way now," said Diana, shooing her off like the rubbish she was.

* * *

"Let's have another cup of tea," said Sylvie.

Marielle laughed. "Sylvie, I can't fit another drop in. And why do you keep looking at the clock? Have you had enough of me?"

"I don't, do I?" Sylvie replied with a laughing apology. Her phone beeped in her bag and she reached down to pull it out. She read the text she'd been waiting for.

She's gone.

Sylvie shoved it back in her bag and prepared to lie. "From Tim. Do I fancy going out for dinner? he says. I don't think so. I'll still be digesting this till Christmas."

"It was a real treat. Thank you," said Marielle.

"You deserve it. You're a lovely friend. Far too nice for your own good."

Marielle laughed. "Okay, what are you after?"

"Nothing. And I mean it." Sylvie leaned over the table, put her extra-serious face on, placed her hand over Marielle's, and said, "Darling, I know."

"Know what?" said Marielle.

"I know that Sabrina took your purse."

Marielle's face dropped. She looked mortified. "I see. And now you're going to tell me I'm the biggest fool to walk God's earth, aren't you?"

"I am so not. You have the biggest heart of anyone I know, and you did more than your duty for her, but it's up to her now to sort herself out."

Sylvie waved over the waitress for the bill, and as Sylvie was getting out her bank card, Marielle's brain started to spin.

"Hang on, how did you know?" she asked her friend.

"I bumped into Flick in the post office yesterday. She was very upset. She told me and I'm afraid that I couldn't sit back and do nothing. I—"

This was getting weirder. "How did Flick know?"

"Cilla told her. They had lunch together on Sunday and apparently it came out in a bit of a row."

Marielle's features squeezed further into an expression of utter confusion.

"What came out?"

"About your purse going missing. Cilla made her swear not to say anything, though, and I had to convince Flick that she wouldn't go to hell for telling me and breaking an oath—"

"Wait a minute, wait a minute." Marielle pressed her fingertips into her temples, thinking hard, backtracking, putting events in order. "No, no, that's not right. That can't be."

"What's the matter?" Sylvie asked her.

"Sylvie, I didn't tell anyone about the purse when I couldn't find it. No one. If I was going to tell anyone, it would have been you, and I certainly wouldn't have said anything to Cilla about it. I've only spoken to her the once recently anyway, when she came up to the house to tell me off the day we went to see Psychic Pat, so this doesn't make any sense because I didn't even know it was missing until long after she'd left . . ."

Her voice trailed off as she replayed the scene of Cilla's visit in her head. Cilla barking at her, Marielle wanting to make peace with some tea. She'd filled up the kettle and put it on. Then she'd opened up the cupboard, hunting around for the best mugs and the matching plate for some biscuits. She would have had her back to Cilla throughout. She'd only discovered her purse wasn't in her bag five minutes before she and Sabrina were going out the door that evening.

"Sylvie, there is only one way Cilla could have known about my purse."

"Oh God, Marielle," said Sylvie. It was her turn now to look mortified.

Chapter 38

It was a foul day, which was good, because nobody in their right mind was on the beach apart from a couple of hardened dog owners, but even they'd make it quick. Through a practiced process of elimination, Orrible had worked out the optimum size of rock he'd need to have any chance of hitting that handbag, which was still hanging tantalizingly. He'd come pretty close to it recently, but today was the day; he was not going home until it was his. He arrived at the site with a bag for life full of rocks and bricks that he'd collected and began chucking them until his arm gave up and he had to stop and roll his shoulder. It was still aching from being twisted the last time he'd been the recipient of one of Square's armbars. He was meant to have it, he knew. It was fate that the owner of the handbag had lost her memory and hadn't gone into Slattercove police station and told them that the bloke who had nicked her car looked like someone who should have been dancing up the yellow brick road with Judy Garland. She'd only have had to mention "floppy hat" and the rozzers would have been round at his house faster than you could say "brain."

The rain was getting stupid now; he picked up one of the rocks that had come tumbling back to him down the cliff face like a homing stone and pitched it, roaring as he did so as if that would help take it higher up, but it didn't work, landing well south of its target. It had become a battle of wills for him: man versus handbag. It was the last thing he thought of at night and the first thing he thought of when he woke up. It was a compulsion stronger even than keeping on the right side of Billy.

He was just straightening up from retrieving the rock at his feet when a seagull mistook his hat for something edible and swooped, screeching at him.

"Oy, you bloody thing," Orrible said as it soared upward, the hat in its beak. He lobbed the rock in his hand, which by some miracle hit the seagull full on in the wing and drove it smack into the cliff wall, but luckily for the gull, the impact was softened by the bag. And luckily for Orrible, the collision caused the branch it was caught on to snap clean off. Orrible watched in joyful amazement as his hat, the seagull, and the bag fell down to the beach in a holy trinity. The seagull gave its head a shake, righted itself, and flew off none the worse for its ordeal. Had it died, Orrible thought he just might have given it a state funeral.

He lumbered up to the road to catch the bus home, though he could have floated there without the need of a vehicle, so euphoric he was about winning this long-drawn-out campaign. He fully intended to save the whole surprise of what the bag contained until he was sitting at the kitchen table with a celebratory can of cold lager, but he'd had a quick dabble inside and found a fabulously fat purse and a passport. He recognized the woman's photo in it. So, she was called Polly Potter then. He thought she looked nicer without all that makeup that she'd been wearing up on the cliff top. He clutched the bag to him for the prize it was and quickened his pace as the bus he wanted was just about to pull in and save him from the rain. Could this day get any better?

The doors *shhh*'ed open and he stood back while a woman alighted. She was carrying a black bin liner, and when she raised her head and her eyes locked onto his, he knew her straightaway because he'd just been looking at her photograph in her passport. *What are the blimming chances?*

* * *

Sabrina registered the scrawny, scruffy man with the string for a belt and the floppy hat, holding a woman's large handbag. She'd seen him before. In a field where her uncle's car had crashed many years before, the black eyes that took in everything, the insects scratching inside him. *Her uncle Ed, her auntie Rina. Would you like to come and live with us? Seagulls and the seaside, the old cat next door, the crash, Benidorm. It's for the best.* Thoughts and feelings and sounds and words burst a dam wall inside her, totally drowning her brain. She couldn't breathe.

She put one foot on the ground and her legs crumpled beneath her.

"Oh Jesus, Mary, and Joseph, not again," said Orrible.

Chapter 39

Teddy couldn't understand why Sabrina hadn't come in to work. He'd been thinking about her all night, and after their chat, he couldn't wait to see her, be in her orbit, know she was close by. It was enough for now. He rang his mum to ask if she knew where she was, but he couldn't get hold of her either. He was debating whether to take a quick drive up to Big Moon when he saw Marielle walking toward the restaurant, and he went to unlock the door for her.

"Teddy, can I have a word in private?" she said, her expression dark, and she swept past Flick as if she hadn't even seen her on her way to the office. Teddy followed her.

"Just shut the door, will you."

"Okay." Baffled, he asked, "What's up?"

"Has Flick said anything to you?"

"Anything to me about what? She's been like a bear with a sore *culo* for days. I had to send her home yesterday." His puzzlement segued into concern. "What's the matter with her?"

"It's not Flick; it's Sabrina."

"Sabrina isn't in. Where is she?" Teddy felt his heart give a thump of worry. "Mamma, what's going on?"

Marielle let out a long breath. "Oh, where to start?"

"Mamma?"

"Just listen to me, Teddy, because this is going to come out in a jumble. My purse went missing at home. I thought it could only be Sabrina who took it, but I never said a word to anyone about it. But then Cilla told Flick that I'd confided in her about it. But I didn't; I couldn't have. My purse wasn't even missing when I last saw her. She came round to the house to tell me how stupid I was for having someone stay in the flat, but it was only later on that day when I discovered it was gone."

Teddy went over her words in his head, putting the info in order.

"You're sure you didn't have that conversation?"

Marielle humphed. "I'm sixty-three, Teddy, not a hundred and three. As if I'd take Cilla into my confidence about anything, for a start. I couldn't find my purse when Sabrina and I were going out to the theater, and that was hours after Cilla had left."

Teddy was straight on it. "So how did she know then? Unless . . ."

"Unless she had a crystal ball, and I think we can safely discount that. There is only one way she could have known."

He knew what she was saying, but he shook his head, unable to understand the motivation behind such an action.

"Why would Cilla take it?"

"To frame Sabrina. So she could then say she was right and Sabrina was taking me for a ride."

Teddy screwed up his face. "But that would be really twisted, Mum."

"I've gone over it and over it and I can't think of any other explanation. And sadly it's entirely believable."

"Where's Sabrina? Have you spoken to her about any of this?"

Marielle sank to a chair. "Oh Teddy, it gets worse. Flick, our darling Flick, worried sick about me, told Sylvie, who whisked me out for breakfast this morning to keep me out of the way while my caring, misguided friends went over to Little Moon and threw Sabrina out. I have to find her, Teddy. I feel terrible. They told her to go to the women's refuge in Slattercove. I'm heading over there now."

Teddy unbuttoned his white chef's tunic and hung it up on a peg. "I'll drive you," he said.

* * *

Flick moved quickly away from outside the office where she'd eavesdropped on their whole conversation, into the loo next door, and sat on the seat with her head in her hands. She didn't think she had ever felt so bad in her whole life.

* * *

Few people knew the address of the women's refuge, but Marielle did because of her hospital work. It was only because they knew she was a person of trust that the manager there gave her the carefully worded discreet information that they had taken no new woman in for days.

They walked along Slattercove front and up the small side streets looking in café windows. On a horrible rainy day like this, Sabrina might have gone in to shelter and think, if she was even here. Maybe she'd holed up in one of the many boardinghouses, even though signs in nearly every window said "No Vacancies" and the hotels would surely be too expensive. Marielle wiped her wet cheeks with the heel of her hand.

She hadn't stopped crying since she'd gotten in Teddy's car. This was finding-a-needle-in-a-haystack territory.

"What about the hospital?" asked Teddy. He didn't want to think it was a possibility, but at least they could rule it out before they tried any other avenues.

Marielle pulled out her phone. She had Sister Tessa's direct number. She answered after three rings. As luck would have it, she was on duty and said she'd ring down to Emergency and call straight back.

Marielle sat in a bus shelter waiting while Teddy checked out a couple of cafés to ask if a lone woman of Sabrina's description had been in. The thought of Sabrina trailing a black bin liner around not knowing where to go made Marielle's heart feel as heavy as a rock in her chest. Then her phone rang in her hand and she almost dropped it in her eagerness to answer it.

"Marielle, she's in Emergency waiting to be seen. Apparently she fainted when she got off the bus in Slattercove and someone called an ambulance."

Marielle waved Teddy over and told him. "Come on then," he said. "Let's go and get her."

* * *

"I'll be back in half an hour, tops," said Flick, grabbing her jacket and rushing out of the restaurant. Antonio and George exchanged looks that said, *What the hell is going on this morning?* First Marielle had rushed in with her face drained of blood, and then she and Teddy had taken off, and now Flick had gone AWOL.

Cilla lived in one of the bigger houses on a nearby estate up the hill from the center of town. Flick ran all the way there to expend some of the excess energy her body was churning out. She wasn't even breathless by the time she got to her mother's; if anything, her energy had grown. It wasn't a nice energy either: it was full of anger and it needed an out.

She rang the bell to be polite, but when her mother didn't answer straightaway, she used the key she still had on her key ring. Cilla was just coming down the stairs in a pink satin peignoir as she barged in.

"What on earth is the matter?" Cilla asked her. From upstairs a male voice shouted, "Everything all right there, Cilli?"

Silly. The word didn't even come close, thought Flick.

She tore into the lounge and opened the top drawer of the dresser in there.

"Where is it then?" she demanded.

"What on earth do you think you're doing?" said Cilla. "Stop that immediately."

Flick ignored her, moved to the next drawer, then the cupboard beneath where Cilla kept her box of important documents. Nothing. She skirted past her mother and into the next room, the pink parlor. It had been a dining room originally, but for some reason Cilla had redecorated it into a place she might receive friends and take tea as if she were the Duchess of Devonshire.

Flick made to open the drawer in the antique cocktail cabinet. Her mother grabbed her arm hard.

"I don't know what your game is, Felicity, but—"

Flick rounded on her. "My game? My game, Mum? *Your* game, you mean."

"You're talking gibberish. I think you need to calm down." Cilla's grip was tightening.

"Open that drawer, Mum."

Cilla slapped her arm hard. "Felicity, get out of my house."

Flick shook her mother off and pulled the drawer so hard that it left its housing. She knew it was where her mother kept her fripperies and pretensions. She tipped the many contents out onto the carpet: old love letters, boxed jewelry, posh invitations she'd been sent in the past, her envelope of emergency money, her checkbook in its gold, monogrammed casing. And, looking quite out of place among them, a battered brown purse. Flick knew it instantly because she herself had bought it for Auntie Marielle. She snatched it up.

"I think you should go, young lady," said Hugo, appearing in the doorway, clad in a ridiculously showy maroon velvet smoking jacket.

"I think you should keep your fucking nose out," Flick snarled.

"Disgraceful language," said Hugo.

"Felicity, don't show me up," said Cilla.

Flick rounded on her mother. "Oh my God. You, you, it's always about *you* being affected, isn't it?"

Cilla made a grab for the purse, but Flick was much quicker and taller and held it out of her reach. She opened it and took out the bank card that sat in one of the slots. The name on it was *Mrs. Marielle Bonetti*.

"It's not what you think," said Cilla, patting her breathy chest.

"It's exactly what I think," replied Flick, her eyes narrowed with disgust. She couldn't look at her mother; she had to get out of there.

"How dare you talk to your mother like that?" said Hugo, as she flew past him and headed for the front door, hot, furious tears sploshing out of her eyes. Behind her she could hear her name being shouted on an exasperated, continuous loop: *Felicity, Felicity.* She'd always hated it. And at the moment, she hated even more so the woman who had given it to her.

* * *

As Teddy and Marielle walked across the hospital car park, they saw an unmistakable figure carrying a bin liner, heading for the bus stop. For a few seconds Teddy doubted his own eyes because the woman seemed so much smaller than Sabrina, and as fragile as eggshell. He wanted to bound across, pick her up, and take her home, but it was his mother who first broke into a run, calling her name, reaching her, throwing her arms around her.

"Oh my darling Sabrina." She couldn't say any more because her throat was clogged with a lump of tears and explanations and apologies.

Teddy took the bin bag from her, and the weight in his hand was significant. This was a woman's whole life as she knew it, right here. He felt a rush of emotion and couldn't have unpicked the various strands that made it up if he'd tried, but he knew that pity and anger and relief were heading up the list of dominants.

"Let's get you home," said Marielle. She took a firm hold on Sabrina's arm, guiding her forward. She looked broken, thought Teddy. He couldn't even guess at what was going through her head.

They walked to the car, barely saying anything. Marielle thought that if she started talking, she wouldn't be able to shut up, and maybe that was better done when they got home. Teddy drove in silence; his mother was sitting in the back with Sabrina, sniffing, beyond upset at the turn of this morning's events. He could almost hear the what-ifs coursing through her mind. *What if they hadn't found her? What if she'd disappeared from them without a trace? What if she'd been so disorientated that she'd had a worse accident?* They were the same what-ifs that were racing through his own brain.

Teddy followed them into Big Moon. He put the bin bag down, then switched the kettle on while Marielle fussed around Sabrina, pushing her onto the sofa, placing a throw over her shoulders because she was shivering. She was so pale. Marielle couldn't believe they had said she could go home at the hospital; if she'd still been a nurse, she would have made a strong case for admitting her.

Teddy put a mug down on the coffee table in front of her and sat down next to her. He took her hands in his own much larger ones and held them, warming them to rid them of the trembling.

"Tessa said you fell getting off a bus," said Marielle, her voice quiet, as soothing as she could make it.

"I saw someone I thought I recognized," said Sabrina eventually, imagining him, the scarecrow man who'd been at the beginning of it all, and now at the end. She raised her head.

"Marielle, Teddy, I know who I am."

DAILY TRUMPET CLASSIFIED ADS
FOR SALE

Burr walnut dressing table ideal for lady with sturdy legs and very roomy drawers.

King-sized mattress, good as new. Only slept on once. Slight urine stain in middle.

Used gravestone, cross-shaped, gray marble. Ideal for someone called Shirley Bickerstaffe.

Complete shed's worth of tools, some brand new including drills, various electric saws, workbench, screwdrivers, spanners. £50 for quick sale. Must be collected before 7 July when lying cheating bastard husband gets back from "golfing holiday with lads" in Tenerife but really with his slag of a girlfriend.

Chapter 40

Sabrina had no idea why the man who looked like a scarecrow should have been the one to blast down the wall in her head behind which so much was hidden. He had been a terrible key, because she knew now that Eddie and Rina had not been her parents but her uncle and aunt, and she'd lost them both years earlier than she'd thought. She hadn't seen them grow old together, enjoying a long and happy life: Those memories had all been false, manufactured by a brain that had seized an opportunity to hold on to them for longer. Their dear, beloved lives had been cut tragically short when she was just a little girl, and the place where they died was somehow linked to a scarecrow in a field. But they had brought her to Shoresend with them once and that's why this place was so special, synonymous with happiness for her, and that's why she had come here again in need of solace.

When she drove to Shoresend, it had taken hours, so she hadn't come from the immediate vicinity. She could remember throwing her car keys on the grass toward someone because she had no choice but to do so. He looked like the scarecrow man at the bus stop—maybe that's why he had sprung the lock—but they couldn't be the same person because the man at the bus stop had helped her, sat with her until the ambulance came apparently. She knew that her mind had a habit of attaching nasty things to scarecrows; they'd become a symbol of darkness for her since that terrible crash which had changed the course of her life.

She knew she was a business analyst, without any question. And she was definitely called Sabrina Anderson because that name fit her like a tailormade jacket. She'd been called after her auntie Rina; she was in no doubt of those few facts about herself.

But there were still great gaping potholes surrounding the few solid chunks of certainties. There was no violent, unhinged fiend that she needed to hide from; God knows where her mind had conjured up that thought from. But then, imaginations often warped and caricatured for their own reasons. She could see the actual man she lived with, but only as a vague outline, and he wasn't someone to fear. Why wasn't he clearer, though, and why did she not have any feeling that she missed him? There was something about a wedding that was pertinent. She thought she might have been a bridesmaid, but surely that was unlikely at her age.

"I know all this and I'm no further forward," she said to Teddy and Marielle. Her eyes were shiny from tears; they spilled over and down her cheeks, a flow that refused to stop.

"I really think you need to rest, darling," said Marielle.

"What aren't you telling us?" asked Teddy gently, sensing there was something.

There was, and she didn't want to say because it would make it real. It would dissolve her one solid treasure in an acid of reality. The truth had already taken her parents away from her, and it hadn't finished with her at that, because she remembered now being in the hospital holding her newborn daughter in her arms, knowing that every minute brought her closer to having to let her go.

"My daughter isn't working her way around Australia," said Sabrina. "She was stillborn many years ago."

Teddy's arms closed around her and his mother's around them both. There was nothing to say for the moment that their embrace couldn't say better.

*   *   *

Sabrina went to bed soon after. She said she was tired, but it was a lie. She just couldn't hold up any longer, not even in front of these dear, kind people. She needed to be alone. She wished she had never met the scarecrow man. She had prayed for the truth, she had thought she was ready for it, but he had brought it to her and she wasn't. She had lost memories she'd never even had. There had been no decades of picnics and barbecues in Ed and Rina's cottage garden, nor happy family Christmases that she'd hoped the truth would wash ashore for her. Instead it had smashed into her skull like a tidal wave and dragged every sweet illusion far out to sea. And Linnet, whom her well-meaning brain had decided to ripen into a vibrant young woman and send to Australia to have adventures and fun, was merely a colorful, beautiful fantasy. All Sabrina had left of her now was that tiny baby with a perfect face and dark hair, whose eyes would never open, whose mouth would never form the word *Mama*, never stretch into her first smile.

She had never fully excised the grief; she had never gotten over the loss. And now she had lost her all over again and it was every bit as painful as the first time. Sabrina pushed her head into her pillow and cried silently and hard until sleep eventually took pity on her and pulled her into a deep, dreamless oblivion.

*   *   *

The next morning, Sabrina was awakened by a quiet tapping on her bedroom door. Then it slowly opened and Marielle appeared, holding a mug.

"You've slept for over sixteen hours," she said gently.

Sabrina threw back the covers and stood up so quickly that she staggered backward. "I'm so late," she said, attempting to stand again.

"I hope you don't mean that as late for work," said Marielle sternly. "There's no way you're even stepping outside today. You're to rest and that's final." She put the mug down on the bedside table. "And you're to drink this. And when you have, will you come through and I'll make you some breakfast?"

Sabrina felt slightly out of it, hungover without the headache; the coffee helped to right her. Her throat was dry from the long sleep. She put on her waffle dressing gown because she had no energy to think about what else to wear. Someone, Marielle she presumed, had emptied the bin liner and hung her clean clothes back up.

Crying had helped. She would cry again, she knew this, but what she had let go of the previous day had been sitting inside her for years, keeping the wounds open. She had hung on to it as if the pain was the only way to feel her loved ones close, and if she cried, if she emptied her soul of grief, they would sail away from her on her own tears. They were still there with her, though, part of her; while she held them in her heart, they would always be with her.

She knocked on Marielle's door, knowing she must look a proper sight, and when Marielle opened up and invited her in, she nearly died of embarrassment. The sitting room was full of the women who had ousted her so rudely the previous day.

"Please come and sit down. No one cares what you look like," said Marielle, catching her arm before she retreated. She knew how her friends had treated Sabrina. She knew they'd done it from a place of kindness to her, but still it hadn't been right. She wasn't as angry at them as she was at Cilla, though, because she was the one who had caused all this. She didn't want to think of what might have happened if they hadn't found Sabrina at the hospital, even though her mind kept wanting to take her down that road.

Sabrina sat crunched up, defensive, her arms wrapped round herself.

Sylvie spoke first. Sabrina remembered her from the fish-and-chip restaurant, but she hadn't been in the posse yesterday.

"I can't begin to tell you how sorry we are, Sabrina. In our defense we were protecting one of our own, but we got it very wrong."

"It's fine," said Sabrina. "Really. I understand."

"It's absolutely not fine," said Diana vehemently. "I was especially vile to you. I was so angry at you, and I'm now ten times angrier at myself. We handled it all wrong. We can't make up for it, but we thought you might like some flowers and chocolates—they're lovely, those, made by a French woman in town." She pointed to the table where there was a large wrapped bunch of mixed blooms and a rectangular gold carton sitting beside a very large square white box.

Bev spoke next. "We've always said flowers are sweeter when women give them to each other. Men too often buy them because they've been caught with their trousers down. Again." She sounded as if she spoke from experience and Sabrina smiled, just a little, but it was enough to break the ice.

"We are all really sorry," said Jackie. "I can't tell you how much."

"Can I get anyone a top-up?" asked Marielle.

"If it hadn't been so early, I'd have suggested gin," said Sylvie, cradling her mug.

Bev twisted her head to look at the clock on the wall. "Can't we nudge the hands forward?"

"You're honored, you know," said Sylvie to Sabrina. "Being allowed into the inner sanctum with the Mad Cows. Cilla's been trying to get in for years."

"Well, she's never getting in now," said Jackie. "I hope you're not going to let her get away with it, Marielle. It needs calling out. I mean, who does that? I can't get my head around it."

"We have cake as well," said Diana. "We didn't know what you'd like, so we brought coffee and walnut, chocolate, and Victoria sponge. Cake of apology tastes especially good."

"They all sound lovely," said Sabrina. "Thank you."

"As Cher said, if only we could turn back time," added Sylvie, "but we can't, and a Mad Cows collective and very genuine sorry from the bottom of our hearts is the best we can offer you."

"Can you forgive us?" asked Jackie.

"Of course," said Sabrina, and she felt the air in the room almost sigh with relief at her answer.

Then she broke bread, or rather cake, with the Mad Cows, and for that morning, at least, all was well with the world.

* * *

At work, Flick was quiet at best, morose at worst. She wouldn't cheer up.

"Go and see her," said Teddy, during their break.

"I daren't." Flick coughed a rasp out of her throat.

"Can I make you feel better?" said Teddy. "If you hadn't said anything, then this lie might never have been found out, so you did Sabrina the biggest favor, though it might not seem like it."

Flick let that sink in. "Do you think?"

"I know."

"Uncle Teddy, I can't believe my own mother could be so flipping evil."

"I think *evil* is pushing it a bit, Flick," even though he thought *evil* might be precisely the right word but didn't want Flick's relationship with her mother damaged any more than it was. This was a big blow to an already fractured connection.

"I thought some really horrible things about Sabrina. I hated her, and I was that far from telling her what I felt about her. I never would have been able to take back the words," said Flick, pressing her fingertips into the corners of her eyes to stop any tears in their tracks.

"But you didn't," said Teddy.

"I really like her," said Flick, her voice now taken over by sobs. "I think that's why I was so mad. She proper listened to me; she didn't just humor me. I loved talking to her and hearing about what she'd do with this place."

Teddy reached over for a paper serviette and handed it to his young cousin before she dissolved herself in salt water.

"Go and see her," he insisted.

* * *

Sabrina hadn't left Teddy's mind since they brought her home yesterday. He had replayed holding her so many times that had it been an old cassette tape, it would have snapped hours ago. She'd been in his world for only a few weeks, but he couldn't remember how they'd coped without her in the restaurant, and he couldn't put his finger on what she brought with her that changed the atmosphere. It was as if, when she was in here, someone had tweaked up the brightness levels. And he felt that effect inside himself too. She wasn't like the usual sort of women he went for who wrote all over his life with a shouty pen; she was a gentle murmur, not recognized until it stopped and then was missed in its absence. And he couldn't work out why her partner wasn't moving every rock and stone to find her, because that's exactly what he would have done—and he wouldn't have stopped until he had.

* * *

Marielle was just washing up the cake plates when Flick arrived at her door.

"Can I see Sabrina? I won't keep her long, Auntie Marielle." She'd been crying, that was clear.

"Go on through, love," said Marielle, taking herself off downstairs so they could speak alone.

"Hello, Flick," Sabrina said and smiled. She was sitting in the armchair in her waffle dressing gown. She looked pale but drained of more than color. *And I've done that to her,* was all she could think. Her practiced, measured apology disintegrated in her mouth. Flick lowered her head, ashamed to look at her. When she felt Sabrina's arms come around her, she pushed her face into the woman's neck and let herself be comforted.

"I'm so sorry," said Flick over and over.

"Darling, it's not your fault; it really isn't."

"Don't be nice to me; it's making me feel worse." Flick sobbed.

"You have nothing to feel bad about, Flick."

Sabrina had prayed to God to bring it on, to give her the truth, answers, shine light on all the mysteries, and now he had; boy, had he.

"Come and sit down." Sabrina pulled her onto the sofa and snapped a clutch of tissues out of the box on the coffee table for Flick.

"I've missed talking to you," said Flick eventually. "I really love our chats. I've been so upset. Please say you're coming back to work."

Flick was holding her hands. She was disgusted that it had been her mother who started all this. She'd almost smashed up a precious friendship by believing her, because despite the age difference, Flick really felt that Sabrina was her friend. "Please don't leave because of this."

"I think it's time that I find out where I belong," said Sabrina. There might be some less-than-ideal things to deal with, but there could be nothing worse than what she'd already found behind the wall in her head.

"Do that and then come back," said Flick. "You belong with us."

Sabrina stroked her hair. She did belong here, with these people. But she belonged somewhere else as well, and she couldn't just pretend she didn't. It would all be so much simpler if she had dropped out of a spaceship and her present place in the world was the only option she had.

The *Daily Trumpet* would like to point out an unfortunate error that appeared recently in our "Healthy Eating" weekend supplement, in which food specialist Don Attercliffe advised people to always wash their vag before it is eaten no matter how clean it looks. We did of course mean "veg."

Chapter 41

Chris was having a birthday tea out at the pub with his sister, brother-in-law, son, and daughter. He really thought Polly would have sent him a card; he would have put money on her using the occasion to ask if she could come over and either get her stuff or worm her way back into his life. He'd been gobsmacked to get only a letter addressed to her in the post, a bank statement, and some junk mail asking him if he'd thought about a cheap cremation, which made him feel great. He opened up Polly's letter, read it, and stuck it behind the clock on the mantelpiece with the other one that had come for her a couple of days ago.

Chris hated living by himself. He hated coming home from work and there being no presence in the house, warming it up in a way that central heating alone couldn't—and no smell of his tea brewing. The bed was too big, and it had taken him the best part of half an hour to put on the duvet cover last week. Nor did it smell of fabric conditioner, but of damp because he'd taken it out of the washer and dumped it on a work surface for days to dry. He was ready for letting Polly back in. He'd had a fling, well, one that she knew about, and she'd had one that he knew about, so that made it even steven. No one had the moral high ground anymore, so that would make it easier to shove under the carpet.

As if his daughter had picked up his thoughts, she asked him, "Have you heard from you-know-who?"

"Oh for goodness' sake, do we have to talk about her?" asked Camay. "You do know how to bring the mood down, Shauna."

It was hardly high to begin with, thought Will. His father was miserable; his auntie Camay was sniffy about the food because on the rare occasions that his father offered to pay, they wouldn't be going to a James Martin restaurant. Uncle Ward wasn't interested in contributing to any conversation either; he was just there to bulldoze his way through three courses and a bottle of house wine like a bloated locust.

Chris answered the question anyway in his best "don't care" tone. "No, I haven't."

"What have you done with all her things?" asked Ward, spitting gravy as he spoke.

"Nothing. They're all still in the room upstairs," Chris replied.

"I'd have made a big bonfire. Very cathartic," said Camay with a huff.

"She'll come back with her tail between her legs eventually," said Chris.

"Or someone else's," snorted Ward, causing Camay to jab him hard with her elbow.

"Surely you won't take her back?" Shauna was horrified at the thought.

"She'd have to have a brass neck to even try," said Camay, spearing a chip with a viciousness that suggested she was stabbing at something living.

She'd have to have a screw loose to even consider it, thought Will, although he didn't want to think that he wouldn't ever see Polly again. She'd always been so kind to him. He referred to her as his stepmum, though Shauna never did.

"Have you tried ringing her, Dad?"

"What do you take me for?" said Chris indignantly. "I think it's up to her to make the first move. She's hedging her bets because her post is still coming to the house; she hasn't redirected it. Today she got a letter from her 'creative writing' class"—he drew the quotation marks in the air—"asking if she was all right as she hadn't been recently."

"Crafty bitch," said Shauna with relish.

"Precisely," said her father.

"Crafty how?" asked Will, confused by that comment.

"Well, she never told me she was going to creative writing classes," Chris answered in a way that suggested Will must be a bit dense for not seeing it. "So what else was she lying about? I think we know the answer to that one. Ha." He nodded the full stop at the end of his sentence.

"Maybe," said Shauna, wagging her fork, "just maybe she got someone to write that letter to make Dad worry."

"Or she might have been attending creative writing classes and hadn't been for a while and so people genuinely *are* worried. How about that as an option, Columbo?" said Will crossly.

"Whose side are you on?" Shauna threw at him.

"Stop this now," commanded Camay, banging a teaspoon on the table. "This is exactly what she'd love—to be playing the starring role in our evening and ruining it. We might as well have set a ruddy place for her at the table. I for one hope she never comes back. She's playing games. She's screwing with our minds."

"By doing absolutely nothing?" said Will.

"Precisely," said his aunt Camay. "Now let's all have a toast. To Chris, who is today a forty-six-year-old eligible bachelor. Happy birthday, baby brother."

Will raised his glass but not with the same gusto as everyone else. For his own peace of mind, he needed to find out that Polly was all right. If she was and she wanted nothing to do with any of them, including himself, that would be her prerogative, but a cloud of worry was just now starting to drift into his peripheral vision.

When Will dropped his dad off after the miserable birthday party, he asked for Polly's mobile number. He rang it, but there was nothing, no dialing tone, no forwarding to voicemail, zilch.

"Well, she must have changed her number," was Chris's explanation.

"It's not proof she has, though," said Will, who felt now that he did need proof.

He asked to see the letters Polly had been sent and he took photos of them so he could do some detective work at home this weekend. He didn't say to his dad that he hoped he'd discover Polly was living her best life with a lover. There were a few alternative scenarios running through his head now, after reading those two letters, that he really didn't want to contemplate, and doing the dirty on his dad by running off with another man at least meant she was still alive.

A late-night search on the internet to find the creative writing group that Polly supposedly belonged to yielded nothing. There was no address, email, or telephone number on the letter, just a linocut-type stamp at the top of the A4 sheet of a quill and underneath it the words "Millspring Quillers." So he parked it until the morning.

The second letter Polly had received was from a company called Business Strength, telling her she was reinstated, which didn't make sense because Polly didn't work for them. She'd worked for the same company since she left college. Or had she? Polly just didn't seem the sort of person to have so much intrigue surrounding her. Will was half expecting to discover she was really an MI6 agent.

He shouldn't have waited this long to make sure she was okay. He was annoyed with himself that he'd accepted the "Occam's razor" easiest answer to where she was. But now, for a reason he couldn't explain other than it being intuition, he no longer believed it.

Chapter 42

Cilla had tried to reach out to her daughter after the row, but Flick had been adamant that she didn't want to hear from her until she'd apologized to both Marielle and Sabrina in person. She wouldn't shift on that, and she wouldn't pick up the phone to her mother after she'd delivered her terms. So, though it was with much reluctance, Cilla drove round to Marielle's house on Saturday morning to say what she had to to get out of the poop. Shoresend was a gossipy little enclave, and she really didn't want people talking about her behind her back in less-than-glowing terms. If they were going to discuss Cilla Charlesworth at all, she would rather it be in the context of her always having a balcony on a cruise and that her lover had been to Eton and owned a Rolls-Royce.

Sabrina was beyond curious to see Cilla in person, the woman who had done such a horrible thing for no valid reason. She was surprised to see how much she was the physical opposite of her daughter, short and compact with thick blonde hair perfectly arranged in soft lacquered curls, creamy pale skin, over-smooth forehead. Her facial features were like little circles: beady blue eyes, a pudgy nose, a cat's bum of a mouth painted dark pink.

Cilla was every bit as curious over this Sabrina person who was the reason she was here, brought to heel, so she wasn't predisposed to be her greatest fan. After all this fuss, she expected to see something more impactful than just a plain woman with brown hair. Her daughter had painted her as some sort of marvelous, kind, and clever paragon, plus other nice words that her daughter never seemed to apply to her—the mother who had carried her for nine long months, not to mention the agony of spitting her out at the end of them. Cilla prepared to deal with this as quickly as possible so she could get on with her life.

For the first time ever, Cilla noted Marielle hadn't asked her if she wanted a cuppa when she entered the house. She was standing up, arms folded; she hadn't even invited her to sit.

"Go on, you can say it to Sabrina first and me afterward."

Cilla took in a breath and then let it go. *And begin.*

"I am really sorry for insinuating that you were to blame for the purse. Please accept my deepest apologies." She nodded at Sabrina, signaling the end of part one, and then turned to Marielle.

"Marielle, I am really—"

"Whoa, hang on there, lady," said Marielle, holding up the flat of her palm. "If you're supposing that it's done with, you have another think coming."

"Well, what else do you want me to say?" asked Cilla with a trill of laughter. "Come on, under the circumstances, you do have to accept that I might have been justified in—"

Marielle cut her off. "There is no justification for stealing from someone in order to cast blame onto someone else. It's just . . . wicked."

"I beg to differ," countered Cilla. "As we have already said in past conversations, you are not the most reliable in terms of character assessment. I could see it coming—again—and I was trying to protect you from further hurt."

Marielle moved her head slowly from side to side. No, she wasn't buying it, however clever Cilla might think herself. Her cousin was an expert at stain removal, and she was prepared for this sort of verbal tripe.

"How could you protect me from hurt by being the one hurting me?"

"Because... I thought a small hurt would save you from a big hurt." Cilla smiled in the manner of someone who thought she'd delivered a cracking answer there.

It wasn't the first time Sabrina had come up against someone like this, someone who dressed up bullshit in a gift box. She thought it could be someone she worked with because she had a flash vision of a man sitting in a large swivel chair, long fingers pressed together, telling her something in an oh-so-genuine tone that she knew was utter garbage. *Dick* came to mind, but she wasn't sure if that was a name or a description. Sabrina had the measure of Cilla, but she could also recognize that it would have taken a lot to come here and face her, and this shambles of an apology was probably all she had in her to offer. It would do. She butted into the increasingly heated exchange between the cousins in a voice that brooked no argument and said, "I accept your apology, Cilla. Now I'm going to leave you both to talk."

As she closed the adjoining door between Big Moon and Little Moon, she could hear Cilla saying, "I don't know why you're looking at me like that. If she's accepted my apology, what's your problem?"

Sabrina's hackles rose at being referred to as "she" in such a disparaging tone. She had meant to put on the television to give them privacy, but the desire to listen was too strong, and under the circumstances, she allowed herself to eavesdrop. She didn't trust Cilla not to say something she'd later retract, and she wanted to be able to back up Marielle if needs be.

"I'll tell you what my problem is, Cilla," Marielle replied. "You might try and convince yourself that your motives were wholly altruistic, but you haven't convinced me."

"Marielle, I can't convince you if you are set against being convinced, but I can assure you I only had your best interests at heart."

"Swear it," Marielle demanded then.

"I will not. It's using God's name for trivial purposes and that's blasphemy. I never swear, as you well know."

Marielle dropped a sarcastic laugh. "Nice swerve. Why did you really do it? Come on, while it's just us two in the room. Tell me the truth and I'll let it go and never mention it again. Were you jealous that your daughter and Sabrina get on so well? Or maybe it's me you have a bee in your bonnet about and that's why you wanted to wreck my friendship with her. Why would you want to try and make me look stupid? This goes back way further than the thing about the purse, and I've had enough of it, Cilla. What has been your problem with me for all these years? Because I've never been able to work it out."

It was Cilla's turn to laugh now. "You think I might be jealous of some woman who cleans for a living and is running rings around you all? Er, no. And if you're trying to insinuate that I'm jealous of you, then you need to have a word with yourself, Mari. What have you got that I could possibly want? You're the jealous one. You resented me from day one and you still do," spat Cilla.

"I did not," refuted Marielle. "I was never nasty to you. I really tried to make you my little sister."

"You hated sharing anything. I remember your screwed-up sullen face when Mum and Dad said you had to let me play with your toys."

"I was an only child when you came into our lives. I'd never had to share before, but I learned," Marielle threw back.

"You did that, all right," Cilla scoffed. "You had to learn to share your husband with God knows how many other women, didn't you?"

"Why are you so bloody bitter?" cried Marielle, wounded now. "No wonder none of my friends want anything to do with you and why my own son tells me to stay away from you because you're poison."

"His father didn't stay away from me, though. Quite the opposite." As Cilla's words died, a terrible charged silence rushed into the space they left.

"What do you mean?" gasped Marielle.

"What do you think it means? You want truth, the whole truth, and nothing but the truth, well, here you go then: Felicity is Salvatore's daughter. There you have it. So now you can deal with it."

By the time Sabrina had opened the adjoining door, Cilla had gone, stormed out most likely, leaving Marielle obliterated.

"I heard all that," Sabrina said, putting her arms around her friend. Marielle was stiff, unresponsive, as if she was frightened to untense herself in case she crumbled to nothing. "I can't believe she said that to you. It's lies, Marielle; she's just saying things to hurt you."

"No, she isn't," replied Marielle, her voice as broken as the rest of her. "I think I've always known."

The *Daily Trumpet* would like to apologize to Mr. George Staley and Mrs. Yvonne Staley for the unfortunate wording "George and dragon" that appeared under a photo of them standing outside their newly refurbished pub last week. We in no way intended to insinuate that Mrs. Staley was a dragon. The wording should have read, "George and Dragon standing outside their newly refurbished George and Dragon pub, Skipton, North Yorkshire."

Chapter 43

Will didn't expect anyone to be working at Northern Eagles over the weekend, but it was worth a try. He needed to hear Polly's voice, even if it was just to say, *"Shove off, leave me alone, I'm happy."* But when he rang the number he found on the net, the woman who picked up the call said, "Business Strength, how can I help you?"

That threw him. "Is this not Northern Eagles?"

"It was, but the name changed recently. Number's the same, though," she explained.

"Ah, I see. I don't suppose I can speak to Polly Potter, please?"

"I'm afraid Polly no longer works for the company."

Will went cold. "Since when?"

"A few weeks, I think."

"Are you sure?" said Will.

"Absolutely sure. I know Polly."

"Do you happen to know where she moved to?" asked Will. This was really starting to get worrying now.

"I'm afraid I don't know."

"Did you say you were called Business Strength?"

"That's right."

"Okay, thank you."

Will put down the phone. That was the name on the other letter Polly had received. The one that said there had been some sort of misunderstanding at work and Polly was to be fully reinstated with immediate effect. So she hadn't changed jobs after all, then, not that that particular revelation helped in any way to solve what the hell was going on. The Millspring Quillers weren't easy to locate either. He rang Millspring village hall as a first port of call, but they'd never heard of them and told him to try the Bees 'n' Cheese Tea Room on the high street as they rented out their room above to some sort of literary club. It turned out to be a dead end as they'd only ever let it out to "Crochet with Caroline," but the woman there told him to try the vicar at St. John's because all sorts of groups met in the church hall. He wasn't in, so Will left a message on the answering machine. And another two hours later, when he'd heard nothing.

Not long after, the vicar's wife rang back to tell him that the Quillers did indeed meet in the church hall and she gave him the number of Jennifer, who ran the classes. She picked up straightaway when he called, which was lucky because he was really starting to get twitchy.

"Hi," said Will. "I'm ringing up about a letter you sent to my stepmum, Polly Potter."

"Oh, Polly, yes. Is she all right?" Jennifer said. "I've been a bit worried about her. I wouldn't usually chase because we get a lot of people dropping in and out, but Polly never missed a class, and then she suddenly just stopped coming."

"Well . . ." Will hadn't a clue how to dress this up and so decided to just come straight out with it. "The thing is . . . we don't know where she is and we're trying to trace her." He cringed at how it came across.

"Oh, I see," said Jennifer, sounding as if she didn't see at all. "I'm so sorry to hear that. You don't think . . . I mean . . . Is she . . . ? I'm sorry, I don't really know what to say."

They needed to start seriously looking for Polly, thought Will now. Too much evidence was banking up that something was wrong. She was a bona fide missing person. He shuddered at the thought.

"Such a lovely woman. And quite a talent as well. She brought in a lovely poem about a cat . . ."

Jennifer was nervous-twittering now. Telling Will about a book Polly was writing and the short story about her uncle and aunt who'd died when she was young that had people crying in the class when she read it out; and the love letter; and the limerick about her boss at work that made them all laugh. "Oh my goodness, will you let me know if you hear anything?" said Jennifer in a very wobbly voice.

"Of course—" *Hang on.* "Jennifer, what was that you said about a love letter?"

"I . . . er . . . set the class a fun challenge round about Valentine's Day to pen a love letter to someone they were having an affair with. I told them to put aside all their values and morals and let rip. You'd be surprised how liberating it can be when you're given permission to loosen your literary corset, as it were. We had some very steamy pieces; I was quite surprised at a few of my writers—they could have given E. L. James a run for her money. Polly's was more romantic than smutty, though. I told Polly she could have been one of the Brontë sisters with her turn of phrase. It's always amazed me how someone with so little passion in their life could write such fervent prose."

Will didn't know if she meant the Brontës or Polly.

"How long was she coming to your classes?"

"About a year, I think. Yes, that's right. She started last June."

Will's brain was spinning. "You don't happen to have any copies of things she wrote, do you?"

"Yes, I have."

"Could I see any of them?"

Jennifer wasn't keen. "I'd be contravening group rules by doing that."

"Please," said Will, surprising himself by how desperate he sounded. "We're going to have to involve the police, and the more information I've got, the better. I'm clutching at straws, I know, but there just might be something she wrote down that might help us find her."

Jennifer sighed at the other end of the line, and Will could tell she didn't know what to do for the best.

"Okay," she relented eventually. "If you think it might help." Will dictated his email address to her. Jennifer said she'd do it straightaway, and she was as good as her word.

Will opened up the first file: "Love Letter—Polly."

> My darling, I cannot live a lie any longer. I have to come to you before my soul fades away and I am nothing. I am yours and yours only. You are the breath in my lungs, the blood in my veins . . .

He recognized it immediately. He remembered his sister reading it out with relish to a horrified but enthralled crowd on the day of the wedding.

It was nothing more than a bloody writing exercise.

Will rang his father to ask if he was in. He wasn't, but he would be in about an hour. Will said he'd meet him at the house and he'd explain why he needed to speak to him urgently when he got there. In the meantime, he read the other files that Jennifer had sent through, Polly's stories and poems. He remembered her telling him about the neighbor's ginger cat whom she used to let into the house when her mum was at bingo and she'd feed him cheese and cuddle up to him on the sofa. And her aunt and uncle who were going to adopt her and take her to Australia, but they died. Polly had a rotten early life. The synopsis of her novel told Will a lot. He was very moved to read that she'd reimagined that the child she'd had when she was only seventeen was alive and traveling. Polly would have made a smashing mum, and reading this, it sounded as if there was an emptiness inside her that still wanted to be filled with a baby of her own. The Sabrina character was obviously based on herself, and it wasn't hard to see where dubious Jasper had his origins. No wonder Sabrina was leaving him.

Chris had the good grace to look uncomfortable as he listened to his son's findings. Will had also been upstairs to where Polly's things were stored and found a folder with the physical copies of the writings which Jennifer had sent him by email.

"Shauna didn't say that she'd found that love letter in with all this other stuff from Polly's classes," said Will, who was furious at his sister, and he'd tell her so. "It would have cast a totally different light on everything if she had and put it in context. She deliberately kept that quiet to shit-stir."

"But even if that letter isn't real, we still don't know that Polly's not with a fancy man, do we? Why was all her stuff packed up if she wasn't going to someone else? She wouldn't have just left me for . . . no one. That doesn't make any sense."

Will rubbed his forehead in frustration because they were going around in circles.

"You do know people can leave their partners without going to someone else, especially if they're really unhappy, Dad."

"Rarely, though," said Chris, who couldn't think why anyone would leap to another lily pad unless there was another frog waiting on it. He was sitting at the table flicking through Polly's papers.

"Who's this Jasper bloke?" Chris asked suspiciously.

"He's a made-up character. Sort of," said Will, wanting to bang his head against the wall. His dad was reading more or less about himself and still couldn't see it.

"I don't understand why she'd want to keep a writing course secret from me," said Chris. "Why on earth would she do that?"

"Maybe she didn't think you'd be interested."

"Well, I probably wouldn't be, but that's no reason not to say anything."

"I think we should go to the police."

Chris rounded on him. "Don't be so bloody silly, Will."

"Dad, this is serious." Chris had watched enough detective programs to know that the police always looked first of all to "home" for the perpetrator. Even though he was totally innocent, they'd investigate him as a person of interest. They'd take his computer away and see he'd made quite a few visits to "naughtysluttyladies.com." He went cold at the thought of a roomful of coppers laughing at that before they started digging up his garden.

"They might frame me for murder."

"Have you murdered her?"

"Don't be so bloody silly, Will," Chris said again, with even more emphasis this time.

"Then you've nothing to worry about."

"Anyway, the police these days are too busy fannying about dancing at festivals wearing rainbows."

"I wouldn't go into a police station saying that, Dad," replied Will.

"If we go to the police, they'll do one of those TV appeals and all hell will break loose. They'll film me and if I don't cry everyone will think I know more than I let on, or if my eyebrow moves in the wrong way, or . . . or I put my arms in the wrong place or I say the wrong word. There's a load of armchair detective nutters out there who will presume I've done her in and come for me. They'll spread a load of lies and wreck my business. They'll paint 'Murderer' on the front door in red paint. I'll be made into one of those memes." Chris was getting himself into a proper state now.

"I don't think—"

But Chris was still in a loop. "And it won't just be me who suffers, because the national papers will get hold of it and rake up the whole of Polly's life and splash it on the front page of the *Daily Mail*. If all she's doing is lying low—and I'll put money on it that she is—then something like that could push her right over the edge."

Will threw up his hands. "Okay then, what's your alternative?"

"I'll email the *Daily Trumpet* and put an advert on their lost and found page for the next issue."

Will blinked. "Are you joking? That's for things like wallets and Labradors. And, Dad, come on, really—the *Trumpet*?"

"They've got a massive circulation and everyone reads it. It's worth a shot."

Will thought about it and then nodded. "Okay, like you say, worth a shot."

It was too, but one of Will's old college pals was in the police and he'd ring her for some advice at the same time. Best-case scenario was that Polly saw the *Trumpet* entry and rang to tell them she was absolutely fine and not to worry. Worst case . . . he really didn't want to think about that.

Chapter 44

Teddy was both gobsmacked and overjoyed to see Sabrina walk into his restaurant on Sunday.

"This place won't clean itself," she said, snapping on her rubber gloves, but she wasn't there because she had a compulsion to clean. She knew change was on the horizon and it scared her stupid, and she would rather be busy than sitting "resting." She didn't want to rest, she didn't want to think, she wanted to *do*. More memories had popped into her mind, their flow increasing since she'd met the scarecrow man. She now remembered that she'd had a large executive desk in an office before it was removed and replaced by one of the ordinary gray ones. She remembered playing some sort of tennis game over the divide with the young woman she sat next to at work, who had dark curly hair and eyes full of mischief. There was a young man somewhere in her life who brought the same sort of warm wave with him, her partner's son, she thought—not her husband's; she knew she wasn't married. And she could see herself loading many, many shoes into bags and feeling an all-consuming rush of anger as she did so. So many small memories with no weight attached had sharpened to full HD color, yet too many big, important ones remained shadowy. The man she had left either temporarily or permanently, for instance; he was there in her head without distinction or definition, and she wasn't sure if she was blocking him unconsciously or deliberately.

Teddy was humming absently as he was food-prepping in the kitchen. He sounded content, without a clue of what was about to fall on him. He didn't know that the previous day Cilla had dropped an A-bomb on his mother's life, how much she'd cried on Sabrina's shoulder that the happy last years she'd spent back in England with Sal had turned out to be a lie, the biggest deception her husband had ever performed. Sylvie was up at the house with her at the moment, talking it through as friends do, helping her to put it in order in her head so she could tell her son that Flick was his half sister, because he had every right to know. God knows how Flick would take it. The onus had been unfairly put on Marielle to make the call whether to share or keep the secret, but once known, it was too big to fit back in the box. Sabrina wondered if it ever would have come to light had she not been there. She didn't want to be the catalyst for something as cruel as that. Why, after giving out so much kindness, did Marielle have to be the one to get kicked in the teeth?

At half past twelve Teddy bobbed his head into the ladies' loo and said, "I've made lunch." And she walked out to find that one of the tables for two had been set for them, rather than the big table where they usually ate. Cannelloni, breads, butter. Simple, thoughtful; she could tell he'd set everything precisely, had arranged the food on the plate the same way, with care.

"Your mum has put a notice about me in tomorrow's paper," said Sabrina to him as he handed over the dish of freshly grated Parmesan. "I don't exactly have a lot of details to give out, but it's a start."

He nodded slowly. "And if no one responds, what will you do then?"

"The police, I suppose. I don't know what made me initially think I might be in danger, but I'm ninety-nine point nine percent sure I'm not."

"Maybe it was your mind forcing you to take time out from whatever it was you left," said Teddy.

"They're odd, aren't they, minds?" said Sabrina. "Hiding things, distorting facts, telling you lies."

"It sounds to me as if you've maybe had a lot in your life that you never really worked through, Sabrina. Your mother, your aunt and uncle, your baby. They might have been a long time ago, but if you never had help to heal, they've just sat inside you like unexploded bombs and . . . they eventually went off."

What he said made sense. Maybe she needed to go back so much further than what had happened to her in the past two months, disassemble herself, restructure, like some of the companies she'd helped along the way. She remembered a sports shop on the brink of collapse. She'd had to strip it down to its basics, excise the rot rather than patch it up, pretending it wasn't there like they'd done in the past, only to fail. But they'd succeeded when they'd rebuilt from the ground up.

From the ground up. Why did those four words make her think of happy Monday evenings spent with like-minded people in a fusty church hall?

"You don't have to go back," said Teddy. "You're welcome to stay as long as you like . . . want . . . need to."

"Thank you." She smiled. She felt that, but she had to find out everything about herself. She needed to be the full finished jigsaw with the picture complete.

Teddy dropped his fork. "I'm putting this all wrong. Of course you have to go back. You have family, possessions, money, friends, your job to reconnect with. But you don't have to stay there if you find you aren't the right shape for that life anymore, Sabrina, because . . ." He couldn't say it: *You are the right shape for us. For me.* It wasn't fair to put that pressure on her. How could she tell what she wanted until she was back where she belonged and in a more informed position to choose? "You know what I mean," he said instead.

"I do," she said. She half felt as if she were on holiday, and the thought of going home brought with it the sort of depression that comes with the prospect of returning to a mundane, lesser existence.

But people did go home, and they settled back in their places, because that's what life was like.

That's why people loved *Shirley Valentine* so much, because Shirley lived the dream, but it was just a fantasy, a story.

"Your mum asked if you'd call in on your way home," said Sabrina then, careful to sound as matter-of-fact as possible, as Marielle had asked her to.

"What for, did she say?"

"Nope, she just asked me to pass on the message."

This lovely man had secrets ready to jump out at him from behind a corner too, and she so wished he didn't.

"Of course," he said, breaking into some bread. Would this be the last Sunday they spent together like this? Her being here had awakened him inside, and he wondered if that had been fate's purpose in bringing her into his life. That and giving him some great advice on the best way for his business to survive when Ciaoissimo opened. Maybe that was all he was meant to have of her, just a small but precious and transient gift.

"This is delicious," said Sabrina, eating the last of the cannelloni.

"I know," said Teddy, "because I made it."

He smiled, a deep curve that made something inside her warm, and she wondered if she had been led here to realize that she should be cared for, that she was worth a man's consideration, and that, if she didn't make someone smile like that, they weren't the one for her. She knew, without a doubt, that if Teddy Bonetti had been in the other life she had left, her brain wouldn't have been able to forget him.

* * *

When Sabrina left the restaurant after her shift, she turned down the lift home with Teddy, saying she wanted to take a walk, but instead of going down to the beach, she headed up the hill to the estate where

Cilla lived. She didn't know the address, but she had picked up from Flick that her mother had one of the largest houses and a pretentious porch with sturdy Greek pillars, lording it above all the others. It wasn't hard to find.

Sabrina walked up the drive, past the showy BMW parked there. She hadn't been told what car Cilla owned, but strangely she had guessed that was what she'd have. She rang the bell and waited. Eventually a clipped voice came through the doorbell speaker.

"What do you want?"

"Can I talk to you, Cilla?" replied Sabrina.

"I have nothing to say to you."

"I'll take up five minutes of your time only, but it will be the most important conversation you'll ever have in your life," said Sabrina. She was prepared to wait here for as long as it took to wear Cilla down into speaking to her. If her presence here was in any way responsible for all this upset, she would do her best to limit some of the damage before she left.

Surprisingly, she didn't have to lay siege to Cilla's house, because the door opened and Cilla appeared. She was fully made up, but the thick layer of foundation couldn't disguise her swollen eyes with the puffy bags underneath. She moved aside so that Sabrina could come in, but it was clear that whatever Sabrina had to say to her had to be done standing up in the hallway.

"Well?" she asked.

"I'm here to talk about Flick," said Sabrina.

Cilla dropped a disbelieving laugh. "How is she any of your business?"

"You're right, she isn't, but I've really come to care about her. You are so lucky, Cilla. She's a gorgeous girl—bright, ambitious—"

Cilla cut her off. "I know what she is because she's my daughter. My daughter. Do you have a daughter?"

"No, but—"

"Then why are you about to tell me how to treat mine, because I can smell that's what you're itching to do and I'm not—"

"My daughter died, Cilla." Sabrina's turn to do the cutting off. Cilla's mouth snapped shut, and when she opened it again to speak, her voice had dropped considerably in volume.

"I'm sorry to hear that," she said, her tone still stiff, still not conceding anything.

"I imagined my daughter would turn out just like Flick. Confident and ready to take on the world." Sabrina smiled, thinking of her beautiful dark-haired Linnet working her way around Australia. She had felt so real, so *vital*, but she was just a figment of a desperately sad imagination that couldn't let her go. "My own mother put everything before me—men, booze, money—and eventually it killed any affection I had for her, because there's no automatic right to love, Cilla, just because you're related to someone. I know my memory is a little skew-whiff at the moment, but when I think of my mother, there is no doubt in my mind that her place was taken by the aunt who was going to adopt me, and I feel nothing for the woman who gave birth to me other than resentment and disappointment and sadness. I'm here as a cautionary tale, Cilla. You are losing Flick; eventually the love she has for you will erode past the point of no return. I would give anything to have a relationship with a daughter. I'm beyond jealous of what you have, and I can't stand by and see you throwing it away."

"I love my daughter," said Cilla through clenched teeth.

"Then show her. Respect her as the grown woman she is, be there for her, tell her you're proud of her, tell her you love her, because all she gets from you are petty criticisms and put-downs, and she sees how much more important men and money are in your life than she is, and trust me, I can tell you how deeply that wounds. You've caused a lot of damage, Cilla, and you are going to end up miserable and alone if you don't put this right. This might well be your last chance to save your relationship with your daughter; don't throw it away."

"Well, thank you for the lecture," said Cilla after a few seconds of silence. But it was bravado, because Sabrina knew that she'd listened, and that was all she wanted, for Cilla to see what she had to lose. She could do no more. She turned, opened the door, and left.

* * *

Sabrina called in at a café on the way home so that Marielle and Teddy had time alone without her arrival interrupting anything. He'd gone by the time she reached the flat. She knocked softly on the adjoining door to check up on Marielle, who invited her through. She looked stronger than Sabrina had expected to find her.

"How did he take it?" asked Sabrina, putting on the kettle.

"I don't think he knew what to think. He was upset for me, he was angry at his father, I had to make him promise not to storm over to Cilla's house because I know my boy, and though he has a lot more control over himself than his father obviously had, he has a very pronounced sense of right and wrong. And he's worried about how Flick will take it because she'll have to know." Marielle pressed on her temples with her fingertips. "What a mess. Halfway through telling him, Sabrina, I wondered if I was doing the right thing. Did he even need to know? I could have saved him the pain just by keeping it to myself. We should have done a paternity test first. Bev's daughter works in a lab and she says if we do one, she'll fast-track the results."

Marielle was getting herself properly wound up. Sabrina abandoned any tea-making to sit with her.

"None of this is your fault, Marielle. Yes, you did the right thing. You shouldn't have to carry all this alone."

"Cilla's husband was pale and fair and slight. I could never understand how two people like them could have produced Flick. She was the tallest girl in her class, the darkest skinned. Cilla used to say she was a throwback, but it crossed my mind more than once about her and Sal because he did like a pretty blonde, and I felt guilty that it had, can you believe?" She laughed and a few tears escaped from her eyes at the same time.

There was a knock at the front door and they heard someone come in straight after.

"I bet that's Teddy," said Marielle. "He went off to clear his head. I knew he'd be back."

But it wasn't. The lounge door opened and in walked Cilla.

Chapter 45

"Anything you have to say to me, you can say it in front of Sabrina," said Marielle when Cilla had asked if she could have a word in private. "But I'm not sure I want to hear it." Cilla didn't protest, though Marielle wouldn't have stood for it if she had.

"I didn't want to come empty-handed, but it's Sunday and there was no place still open to buy flowers," said Cilla.

"Cilla, if you'd brought me flowers, I would have rammed them where the sun doesn't shine," replied Marielle coldly. "Now what do you want?"

"You don't know how sorry I am for what I told you," said Cilla.

"I won't ask you to swear that on the Bible."

On cue, Cilla reached into her handbag and took out a small Bible, which she put on the dining room table.

"Anything you wish me to swear to, I will." She took in a breath as if to strengthen herself. "You might be glad to know that you were right. About Hugo."

She told them that when she'd been putting everything back in the drawer that Flick had turned out, she noticed that her checkbook had a couple of stubs in it without checks attached. She couldn't remember the last time she'd used it—who used checks much these days?—but she certainly wouldn't have torn checks from the back before using the next one in line.

"I rang the bank. The checks were made out to some woman. I hadn't even noticed. Six thousand pounds. I should do my banking more often, shouldn't I?"

Marielle remained impassive.

"Other things had gone missing too, when I looked around. I didn't want to believe it. I'm not trying to use any of this to excuse myself, but I thought I'd tell you anyway. The police came to arrest him this morning. He hadn't a clue it was coming. Quite the floor show for the neighbors."

Hence the swollen eyes, thought Sabrina, but no, what had been going on in Cilla's life over the past days wasn't an excuse for what she'd thrown at Marielle yesterday.

Cilla left a silence, maybe for an entirely justified "I told you so," a gloat, a laugh of ridicule, but Marielle was above that. She just let the silence linger until Cilla was ready to break it. "What happened was all my fault, and I promise you, it just happened the one time. Roy was having a fling with a barmaid. I was upset, I cried on Sal's shoulder, one thing led to another. Both of us were disgusted with ourselves afterward. And yes, it was as base and vulgar as it sounds. I was ashamed because I'd committed adultery, I'd lost my moral high ground, but Sal was completely beside himself at what he'd done. I know you had a new start when you left Italy, and he felt he'd smashed it up. He told me how much he loved you and begged me not to say anything. I swore to him that I'd never hold it over him, he had nothing to worry about. Felicity couldn't have been anyone else's, but I said she was Roy's and he wasn't around to disprove it, seeing as he died not even knowing I was pregnant. Sal once asked me outright if Felicity was his and I lied and told him absolutely not. He loved her because she was family, but he never knew she was his daughter."

Cilla placed her hand flat on her Bible then and said, "I swear that everything I've told you is the absolute truth. I haven't dressed it up, I haven't taken anything away. That's how it happened and I could not be more sorry. I'm sure that if a psychiatrist had a good look in my head, they'd find some very errant wiring in there. I've always wanted to be better than everyone else, but as you can see, I've never managed it." Cilla was crying, real tears. Marielle knew they were genuine because they were just rolling out of her eyes; she wasn't drawing attention to them, hiccupping sobs, artfully dabbing her cheeks. She picked up the Bible, put it in her handbag, and took out a folded tissue.

"I'm going to tell Felicity now. I wish I didn't have to."

"It's her truth to know," said Marielle.

"As if she doesn't hate me enough."

"She doesn't hate you, you silly woman," said Marielle. "But make yourself a little bit easier for her to love. You have to try before it's too late."

Cilla nodded and then put the tissue down on the table. "I said I didn't want to come empty-handed. These aren't mine. I never should have had them. I'm sorry."

She walked out before Marielle had the chance to get up and see what she'd left. Inside the tissue were Marielle's mother's engagement and wedding rings.

Chapter 46

LOST AND FOUND

If anyone knows the whereabouts of Polly Pocket, last seen Saturday March 20, of Penistown Barnsley, S Yorkshire. Contact Christ Barrett. LF28

Found in Lower Poppleton wood, Thursday 29 June, large blue parrot, yellow detail around eyes. Friendly, affectionate, says a lot of swear words. Being presently cared for by person with lots of parrot experience but owner must be worried. LF29

Lost tabby cat, Brightside, Sheffield. No teeth, has limp, only one eye (left), right ear half-missing, tail broken at end. Answers to the name Lucky. LF30

Lost, Wednesday 28 June, blue parrot, yellow around eyes, Lower Poppleton, York. Very friendly and dearly missed. Large reward for return. Please contact Reverend Robert Marlow, Church of St Francis, Lower Poppleton. LF31

Looking to find the family and friends of Sinitta Hanson who has been in Shoresend/Slattercove since mid-May. Please contact Mrs. Marielle Bonetti. LF32

Chapter 47

There was a weird vibe at work the next morning when Sabrina arrived with her copy of the *Daily Trumpet* to check the entry. Teddy was on the phone to them when she walked in, shouting at someone down the phone about getting something so important so wrong. It didn't sound like him, and she knew he was stressed. And Flick was playing at being normal. She smiled as she said good morning, but something about her was off.

"Have you seen the lost and found page?" she asked.

"Not yet," replied Sabrina.

"I wouldn't get your hopes up. They've really cocked it up. Unless you're a parrot—then you've got a great chance of being reunited with your family."

"*Goodbye.*" Teddy ended his call and let rip a string of Italian words that might have given the foul-mouthed parrot a run for its money. "They're running a corrected piece on Wednesday, if they have the room. They'd better have the room." He looked enraged, but as he passed Flick, he squeezed her shoulder tenderly. Sabrina read from the gesture that they'd spoken, that they knew they were more closely related than they thought they were.

"We get to keep you for a bit longer," said Flick. She smiled, but Teddy's touch of affection had weakened her frail composure and she strutted off in the direction of the office before emotion overtook her.

Sabrina wasn't sure if she was supposed to know or not, so she kept her head down, scrubbed, mopped, and wiped. Then just after Niccolo and Roberto arrived for their shift, Teddy left the kitchen, stood in the middle of the restaurant, and clapped his hands.

"Everybody, come in here, I have an announcement to make. Come on, all of you. Sit down." George and Antonio wandered through; Sabrina sat, as did the waiters. Teddy stood behind Flick, his hands on her shoulders.

"I wanted to wait until you were all here. Yesterday I found out that Flick is my sister. There, that's it. Announcement over."

There followed a stunned silence. Niccolo broke it, speaking in Italian, and Teddy replied to him in Italian.

"If you're going to talk about me, can you at least do it so I can understand it?" said Flick impatiently.

"I'm sorry," said Teddy. "He asked me how and I said that I think he could guess without all the graphic details."

"Oh my God," said Roberto, clamping his hand over his mouth. "That means I am also directly related to you now, Flick. As if my life couldn't get any worse."

"*Cristo*," said his brother, equally horrified. Then both of them and Flick exploded into laughter. They'd handled it perfectly, lightly in a way that Teddy couldn't have, because he was too close, his loyalties and emotions tangled. George and Antonio gave her a hug—and playful commiserations—and the tension that had been weighing down the air all morning was gone. At least where that was concerned. Teddy, once again, had to go out and remonstrate with builders who had parked up on their private land to work on the property earmarked to be the new Ciaoissimo.

Flick came into the ladies' loo when Sabrina was mopping the floors in there after the lunch customers had left.

"You'll be back working at your desk soon and cleaning our bogs will be a distant memory," she said, leaning against the sink and smiling, but it was a sad sort of smile. When Sabrina looked up at her, she thought that she seemed to look even more like Teddy Bonetti since the news broke.

"Vital job, Flick. Do you know how important it is to have spotless toilets in restaurants?" Sabrina said. "People seem to equate the state of the loos with the state of the kitchen. Also, restaurants are very much judged on their dessert offerings too. Women especially turn to the puddings on the menu before they ever look at the mains."

"Oh my God, I do that," said Flick. "If there's no cheesecake on there, I just want to leave." She laughed but then became suddenly serious, and Sabrina knew that she hadn't come into the toilets to talk trivia.

"Did my auntie Marielle tell you what my mum did?" she asked.

"Well, it wasn't just your mum, was it?" replied Sabrina. It wasn't fair that Cilla should take the entire blame. "How do you feel about it all?"

Flick tilted her head one way, then the other, as if that would help her answer.

"I don't know; it keeps changing. I never knew my dad . . . well, the dad I thought I had. He didn't have any relatives, so I didn't grow up with any of his family in my life; I only ever knew Mum's side. Teddy said that his dad really loved me, which is nice, isn't it? I suppose I'm expecting to feel different, but I don't."

"You haven't suddenly changed through this news, Flick. You are who you have always been."

"I don't know what I feel about my mother, though. How could she have done that to someone she thought of as a sister? But then, she didn't try and excuse it. She didn't do her usual trick of trying to blame it on anything or anyone else, which was really weird."

"Give yourself time to unknot your feelings, Flick." Sabrina snapped off some toilet roll and handed it over because Flick was sniffing.

"Hugo's gone. She had him arrested."

"I heard," said Sabrina.

Flick blew her nose loudly, then said, "I don't think I'll ever trust a man."

"Yes, you will, one day, when you find someone worth trusting," Sabrina replied, though she couldn't say for sure if she'd ever found that person for herself.

"Sabrina, will you stay in touch with me when you go?" asked Flick then. Her voice was so wobbly that Sabrina dumped the mop in her bucket and went over to her, giving her a hug, and just for a minute, she let herself believe that this was what hugging Linnet would have been like. This was how a daughter felt in a mother's arms. Cilla was a fool to have this and not recognize how special a relationship it was.

"Of course. I promise. I'd like to know how you're doing at university." Flick's hair smelled of apples. Linnet would have used a similar shampoo, something fresh and clean. Sabrina pushed her out to arm's length before the scent pierced her tear ducts.

"Both of us have to leave our comfort zones and that's going to be a bit scary, Flick. But it's for the best."

For Flick, Sabrina knew that for certain. She would excel at uni; she would thrive and grow. For herself, stepping back into her other existence was a necessity she couldn't avoid. And only time would tell if it was for the best or not.

* * *

Orrible was in the best of moods. Even the fact that he'd been summoned to Billy the Donk's house could not dampen his spirits, because he was definitely in for brownie points. In the past four days he had delivered a top-of-the-range, brand-new Range Rover Sport SVR to Shifty Smith's garage in Middlesbrough and had become an engaged person. Okay, he'd become a bit giddy after finding that the handbag of dreams contained some nice bits of gold jewelry and a wad of money in the purse. He wasn't usually a gambling man, but after seeing that a horse called

Handbags at Dawn was running in the two thirty at York, he'd flung a ton on it and it had come in at fifty to one. He'd had too much celebratory *herb* and then proposed to his girlfriend Tina, but he hadn't woken up and regretted the decision—far from it. He doubted he'd find anyone better than his Tina. He doubted he'd find anyone else really.

Also, he'd had definitive proof that the fainting woman hadn't recognised him; he was in the clear. He'd caught her when she fell and saved her from bumping her head this time, and sat with her while the ambulance came, like a Good Samaritan. She'd even thanked him as she got in it.

There was a bag of brooches in the bottom of the bag, cheap tat, and the phone was prehistoric, no good for selling. There was an envelope with documents in it: birth and death certificates, stuff like that. He supposed he could have done something with them at a push, but his engagement had made him feel a bit mushy. The woman—Polly— had had a bit of a rough deal at his hands. Taking everything from her would sour the blissful state he was presently in, but a little giving back would entirely salve his conscience.

He strutted into Billy's office swinging a carrier bag and smiled at him.

"Put that smile away, Orrible, you're bringing up my breakfast," said Billy, averting his eyes.

"You're happy, aren't you, Billy? I did good, didn't I?"

"Yes, son," said Billy, "you have indeed come up trumps. Pay the man, Charlie."

Big Charlie tossed Orrible a roll of notes. He teased a twenty out before putting it in his pocket and placed it on the desk.

"It's for the donkeys," said Orrible. "Will you pass it to them?" Billy, Big Charlie, and Square all exchanged glances of amused shock.

"I will indeed," said Billy. "That's very kind of you, Orville."

Orrible grinned. Billy had called him by his real name, which was testament to how chuffed he must be.

"A little birdie tells me that congratulations are in order," said Billy, leaning back in his chair, templing his fingers.

Those little birds Billy knew didn't half have bloody big beaks, thought Orrible. And they were everywhere. He just hoped one of them wasn't the seagull he'd clobbered with a rock.

"Yep, me and Tina are now fiancé and Beyoncé." Orrible chuckled.

"Every king should have a queen," said Billy, nodding. "Even if she is Anne of Cleves."

Square snorted and covered it up as a cough.

Orrible's grin was now so wide, full-sized letters could have been mailed through it.

"Cheers, Billy. She'll be really 'onored you called her a queen."

"Now, Orville, before you jog on your merry way, we must address the small matter of a handbag," said Billy, his eyes darkening, even though his mouth was holding a smile. "The one that was lodged up on the cliff. The one that isn't there anymore."

But Orrible was fully prepared. Hardly anything got past Billy; it wouldn't have done to pretend that the bag disappearing had nothing to do with him.

"You mean this bag. Da daaaa." He tipped it out of the carrier he was holding, like a rabbit out of a magician's hat, and put it down on the desk. And what's more, when he told Billy the story behind it, he'd be telling the truth—albeit with a few tiny tweaks—as Billy, who could spot a lie at fifty paces, would be able to confirm.

"I was walking on the beach, only to check if it was still up there, mind, and a seagull swooped on me and nabbed off with my hat, so I shouted at it and I must have scared it because it went splat into the cliff face. But guess why it didn't hurt itself, Bill? Because it only went and crashed into the bag, breaking the branch it was hanging on, and it tumbled down and fell at my feet along with my hat. The bird flew off, in case you're wondering. It was a blimming miracle," Orrible concluded. "And I brought it to you. Oh, and I swilled it in seawater first because that gets rid of any DNA."

Billy studied this chuckling creature before him and, blow me, it was telling the truth. He was sure there must have been a *leetle* bit more to the story, but he could let it go on this occasion, seeing as Orrible had come through for him with a beautiful Range Rover Sport SVR. Billy took a pair of disposable gloves out of his desk drawer and dragged the handbag toward him. This wouldn't be gracing any lady's arm again. He rifled through the pockets, found the usual women's detritus: makeup, pen, brush, and a model of phone that came out before the last brontosaurus had perished. He drew out the purse. There was a debit card and a Visa and a five-pound note in the money slot. Billy smirked. Orrible's attempt to "prove" he hadn't touched any money and was as honest as the day was long. He pulled it out and tossed it toward Orrible. "You might as well have that . . . as a reward for your scrupulous morals."

"Aw, cheers, Billy. I didn't notice there was anything in the purse." Orrible didn't wait to be asked twice.

There was a bag of small brooches and a note in with them. Billy unfolded it and read it. From someone called Will, thanking someone called Polly for helping him get through his exams when he didn't think he would. It brought a proper lump of emotion to his throat.

He took out the passport and looked at the photo of a woman staring straight ahead with lovely light eyes. The woman who had given him a bit of a headache these past weeks, even though she hadn't known a thing about that.

"Polly Potter. She looks nice, doesn't she? I mean, not as nice as your Tina, of course, but I think she'd like to have her bag returned to her. One of my little birds tells me she's working at the Italian in Shoresend. She never did get her memory back, so I think being reunited with herself would be a good, Christian thing to do, don't you? Kind of leveling things up a bit. Take with one hand, give with the other; that's what we do and that's why the universe is balanced. I'm presuming all her cards are present and correct and that no one has been flashing them around buying things contactless and being captured on CCTV cameras, because that would be very, very stupid, wouldn't it?"

"Didn't touch 'em, Billy." Orrible nodded and produced his most honest smile.

"Good boy. Well, I'll make sure this gets to her. Sorry to hear about your uncle Benny's hand. Tell him when you see him that I hope he recovers soon."

"I will, Billy." He'd rather have had Uncle Benny's hand than the other fella's face. Orrible was really glad he'd been distracted from trying to blackmail him that day when he nicked Polly Potter's car at the beauty spot. He was indebted to her really, hence why he was here with the bag full of her things. Like Billy said: *balance*.

"So, Orrible, our business has concluded," said Billy with his big-toothed crocodile smile. "Our association is at an end. Off you go. Have a nice life."

Orrible almost skipped to the door, where he turned. "Billy, do you think when me and Tina get married next year you'd consider being my best m—"

"Bye, Orrible."

As Orrible sauntered out into the bright and beautiful day, he thought how life-affirming it felt to do a good deed. Not as life-affirming as getting Billy the Donk off his back, but in a week when he'd done both and become an engaged man, he felt as if the sun had come out especially to shine on him.

* * *

Will never shouted at people over the telephone, but today he made an exception. He'd given whoever had picked up the phone at the *Daily Trumpet* both barrels. His father had been totally misguided suggesting the *Daily Trumpet* as a way of contacting Polly. Polly Pocket? Could they have gotten it any more wrong? And as for calling his father Christ . . . They'd put the wrong month in too—she'd been missing since May, not March. He just hoped that poor old Sinitta had more luck finding her family, but at least there was plenty of hope for the foul-mouthed parrot. She'd promised to refund him and put in a correction on Wednesday, if they had the room, she said. He said that they'd better have the room, then apologized for snapping at her when it wasn't her fault. He reckoned that anyone who handled calls from the public for the *Trumpet* must be hard as nails, and he just hoped they were paid well for the flak they must take.

First thing in the morning, he and "Christ" were going to the police station as his pal on the force had advised him to.

Chapter 48

The sunny weather had brought Teddy's restaurant extra business, as people weren't ready to say goodbye too early to the day and had started their week off with a teatime treat. They'd had to set up tables outside to accommodate everyone. There were a few repeat customers who had posted reviews and presented their vouchers for free desserts or coffees, which was good. The flow of troll reviews had slowed down, but it hadn't yet stopped; some were still getting through. They were obvious fakes because when Flick answered them asking for details of their bookings, they didn't respond.

Marielle had walked down to check on Flick and ended up being drafted to help wait on tables. It did her good; it took her thoughts away from a past she couldn't alter and into a present where everything was better than she'd imagined it might be when she was sitting at home worrying. Flick was still sorting things out in her mind, but there seemed to be more advantages than disadvantages for her to the disclosure. If Teddy was her brother, then that made Marielle her sort-of stepmum, and she was well happy with that.

They closed the doors just after ten thirty. The waiters got straight off because they were going to a nightclub in Whitby. Marielle envied them their energy. She started to strip the tables with Sabrina, who told her she could manage but George could do with some help in the kitchen.

As Sabrina was taking a bag of rubbish out to the bins outside, she heard George say, "Marielle, I don't know if this would be of interest to you, but I have two tickets for the theater to see *My Big Fat Greek Wedding* . . ." And when she came back in, George's face didn't read that Marielle had turned him down. She grinned. Dear George and Marielle, they just needed a little push toward each other to start things off, and then they'd be fine, she was sure of it.

Teddy's eyes locked with hers as she was wiping down the hatch.

"Are you okay?" she quizzed him.

"*You're* asking *me*?"

"Yes, I am," she said. "I know that Flick and your mum have had a lot to take in this weekend, but it can't have been easy for you either."

He looked at her, really looked at her, into her beautiful, unusual gold-flecked eyes, at her hair caught up in a ring of elastic and her flour-splattered black top, and he could so easily have reached through the hatch, placed his hand on the back of her neck, and pulled her soft, full lips toward his own. She had stirred up his life by doing nothing really but being in it; his feelings for her were strengthening day by day, and he was about to lose her anytime soon, he could feel it. He knew his mum was hurting, he knew that Flick was trying to get her head around it all, but Sabrina was the only one who had seen through his facade and realized that he, too, might be sorely affected by what had happened all those years ago between his father and Cilla.

"I'm disappointed in him," said Teddy, careful not to let his mother and George behind him hear. "He thought he was a good father and he was, but when he hurt my mother, he hurt me too, and I'm not sure he ever thought about that. He saw us as two separate pieces of his life. I wish I could have said this to him, got it all out in the open instead of keeping it inside me. You always think you'll have more time, though, don't you? We should say the things that are important . . . before it's too late."

He was looking at her so intently, as if he had something important to say to her. Then Flick appeared at her side and the moment was lost.

"I forgot to give you this, sorry, it was just so busy earlier on. Someone dropped it off for you on a motorbike. Said it was a present from a well-wisher. Sweet."

She had a parcel in her hand and on the front was written in Sharpie, "For the lady who has lost her memory."

Sabrina tore off the brown paper to find a leather handbag with white waves of salt stains covering it. Puzzled, she unzipped it and pulled out what was inside. Teddy watched her reach for the passport and open it slowly. He saw her breath catch in her throat as she turned to the back, and he registered the moment when she saw her own face staring up at her from the page.

Chapter 49

Sabrina didn't sleep well that night. The name "Polly Potter" rolled around in her brain as if it were a sole piece of laundry caught up in a very fast spin cycle. She couldn't be Polly Potter. Polly was someone different. She'd worked with her in the past, she was sure. She was a business analyst too and had a partner called Chris and he had a sister who was a bit of a nightmare and Chris had a son whom Polly really liked and a daughter she was wary of. She remembered more about Polly than she did herself. And Polly used to live next door to people who had a ginger cat and she'd feed it cheese and . . .

Sabrina groaned into her pillow. She *was* Polly; all the facts said so, but she didn't feel like her. They were like different people, but at the same time one had obviously become the other; they blurred and crossed, switched and swapped. So where did Polly end and Sabrina start? None of it made any sense, and besides, Sabrina Anderson was her anchor in this madness; her identity was one of the only things she had been sure of, and yet it had been a lie. Where did that leave her?

There was an emergency number in the passport for Will Barrett. Sabrina would ring him first thing in the morning; it was too late by the time they got home after work. Teddy had driven her and Marielle home in a strangely somber mood after such a jolly evening. She knew how he felt. Finally knowing who she was should have been a cause for celebration, and yet all she felt was confusion and dread.

"You don't have to go back yet," Teddy had told her before he left. "I for one don't feel comfortable placing you in the hands of people you might not even recognize. Stay and build the relationship from here, if that's what you want to do."

She didn't want to go back, but the time had come when she had to. Her head hurt thinking about it: being sure she was one person when in fact she was another, remembering things that hadn't happened, forgetting things that had. She was sick of it all. She couldn't live being more holes than whole; she needed to fill in the missing spaces, and it was taking too long to do that being so far away from wherever she—Polly—came from.

What really swung it for her was that these good people had their own lives to attend to, especially given the dynamite that Cilla had thrown into the middle of them. They needed to concentrate on recalibrating and repairing after that, not worry about her anymore. They should prioritize themselves, not her. She had to help herself from now on.

So lying awake, staring at the ceiling, she formulated a plan she would stick to. Tomorrow she would go back to the life of Polly Potter and take it from there. The doctors at the hospital had already warned her that the restoration of emotional connections might lag behind everything else, but with self-imposed psychological blockages, there was no definitive guidebook, no logical order of how things would play out, no promises or guarantees. Her best shot at full recovery was going home, even if by the definition of the word, home felt like where she was now and not where she was bound for.

Part Three

I am not what happened to me, I am what I choose to become.

—Carl Jung

The *Daily Trumpet* would like to apologize to Sir Melvyn Powdery-Hall for an unfortunate error in a profile piece we ran in May in which we referred to Sir Melvyn as a retired city wanker. We did of course mean that Sir Melvyn was a retired city banker. Sir Melvyn would also like us to point out that he retired from wanking in 2000 and not 2020 as stated.

Chapter 50

The next morning Sabrina sat in Marielle's lounge, an untouched mug of coffee in front of her. Teddy had wanted to be there when she rang Will Barrett, and though he didn't say so, if her folks were any less than ecstatic about her getting in contact, he would do everything in his power to keep her here.

He noticed her hand was shaking when she tapped the number into Marielle's phone, making a mistake the first time. She put it on loudspeaker so Teddy and Marielle could hear.

The phone connected after two rings.

"Hello," she said. "This is . . . Polly." It sounded wrong, as if she were lying.

"Polly? Oh my God, Polly." A male voice, familiar to her, a kind voice, thrown into shock. The young man she remembered. A blur of questions: "Where are you? Are you okay? Where have you been?" Relief coursing down the line like a tidal wave.

Another voice now, older, less effusive but in the same state of disbelief.

"Polly, it's Chris. We've been worried sick about you, love . . ."

Chris. She saw him in her head as if his voice had lifted him out of a fog. Tall, handsome, short sandy hair.

Teddy asked Sabrina if he might take over because she didn't know what to say. He introduced himself and delivered a potted history of the past weeks, that she'd been mugged and in hospital and that her memory was lost but was slowly returning. He didn't say that he was falling fast for her and that he had lately discovered he was at his happiest when she was around him.

"What do you mean her memory's lost?" Chris asked, incredulity in his voice. "Polly, can't you remember me? We've been together over eight years."

"Yes, of course, but there are a few gaps." Which was putting it mildly.

"Can you remember why you took off?"

"No, I can't remember that."

"Can you remember the day you left?"

"I can't remember that at all." At the other end of the phone, Chris puffed out his cheeks.

Well, that's handy. He wished he could forget it as well. "It was just a daft misunderstanding, love. We've been out of our heads with worry. We drew a blank with every avenue we looked down trying to find you. We'd just started to up the ante."

Will gave his father a look.

"It'll be good to get home," said Sabrina, hoping she sounded more convincing than she felt.

"Aw, it'll be smashing to have you home. You still on speaker? If so, can you give us an address, Mr. Bontempi?" Chris went on. "We'll be setting off soon as we can to pick her up. I can't believe it. Thank you . . . so much for everything you've done for her."

Teddy looked at Sabrina and mouthed the words *Is that what you want?* to her. And she nodded and forced out a smile that she hoped would convince him it was.

* * *

Chris put down the phone. His first thought, though he wouldn't even have admitted this to his son, was a palpable sense of relief that he wouldn't have to go to the police station now, as they'd intended to that morning, and admit that his partner had gone missing six weeks ago and he'd just decided to report it. He couldn't have scripted this better. Polly was coming home, so all would go back to blessed normality, she couldn't remember that she'd been planning to leave him, and he wouldn't end up on one of those TV crime documentaries.

But he did let Will into his second thought.

"What was she doing at the bloody seaside? She must have had some sort of a breakdown."

"It was a special place for her, Dad. I read about it in her creative writing file," Will answered. "Maybe she went there hoping to be happy again because her brain must have been ready for blowing up."

"I know how she feels. My brain blew up when I got your auntie Camay's bill for that sodding wedding," Chris grumbled. "I knew she hadn't left me for another man. I don't think she was leaving me at all, you know. I've thought about it and I think she was just bluffing, wanting to make me sit up and notice her. I know I work too many hours and she must have felt neglected. But I was hoping the wedding would prove how much I appreciate her."

"Don't you mean *love*?" asked Will.

"'Course I mean love. She's obviously had some trouble at work which pushed her over the edge."

Will almost said that if anything had pushed her over the edge, it was probably turning up at her own wedding which she knew nothing about, but it would have sounded rather snippy and his dad looked as contrite as he'd ever seen him, so he kept schtum.

"She loves the sea."

"Does she?" asked Chris.

"Yes, Dad, she does." Will tried his best to keep the impatience out of his voice and be constructive. "Maybe when Polly comes home you should start to pay her more attention, or you're going to lose her for good. You obviously don't know her half as well as you think you do.

If you did, you'd have been to the police weeks ago and she'd be home now."

"You're right, son. This has been a massive wake-up call for me," said Chris adamantly. "Let's go and get her."

* * *

The three hours that followed, Teddy likened to waiting to be executed. He didn't want Sabrina to go, but he understood why she had to. He didn't want her to be lost anymore, for her own sake, because a cycle of deep frustration and depression was waiting to pounce on her from around the corner if this continued; he'd read all about it. Whatever it took for her to heal quickly was what he wished for her. Even if it took her away from them. From him.

Marielle was standing by the window looking out for a large black Mercedes van. It would be here any minute.

"Well," said Teddy, for the want of anything better. He was never usually stuck for words, but he was now.

"Thank you for everything," said Sabrina.

"You know that if you're ever around here, call in and you can have a pizza on the house," Teddy said, berating himself because it sounded lame, and it wasn't what he wanted to say at all, which was, *Don't go.*

"Thank you, I'd like that." Her smile was very watery and wavery. Teddy opened his mouth then to say, "*And if you don't fit back into the space you left, come back here and we will make you belong with us,*" but his mum got in first.

"I think they're here, love."

Teddy and Sabrina both jumped to their feet as Marielle went to the door. The blood inside Sabrina was galloping through her veins like a racehorse. This was it then, the new beginning, though it felt too much like an end.

In walked the young man Sabrina remembered. This was Will,

someone she liked very much, and he bounced forward and embraced her hard.

"Oh Polly, thank God you're all right, you're safe," he said. The man who followed him in hadn't pushed his son out of the way to grab her first, as Teddy knew he would have done. Tall, slim, good-looking, stiff. He approached Sabrina more warily.

"I don't know what to say to you," he said. "Come here." He opened his arms and when Sabrina walked into them, Teddy thought they looked like two robots trying each other on for size. He forced himself to concede that this was not a normal situation; who knew how to react, who knew what to say or do?

"I've missed you so much, Pol," said Chris. "It'll be good to have you at home again. I've been wandering around in it talking to myself like a lost soul."

"Thank you so much," said Will to Marielle and Teddy in turn. He looked genuinely relieved to see her again.

"We're just glad we could help," said Marielle. She wouldn't have put Chris and Sabrina together had she been matchmaking. He should have embraced her like his son had, she thought.

"Were the police looking for her?" asked Teddy. He noticed then how father and son flashed a glance at each other.

"Yes, we reported it," replied Chris, which was a bit of a stretch, seeing as all that had happened so far was Will had had a casual word with his mate on the force for some advice. But they were going to report it that very morning, so it was sort of true. "We've been worried sick waiting for news."

Chris hadn't imagined Mr. Bontempi to look like that. He thought he'd be an old bloke, not someone quite so Italian-looking, with thicker hair than him, taller than he was even. He put his arm around Polly, a territorial gesture more than an affectionate one.

"I think our Pol must have had a breakdown," Chris went on. "She lost her job and it must have been too much for her head. That job was her world. As she is mine." He turned to her and smiled, and at that moment Chris meant his words because he really had missed Polly. She was a good, faithful girl, and living out the rest of his life with her didn't come with any negatives. He didn't enjoy coming in to an empty house of an evening; she was a good cook, she never nagged him to turn the TV over from the footie, and she kept the house clean. They'd have another stab at the wedding thing, but it would be Gretna Green next time, no guests or fancy stuff, and he'd arrange it himself.

"Would you like something to drink?" Marielle asked her visitors.

"Marielle, I think it might be best if we get straight off," said Sabrina. She didn't want a protracted goodbye. If she didn't go now, her carefully formulated plan might crumble to dust.

Marielle squeezed the living daylights out of her.

"Don't be a stranger to us," she said, releasing her and then pulling her back in for a second hug. She thought it was way too early for her to leave them, but she shouldn't interfere.

Chris picked up the suitcase that Marielle had packed Sabrina's stuff into and stepped toward the door.

Teddy kicked against his urge to crush Sabrina to his big Italian chest. It wouldn't have been respectful, but more than that, he was worried he wouldn't be able to let her go. Instead his hands came up to cup her face and he held it as if it were a precious thing.

"You know where we are if you ever need us," he said.

And she couldn't answer because she had no breath in her body. Such a small gesture, yet it lit up every fiber and tissue, every nerve and neuron in her body.

Teddy and his mother watched the van drive off and waved and stood long after it was out of sight, and Teddy hoped she would fit into the Polly Potter–shaped hole she had left. It was going to take some doing, and he wished he could be the one to hold her when it got too much for her head, as it inevitably would, because it was already too much for his and he needed her to hold him too.

There was an unfortunate error in yesterday's *Daily Trumpet* in which we referred to Mr. Brian Cherry as acting chief defective in the Middlesbrough police force. This should have read that Mr. Cheery is acting chief detective in the Middlesbrough police farce.

Chapter 51

The house, when they got to it, was as familiar to her as if she had merely been on holiday for a couple of weeks and had returned home. It was odd how much was flying back to her now, like old photographs being developed in chemicals; shapes were forming, blurs crispening. She looked around at the kitchen, taking it all in, noticing the chipped tiles and thinking they needed replacing and the cupboard door which wasn't square in its frame. This was Polly's world. She was Polly Potter, not Sabrina Anderson, and she had to get used to being her again.

Will put the kettle on while his dad took her things upstairs. "It must be beyond strange to be back," he said, watching her eyes roam around the room and wondering if she was comparing it to the light and cheerful house they had collected her from. His mouth was crowded with questions, but he didn't want to deluge her with them. It would all come out in time. And so would the fact that for six and a half weeks no one had tried to find her because they thought she was living the life of Riley with a lover somewhere when in fact she'd been robbed and attacked, and God knows where she would have ended up if those nice people hadn't been looking after her. Teddy Bonetti said that someone had found her passport and that's how they'd finally managed to get in touch, and Will then wondered why they hadn't gone down the police route either. Surely they would have been able to get her back here sooner if they had.

"We'll have to get onto the insurance about the car," said Chris, appearing at the bottom of the stairs.

"That can wait a bit, surely," said Will.

"I'll sort it. I don't expect Polly to if she's . . ." Chris tapped his head. Will cast him a look.

"The important thing is that we draw a line in the sand and start afresh from here," said Chris. "We'll patch you up good as new."

I really hope you keep to your word, Dad, thought Will. *You nearly lost her twice, so look after her this time.*

* * *

Polly slept in the small room at the back of the house where most of her things were in boxes and suitcases. Apparently losing her job had affected her greatly, Chris told her; that was why she'd packed all her stuff up but then run away without taking it, which certainly illustrated her state of mind at the time. He handed a letter to her which had the company name Business Strength in red lettering with a bull logo, which wasn't at all familiar. Chris said he'd opened it hoping it might give them a clue where she'd gone. She didn't recognize the name of the firm, but she did know the name at the bottom of the letter: Jeremy Watson. She could bring him to mind, tall and angular and sarcastic, and he came with a rush of bad feeling. The letter said he would like to address a misunderstanding and reinstate her to her old position with immediate effect, and could she please ring HR at her earliest convenience to confirm she would be returning. She remembered Sheridan, whom she used to sit next to calling him Jeremy Twatson, Germany, Jiminy, Jeremeny, and she let loose a burst of laughter. She was mending; she was getting it back at a rate of knots now, Polly's life, even if it did seem so much less bright than Sabrina's.

Over the next couple of days, Polly emptied all the boxes in the spare room and put everything back where she presumed it once lived; she pressed the creased clothes and hung them up. Then she set to cleaning the house, which badly needed a spruce. Mopping the floor made her think of Teddy's restaurant, the coffee-filled air, the music playing, the cheery banter, Flick quizzing her about things to do with how businesses operated as they set the tables together. She wondered if Cilla was working hard to repair their relationship, if Marielle was being looked after by her friends . . . and if Teddy was okay. She missed them all, but especially him. She closed her eyes and thought of walking alongside him that day on the beach, their toes pushed into the sand. And she thought of her face in his hands, looking into his kind blue eyes, wishing he would lower his lips to hers. They'd forget her far more quickly than she would forget them; she was a mere short interlude in their lives. One day she would go and visit them, but it wouldn't be the same as being part of them. She found the file with all her creative writing in it and she half laughed reading about evil Jasper, the shadowy figure she'd thought she was running from, who was just a character from her imagination. But if she'd known that, she probably would have sought a quicker route back home and not grown as close to the Bonetti family. Would that have been better than becoming attached and then having to wrench herself away from them? There was her poem about Tom, the lovely old cat next door. She could see him now clear as day, stretched out blissfully on her young-girl knees. Such moments of brightness only shone like diamonds because they were surrounded by such a sea of sadness. No wonder she had built her own world in her imagination where Ed and Rina and Linnet had breathed and loved and laughed for longer.

As for Sabrina, no wonder she had imagined she was her. Sabrina was herself augmented, braver and ballsier, the woman Polly wished she was, enough to have become her. Even if it had just been for a few glorious weeks.

She rang Business Strength and spoke to the HR department and made an appointment to go in and see Marjorie Wright herself the next afternoon, the head honcho. She could remember her clearly, her suits with the *Dynasty* shoulder pads and no-nonsense manner tempered with innate fairness. Someone she associated with a better past of the company, when it had been Northern Eagles.

That evening she made a meal for two for herself and Chris. She needed to get to know this man again, the man she had been with for eight years but didn't have eight years of memories with. He came home from work with a bunch of flowers for her and apologized that they looked half dead, but it was the last lot in the shop. She tipped some dried pasta into the pan and her mind teleported over to the restaurant where the pasta was fresh, where the air was scented with garlic and the ragu sauces bubbled. Polly Potter felt like a coat she had taken off, left aside, and then put back on to find it no longer fit. But it was her coat all the same, it was her life, and she'd have to adjust it to make it fit. It was Sabrina Anderson who was made up, imagined, so why did she feel so much more solid than the "real Polly"?

"This is nice, like old times," Chris said. "I've missed us eating together. We did it nearly every night." Sabrina noticed how fast he wolfed it down, barely tasting it. She'd only eaten half hers when he got up, shoved his plate in the sink, and said that there was a football match on he really needed to see, was that all right? There would be plenty of other nights when they could draw it out a bit. And she answered that it was fine because she didn't have that much to say to him anyway.

* * *

Polly caught the train into Leeds the next afternoon, wearing a newly washed and pressed black suit. She teamed it up with a pale blue shirt, one with thin stripes, vertical, not horizontal, not like the Breton top she'd worn for her spy mission with Teddy. *Teddy, Teddy, Teddy.*

All roads seemed to lead back to him, and to the people by the seaside who had embraced her. There was an incongruence between her memory and reality as she approached the place where she had worked for so many years. The massive, kickass blue signage with the flying eagle had been replaced with a black bull's head, which looked more demonic than animal, and red lettering: "Business Strength." She thought how bland it seemed, how weak compared to the old name, which she knew rang with a long history of excellence.

She walked into the building, through reception, and up the stairs, turning left through the double doors. Her legs remembered where to go as if she'd been there only yesterday. A mini-bomb of thoughts exploded by the coffee machine there as she imagined the mighty figure of Alan Eagleton hitting it with his fist when it didn't deliver. *"It's got a grudge against me, this bugger."* He used to say it was haunted by the spirit of his ex-wife, even though she was still very much alive, and Polly thought that it was good to have such memories of him returning to her again.

Marjorie's PA walked Polly into her office where Marjorie herself greeted her warmly, produced her hand, and held Polly's, rather than shaking it. They sat down then. Marjorie's office felt like part of a comfortable past where she was as happy as she was with the Bonettis, because it was the people who made the magic.

"I haven't seen you to talk to properly for so long," said Marjorie, her voice brimming with genuine concern. She thought Polly looked different somehow. She'd taken to wearing a red lipstick that suited her, even changed her. Or maybe it was just being away from this hellhole for a while that had done that.

"I'm so sorry to hear you've . . . had a few problems that you really shouldn't have had."

Polly hadn't mentioned anything about her loss of memory, not yet, so she let Marjorie enlighten her on what those few problems were.

"I'm on a mission to stop this culture of misogyny. To my shame, I admit I had no idea how bad it was in certain departments. I think the word that comes to mind is *critical*. Of course once one little birdie chirped, we had a whole gospel choir of them. Have you received an apology from Jeremy Watson?"

"Well, not really, just a letter asking me to ring HR to confirm that I agreed to be fully reinstated."

Polly watched Marjorie's lips shrink back from her teeth, only for them to mutate into a tenuous smile.

"Then he's evidently intending to do that in person. So let me be the one who formally welcomes you back to . . . Business Strength." The pause before the company name was a derisive one, Polly thought.

Marjorie slid across the table an amendment to her job contract. Polly was to be elevated to managerial status with all the benefits and perks and bonuses that entailed, backdated to include all the work she had done for Nutbush. It was quite the improvement. It was the least Marjorie could do for people she liked in her remaining term in the job. Every mention of Jeremy Watson made her think that her early retirement couldn't come fast enough.

"It's what you deserve, Polly. I want you back at your desk. They've already lost Auntie Marian's Bread as a client since you were last here, and Arthur Peach has made a very noisy exit. Can we say Monday for your return?"

Polly nodded slowly. "Yes, I'll be in on Monday."

Marjorie stood and put out her hand again, and she didn't let go of Polly's hand after she'd shaken it.

"Alan thought a lot of you, you know. If he'd still been here, he'd have put you in the driving seat and we wouldn't now be in this era of BS."

She spoke so sincerely that Polly felt choked by emotion. Alan had been a wonderful man, she knew, and she would welcome each new recollection of him as it came to her.

As she was walking out of the door, Marjorie called her back.

"One more thing: I'm sure you remember Phil Bowery and Dave Deacon, don't you?" Polly did remember. Her old friends who were part of Alan's inner circle and who'd been rudely shoved out in the takeover.

"They've set up a company together, not before time, and they're doing very well," said Marjorie. "They've called themselves Yorkshire Eagles. Phil contacted me last week to see if I knew anyone of good caliber who might be interested in pastures new. It's over near Whitby though, so quite a distance, but . . . I said I'd keep my eyes and ears open, of course. Thank you, Polly. Enjoy your weekend."

When she had gone, Marjorie returned to her chair and grinned to herself. She'd just park that there with Polly. She wouldn't have been a *sister* if she'd kept that little nugget to herself.

Chapter 52

When Chris came in from work that night, he kicked off his boots and dropped his bag and then disappeared upstairs to change. Polly, grating cheese for a sauce, went to move the bag to the side, and as her fingers touched the handle she was filled with a surge of anger that was almost too big for her to contain. She'd been here many times, she knew, and picking up this bag and shifting it was just a little thing but one of many little things that had made her unhappy in this house. She had walked out of it and then somehow stumbled into her own work of fiction and become the character who was ready to begin a new life. But here she was back in the old one, like a snake that had crawled into its discarded skin and found the fit tight and uncomfortable.

Will came round to see her that Sunday. He'd put Shauna off coming with him because he knew she just wanted to gawp. And an absolute no to Auntie Camay, who was still smarting about the wedding that never was and was itching to let rip about it to Polly's face.

His dad was at the garage and had been all weekend—again. Will had told him to take some time off and book a night away or a meal out, but Chris had said he was too busy. He'd laughed when Will then suggested a holiday. He said Polly was happy as she was. They'd have a holiday in a bit, when she was fully better. Maybe. His dad was a fool who fooled no one. He'd thrown a bunch of flowers and a box of dark chocolate at

Polly and expected it to be enough glue to hold together the structural break. Just like he'd done when he'd nearly lost her last year. And how come his dad didn't even know that Polly disliked dark chocolate?

"So you're returning to work tomorrow."

"Yes, I'm back to it." She smiled at him.

"Have you heard from the people you were staying with in Shoresend?" asked Will, poking around in the cupboard for some biscuits.

"I had a text from Marielle to check that I was okay."

Polly had replied that she was, with a "speak soon" tagged on the end, but she didn't think she was up to calling her just yet; it would feel too raw. She'd deliberately distanced herself, for a while at least, so she could get her head straight in Polly's world. But it was impossible to stop her thoughts wanting to fly to them, as they so often did.

"They seemed like good people," said Will.

"They were very kind to me."

"Have you told them at work what happened to you?"

Polly shook her head. She didn't want to give Jeremy any ammunition to manipulate her. She was pretty sure her professional capabilities weren't affected, so there was no reason to have that conversation. She'd tackle it if it came up, but such information given would be on a need-to-know basis.

"You love your job, don't you?" said Will, thudding his body down on the chair at the table. "You're lucky. I hate mine."

"Then change it," said Polly. "What is it you want to do?"

"Social work. I want to help kids," said Will, his voice whispery because he half expected his dad to suddenly manifest in the room and say, *"You must be bloody daft."*

"Then why aren't you doing it?"

"I'd have to get a degree first. Is it too late to start when everyone else my age is graduating?"

"You're only twenty-one, Will. Even people older than me decide to go to university." He opened his mouth to tell her something, then pulled it back, but Polly reached over and shook his arm.

"Say what you were going to," she insisted.

"Okay . . . I applied at Bournemouth for a place and I got in."

"Then do it, Will," said Polly. If ever someone was suited to a career helping kids in need, it was this caring boy.

"Dad would say I'm going backward."

"You wouldn't be going backward; you're preparing for a running jump. Am I convincing you?"

Will smiled. "I want to be convinced. Living by the seaside would be nice, wouldn't it?"

Polly remembered the hush of the sea and the gently foaming waves, the warm sand, the fresh salt air in her lungs, the seagulls wheeling above her head.

"Yes, darling Will, it really is."

Will swallowed a lump of emotion caught in his throat. He wished Polly could have been his real parent. He thought more of her than he did his own combined. And he owed her. "Polly . . ." He had to say something, he had to tell her how it had been before she left and why he thought she had packed up to go.

But this was his dad. And Will really wanted him to step up and make his relationship work. Polly was the best thing that had ever happened to him. He didn't want his dad to lose her again. Will didn't want to lose her again.

"I . . . I know that Dad is glad you're back. He's not great at showing his feelings."

"Thank you for that, Will," she said. And she placed her hand on his cheek and he felt really shit then that he'd chickened out from telling her how bad it had become.

Chapter 53

Polly walked into her old department on Monday morning with a sped-up heart rhythm and strides powered by anxiety. She could recall that the last time she'd seen Jeremy they'd had some sort of altercation, presumably the "misunderstanding" that he'd referred to in his letter. The jigsaw puzzle of her mind was mostly completed, but there remained plenty of missing patches where the detail wouldn't materialize, and this was one of them.

Familiar faces in the department turned to say hello or give a smile as she headed for her desk. The drawers were empty, as was the top apart from a PC and a keyboard, as if she were coming to it for the first time. There was no desk next to it as she remembered there used to be, where Sheridan sat and they'd throw things to each other over the divide: sweets, tissues, biscuits. She'd sent a teddy bear to her for the baby and a note to say she was sorry she hadn't been in touch but she hoped to see her soon, which was true, because Sheridan's friendly face would be like medicine to her.

"Hello, Polly." She turned, hearing the voice behind her, to find the tall, lean, mean figure of Jeremy Watson. "Before you get yourself re-established in the department, could I have a quick word in private?"

"Certainly."

She followed him to his office, and as he sat down in his huge swivelly chair, she remembered the large portrait of Alan that used to hang on the wall before this strange, pointy one of Jeremy.

"Please sit." Jeremy smiled and gestured toward the chair at the other side of the desk. "How are you?" he asked, tilting his head at a concerned angle.

"I'm fine, thank you."

"Good, good. I didn't want there to be any awkwardness between us. I think now that we've both had a little time to reflect, setting out on a new footing is what should happen. I'm"—a huge deep breath needed for the next words, which were forced out of him under obvious duress—"very sorry if you ever felt you were being sidelined or overlooked. I think with the new BS name above the door, what remains of the old Northern Eagles history should be buried with it. Onward and upward, don't you agree?"

"I do," replied Polly.

"Good, good." His obligatory apology was expended and it had been easy enough, though meek and mild Polly wouldn't exactly have had the front to make it difficult; now they could get down to business as usual. "Not sure what Marjorie told you. We lost Auntie Marian's Bread. We never could have made them into the next Warburtons; Peach just wasn't prepared to listen and we do need some pliancy to work with. But we do have other companies ready for you to cast your spell on." He nudged forward a stack of files that sat on his desk.

"Mandy's Handbags, not a huge concern. They haven't got a lot of money to play with, but I think we . . . you can give them some of your valuable insight. Mr. Waggy, dog food. Wants to be the bargain-basement version of Pedigree Chum. Good luck with that one because their ingredients are floor-sweepings and even the basement is aiming a bit high. And you might remember this one. I gave it to you in error, but I think in retrospect maybe it was meant to be yours all along. It's . . . tricky, and to say they haven't been happy with our recommendations so far is an understatement, so we do need you to get to grips with it and come up with the goods."

"Thank you," said Polly, picking them up and standing to go.

"If you're putting the kettle on, Polly, I'd appreciate . . ." Jeremy started to say, but something in the way she looked down at him made the words wither on his lips. For a second there, she looked like someone else, not Polly Potter at all.

How very odd.

"I'll ring Brock for that, shall I?" he said, a strained smile on his face.

"Good idea," she said, and continued on her way. Because it was the old Polly who put the kettles on for everyone; this shiny new version of herself definitely didn't.

* * *

She found the place in the canteen where she presumed she always sat. Muscle memory was an odd thing, bypassing the conscious mind, taking the reins. *So much information must be stored in my neurons*, she thought. That's why her ability to perform her job wasn't affected, why she instinctively knew that George's pizza oven should be moved into the main kitchen, that the hatch should be made wider, that Ciaoissimo had way too many offerings on their menu.

But her heart was a muscle too, and yet there was no memory for the man she had supposedly loved for eight years lingering there, no reflex to open her arms to Chris, no longing to feel his lips upon hers.

She leaned forward, suddenly weary and steps away from tears. She was trying hard to be Polly Potter again, but it wasn't working. It felt as if she was trying to be a stranger, not herself, even though it was herself. It weighed down her brain like the worst sort of puzzle.

She breathed in deeply, dragged over the first folder and opened it. Mandy's Handbags. The vibe she got was that they were a small firm but energetic, and they'd be on board with whatever they were advised to do. They weren't expecting to be the new Lulu Guinness, but a bigger share of the market would be a great start. They'd be good to work with; they should aim at primarily young people, she thought.

Mr. Waggy would need a complete overhaul. Their fat-to-protein ratios were all wrong, too many cheap fillers. They were a two-star that could be a four-star bargain brand and still make a good profit.

She put them to one side and picked up the third file, the biggest one. She opened it and had a flash of déjà vu when she saw the name at the top of the page.

Ciaoissimo.

Chapter 54

Over the next fortnight, Polly worked on researching her three clients, but mainly Ciaoissimo; the mills of God couldn't have ground finer detail. She poked into every nook and cranny of the business; she investigated every member of the board down to what color socks they wore and what sort of pet their dental hygienist owned. She took her research to obsessive levels, getting in after Chris some nights, which he wasn't happy about. They still weren't sleeping in the same bed, even though he said that if they did maybe that would bring back a few memories. She refused to be hurried. She recognized that work had become her respite again, as it must have been before, because there was nothing outside it, nothing to come home to other than rattling around inside four walls with someone who did nothing to dispel her loneliness.

She'd just walked into the house, having had a very successful meeting with the Mandy's Handbags people, when there was a knock on the door, and straight afterward Will flew in. His eyebrows were lowered in a worried frown and she remembered a younger version of him, convinced he was going to fail his exams, wearing the selfsame expression.

"Polly, I need to talk to you," he said. "I'm not sure if I'm doing the right thing, but I have to do it."

"Then sit and talk to me."

Polly pulled out a chair from under the table for him and he threw himself down on it.

"Are you okay?" she asked. He didn't look okay. He looked stressed. He was stressed; in fact, Will couldn't remember being more stressed in his life. He had talked himself in and out of this more times than he could count. He felt as if he'd been at war with himself for the past couple of weeks.

"Polly, what do you remember about the day you left?"

"Not a lot."

"Do you remember the wedding?"

Polly jiggled her head, unsure. "I thought I remembered a wedding. I think I was a bridesmaid, but I'm not sure that's right."

"No, Polly, you were the bride. On the day you left, you were getting married. You didn't know you were; you thought you were my auntie Camay's bridesmaid. It was all supposed to be a big surprise."

He pulled out his phone. For once he was glad that his sister was a class-A bitch and had filmed it, probably for nefarious reasons, but he'd warned her right off using any footage. He started the video and Polly heard violins playing, saw herself walking in between chairs, people's heads turning, the close-up of confusion on her face hardening to something akin to horror.

Images slammed into her brain like asteroids. She remembered it all in one God-awful agglomeration of facts. Shauna's sneery face, the long, baggy dress, Camay and her plum satin, the gripping hand of panic at her throat as she realized why she was there. Kicking off her shoes and picking up her dress to run. Stan and the limo; angry, sweary texts on her phone. Her hands shaking as she tried to put her key in the car ignition to go, leave, now. She had to get away, her foot on the accelerator.

Will watched her eyes flickering and could only imagine the brain activity going on behind them.

"Everyone thought you'd gone because you were leaving Dad for someone else. That's why it took us so long to look for you. Oh Polly, I'm so sorry."

"*Me and Mrs. Jones.*" *A receipt for fillet steaks and porn star martinis.* Chris had had an affair. No wonder she hadn't remembered him with any emotional content, because there was none. He'd killed her love for him with a thousand small cuts and one massive coup de grâce, and he hadn't valued her enough to try to put it right. She had walked out because she didn't want to be with him anymore. She had packed up all her possessions because she was leaving him, not because she'd gone barmy after losing her job. But she'd driven off with only the bare essentials because the wedding had derailed all her plans, and she'd fled to the coast to start again with no intentions of going back.

Will sniffled; embarrassed, he wiped away a tear that had dropped onto the tabletop. "You must have been so unhappy. I half wish we hadn't found you because Dad's still not making any bloody effort to keep you. I know he's my dad, Polly, but I had to tell you the truth. I love you and I think you deserve so much better."

Polly put her arms around him and held him. This dear boy whom her heart had remembered with smiles when it couldn't remember his father at all.

Chapter 55

Alan Eagleton said once that sometimes you have to think of a task in hand like an unstable bomb in a box. Every bit of your concentration, every scrap of your energy has to be screwed to it to stop it going off. Nothing is allowed to get in the way of you delivering it intact to its destination. Then and only then can you let anything else into your brain. Polly couldn't remember what he'd said it about, but that's what came to her mind when she was making her final notes for her presentation to the big boys of Ciaoissimo. Every thought she'd had, every sentence she'd written recently had been around them and how she was going to "take them to where they needed to be"—*their words, their instruction.*

She'd booked the boardroom. She'd arranged the caterers personally rather than leave it to her junior, Brock, because there were to be no mistakes, no compromises, and she'd deal with the consequences of her actions later. Jeremy's eyeballs would bulge at the expense, but he was in for as much impact as he could handle. After all, his direction had been crystal clear: Give them everything you've got. *His words, his instruction.* All of the big five from the germinal Italian restaurant chain turned up to witness the big bang they'd been promised. Brock showed them up to the directorate where Polly was waiting to charm them. She could hear them laughing as they approached, the smug guffaws of fat cats already counting their creamy dividends.

"Polly Potter, how lovely to meet you," she said, greeting them on their arrival. Her own name still tasted odd in her mouth, like a fish-flavored fruit pastille. "I've read so much about you that I feel as if I know you already." She chortled, but it was true. She knew more about them than they did themselves. She'd dug deep down to their very core, although they'd helpfully left enough rot on their surface because it was amazing how careless people could be who thought themselves untouchable, whose hubris blinded them to their fallibility; one only had to see the sleaze surrounding some celebrities and footballers in the papers to know that. Richard Pound was the first to introduce himself to her.

She recognized him as the customer who had made a fuss about his steak in Teddy's restaurant and "found" glass in the zabaglione. He had a crushing handshake intended to intimidate. Then she shook the hand of Councilor James Stirling, joint owner of the shitting spaniel, and Nicholas de Massey, company secretary. Peter Hore, who intro'ed himself as "I'm the money." And finally there was Donald Devine, who was dapper and ancient and didn't seem to know what day it was. If he sneezed, Polly half expected a pound of powder to fly off his rather obvious toupée.

The catering staff had started to serve, and Polly asked everyone to take their seats at the table. They'd eat first, before her presentation; she wanted them oiled by rich food—but mostly wine. There was a lemon-gold white and a serious red; she'd chosen them because they were quality, Italian, and also had high alcohol content. Any stronger and they'd have been a petrol.

"Well, this is jolly nice," said Richard Pound, settling into being schmoozed. By the time she'd eaten her first forkful of lobster thermidor salad, he'd already told her he'd just bought himself a Bentley and that he had an MBE for his services for charity. Polly wondered how much he'd paid for that in backhanders. "Yes, top-class bit of crustacean."

"I'm glad you like it. I designed the menu very carefully," Polly agreed, and topped up his wine. He'd downed the first one like a parched whale.

"So, *Polly*," said Councilor Stirling, seated on Polly's right side. He'd introduced himself as "Jim, Just Jim" in the manner of "Bond, James Bond."

"What businesses have you turned round then, little lady? Seduce us."

He was greasy, shiny with sweat, and bloated, and he reminded her of Camay's husband, also a business fat cat. She was tempted to check the carpet to see if he'd left a slug trail where he'd trodden. She wouldn't have put "Jim, Just Jim" in a couple with the glamorous woman with the defecating dog.

Polly smiled, leaning forward onto her elbows. "Well, where does one begin: Nutbush sports, Knock Doors, Richmond and Harris furniture, Planet Insurance, Kitty-Kitten Heels, Mr. Shine . . . the Fish Fillies." She knew all those names would score for anyone in business. Especially the Fish Fillies, who had wanted to give Harry Ramsden's a run for their money and she'd made them even bigger.

"The Fish Fillies? That was you?" said Peter Hore, clearly impressed. Someone else officially took the credit, of course, but yes, it was all her own work all right. She nodded bashfully.

"Gentlemen," Richard Pound announced to the rest of the table, raising his glass. "I think we are in safe hands."

Over Chateaubriand, carved and served artfully by a chef in front of them wielding a knife that a pirate would have been happy with, the Ciaoissimo party laughed about how they'd bulldozed all opposition in their way so far, how unbeatable they were with their combined dark strength. And Polly edged the conversation around to their new intended flagship restaurant as the waiting staff fulfilled their instructions to keep those glasses topped up.

"Massive potential for clientele," said Richard, as he tore into his beef without any complaint about how it was cooked. "There's a smart little Italian nearby that, alas, we're going to blow out of the water. But there can only be one head lion in a pride. All's fair in love, war, and business."

"That is exactly my mantra," Polly agreed fervently. She lowered her voice conspiratorially. "Have you started an active campaign, if you know what I mean?"

Richard didn't answer immediately, but his jaw was working on his lunch as if he were chewing on far more than just the meat.

"This is all totally confidential, isn't it?"

"Let me just say," replied Polly, "you have no idea of the depths I've had to swim to in order to put my clients in their rightful place."

Richard smiled as if this was music to his ears.

"I always think," Polly continued, "in business, you have to do what you have to do." Richard held up his glass and Polly chinked hers against it.

"Dog eat dog," he said and winked.

"Dog eat dog," said Polly, praying that the recording device she had secreted about her person was getting all this. She knew the four boardroom cameras were because she could see the red light of the one directly ahead blinking as if to assure her. The footage, thanks to fellow psychopath Len Champion, who'd rigged up all the equipment, would download directly to her laptop from all the varying angles so they could catch *everything*, and would be stored safely in the cloud. There was less filming equipment on *Love Island*.

"Well," began Richard, before confiding in Polly what they'd done to close down the Italian in Scarborough which three generations of the family had run. It was clear the power had gone to their heads, especially as no one had stopped them so far, and as such they thought they were invincible. He told her then about the compulsory purchase order they'd just had served on a restaurant in Bridlington and the pathetic efforts of the family who'd owned it to try to stop them. "*No pain, no gain*," he snickered, even though it was someone else's pain that enabled the Ciaoissimo crew to gain. Jeremy arrived just as dessert was being served: zabaglione accompanied by a sugary Torcolato dessert wine. He shook everyone's hands enthusiastically and absorbed that talks between BS and Ciaoissimo were going very well. He did a double take at the number of wine bottles on the table.

Luckily he didn't know the half of it, thought Polly. That beef didn't come cheap. Or the lobster.

"Yum yum, zabaglione." Richard Pound nodded approvingly. "I wish I could confess what I did to some of this stuff recently." He chuckled to himself.

"Oh, do say," replied Polly in her best silky voice. She'd chosen the dessert deliberately, hoping it would entice a tongue to wag.

Richard was about to, then thought better of it. "No, I couldn't."

"Then I'll never know; what a shame." Polly appeared to give up asking, knowing he really wanted to tell, and he fell for it.

Richard Pound looked behind him as if expecting to see a spy lurking, then whispered, "I shouldn't really share, but I was a bit naughty. Slightly low blow."

"How low did you go?" Polly widened her eyes in anticipation of being thrilled.

"Snake's belly low," said Richard. "We aren't people you mess with, if you know what I mean." He raised his eyebrows knowingly, but he couldn't quite pull off the hard-man effect. "We aren't averse to a smear campaign or two." He nodded across the table at Nicholas de Massey. "Old Nick there is our dedicated review writer. He's got his whole family onto it. Nephew's a bit of a whiz on the net and he can bounce things off servers so nothing's traced back."

"You mean like . . . fake restaurant reviews?" suggested Polly.

"Indeed I do," said Richard, impressed by her "lucky guess."

"Effective?"

"They work a treat on the 'no smoke without fire' principle. We've managed to crash and burn one competitor by those alone. We're having to up the ante with the new venture as it's quite popular. I thought I'd try it out. Tidy little place; shame it has to go." He sighed as if he cared. "Ended up cutting my lip on some glass in a pudding. Haven't a clue how it got there, of course, but four of us ended up eating for free. Result." He winked.

"Oh my goodness," said Polly, hands flying up to her face in shock. "Don't tell me that's your level of sabotage?" She laughed, impressed.

"Despicable, wasn't it? I'm almost ashamed. No one wants glass in their dinner, do they? It had quite the ripple effect round the room. Damage!"

"You're such a player," said Polly, not sure how long she could carry on smiling at this vile creep. "Playing devil's advocate, couldn't you coexist with this... other Italian restaurant? It would get you brownie points with the community, surely."

"Fuck the community," said Richard with gusto. "Every meal someone buys in that place they aren't buying in ours."

"Surely Jim must care? He's a councilor."

"I think you have the wrong idea about councilors, my dear. They don't exist to *care*." Richard Pound laughed heartily again, but Polly had encountered a lot of people on Slattercove and Shoresend council who cared a great deal and wanted nothing better than to rid themselves of the gangrene in their ranks.

"Peter Hore there, opposite you, is the money man. He hasn't a clue what he's doing businesswise, but he thinks he does. Rich as Croesus and a harmless chump. Genius on the stock market, though it does help if you have a pal who gives him insider tips on what to buy, for a generous backhander." Polly knew this, of course, because she'd done her homework. And it wasn't hard to trace who that friend was when you didn't think you'd be found out and were incautious with information.

"Isn't that... illegal?"

"Oh God, yes. Don't say I told you this, but invest in minerals. That's straight from the horse's mouth. Tank Uranium Corporation in Canada. We've all done very well out of that one thanks to Peter's friend Ni—oops." He covered his mouth before he could say Niles Rillington, a name that Polly was already aware of.

"I appreciate the tip. What about Donald? What special skills does he bring to the table?" Polly jerked her head toward the eldest man in the group, who looked like a doddery old white-haired uncle who was totally oblivious to everything. He seemed to be happy eating and drinking without the bother of conversing, even if Jeremy to his right was doing his best to engage.

"Don't take any notice of him," said Richard, flapping his hand. "He's got a hereditary title and sits in the House of Lords, and it's handy to have one of those on the board even if he's virtually inbred. Plus he says yes to everything because he can't think for himself. Not a bit of gray matter in that weird-shaped head of his."

But Polly knew that Donald wasn't as bumbling as he appeared. He had been living a double life for thirty years and had a mistress and two children who were ensconced in a secret vineyard business he had in France. Lady Celia Devine would have a lot to say about that if she found out.

Polly couldn't believe her luck. Richard Pound was the gift that kept on giving. She had plenty to sink the lot of them, but he was providing her with enough to keep it sunk for eternity.

"What I can't find is Councilor Stirling's name on anything," Polly asked then. "Why is that?"

"Well, he can't be seen to have a vested interest, can he, being a councilor," answered Richard, his tongue wonderfully loosened by flattery and fine wine. He lifted his fingers to his lips. "Shhh. It's all in the name of his daughter. My, the power that man wields, everyone calls him James Stalin, not Stirling. They're all terrified of him, with good reason. He makes up the rules as he goes along, and he's got some dirt on the leader of the council, so he's untouchable. Pushing people higher up on the housing list for a blow job, that sort of dirt."

"No way!" exclaimed Polly.

"Oh yes. And old Jimbo isn't averse to a little fumble for favors either. Do you know, when you lean toward me I can see right down your top."

Polly forced out a tinkly laugh while slapping her hand to her chest to close down any gaping at her neck.

"Seriously, after this, I know a very nice hotel in Leeds if you'd like me to continue filling you in. I think you know what I'm saying." Richard winked and picked up a strand of her hair, tucking it behind her ear. Polly tried not to shudder.

"Let me do my presentation over coffee, and then we'll see where we are," she said, standing and signaling to the waiting staff that it was time to bring out the Yorkshire Wensleydale, cafetières, and Betty's best mints while she made some quick amendments to her script.

Coffee and cheese were served up, as were more revelations. Richard Pound seemed to be under the impression that the more he thrilled Polly with gossip about their dirty deeds across the whole county, the more chance he had of getting into her pants, and she didn't exactly tell him he was wrong. She could still feel his hand on her knee minutes after she'd removed it, coyly but firmly.

Finally it was time. The lights dimmed, the screen dropped from the ceiling, and Polly took her place by her standing desk from where she would control the PowerPoint on her laptop.

"Good afternoon, or should I say *Ciao*?" A titter of laughter. "Welcome to BS, and you are very welcome to it. In the course of this presentation I hope to prove to you what Ciaoissimo can expect from the future, what I can make happen, giving you everything I think you as a company deserve."

She pressed a button and the screen was filled with the first page of her research. A company profile. Then another: a drilling into their finances, growth, gross and net profits, and what the potential could be. It all looked very exciting. There followed photos of their establishments and several bullet-pointed slides that highlighted all their "best practices": the extensive choices on their menus, the functional cheap furnishings, the zero-hour staff contracts, and masterful corner-cutting at every turn. The most BS that it was possible for an employee of BS to drum up.

Then the next slide: a photo of the road in Shoresend where the new Ciaoissimo restaurant in the making and Teddy's restaurant were situated.

"Both restaurants at a push could coexist," said Polly, as James Stirling made a boo noise. "But we all know that is not going to happen: One has to be kicked to the curb for the trash it is."

Polly moved to the next slide: Teddy's restaurant. "This one, of course, has to . . . stay." Richard Pound guffawed, presuming it was a joke. The next slide: James Stirling's formal council photo.

"Councilor James Stirling"—she pointed to him—"there he is. We do need to address your undeclared interest in the Ciaoissimo chain. I mean, what's going on with the proposed compulsory purchase of the Teddy's restaurant car park? Manipulation of rules for personal benefit. Or fraud, I think it's better known as. And of course let's not forget the sexual harassment claims from council staff which have been made to disappear with a combination of threats and hush money paid from council funds."

It was amazing how many people couldn't stand James Stirling, and yet they had no chance of complaining if they were to keep their jobs, because the head of HR was a puppet on a string for him too. People couldn't wait to dish the dirt once they realized it might actually lead to the toppling of his statue and not the loss of their pensions.

"What the . . ."

Polly heard his cry, but she plowed on regardless and put on her next slide: a choice selection of the duff restaurant reviews.

"All false," she said, "a targeted attack to close Teddy's restaurant in Shoresend. However, for every clever fake reviewer who thinks they're untraceable, there's an expert computer genius who can trace them. And guess what . . . I have a source address record of where every single one of these was sent from which makes for very interesting reading." She looked pointedly at Nicholas de Massey, whose stunned expression was priceless. It was a bluff on her part, but it didn't sound like it.

"Polly, can I have a word, please," said Jeremy, getting to his feet.

"In a moment, Jeremy. When I've finished. You did want me to get right to the heart of Ciaoissimo, so that's what I've done. My, what a tale of skulduggery, deception, sabotage, insider trading, blackmail, sleaze, fraud, second families living in French vineyards, adultery, bullying, sexual misconduct, intimidation . . . I could go on, but I think that's quite enough for now. I know all my findings will be most welcomed by the community of Shoresend and far beyond. Fleet Street in particular."

She pressed her button a final time and hoped she'd cued the sound up correctly. Out of all of this despicable crew, she wanted Stirling to be rattled the most. Richard Pound's voice came through the speakers at deafening decibels.

"Well, he can't be seen to have a vested interest, can he, being a councilor. Shhh. It's all in the name of his daughter. My, the power that man wields, everyone calls him James Stalin, not Stirling. They're all terrified of him, with good reason. He makes up the rules as he goes along, and he's got some dirt on the leader of the council, so he's untouchable. Pushing people higher up on the housing list for a blow job, that sort of dirt."

"No way!"

"Oh yes. And old Jimbo isn't averse to a little fumble for favors either. Do you know, when you lean toward me I can see right down your top."

Polly bowed. "Thank you for your time, gentlemen. I do hope you've enjoyed my presentation. I look forward to your downfall and I know I won't have a long time to wait."

"You fucking bitch," said Richard Pound, putting a very brave face on a very rattled body.

"Ciao," said Polly, then she swept up her laptop and handbag and strutted out the door.

Chapter 56

Polly opened the door to Chris's house and her own loneliness rushed out at her with the quiet. For the past months, since she had woken up in hospital, she had been guided by her feelings and instincts; they steered her through the seas of uncertainty in which she found herself. If common sense had been her only pilot, she knew she wouldn't have done what she did today, and she was rather glad it had been forced into a corner and told to shut up. She hadn't exactly handed in a formal resignation, but she reckoned there would be no future letter asking her to have a meeting with HR, because there could be no excusing this time what had just occurred. She hadn't just blotted her copybook; she'd ripped it up and chucked all the pieces on the fire, but she'd sleep more soundly in her bed for doing it. Not the little bed upstairs; she wasn't sure which bed she'd be in tonight, but she'd spent her last night in this house, and this time she wouldn't be back.

She'd picked up the hire van on the way home after dropping off the hire car she'd been using. She arranged for the swap to happen today, to follow the throwing of Ciaoissimo to the wolves, for the people she loved. Now that was done, she was free to help herself. It hadn't taken her long to pack up her things, just as she had done twelve weeks ago to the day. It felt a lifetime away, because it was really. So much had happened in those three months, both bad and good, but she'd had to be lost to be found.

When Chris came in from work that night, he wondered whose white van was parked outside and why Polly's blue hire car wasn't in its spot. She was in though, thank goodness, because it always put him in a bad mood if there was no one home before him. The light was on in the kitchen and she was sitting at the table with a jacket on. He couldn't smell any food cooking, and he thought that if she was going to announce they were going out for dinner, she'd be sadly disappointed that he wouldn't be joining her.

"What's going on?" he asked. He dropped his bag on the floor in that same place, and if ever a single, tiny, lingering doubt remained that she was doing the right thing, it was snuffed out there on the spot.

"I'm leaving you," Polly said, no regret, no recrimination in her voice; it was delivered as a straight fact. "I wanted to tell you to your face."

Chris stood there arms akimbo, his expression pure *What the hell now?* "Is this because I haven't booked a cruise or chucked presents at you since you've come home?"

"No, Chris." It was because he'd been with her for eight years and he didn't know how she took a cup of tea or that she didn't like dark chocolate and he dumped things expecting her to shift them. It was because he'd never walked with her barefoot across sand or held his arm out for her to link. And it was because he had never taken her face between his hands. She was leaving him because he didn't see that the little things were important. The bad little things and the good little things.

"Polly, love . . ." A sigh of exasperation from someone who absolutely didn't need this after a hard day's graft. "See sense. Give it time for us to get back to how we were. I know you can't remember properly, but trust me, it was good."

"I can remember. We are already back to how we were, Chris, and it really wasn't."

"Okay." A note of desperation in his voice. "Let's get married then, if that makes you feel more wanted. Properly this time. You pick your own frock and we'll go away and do it, just you and me."

"No, Chris." She shook her head slowly.

"Look, I'll go upstairs and change, and then I'll come down and we'll talk. Okay? I'll be five minutes if that. You put the kettle on, Polly."

He raced up the stairs, but she wasn't fooled by his urgency. He didn't want her; he wanted someone, *anyone* who would warm up the house with their living presence without having to give back anything in return but illusory promises and procrastinations. Chris was one of life's takers, not a giver like his son, like Marielle and Teddy Bonetti. She wasn't sure there was a place still waiting for her with them, but there was nothing for her here.

She took out the notepad and pen that lived in the drawer in the table. Then she turned to a page and wrote:

Take good care of yourself and be happy, Chris.

Love, Polly xx

She tore out the sheet and propped it up against the salt pot; then she stood and took a last look around at the kitchen with the broken tiles, the missing slat at the window, the incomplete dining set, and the big work bag in the middle of the floor.

"Goodbye, Polly Potter," she said.

Then she opened the back door and walked out into the night air.

The longest-serving reporter Bill Thompson retired from the *Daily Trumpet* today and was presented with an engraved gold cock by the newspaper owner Sir Basil Stamper, who set him on in the post room on his sixteenth birthday. In an emotional speech, Bill said that every time he looked at it sitting on his sideboard, he would think of Sir Basil.

Chapter 57

Three days later

Teddy dropped the metal shutters, pressed in the alarm code, and locked the door behind him. The restaurant had been full tonight, and the overflowing tips jar sang a sweet song of satisfaction. Niccolo and Roberto had upped their gesticulations. Sabrina had been right—the customers loved it, and repeat bookings were up. He'd warned his cousins, though: no broken hearts. It was bad for business. If he *had* a business for much longer. In saying that, oddly, he remembered there had been no builders' vans causing their obstructions on the road today, no activity at all next door. He'd had to check his calendar to see if he'd missed a bank holiday. It wouldn't last. They'd be back tomorrow, of that he had little doubt.

He just wanted to get to bed, but he'd promised his mum he'd call in on his way past. She had something that would cheer him up, she said. He hoped it was a pint of grappa. He couldn't stand the stuff actually, but it would give his brain blessed oblivion while his body was wondering what the hell his mouth had just let in.

He pulled up outside his mum's house and knocked. She greeted him with *that* look on her face. The one that said, *"I hope you aren't going to be cross with me Teddy, but . . ."* He felt the hairs on the back of his neck rise in response.

"Teddy, I've let out the flat again. Bear with me, though, I'm doing it properly this time. I thought it might be wise if you met the person straightaway so you could suss them out."

"Mamma, really, at this time of night?"

Marielle knocked softly on the adjoining door and called through it, "Could you just come through, my lovely, and meet my son? If you're going to be staying here for any length of time, he'll need to give his approval."

The door opened; Teddy prepared himself to smile politely, and because he wasn't expecting her, it took him a long second to register who she was. And then he cleared the distance between himself and Sabrina in two long strides and picked her up in his big, strong, Italian arms.

* * *

No grappa was needed; he didn't want any oblivion, he wanted to feast on the sight of her. He sat on his mum's sofa next to her, holding her hands between his own.

"I have wanted to call you so many times," said Teddy. "You have been on my mind every day."

She could have said exactly those words back to him. They'd had to distance themselves from each other. They were decent people and she'd been in a long-established relationship, although neither of them knew how crumbled and broken it was. She'd needed time and he'd had to give it to her. But she didn't need it anymore.

She'd driven to the Premier Inn in Slattercove the night she left Chris and spent the next couple of days devising a plan of action. She'd been in touch with an estate agent who was now looking for a house for her to rent, although when she'd rung Marielle and told her she was back, the offer of Little Moon was there for as long as she wanted it. Then Sabrina had emailed Phil Bowery at Yorkshire Eagles to ask if he remembered her. He called her within the hour.

"Remember you? Of course I remember you, Polly. You're not looking for a job, are you, by any chance?" He made it that easy. The change of her name she'd explain to him when they met up tomorrow.

"I have to confess something to you, Teddy," she began earnestly. "I have been working with Ciaoissimo. They paid us a fortune to overhaul them and I was assigned to be the one to turn them into what they should be."

"Oh . . . right," said Teddy, pondering, brow creased, but he did not let go of her hands because his heart trusted her.

"So that's exactly what I've done. My findings are filtering through to those who need to see them as we speak."

Teddy's sky-blue eyes met with her lovely golden-brown ones and he saw the light dancing in them.

"Oh Teddy, what a nest of vipers. And I have all the evidence of it in glorious Technicolor: admission of sabotage and smear campaigns, and some fabulous dodgy and insider dealing, not to mention enough dirt to line the whole of Yorkshire's chimneys. I'll tell you everything in due course, but I can assure you of two things—Councilor Stirling is finished. And Ciaoissimo will not be opening up next door."

"I don't care how late it is, I'm having a celebratory glass of wine," called Marielle, tripping to the cupboard for glasses.

"So you'll be sticking around for a while then . . . to fill me in with the whole story?" asked Teddy. "Until tomorrow, at least."

She smiled and his own smile widened. It felt welded to his lips.

"You lost your job, I presume?" he asked.

"As one door closed, a much nicer one opened," she replied. She'd enjoy working with Phil and Dave. She'd enjoy living by the sea and hearing the seagulls every day, birds that carried so many happy memories on their wings.

"How am I going to thank you?" he wondered aloud.

Sabrina resisted the urge to say she could think of a few ways.

"I think you all thanked me in advance," she said instead.

"Oh my God, I've missed you," he said. There were so many things he wanted to say to her—how much he wanted her, how much he thought about her, how happy he felt just being near her—but there would be plenty of time for that, because now that she was back, he wouldn't be letting her go again. Not ever.

Epilogue

The following summer

"Do you remember when I said to you that I wish you were having a baby at the same time as me so we could meet up for lunch and other stuff and I told you to go and find someone and get up the duff?"

"I do." Sabrina laughed and nudged the woman at her side affectionately as they strolled. "You can't say that I didn't listen. Oh, it's so good to see you again."

It *was* good to see her too. Sheridan and baby Alexander. And her soon-to-be-born second son, giving her more sciatica fun.

"I need to sit," said Sheridan. "Quick, let's nab that bench." They sat down on it and Sheridan applied the brake to the pram. Alexander was fast asleep, knocked out by the warm sea air.

"You look happy, Sabrina Bonetti," said Sheridan, giving her friend the once-over. "I wondered if I'd get used to your new name, but it was easy. And you look happier than Polly Potter ever did. Although if you had married Chris, your name would have been Polly Barrett, which would have been comedy gold." Sabrina hooted with laughter. A lucky escape then, in more ways than one.

"I am happy," she said. She'd had fun arranging her own wedding, picking her own dress—ivory and fitted—and they'd had a pizza and pasta reception in the restaurant. Flick had been her bridesmaid—in sage, not beige—and George had been Teddy's best man. Sheridan and Dmitri had been there, and Will had come up from Bournemouth for it. He was living his best life down there and was forever grateful she'd helped him find the confidence to take the leap of faith.

"This is bliss. I might have to come here a bit more often," said Sheridan, tilting her head back and letting the sun warm her face.

"You're welcome anytime."

Sabrina looked across the road at Teddy's and the tables on the pavement full of people eating, drinking. Inside the restaurant the hatch had been widened so that diners could see the internal workings of the kitchen and the big, handsome chef putting his all into every dish he made and the Greek pizza chef flinging circles of dough into the air like a seasoned circus performer. Occasionally they'd bicker loudly that each was in the other's way and George would tell the chef that it wasn't his idea to have his pizza oven moved and he preferred it in the back where he didn't have to see his stupid Italian face so much. And so often the reviews on Tripadvisor would read that this double act should be on a stage.

The "Ready Teddy Go" takeaway service had been a huge success. They'd had to take on more staff to cope with demand: one from Rome and two from Athens. All three of them suitably loud.

George and Marielle had been a solid item since he'd escorted her to the theater to see *My Big Fat Greek Wedding*, with a meal afterward—Greek, of course. He said that he wanted to take her somewhere decent to eat for once.

Flick was home for the summer after her first year at university. She knew as soon as she landed there that she was in the right place and she was always on the phone to her new sister-in-law talking over her assignments and asking advice. Relations with her mum were improved. Cilla would always be a pain in the arse, but she was at least trying not to be one all of the time.

The shop that was once going to be a Ciaoissimo was now a popular antiques center. Ciaoissimo was no more. Its ship had sunk into its own murky waters and taken its crew with it, but its story kept the newspapers fueled for months. The winds of change had blown through the council, and by all accounts, it was a far better place to work these days with councilors being voted in in the local elections who cared very much about their constituents.

"So do you fancy doing a bit of virtual admin work for us then?" asked Sabrina.

"Abso-flaming-lutely," replied Sheridan, opening up one eye. "I need something adult to do. I'm at the stage where I want to hunt down Peppa Pig with a sawn-off shotgun."

"It'll be great to have you on board." Sabrina grinned. "Only if we can have some sort of online version of confectionery tennis, though."

"Deal."

Working with Phil and Dave again was like being back in the old days with Alan Eagleton. They'd called themselves Yorkshire Eagles in Alan's honor, they told her. No one better to be with them in spirit.

Sabrina sometimes did some creative writing. She'd joined a class in the next town: the Slattercove Nibs. She didn't need to finish her novel, though, because Sabrina Bonetti couldn't write a happier ending for Sabrina Anderson than she was already living. Her own story now included a house she and Teddy were about to complete on, with thick stone walls, a creaky staircase, and a cottage garden overflowing with roses of all colors. And a kitten that Teddy had given her for her birthday, naughty and ginger and partial to a lump of cheddar. They'd called him Cheese.

Sabrina felt a quiver inside her. Baby Bonetti was growing a little more every day. She was the size of a *pomodoro* at the moment. Teddy had put a poster up in the restaurant so they could chart the progress in Italian fruits.

She followed her friend's lead, leaned back against the bench, and let the sun take her face between its hands, like Teddy Bonetti often did before he kissed her and told her that she was all of his best dreams come true. She wasn't sure it was legal to be this content, but she was milking it for all it was worth. She was a living lesson to anyone who was lost that they could be found, that changes could be messy and scary but ultimately magnificent. And that there was a right place for everyone, where they could live their happiest-ever-afters—and this, here with these wonderful people, was hers.

DAILY TRUMPET, 19 AUGUST
GROOM ATTACKED BY SEAGULL IN HOSPITAL

When newlywed Orville "duck" Bell walked out of Shoresend registry office on Saturday he did not imagine he would be spending his wedding night in hospital after a seagull dropped a rock on his head, giving him concussion.

"It was deliberate," said Mr. Bell. "I know that bird and it's got a right grudge against me."

Acknowledgments

What a lucky woman I am to have such a fantastic team behind me. It's never "one size fits all" in this business, but I have the perfect combo of publisher and agent and feel in very safe hands. So big thank-yous to these splendid people. My publishing family, who I drive insane afresh with every book, but they never fail to do their best for me—and it shows. The inimitable Sara-Jade Virtue, Matt, Gill, Rich, Maddie, Jess, Dom, Heather, Louise, Sarah. And, of course, Ian "God" Chapman and my fairy godmother Suzanne Baboneau.

A special mention to my fantastic editor, Clare Hey, who is blimming fabulous and a proper guide. My books are ALWAYS better for her input. A writer who doesn't listen to a good editor is just plain daft.

Sally Partington, my copyeditor extraordinaire. I can't work without her, she's my talisman. When I get the seal of approval from Sal, all is well in my world.

My agent Lizzy Kremer, the woman who has my back at all times. I wouldn't swap her for anything. And also the indispensable people at David Higham: Maddalena Cavaciuti and Margaux, Ilaria, Clare, Kaynat, Orli, Rhian, and everyone else there working behind the scenes for their authors.

My PR team at ED PR, Emma Draude, Annabelle Wright, and Courtney Jefferies. They have added so much to my career and are as essential in my life as red lipstick and oxygen.

Thank you to the lovely lot at Harper Muse who have brought me across the pond. I can't wait to see what we can do together—I'm so excited about reaching a new American audience. Special thanks to Lizzie Poteet (waves fondly), Savannah Breedlove, Jennifer McNeil, Caitlin Halstead, Becky Monds, Amanda Bostic, Kimberly Carlton, and Laura Wheeler.

To all the booksellers who promote me, especially Mike's Famous Bookstall in Barnsley Market and The Book Vault in Barnsley (@thebookvault07), an independent shop that supports authors local and otherwise so generously, offers a stellar service, and will post books out to those who can't get into the shop.

To the press who have been great, headed up by my buddy Andrew Harrod at the Barnsley Chronicle, whom I'd consider a true friend while he might pretend he's never heard of me if asked. Ha.

To Stu, my website bloke, who is a marvel. And a mate. He would also deny this.

The generous-hearted blogging and reviewing stars: Anne Cater, Yvette Huddleston, Natasha Harding, Linda Hill, Annette Hannah, Zoe West, Kay Ribeiro, Lisa Howells, Susan Watson, and Amy Rowland. Thank you to the Books and the City community who are always so generous with their time and support of my books.

To my writer friends who are like the sisters I never had. It's a weird job where your closest rivals are often your best buddies. The dearest of women: Cathy Bramley, Phillipa Ashley, Trisha Ashley, Carole Matthews, Jane Costello / Catherine Isaac, Lucy Diamond, Jane Fallon, Veronica Henry, Paige Toon, Lynda Stacey, Jenny Woodall. We all manage to rescue each other from the brink sometimes, workwise and otherwise. And last but by no means least, the queen of writerly friends: the wise, wonderful, and very talented Debbie Johnson. I'm not sure how I ever managed without her.

And my SBC group: Judy Astley, Katie Fforde, Catherine Jones, Bernie Kennedy, Janie Millman, AJ Pearce, Jo Thomas, and the sadly missed Jane Wenham-Jones. A special big thank you to group member Jill Mansell for her guidance on loss of memory via psychological trauma. I didn't want to get it wrong, and she steered me away from the pitfalls with her very extensive knowledge. Yep, we all had very different jobs before we joined this crazy writing lark.

To the "Daily Trumpeters" who paid to have names featured in the entries (Jill Mansell's idea—she was on a roll with this book!). The money all went into the coffers of yorkshirecatrescue.org, of which I am a proud patron.

It's not always easy to explain this job to those who aren't in it, or for those not in the writing game to understand that you can't be out playing on a Friday night because you've got an edit to do that simply will not wait. So I'm blessed to have Traz, Cath, Rae, Kath, and Maggie, who have unlimited reserves of patience. And in memory of Nancy Scrimshaw, who, as part of our Golden Girls group, taught me how women's friendship knocks down so many barriers, especially age. She was prudent and funny, no frills, straight as an arrow, and I will miss her so much, especially laughing anew at the story of the flying mince pie which was still going strong after thirty-five years.

To the people who support me in my local town and God's county of Yorkshire, because they really have built me from the ground up: buying my books, doing the best PR job on the planet for me. You can't buy support like I have from them.

And to my family: Pete who is the oil in the machine, Tez and George who are my best creations. I hope you'll always think of me as the mad imperfect bag who loved you more than life itself.

Finally, a few more words about the dedication in the front of this book. Writing is not an easy profession. It is the most unlevel playing field, it is brutal and unforgiving, a minefield at times, and we authors, who take it seriously, are all at the mercy of unfair winds. It is also a true vocation and hard to ignore when it calls. But writers of romance have more of an uphill struggle. Mainly because most of us are women.

There has been so much snobbery about romantic fiction being somehow "lesser" than other genres over too many years. Nonsense, of course. The massive book sales speak for themselves. The money gained from romantic fiction novels props up the industry. You cannot respect the revenue without respecting those hardworking novelists who spin it. There are good books and bad books in every category.

But everyone I know puts their heart and soul into their romantic fiction novels, which are smart and insightful. They are as deftly plotted as crime novels, they are as beautifully written as literary novels, often more so. A happy ending does not make it a weaker book. We set out to entertain but end up giving our readers respite and guidance, solace and inspiration. We know this because they write to tell us as much. Our books change lives. Sometimes, as our readers' own stories tell us, they save lives.

Our books are not a "guilty pleasure"—just pleasure will do. So parade them, show off your favorite reads, and don't let anyone tell you your choices aren't valid. I've lost count of the times people in Barnsley have shouted across the road to me: "Oy, you got me through Covid," and I'm proud of that. Our book sales increased by over 49 percent during the pandemic, and that demonstrates what we gave to people: comfort and familiarity and a place for their troubled heads to go to. Readers, don't let anyone make you feel inferior because you prefer a romantic fiction story to a lauded classic that you can't get to grips with. Read for pleasure and sod the snobs. Fiction should not be devalued for being popular. It's popular because it's good stuff.

The walls of prejudice in the industry are slowly breaking down, not before time. It takes serious skill to keep a reader enthralled; we don't just chuck words at a page hoping some of them will stick. We pour ourselves into our stories; we harvest experiences and emotions. We deliver the best we can; we are proud masters of our craft. I say it again: We do not write lesser books. We are not lesser writers.

To everyone who loves us and reads us, buys us, borrows us from libraries, tells people about our stories, you are not lesser readers for that; you are discerning and selective and in charge of your own choices. In short—you ROCK, and I can't thank you enough for your support.

Love Milly xxx
#RespectRomFic

Discussion Questions

1. *The Accidental Rewrite* explores themes of self-discovery and starting over. How do Polly's actions, such as leaving the surprise wedding, reflect her desire for a fresh start?
2. The story features elements of both humor and tragedy, from misprints in the *Daily Trumpet* to deeply emotional moments like Polly's memories of her uncle and aunt. How does this blend of tones affect your experience of the book?
3. Several characters in the book grapple with significant personal changes. How do these transformations impact the storyline and relationships between the characters?
4. Polly's dissatisfaction with her professional life leads to a series of significant changes. How does her character evolve over the course of the story?
5. How would you describe the relationship between Polly and Chris? Do you believe there are any redeeming qualities in Chris's character?
6. Characters like Jeremy Watson and Charles Butler are portrayed as antagonistic forces in Polly's professional life. Do you think they served as catalysts for her eventual departure, and were their actions justified in any way?

7. The novel features a number of quirky and flawed side characters, such as 'Orrible and Benny. How do these characters contribute to the overall tone and narrative?
8. Locations like Shoresend play an important role in Polly's memories and her fresh start. How does the setting shape the story and Polly's decisions?
9. The restaurant Teddy's serves as a symbolic place of community and healing in the book. How does this location contrast with Polly's previous workplace?
10. The book explores complex family dynamics, such as Polly's relationship with her Auntie Rina and Uncle Ed. How do these memories influence her actions and decisions?
11. Camay and Ward's vow renewal ceremony becomes a pivotal moment for Polly. Do you think their intentions were misguided, or were they genuinely trying to support Polly and Chris?
12. The book uses humor, such as the misprints in the *Daily Trumpet*, as a narrative device. How does this humor enhance or detract from the story's emotional depth?
13. The title *The Accidental Rewrite* suggests a theme of unintentional transformation. How do you interpret the title in relation to Polly's story?
14. How does the inclusion of Polly's creative writing, such as her limericks and love letters, add depth to her character? Do these elements affect how you perceive her?
15. If you were in Polly's shoes, would you have made the same decision to leave the surprise wedding? Why or why not?
16. The book highlights the courage it takes to leave an unhappy situation and pursue a new path. What lessons can readers take away from Polly's story?

About the Author

Copyright @ davidcharles.com

MILLY JOHNSON was born, raised, and still lives in Barnsley, South Yorkshire. A *Sunday Times* bestseller, she is one of the Top 10 Female Fiction authors in the UK and has sold millions of copies of her books across the world. *The Accidental Rewrite* is her twenty-first novel.

Milly's writing highlights the importance of community spirit and the magic of kindness. Her books inspire and uplift, but she packs a punch and never shies away from the hard realities of life and the complexities of relationships in her stories. Her books champion women, their strength and resilience, and celebrate love, friendship, and the possibility and joy of second chances and renaissances.

* * *

Connect with her online at www.milly-johnson.com
Instagram: @themillyjohnson
Facebook: @MillyJohnsonAuthor
X: @millyjohnson